RAVELLED
SEPH GANNON

Enjoy the journey!

Seph Gannon

RAVELLED

First published in 2019 by
BLE Publishing Group USA

978-1-9161840-3-9 (paperback)

Blepublishinggroup@yahoo.com
PO Box 3906
Fredericksburg,
VA 22402, USA
www.blepublishinggroup.com

Other available formats

978-1-9161840-1-5 (hardback)
978-1-9161840-5-3 (audiobook)
978-1-9161840-4-6 (e-book)

For author releases, book signings, interviews
and other information go to

www.sephgannon.com

This story is
for those who know love,
or have forgotten it;
who have faith,
or need it.
No one is ever alone.

Dear Reader,

Just a little helpful information to make discussing this story with your friends consistent and avoid spending time on how to say the names. Without further ado—

Hagen—HAH-gin, hard g. Think Häagen Dazs.

Mathilde—Mah-TIL-da, no "th" sound'.

Georg—GAY-org. Both gs are hard gs. Think Georg Von Trapp from the Sound of Music.

Ryfka—RIF-kah.

Zelik—ZEH-leek.

Piotr—P-YOH-treh.

Krystyna—kris-TIN-nuh.

Morawski—Mor-AHF-skee.

Varsaci—Var-SAK-ee.

Eóin—OW-in. I love Irish Gaelic, don't you?

Brobdingnagian—BROB-ding-NAG-ee-un. From Gulliver's Travels. It means, really, really BIG!

Enjoy the journey,

Seph

The Beckenbauers

Family tree

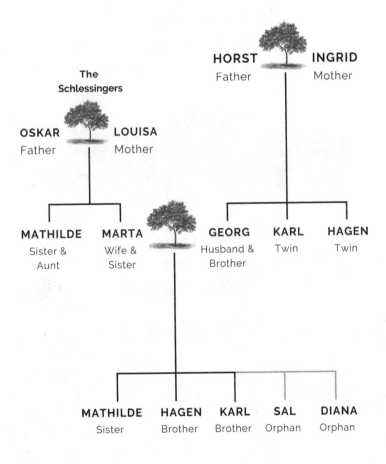

HORST
Father

INGRID
Mother

The Schlessingers

OSKAR
Father

LOUISA
Mother

MATHILDE
Sister & Aunt

MARTA
Wife & Sister

GEORG
Husband & Brother

KARL
Twin

HAGEN
Twin

MATHILDE
Sister

HAGEN
Brother

KARL
Brother

SAL
Orphan

DIANA
Orphan

"I like trains.
I like their rhythm,
and I like the freedom of being
suspended between two places,

all anxieties of purpose taken care of:
for this moment I know
where I am going."

—Anna Funder

Lamy Train Station
New Mexico
February 16, 1998

The sun was on its descent towards the western horizon and a group of people were gathered on the platform of a tiny train depot, a little south of Santa Fe. They were motionless and silent as their lengthening shadows crept slowly eastward.

In the distance, a train horn heralded its imminent arrival. It was 3:56 p.m. and the train was eleven minutes late. No one seemed to care. No one looked at their watch. They remained still, standing in the cold New Mexico breeze as the smells of winter wafted down the tracks; aromas of cedar, mesquite, and piñon woods burning inside the kiva fireplaces of distant houses. When the train arrived, the passengers on board saw the platform and the people standing on it like statues in a wax museum. It wasn't so much their stillness that made passengers on the train stop talking or eating or looking at the scenery. It was the composition of the gathering that held them in its thrall.

Thirty or so people stood there, finely dressed, mostly in black, very few colors. Men in dark suits and overcoats were standing side-by-side or arm-in-arm with women in finery and furs. They shared the platform with a small formation of retired servicemen, wearing WWII era, military dress uniforms. It would not have been too terrifically odd— maybe just plain odd—if they were the only ones waiting for

1

the train. What upped the oddness was what waited on the platform between them. The centerpiece of this tableau was the Stars-and-Stripes draped casket that rested atop a metal cart, perpendicular to the tracks. It was the object of everyone's attention, on and off the train. Of the fifty-or-so gathered that day, only two would be traveling.

The train stopped. Nobody moved. A few moments later, the train inched backward. The *clack, clack, clack* sound of the cars echoed from the surrounding hillside as their connections compressed together. As it reversed, it went off to the right, down a divergent spur of tracks. Most of the passengers were unaware, due to the captivating effect of the casket *et al*, of what sat one hundred yards up—a single railcar, itself a passenger, waited for its turn to board. It was unlike any railcar that anyone had ever seen, and it belonged to no company.

Just like rock bands have enormous RVs and tycoons have private jets and mega-yachts, someone had converted an Amtrak Superliner into a house on rails. It only resembled its stock originality in that it was long, had two levels, and had wheels. Its windows had been rearranged and replaced to suit the interior. A section in the upper level resembled an observation area, almost completely glass, looking more like a greenhouse than a room. At the end of the car, a section had been cut away to make a covered patio. Bogie skirts covered the wheels, and the whole thing was a deep midnight blue, with two gold initials, **SH**, monogrammed on the entrance door. People on the train stared open-mouthed, their attention diverted away from the platform, as their train snaked closer to the blue beauty.

At a walking speed the train reversed. When the distance had closed to about fifty feet, a brakeman hopped down and walked alongside to supervise the impending mating as he communicated with the engineer via walkie-talkie. As the Amtrak train approached the waiting rail yacht, it slowed to a crawl until the couplings touched and then clasped each other in a mechanical handshake. Walkie-talkie static, the train stopped, then crept forward; *clack, clack, clacking* as the slack between all the cars was taken up. Then the train slowly moved forward until the private car neared the platform. One final staticky cue from the brakeman and the train stopped, positioning the railcar directly in front of the platform and its motionless occupants.

Movement on the platform began when the train stopped moving. Eight of the uniformed men broke rank and took up positions around the casket, each grasping one of its silver handles. From the remaining formation came the call to arms and the final salute began. Right arms slowly raised in unison as the eight men walked towards the railcar, the cart and casket keeping pace with them. Eight feet from it, they stopped. One of the servicemen walked to the side of the car, pressed some buttons on a keypad and a cargo door opened downward, becoming a ramp. The men began moving forward with the casket, rolling it up the ramp and inside. After securing the cart in place, they exited the cargo hold and joined the larger formation as their arms slowly came down, finishing the salute. Stillness took over again; the only things moving were the state and national flags occasionally *whip-cracking* in the breeze high atop the station's flagpole and a few of the women dabbing handkerchiefs to their eyes.

"COMPANY... DISMISSED!"

Everyone on the platform moved about freely, their attention now directed at one man. He was tall, older, and distinguished and wore a long, black, camel hair overcoat that accentuated his height. His snow-white hair contrasted against his black, rabbit hair Homburg hat. His right hand gripped a platinum lion's head that crowned a long, mahogany walking stick. The rest of the group, mingling military personnel and civilians, gathered around him. There were hugs, handshakes, and tears as they said their farewells, then peeled away from the gathering, one-by-one, two-by-two, until one man remained facing the tall man.

The other man was Navajo. He was shorter, wore a black suit, no overcoat. Silver tips on his black, leather, western boots glinted in the setting sunlight. A sterling silver Thunderbird bolo tie, intricately detailed and inlaid with red coral and blue turquoise, spread its wings at the collar of his white shirt. A single eagle feather protruded from the top of his long, grey, waist-length ponytail. A few words were spoken, they embraced, then the Navajo man backed up a step as the man with the cane turned to face the train. He pressed buttons on the side of the railcar and stared at the casket as the cargo door slowly closed. His shoulders rose and fell with a sigh. Leaning on the lion's head, he walked to the entrance, pressed a code into another keypad and the entrance door opened. Slowly the man climbed on board, turned and pressed a button on the inside wall, and he and the Navajo nodded to each other as the door closed.

The tall man stood there for a moment, staring at the inside of the door, his heart thumping in his chest, then turned and gazed in the direction of the cargo hold. He let out another sigh, then got into the elevator and went to the upper level.

He walked to his bedroom at the rear of the railcar, hung up his overcoat and suit jacket, took off his tie and kicked off his shoes. Opening the door to the patio at the far end of his room, he walked outside, sat down on a dark brown, leather recliner and picked up a wireless remote from the side table. Pressing a button on the remote commanded the large panoramic windows to descend into the three outer walls. The cool, dry breath of New Mexico blew in as the patio exhaled stale air out into the dusk. Soothing desert air filled his lungs again. He took a deep breath, then another, then a third.

From the opposite end of the train, the engine blew its horn. The man smiled. He loved the sounds of trains; the wheels on the tracks; the *puff-puff-puff* of the old steam engines. Over the years he had witnessed the evolution of train engines as they progressed from steam to diesel; their voices changing from high-pitched whistles to the sonorous chords of the air horn. They were like the chimes played in a theater lobby announcing the end of intermission and the continuance of the play. A few moments later, his car jerked forward with the initial tug as it began to move, then accelerated smoothly, slowly; the tracks retreating behind him as the sun said farewell and ducked behind a hill. It had been a long and emotional day. He reclined as the wheels clicking on the tracks Morse-coded a message—*RELAX-relax, RELAX-relax, RELAX-relax.*

"At times the world may seem an unfriendly and sinister place, but believe that there is much more good in it than bad. All you have to do is look hard enough. And what might seem to be a series of unfortunate events may in fact be the first steps of a journey."

—Lemony Snicket

A New Chapter

A phone on the side table rang. At the other end of the railcar, a young woman in her twenties, dressed in an Amtrak uniform, stood at the locked entrance. She was holding the receiver of the phone mounted on the wall next to the door, staring at the push button keypad above the door handle.

The man sat upright and answered the phone. "Hello, this is Hagen Beckenbauer."

"Good evening, Mr. Beckenbauer. This is Emily, your service attendant for your trip to Philadelphia. I apologize for interrupting you, but I'm at the entrance to your car and I don't have the combination."

"Oh, yes Emily, good evening. The combination is 1–4–3–0. Please do come in. I will meet you in the kitchen in a few minutes."

"Thank you, sir."

He hung up the phone, got up from the recliner, went back inside, and switched on the lights in his room. He walked over to the dresser and looked in the mirror, pulled a comb from his back pocket and ran it through his thick, white hair. In the mirror, he saw the reflection of the bed behind him and the hand-woven Navajo blanket laid on top. He went over and sat down on the bed. His fingers touched the blanket, felt the weave, the fibers, the memories. Another sigh. He slid his feet into his slippers, leaned on the lion's head to stand up, and left his room to go meet the young woman waiting for him in the kitchen.

Emily entered the combination into the keypad, turned the handle and slid the door open. She walked in, closed the door behind her, then turned to look at the kitchen. She marveled at the room. It was a scaled-down version of what might be seen in a restaurant. There was a lot of counter space, a lot of windows, a big gas stove and a refrigerator. At the far end in the left corner was a four-person, corner banquette and in the right corner was the door leading to the rest of the car. She was taking it all in when its owner entered.

The man approached her with an extended arm. "Good evening, Emily. I am Hagen Beckenbauer."

Wow, so polite and refined; and those eyes, so blue. She took his hand in hers and found his grip to be firmer than she'd expected as he took control of the handshake. "Good evening, Mr. Beckenbauer. My name is Emily Connolly. It's a pleasure to meet you."

He appreciated the young lady's appearance: well-kept uniform; very little makeup or jewelry, aside from a plain Timex on her left wrist; her shoulder-length, dark brown hair in a neat ponytail.

"The pleasure is all mine, Emily." He gestured to the banquette in the corner. "Please, have a seat. Let's chat."

They sat down across from each other and Mr. Beckenbauer began. "Well, my dear, you are probably wondering why you are here. I am usually quite self-sufficient. I know how to cook. I can make my own bed. I can dust and vacuum." Sensing the tension of the initial client/employee meet and greet, he put both arms on the table and leaned forward. "But I do not do windows." He grinned. Emily squinted confusedly. "No Emily, you are not here to clean my windows," he said. "That was my poor attempt at jocularity. I apologize."

Her expression went from confused, to pensive, to completely serious. She wiped her brow. "Whew! I was trying to figure out how I was going to repel off the side of the train while speeding down the tracks at a hundred miles an hour and still hold a bottle of Windex." She looked straight into his Caribbean-blue eyes, poker-faced. He looked right back into her espresso brown eyes, just as straight-faced as she. The stare down did not last long. Smiles broke out on both sides. The ice was broken.

He continued, looking into her eyes, this time completely sincere. "Emily, this trip is different than others I have taken. I am sure you saw us on the platform in Lamy."

"I think everyone on the train saw you, sir."

"I can only imagine how it looked," he said.

"It sure was a sight. I mean, it's not every day you see something that spectacular at a train station in the middle of nowhere. And what makes it even more awesome is this," tapping the table, "this railcar. I have never seen anything like it." Emily winced with embarrassment. "Oh, Mr. Beckenbauer, I am so very sorry for your loss and I apologize that I didn't greet you with condolences first before commenting on how you looked on the platform."

"Oh, my dear, please do not apologize. I appreciate your kind words, but today has been so very serious. I have been surrounded by somber, serious people all week and it is a refreshing change to talk to someone about something not hospital- or funeral-related. Which brings us back to why you are here."

"To be honest, Mr. Beckenbauer, I am wondering that myself." She turned her head in the direction of the engine then back to him. "I've never heard of an Amtrak employee working on a private railcar. Heck, I've never even seen a private railcar before today."

"Privately owned railcars are uncommon, as is hiring Amtrak personnel to work on one. You have been assigned here, at my expense of course, because I do not want to be around people right now who know me. I did not, *do not*, want to be coddled, and doused with sympathy. I simply want someone to be a liaison between me and Amtrak, bring me food, keep things tidy and maybe keep me company on our journey east. I do have on-call staff who accompany me when I take to the rails: a cook, a maid, a valet. But this time, I did not want to deal with multiple personalities surrounding me with their multiple sympathies, walking around on eggshells waiting for me to melt down so they can mop me up. Instead, I wanted an assistant who does not know me personally, someone who also knows their way around a train. I spoke with Warren about my situation and he was very sympathetic to my needs. He suggested that I utilize one of his employees before I could ask for one. *Et, voilà*, here you are. I want you to *not* tiptoe around me like I am going to break down at any moment. Yes, I am sad; this is a very sad time for me, but I know all things must, in their own time, end. Life goes on and I, the last time I noticed, am still breathing. So, Emily Connolly, can you do this for me? Take off the kid gloves and be yourself? I promise you that this will not be a difficult assignment."

"Yes sir, Mr. Beckenbauer. I believe I can handle this assignment. Besides, I hadn't put the left kid glove on yet."

He smiled at her quick sense of humor. "Very good. Now, we must get one thing straight if we are to get along. I have one stipulation for this position. It is a requirement for you to stay on for this journey."

Emily found no evidence of humor now in his demeanor. She sat completely upright and braced herself for his stipulation. She was generally not a pessimistic person. Her glass was always half full. But she also wasn't the naive little girl her overprotective mother shielded from the horrors of the real world, either. She had heard about some of the weird stuff that old, rich men liked to get into. *And this guy wasn't just rich, he was uber-rich. This man had his own train and on-call chefs, maids, and valets. He was even on a first name basis with the company's CEO!*

And I am going to be all alone with him in his private railcar.

No one can hear me scream from in here.

Oh, God! Oh GODDAMMIT!! shouted her brain. All the shit she'd either seen or heard of whizzed through her mind like a giant, pornographic slide show. *Is he wearing women's underwear right now? Or, is he going to pull a French maid's outfit out of one of the cabinets and tell me to try it on for size? He seemed so nice, so sincere. He sure knows how to make you feel at ease before knocking you over with his creepy fetish.*

OK, get ready to run, whispered her brain, while at the same time ordering her guts to speed up the churning of her late lunch. *Damned fight-or-flight response.* She so regretted getting off the train in Albuquerque and eating that carne adovada burrito.

She glanced at the exit. "Yes, Mr. Beckenbauer?" The words came out like someone waiting for the doctor to tell you how much time they had left to live.

"I want you to call me Hagen; no more 'sir' or 'Mr. Beckenbauer'. I can tell that you are very professional. But sometimes one must be able to go against the professional grain at the behest of the employer."

Emily was so relieved and at the same time so damned embarrassed at herself for all those vile images that had screamed through her head in the past few moments. Her face had flushed. Her palms had gotten sweaty. Her forehead glistened with perspiration. And she really needed to use a restroom. That burrito made a mad dash to the end of the trail. *DAMMIT, what the hell is wrong with me!?*

"Yes sir, Mr. Beckenbauer, sir. I will call you Hagen, sir." She gave him a goofy salute as a sense of relief replaced her dread. She was trying to lighten the mood that she had weighted down with her fears. Hagen had noticed her postural change and her dilated pupils when he mentioned there was a stipulation. The big giveaway was the perspiration beading on her brow. Mr. Beckenbauer was not ignorant to the ways of the world either, and could see that Emily had been waiting for bad news.

"Are you alright, my dear? You look like you've just seen a ghost." He smiled a smile that said, *I know what you were thinking.* Leaning on his cane, he rose from the table and walked over to the refrigerator, opened the door and pulled out a bottle of Evian and then ripped off a piece of paper towel from the roll on the counter. He placed them in front of her and sat back down in his seat. "Drink some water, dear, and dab your brow. You're dehydrating right in front of me."

"I'm fine, sir... uh, Hagen... thank you. It's just my spicy burrito from lunch making the rounds." She winced again with embarrassment. "That was gross, sorry." The flush in her face returned again in full force. She opened the bottle and took a big gulp. The coolness spread out from her core, calming the meltdown in her gut.

He laughed. It felt good to laugh. And he was glad that, although it was quite evident Emily had been scared out of her wits for a moment, she could recover with a comeback about her distressed bowels, whether they were distressed or not.

"Let me put your mind at ease. I am old and I am quite harmless. I have had one hip replaced and I use a cane to help me get around. You have nothing to be afraid of."

It was quite apparent to Emily that he had seen through her attempt to hide the high tide of anxiety that had washed over her. "Was it that obvious?"

"Like Rudolph's nose. And if you're wondering… no, I wasn't offended. You have every right to be on your guard." He held out his right hand. "Friends?"

She wiped her sweaty palm on her lap then shook his hand. "Friends."

"Good." He released her hand and placed both of his flat on the table.

"Now, I have a proposition for you." He waited to see if Emily's alarms went off again, but no; no dilating pupils, no perspiration, and no apparent gastric distress.

"I'm fine, *Hagen*, you don't scare me… *anymore.*" A Cheshire cat grin spread across her face.

"Well, good." He smiled, happy to see that she was feeling more at ease. "When I have members of staff with me, I procure accommodations for them on the Amtrak train as I only have one guest room. Since you are only one person, and you will be spending most of your time assisting me, I thought you might want to stay here, on my car, until we reach Philadelphia. It might save you from all the extra back-and-forth, and I am almost positive that my accommodations are a bit more comfortable than Amtrak's."

He could see from her expression that it wouldn't take her long to decide.

The Cheshire cat encored.

"I… I… really? Are you sure?" Emily was hesitant and excited. What a nice change it would be; what an adventure!

"Yes." Mr. Beckenbauer nodded once. "I am quite sure."

"What about Amtrak? Are they going to let me stay here?"

"I had already cleared it with Warren before you got on the train in Los Angeles. He was made aware that I planned to offer the guest room to whomever was assigned to me. They also know you have the option to decline the offer and

13

come to work every morning and go back to your cabin in the evening."

"Wow!" Emily almost giggled. "I would love to. Thank you. Boy," this time she did giggle. "Eddie is going to be so jealous. I accept your offer. Not because it's going to make Eddie jealous, but because this isn't something that happens every day."

"Wonderful. Why don't you retrieve your personal effects and I'll give you the grand tour when you return?"

"Yes, *SIR*!" Emily stood, winked, and gave him another goofy salute.

"Just use the code to come back in. Do you remember it?"

"1–4–3–0, easy to remember."

"Yes, it is."

Hagen watched her leave through the door and disappear into the Amtrak car. Leaning on his cane, he stood up and went to the fridge, grabbed a bottle of water, and went through the door that led into the rest of the car. He walked through the dining room into the observation area and sat down in a leather recliner, twisted the top off the water bottle and took a long, cool drink. He pressed a switch on the table next to the chair and the entire room went dark except for three small spots illuminating a painting in the dining room. He looked out of the window into the New Mexican darkness. It was pitch black out there, a moonless night. An occasional light from a house in the distance appeared, flickered off and on from behind a rock or a tree, then disappeared altogether. He reclined the chair all the way and looked up at the night sky through the clear roof.

The middle-of-nowhere New Mexico is a stargazer's delight. The Milky Way sprayed Heaven with its billions of stars; God's graffiti. Recent events—hospitals, doctors, IVs... last breaths; they all left hot, red impressions on his soul like handprints from a hard, backhanded slap. The whispering of the wheels on the tracks and the beauty of the New Mexican night sky were healing, soothing.

Emily closed the door behind her and walked quickly to the cabin which she shared with another service attendant. The pep in her step was not so much fueled by the excitement at the thought of staying in Hagen's railcar, as by the fallout from the bomb that had gone off in her stomach ten minutes before. She mad dashed it to the restroom in her cabin and was happy that her cabinmate was on duty in the dining car. She was comfortably alone. When she finished, she gathered her belongings and went to the dining car to get menus for Hagen, then returned to the blue beauty.

In the kitchen, only the lights over the stove were on, casting a soft glow throughout the entire room. She put the menus on the table and went through the door into the dining area. It was very dimly lit in there, the only light-source coming from three mini spotlights that were aimed at a painting which hung on the wall that separated the kitchen from this room. Under the painting, against the wall, was another corner banquette, like the one in the kitchen, but larger. It was all a rich, dark brown leather, supple and elegant. It took the *booth-ness* out of the booth. There were two chairs, upholstered in the same elegant leather, on the outside edge, allowing for six people to dine comfortably.

But it was the painting on the wall that stole her attention. It depicted the westward side of the Sandia Mountains as the setting sun lit up the rocky face with a pinkish-orange glow. The moon, full and enormous in a denim blue sky, hovered just above the crest. In the lower left corner were two initials—*HB*; and a date—1963.

From the darkness behind her came Hagen's voice. "What do you think?" He got up from his recliner in the dark and walked into the dining room.

"Wow, Hagen, this is incredible. You painted this?" She put her bags on the floor and folded her arms as she continued admiring the painting.

"I take it you like it, and yes, that is my work."

"It's stunning—the colors, the detail!"

"Thank you. I like it, too. It reminds me of the first time I experienced Albuquerque. It was a brief stop on my way home after the war. I got off the train, it was late afternoon and the sun was just touching the volcanoes in the west and illuminating this enormous mountain in the east. The full moon had just cleared the crest. It was breath-taking. It moved me spiritually, and it stopped me in my tracks, no pun intended."

"None taken. It really is beautiful." She looked from the painting to Hagen and opened her arms wide. "Well… here I am."

"Yes, yes you are." He pressed a light switch on the wall nearby and the entire area, dining and living rooms, lit up with a glow from wall sconces and table lamps.

"Welcome to my home, Emily. Let me show you around. It's not palatial, but it is my castle. The kitchen you have seen. This area is the dining room. Over here," he walked to the lounge area, "is what I call my appreciation room. The windows are continuous from one side of the car, extending overhead to the other side, and are made of ultra-clear glass. I wanted unobstructed views of the passing world and the night sky."

"Why do you call it the appreciation room?"

Hagen shut off the lights. The room went black.

Emily looked up at the Milky Way in all its blazing glory. "Whoa, that's amazing!"

"I have to agree. I call it the appreciation room because I will recline, turn out the lights and look up, and appreciate what Nature has created. It helps me clear my mind and reenergize. That is what I was doing when you returned. These past few days have been somewhat… draining."

"I can only imagine." She tried not to sound too sympathetic. "Do you want to continue appreciating? We can finish the tour later."

"No, no, I'm fine. Maybe after dinner."

He turned the lights on again. "Alright, over there," he pointed to the wall at the other end of the room, "is the elevator. I used to have an elegant spiral staircase in that corner. Unfortunately, logical necessity overrides elegance when you get old and your hips fail to perform properly. If normal stairs are unfriendly, then spiral staircases are belligerent. One of my friends had suggested that I install one of those," he up-and-down wave-motioned with his hand, "motorized chairs that you sit in, that *hummmm,* glides up and down stairs along the bannister. That notion went out the window when I envisioned a zaftig, caftaned, turbaned me spiraling up and down like Dame Edna on a geriatric roller coaster."

Emily had to laugh. "You are too funny."

"I'm here all week. Don't forget to tip your waiter." He took a bow. "Anyway, so I installed an elevator, with music."

"Elevator music?"

"Yes, elevator music. I know how ridiculous it looks to have an elevator for only two storeys. It's totally cliché. I love it and my guests get a kick out of it."

"I think it's brilliant!"

"Thank you. I think so, too." He continued the tour. "The hallway on the right leads to my room at the end. The door on the left is the master bathroom and is accessible to guests as well. The guest bedroom and bathroom are downstairs along with a small laundry room and some extra closet space.   If you have any clothes you wish to launder, please feel free to use the washer and dryer."

"Thank you, I appreciate that."

"My pleasure. Now, if it's alright with you, would you mind settling in after dinner? I don't know about you, but I am famished. I haven't had anything since breakfast."

"No, not at all. I picked up some menus from the dining car on my way back. I left them in the kitchen, I'll go get them."

"That was good thinking. But how do you feel about eating in tonight? I'm comfortable in my slippers. We can order from the restaurant tomorrow. Besides, my refrigerator is stuffed with food. I don't know what it is about funerals and food, but I have a veritable buffet in there."

"*We*, eat in tonight? That is nice of you to offer, but my job is to serve you and your job is to do nothing except relax and enjoy the ride, not feed the help."

"Emily, I don't think of you, or anyone who has ever worked for me, as *the help*. I appreciate your dedication to your profession. But, if you remember, I did say during our initial meet and greet that all I require from 'the help' is for them to feed me, clean up a bit, and maybe keep this old man company. There was nothing specifically said about where the food comes from. And, I believe that dining with me falls under the umbrella of keeping me company."

Emily looked him right in the eye. Her expression went from a squinting, *thinking-of-a-comeback-but-can't-find-the-words-to-say* look to a relaxed, smiling, *I give in* look.

Emily conceded. "Checkmate, Hagen, you win."

"I usually do, my dear, I usually do. Now, let's go into the kitchen and raid the fridge."

"Okey-dokey, boss."

They went into the kitchen and Hagen walked over to the booth in the corner and sat down. "I hope you don't mind too terribly if I let you raid while I watch. My other hip, the remaining original one, is moody tonight."

"Absolutely not, I don't mind at all. It falls under the umbrella of feeding you."

"Touché!"

She smiled a wide *gotcha* smile. "OK, let's see what I have to work with here." She pulled open the refrigerator door. "Well, you weren't kidding. You could feed the whole train."

"I told you. And more will be stuffed in there when I get to New Jersey, so we need to make room."

Emily looked at him quizzically. "New Jersey? I thought you were going to Philadelphia?"

"My family's farm is in New Jersey, across the Delaware River, and a little north of Philadelphia. The railroad tracks run conveniently alongside the western border of our property, and I built a spur that runs through the farm to an area near the house."

"Talk about door to door service!"

He laughed. "It does seem that way. OK, let's talk food. What gastronomical goodies are you finding in there? I know that Lydia Dominguez' enchilada casserole is in there. And Carol Riccardi's ten-pound lasagna; tossed salad; a bowl of cut-up fresh fruit. Oh, and Vera Kirk's fried chicken. I have no idea what else got stuffed in there. It was like *Chefs on Parade* in and out of my kitchen the past couple of days."

"What sounds good to you?" Emily's head was deep in the fridge.

"You choose. I'll eat whatever you feel like having. I'm not making any decisions tonight."

Enchiladas sounded good to Emily, but after today's carne adovada encounter she thought Mexican this soon might not be the best course to take. She pulled out the lasagna and put it on the counter next to the refrigerator. *This is twenty pounds if it's an ounce.* She took out the bowl of tossed salad and put it next to the lasagna. With some verbal guidance from Hagen, she located plates, bowls, olive oil, balsamic vinegar, a chunk of Parmigiano-Reggiano, and a cheese grater. Two nice chunks of lasagna went onto a plate and into the microwave. The salad was tossed in the oil and vinegar. She set the table: salad and salad bowls, napkins, silverware and drinking glasses.

Hagen watched her. She seemed quite at ease as she assembled their meal. There was also something familiar and soothing about someone moving around in his kitchen.

"Alright, dinner is served." She set a plate of the lasagna down in front of Hagen and one at her place. "Ooh, hold on a sec." She went back to the refrigerator and got a large bottle of Evian, opened it and filled their glasses.

"Thank you, Emily. This looks delicious. What would you like to drink?"

"Um, water? Unless you replaced the Evian with vodka."

"Very funny. I meant besides the water. How about some wine to go with the lasagna?"

"For you, sure, but I'm on the clock, remember?" She looked him dead in the eyes.

"Have you forgotten that I always win?"

"Uh-huh. But this pushes the professional borders a bit much, don'tcha think?"

Hagen gave her a look that said *I'm not budging on this one, either.* "You might be an employee. But technically, you're my employee and I just clocked you out."

"I'm just never going to win with you, am I?"

"Oh, you are just too easy." He scrunched his nose and squinted.

Emily huffed a sigh and folded her arms. "OK, what do *we* want?"

"You'll see. Go into the dining room. Against the wall, to the right of the booth, there is a rectangular, wooden box standing on its end, about three feet tall. On the wall above it is a keypad like on a telephone. Punch in 9–1–2, then the "Enter" button. You will hear some movement, then two doors will open as a bottle of wine emerges from the top."

"You're joking?"

He gently shook his head *no*.

"OK, I'll be right back from the Starship Enterprise."

She went into the dining room, found the box, entered the numbers on the keypad and laughed as a bottle of wine magically rose up in front of her.

"This is too wild!" he heard her say from the other room. She came back into the kitchen holding a bottle of wine. "You have a wine machine? Next thing I know you're going to beam us up to the mother ship."

"I haven't quite perfected that technology… yet." He smirked. "And if I had, why would I need the train?"

"Hmm, you've got a point."

"You'll find wine glasses hanging in the cabinet to the left of the sink and a wine opener in the drawer below."

Emily retrieved two Bordeaux glasses and the wine opener and went back to the table.

"I haven't heard of this wine before." She held up the bottle and looked over the label. "Sah-si… Sah-suh…."

"Sassicaia. It is a luscious wine from Tuscany. 1985 was an excellent year. Probably my favorite Italian."

Favorite Italian.

Hagen's thoughts drifted to the casket below.

Emily opened the bottle and poured a little wine into Hagen's glass. She held the bottle like a sommelier as she waited for him to taste it.

"I know what it tastes like."

"Oh, for goodness sake, humor me and let me at least pretend to work for my supper."

Feigning an aristocratic, snobbish air, Hagen picked up the glass, swirled the wine around, took a sip and swished it around in his mouth. He put the glass down. "Swill, I tell you. Send it back!"

She laughed. "I wouldn't know how to send it back if you were serious."

"*Touché* again, Emily. *Touché.*"

She poured more into his glass and then some into hers and sat down.

"*Bon appétit, monsieur.*"

"*Merçi, mademoiselle.*"

She sipped the wine. Hagen watched as her eyes lit up. "This is delicious!"

"Only the best for my guest… and Carol's lasagna."

Emily raised her glass. "To the chef."

Hagen raised his glass and touched it to hers. "And her lasagna."

And my favorite Italian.

They began to eat, both commenting on the deliciousness of the lasagna. After a few moments of quiet, Hagen broke the silence.

"Tell me, Emily, how long have you been working for Amtrak?"

"Just over two years now."

"Do you like it?"

"I do, for the most part. It has its ups and downs."

He washed a bite of the lasagna down with a sip of wine and dabbed his mouth with a napkin. "OK, tell me what the ups are, if you don't mind."

"I like the traveling. I like seeing the country and meeting new people. I love photography. Sometimes I get lucky and get in some good shots."

"Is photography just a hobby or do you aspire to become a professional photographer?"

"I would love to do it professionally. I wanted to be a photojournalist. I have always envied those National Geographic photographers. They get to go all over the world, taking pictures of exotic places and people. Maybe one day. For now, I'll work for *Amtrak Geographic* and make the best of it."

"If that is your passion, then you should pursue it. Life is too short to waste time second-guessing, saying *maybe one day*. Never doubt yourself. Follow your gut instincts."

"I want to, I really do. I know I'm a pretty good photographer. I'm just sort of… in limbo with life right now."

"I certainly can understand that. I'm feeling a little limbo-ish myself."

More silence, slightly awkward for Emily. *Of course, he's feeling limbo-ish; someone died.* Hagen sensed the elephant in the room and resumed his inquiry about her work.

"You said, ups *and* downs. Tell me what about working on the train does not suit you?"

Emily swallowed another mouthful of salad, then sipped her water. She pondered. There really were more pros than cons—only one con, actually. "Probably, the lack of privacy. You live at work and everyone knows your business. That's probably why I jumped at the chance to stay here with you until Philadelphia. I'll still be living at work, but I'll sleep alone for the next two nights and I'll have a bathroom to myself."

"I completely understand wanting some privacy. I was in the military and there is no such thing as modesty in the Army. When I returned to civilian life, I had some privacy for a while, but as our careers grew and our work became more public, our lives became less private. Everyone wants to know everything about you once you are in the spotlight. They feel they deserve to know all the intimate details about you in exchange for their admiration."

She shook her head. "Nothing is sacred." She was very curious to know more about him but did not want to pry. She thought about the casket in the cargo area. If Hagen wished to talk about his life, then it would be on his terms.

"No, nothing is sacred. It is not as bad now as it was when I was younger and more active with my artwork. I couldn't even go to the barber sometimes without someone following me with a camera or tape recorder. After a while, they get enough of you and when you stop giving them fodder, they eventually move on to the next victim."

"I'm sorry I'm not too familiar with your work." Feeling more comfortable around him, Emily got a bit bolder. "What did you do that earned you your fame and fortune?"

"I don't expect everyone to know who I am. It is not like I am a movie star or politician. I am an artist and an inventor. I have acquired most of my wealth from several patents which I hold. And, over the years, several galleries have shown and sold our artwork as well."

"Very nice. When I came back to your car, you said 'welcome to my home.' Do you live here, or just stay on it when you travel?"

"I live here full time. When I decided to purchase my own railcar, I built a spur of track connecting my land to the main rail system. You saw it when I joined on at Lamy Station. If you ride a few miles up the tracks, you will arrive at where I park my home. When I want to travel, I push out to the end of my tracks, close to the main line, and wait for the pickup."

"It seemed pretty secluded and very peaceful. Do you live all alone out there?" She paused, realizing that she may have sounded a bit nosy. "Sorry, I'm not trying to paparazzi you."

"That's alright, my dear, it is a valid question. I did not live alone until..."

He paused to find words.

"...until quite recently." His expression and tone of voice waxed melancholy.

Emily understood the reference to the casket resting just below them. The way he said it spoke volumes about how much the deceased meant to him.

"I really am sorry for your loss." She reached across the table and put a hand on his; her kind touch triggering an emotional response in him, almost. He didn't want to cry in front of her; not now, anyway. "And I didn't mean it when I said all you had to do was sit back and enjoy the ride. I know this isn't a pleasure trip."

"I knew what you meant. And please stop worrying yourself over possibly saying the wrong thing. Remember, I said no eggshells."

"Alright, no eggshells." She sat back and forked another piece of lasagna.

Hagen didn't want to think about it right now. He had the remainder of his life to think about it. He needed a distraction. "But, enough about me. Tell me something about you. Entertain me with a story about Emily Connolly."

"Me? I don't think I have anything to say that could even come close to what you've accomplished."

"It has nothing to do with accomplishments, or accolades. Experiences make the person. Certainly, you must have had some experiences worth retelling, at least one." He looked at her over his glass of wine. She just shrugged and made an *I got nothin'* face. Then Hagen asked, "how old are you?"

"I'm twenty-five."

"I cannot think that you spent the last twenty-five years under a rock."

"I don't think there really is much about me that's exciting."

"That is a shame, Emily." He wanted to hear something, anything, to take his mind off the casket right underneath them. Emily stared blankly at a place somewhere in the middle of the table while she tried to dig up something worth telling, to give him something. She was never all that comfortable talking about herself.

"Maybe… maybe if I just tell you things as they come to mind it might spark something of interest. But I doubt it."

"That's fine, don't doubt yourself. I have spent my life listening to people's stories. Remember, 'Art Imitates Life' and some of my better works were inspired by listening to someone talk. Oftentimes, something wonderful emerges in the telling of a life event; something you may have forgotten about. I would like to know a little bit about you. But, if it makes you feel uncomfortable, please, don't force it on my account. I don't want you to feel pressured."

"It's OK. I don't feel pressured."

"You never know what might come up." He sipped some wine. "Remember, we are our own worst critics. What might seem banal to you may spark interest in the listener."

Emily thought a little more. "OK, I'll start from the beginning, I guess. I was born January 23, 1973 in San Diego, California. My mom was a stay-at-home mom. My dad was in the army. He was a helicopter pilot in Vietnam. I don't have any real memories of my dad. I never met him. He died when his chopper was shot down in 1975, just a few months before the ceasefire. I was two years old. What I know of him are things my mom told me. She showed me photos of him with her before I was born, even a few while she was pregnant with me."

"What is your earliest memory?"

"Hmm, let me think..."

Hagen ate slowly as he listened to Emily, paying close attention to her facial expressions for emotions that might surface. Other than the occasional looking down at his plate, he gave her his undivided attention, never interrupting.

"My earliest memory of anything is... is opening a package that arrived in the mail for me a week before my second birthday. I remember... I was in my room, on my bed, playing with something, but I can't remember what it was. My mom came into the room holding this big box," Emily held her arms out, spread widely, "all wrapped in brown paper and tape and covered in stamps. It was from my dad; a birthday present. He was still over in Vietnam. She put the box in front of me on the bed and we ripped it open together. We lifted the lid and inside was a doll; a geisha doll. She was so pretty. I picked her up and hugged her, but she was very stiff. Her arms and legs didn't move. Her face and hands were made of porcelain. She wore a long, black, silk dress with embroidered flowers and she held a paper fan in one hand and a drum in the other... and she had a piece of wood, a stand, stuck to her feet. I tried to play with her, she didn't play back, so I gave up. I went back to playing with... what the heck was it? Oh, I remember what it was; a *See 'n Say* with farm animals, you know, the cow goes *moooo*?"

Hagen simply nodded and smiled, completely caught up in her story.

"I never played with the geisha doll again. My mom put her on the dresser in her room, where she stood for years." Emily stopped there, picked up her wine glass and took a big gulp.

Hagen waited a moment to make sure she was finished. "That is an important memory, a beautiful memory. Thank you for sharing it with me. Tell me, does your mom still have the doll?"

"She did have it, for many years. The doll was *my* present, but mom kept it safe with her. Years later, when I was old enough to understand, she told me how much it had meant to her, and why. Five days after my second birthday my father's chopper was shot down. The entire crew was killed. That doll was one of the last things he ever touched. My mom said it was my mine but asked if it was alright to still keep it in her room. I couldn't refuse her request. I knew what that doll meant to her. It was the last thing we ever got from my dad." She paused to collect her words. "Every morning when she got up and every night before she went to bed, she would touch that doll. It was her tactile link to my dad." She paused again and closed her eyes, trying to clench back the tears. "My mom died two and a half years ago, and now the doll sits on *my* dresser."

"That is a wonderful story. You might want to write that one down. I'm sorry for your loss."

"Thank you. I miss her very much. She was my best friend."

Hagen could feel Emily's melancholia bubbling up to the surface. "Do you have friends, someone to rely upon, talk to?"

"I have some acquaintances. No best friends. I applied for this job after mom died. I just wanted to get away from everything; not be stuck in one place. After selling mom's house and paying off the mortgage, I took what was left, rented a little apartment, bought a Nikon and hit the railroad. I stay at work as much as they will let me, then I go home and touch the doll."

Hagen was moved by how much Emily was opening up to him. "May I ask, have you any other family?"

"No, it's just me now. My mom's parents died in a plane crash before I was born. I barely remember my dad's parents, but, they're gone, too."

"I am sorry to hear that. I have never known what it is like to be alone, without family, or friends. I still have my brother and sisters. I look forward to seeing them again, even though the circumstances are not festive. Family sticks together and we need each other in good times and in not so good times. They are all gathering at the farm in New Jersey for the service."

Emily finished her last bite of lasagna, followed by the last sip of her second glass of wine. She was not a heavy drinker; a six pack could last three weeks in her refrigerator, if she stayed home for three weeks, which she never did. She was feeling the effect of the wine. Her face flushed, radiated heat. She was more talkative about her past than she would normally have been, especially around a stranger, doubly so with someone like Hagen. They had only just met that day. He was technically her boss. She opened up to him more than she wanted, but he had a way of making it easy to feel comfortable in his presence.

"Well it's obvious from your stuffed refrigerator that you have good friends," she tapped the empty plate with her fork, "who sure can cook."

"Yes, I do have good friends. One thing is for sure, I will never go hungry."

"No, you will not; not on this trip anyway." Emily went quiet. Her dredged up memories were swimming in her wine-soaked mind. Her mood was shifting.

"Thank you, again, for sharing those personal moments," said Hagen.

She picked up the empty wine glass and waggled it in mid-air. "Well, ply me with alcohol and I'm an open book." She put the glass down and stared at the table again.

Coming back to the reality of her position made her feel suddenly awkward and out of place. Hagen got her to talk about her past and now she felt strange about it. She no longer wanted to feel comfortable because she knew it would end in two and a half days. Her little humdrum world got caught in the gravity of Hagen's enormously dense and brilliant star. Like a comet, she would briefly orbit Hagen's sun, just long enough to enjoy it and blaze in his solar wind. Then she would be flung out into the cosmos of her own life to wander the universe and float aimlessly in the void, again.

"Dinner was delicious." Emily got up from the table. "My compliments to Carol Riccardi when you see her." She picked up the empty plates and salad bowls and put them in the sink.

"Just put them in the dishwasher." Hagen felt her mood shift. It got a little chillier in the kitchen.

After rinsing their plates and wine glasses, she put them in the dishwasher and walked over to the table. She stood there, falling into waitress mode, getting re-comfortable with him as the boss and her as the help. Her emotions were caught up in the momentary soup of self-awareness, self-pity, self-doubt, and expensive wine. Emily was not willing to be deluded into thinking that she belonged there in any capacity other than that of an employee. No matter how she looked at it, she was the help. She appreciated Hagen's generosity; sharing his food and wine with her. Inside she was telling herself that this would be the only time it would happen. From now on, she would fix his meals or get them from the dining car but eating with him was no longer an option. She might even go back to her cabin on the Amtrak train. If he was at all sensitive to anyone's wishes, then he would allow her to do what was comfortable for her.

She put her hands on her hips and looked down at her boss. "Do you want anything for dessert?"

"No, thank you. I am quite full. You did the lasagna justice with that very generous piece you gave me. Would *you* like something for dessert? I think there might be a key lime pie hiding somewhere in the refrigerator."

"No, thank you. I'm quite full, too."

"Is everything alright, Emily?"

She folded her arms. "Yes... no." She sighed and looked down at the floor briefly then back at Hagen. "I don't know." She didn't want to say what she was feeling without it coming out sounding silly and selfish. "Maybe it's the wine. You had me talking about my past, things that I hadn't thought about, at least that deeply, in quite some time."

"I apologize if I made you do something uncomfortable. I just wanted to know a little about you. It was not my intention to upset you."

"I know it wasn't, Hagen. I'm just feeling a little sorry for myself, I guess. And I know I don't need to. But I do. I blame the alcohol, not you. I'm sorry that I am such a party pooper." Feeling that this was an opportune time to say it, "Maybe I should leave you alone tonight and sleep in my cabin." She looked down at the floor again, her arms still crossed.

"If that would make you feel better. Like I said, it's your decision. But I don't see the reason why. You have not offended me whatsoever, and you have not pooped on anyone's party. If you did anything, you brought life to it."

Emily looked up from her downward gaze, into his eyes. He could see right into her; she felt it.

"Let me confide in you Emily, if I may. Sit, please." He waved his hand to the banquette.

She sat back in her seat; arms still folded.

"I have always had the ability to sense someone's feelings and emotions. I know when someone is sad, or happy. I can tell when someone is being truthful or is hiding

31

something. No, I am not a mind reader or a psychic. I happen to have a sixth sense that's a bit more sensitive than other people's. We all have it. We call it a gut instinct. Have you ever met someone and for some reason you just didn't feel comfortable near them?"

"Yes. I work with someone like that."

"Let me guess, the jealous Eddie you mentioned."

"I don't know how you figured that one out, but yeah, Eddie."

"And, haven't you ever met someone, who even before they speak, you felt like you wanted to be near them?"

"Yes, I have. I've met some passengers that I just liked a lot, and for no other reason than a feeling I got, or they just seemed nice. I'd go out of my way for them, do extra things for them." Emily was including Hagen in that group of people who she liked at first sight, but she wasn't going to say that out loud.

Hagen felt who Emily was, too. "When I first met you, I knew you were a good person. You have a big heart and you give off a lot of very positive energy. People like to be around you."

She wished he hadn't said that. Her emotions were running rampant and crying in front of him was not an option for her. Managing to keep her emotions in check, she said, "Thank you, Hagen. I can tell that you have a big heart, too."

"Thank you, my dear. Now, if I may be so bold, I think I know what you are thinking. You are afraid of getting comfortable here. You want to put a more professional distance between us."

"I thought you said you couldn't read minds."

"I cannot read minds, but I have had a lot of experience with human beings, and combined with my gut instinct, it simply makes me very intuitive. I am right though, am I not?"

"Yes, yes you are. There's no sense trying to lie to you."

"Emily, listen to me." He leaned forward, his elbows on the table. "In your travels, you are going to meet thousands of people from all walks of life. Some will be brilliant, some will not. Some will be rich, and some will not. They will present themselves to you in all shades of colors with all types of personalities. If you try to pick and choose those who you wish to know and toss the others aside, then you will be cheating yourself. You will be cheating yourself out of life. If there is one thing that I have learned in my seventy-four years traveling around the Sun, it's that when the Universe puts something, or someone, in front of you, it is telling you to learn from it. If you feel that not staying here for the next couple of nights is better for you, then by all means, do what is best for you. I do hope, though, that you will still be my attendant for the remainder of my trip. And if you change your mind about staying here, the offer is always on the table."

"You certainly have a way with words." Her cheeks flushed with embarrassment. "I'm sorry if I got silly. I'll stay tonight. Maybe tomorrow you can tell me about you, *quid pro quo* and all that."

"Absolutely. You must have been reading *my* mind this time."

"Just a gut feeling." Her smile sincere, a smidge apologetic.

"I told you, it works." He returned her smile; his blue eyes were captivating.

She looked deeply into those eyes. There was something there, a knowing. Was it just age and experience, or could he really read minds? One thing she could see was that he looked drained. "You look tired, Hagen. Shall we call it a day?"

"Yes, let's call it a day. It has been a long one, and a filling one. I haven't eaten that much in one sitting in a long time. Why don't you go get settled in downstairs and I'll see you in the morning?"

They left the kitchen and walked into the dining area where Emily had left her things.

"Good night Hagen, and thank you."

"No, thank you."

"When do you usually get up in the morning?"

"I grew up on a farm, so I have always been an early riser. I don't expect you to get up when I do."

"I can be up for you whenever you need me to begin my day. I'm used to it."

"Alright, then. I will expect you at your post by eight thirty."

"Aye, aye, Admiral." She saluted, but not comically this time. "I will see you on the bridge at zero-eight-thirty-hours, sharp."

He returned her salute. "Dismissed, Ensign."

She smiled, gathered her belongings and walked to the elevator. The door was open. She went inside and looked around. It wasn't like a regular elevator—there were no buttons to press. Hagen, seeing her confusion, walked over to assist her.

"Sorry, I should have given you a lesson. It is quite simple. See that lever on the right?"

"Yes, I see it."

"After you slide the door closed, you will move the lever to the *down* position. Once you get to the bottom you can open the door and exit the lift. To come back up, close the door and move the lever to the *up* position. When you arrive, you open the door and get out. It's a very simple design, completely silent and pneumatic; one of my patents, by the way."

34

"Sounds easy enough. Oh, one more thing. Are you a breakfast person? Coffee in the morning?"

"I am most definitely a coffee in the morning person; breakfast sometimes, it depends on the occasion. Maybe toast or a pastry of some sort. Why do you ask?"

"OK, mind reader, you couldn't figure that one out?"

"I figured it out when you asked me what time I get up. We can discuss breakfast in the morning."

"Alrighty then. Let's go for a ride." She closed the door and moved the lever to the down position. *Feels So Good* by Chuck Mangione began to play. "Good night." She waved as the elevator descended to the lower level.

"Good night." He waved back. He walked over to a wall switch and turned off the lights as Chuck Mangione's flugelhorn and Emily's laughter faded into the floor, then walked down the hallway to his room to get ready for bed. After changing into his pajamas, he sat on his bed. He closed his eyes and memories played in his mind as his fingers felt the weave in the Navajo blanket, like a blind man reading brail. Fifty-three years of memories; another big sigh. He pulled the covers down and climbed in. It didn't take long for him to drift off to sleep and for the dreams to begin.

When the elevator reached the lower level, Emily opened the door and carried her things to the guest room. A hallway like Hagen's led to the bedroom door at the end, with a bathroom door on the left. When she turned on the lights in the bedroom, she was greeted by a room filled with furniture you would not find on a regular passenger train. A beautiful, queen-size cherry sleigh bed was against the far wall with matching nightstands. Against the left wall was a matching dresser and mirror. A walk-in closet and chest of drawers were against the wall that separated the bathroom from the guest bedroom. You would have no idea you were on a train if it weren't for the gentle rocking and the sound of the wheels click-clacking on the tracks. The walls were adorned with paintings and photographs. All the paintings had the same initials—*HB*—in the bottom left corner. She remarked to herself how talented Hagen was. His ability to transfer to canvas such detail was extraordinary.

The photographs were also quite beautiful. Some were scenic and some were of people. They captured beautiful landscapes, mostly of the southwest. The people shots were candid—a lot were of Native Americans—and caught the subjects in action at just the right time to tell a story. *This guy is good.* There were initials in the bottom right corners— *SC. I wonder who SC is. Is SC in the casket?*

She unpacked her clothes and put them in drawers and in the closet. She put on her long nightshirt, grabbed her toothpaste and toothbrush, and padded barefoot down the carpeted hallway to the bathroom.

What she found there was just another example of what you don't normally find on a train. There was a full-sized, marble-walled shower with glass doors and a window with privacy blinders that looked to the outside. The sink was a work of art in itself. The basin was blown glass with swirls of colors set into a basalt countertop with a waterfall faucet.

The toilet looked totally alien. There was no tank, and when you approached it, the lid rose automatically and a control panel on the wall next to it illuminated. *Hagen sure does like his control panels.*

"Well, let's give it a go." She giggled at the unintended pun and sat down to do the deed. After the deed was done, curiosity got the best of her. The alien throne also had an integrated bidet. She had never experienced a bidet before. She knew what they were and had always been curious to experience one. She pressed the "Bidet" button and the process began automatically. She giggled again. "I hope a bottle of wine doesn't come popping up." She was quite impressed by the bidet function, thoroughly enjoyed it, and wondered why Americans never really got on board with it.

She brushed her teeth at the sink, feeling sinful spitting into something so beautiful, then went back to the guest room and crawled under the covers. She was experiencing a slight sensory overload—visually with the artwork and the appreciation area; gastronomically with the food and wine; and tactilely with the bidet and the fifteen-hundred thread-count, Egyptian cotton sheets; like she was sliding into a Teflon lined bed. It was a busy and filling day for Emily, and it didn't take her long to nod off into dreamland either.

Above her, Hagen slept deeply. Dreams and images whispered their way into his subconscious, like morning fog through trees. He would occasionally stir when something unsavory came to the forefront, but would easily slip into the depths again, surrounded by the insulation of good things past and yet to come. At one point, a woman entered his dreamscape. She was barefoot and wore a white, flowing dress. Behind her, shrouded in the mist of dreams were the shapes of other people. They stood there, faceless, without moving. She didn't seem to be aware of them. She smiled, held out her right hand and took one step forward. He couldn't tell if she was offering to take someone somewhere or accepting the offer to be taken. She waited with an arm outstretched. Then she spoke.

"Let's go home." She signaled to whomever it was she was talking to, to follow her, then she turned around and disappeared into the mist with the other figures.

Hagen stirred. He woke up, halfway opened his eyes and looked out into his room, expecting to see someone standing there, beckoning. No one was there, but he had the feeling he was not alone. He could smell the faint aroma of peach blossoms. It was not the first time he had the feeling that he was not the only one in the room, and he knew from experience that if he turned on a light to see the room clearly that he would find no one there. He lay back down and drifted off, the train rocking him back to sleep like a giant bassinet.

Emily fell fast asleep. She dreamed as well, but hers was a straightforward dream, inspired by the memories that she'd exhumed for Hagen over dinner. Her mother was in this dream and she was holding the geisha doll. But this dream doll wasn't stiff. She was fully movable and wasn't tied down to a wooden base. Emily's father was also there, in his uniform. His face was blurry, showing only vague features she'd gleaned from the photos her mother had of him. Her mom put the doll down on the dresser and held one hand while her father held the other. They let her hands go and she danced around the dresser, banging her drum. Suddenly, she stopped dancing and looked up at Emily's father. She banged her drum… three… more… times.

Bang... Bang... Bang!

On the third bang, a loud explosion sounded somewhere off in the distance and he vanished into wisps of smoke. Her mom watched her husband's soul float away on a breeze as tears rolled down her cheeks. She leaned over and kissed the little doll on the cheek, stood up, looked over her shoulder in the direction of the explosion, and then noiselessly faded into a mist and floated away on the same breeze with her husband. The little geisha doll stiffened into a pose, hands in mid-bang on the drum, feet stuck to the wooden base. That was Emily's only dream that night. The rest of her sleep was deep and silent.

The Morning

It was 6:15 a.m. when Emily opened her eyes and looked at her clock on the bedside table. She hopped up as soon as she could think clearly, wanting to be up and ready before Hagen. She quickly dressed in her work uniform and went to the bathroom down the hallway to freshen up. That big, beautiful shower called to her. She wanted to take a shower so badly—a real shower; not one of those micro, all-in-one closets she had to share with someone. She didn't want to waste too much time, so she washed her face, brushed her teeth, and tied her hair in a ponytail. She figured she'd enjoy a shower after breakfast, maybe take Hagen up on his offer to use his washer and dryer.

She left the bathroom and got into the elevator. This time she shared the ride with Kenny G. *Interesting choice in elevator music.* As she rose to the upper level, she peered through the elevator's glass windows into the appreciation area. There, in a recliner, sat Hagen, smiling ear to ear.

Emily opened the elevator door and walked out into the room. She put her hands on her hips.

"Good mornin' farmer Hagen. *I don't s'pose ya already milked the cows an' fed the chickens, didja?*"

"Well, good morning to you, Emily. The cows are full of milk, and the chickens are hungry. I thought you might want to do those chores *ya'self, seein's how ya fea-ul 'bout workin' fer yer supper, an' awl thayut.*"

"Ha-ha, very funny. But to be honest, I've never done either of those things. So, if you value your livestock, you

39

might want to find something less *farmy* for me to do."

"Well then, why don't we have some coffee and discuss breakfast?"

"Sounds good. But maybe we should talk food now, so I can get everything on one run to the dining car."

"I have a better idea." His cat-that-ate-the-canary grin told her he was up to something.

"Uh-huh, I'm sure you do. And I bet it doesn't involve anything from the outside."

"Well, you're half right. We can make coffee here. No sense in walking three hundred feet to and fro just for that."

"OK, how am I half wrong?"

"Wait—you'll see." He couldn't help grinning, giving away his having something up his sleeve.

"Uh-huh, we're going to be docking with the mother ship, right?"

As they were bantering back and forth, the train pulled into the Kansas City station and came to a smooth stop in front of the platform.

A few moments later—*DING DONG!*

Emily scrunched her face and cocked her head. "Was that a doorbell I just heard?"

"Yes, my dear, it was. Let's go see who it is, shall we?"

"I think you know who it is, but I'll play along."

They talked on the way down as Johnny Mathis sang *When Sunny Gets Blue*.

"I hope you don't mind that I ordered out."

"Why would I mind? I'm beginning to forget that I'm an employee, you know. I put on this uniform this morning," she plucked at the fabric of her left sleeve, "to keep myself, and hopefully you, reminded of that fact. Am I ever going to actually do some work around here?"

"It might not seem like it, but you are working right now, and have been from the moment you came on board.

40

Also, it's not necessary to wear that uniform. It's perfectly fine to wear your civvies. I should have mentioned that last night."

She shrugged. "Whatever you say. You're the boss."

They arrived at the lower level. Emily opened the elevator door and they walked to the entrance. Hagen pressed a button on the wall and the door swung open outward. Standing out in the cold winter air were six people: three generations—two parents, two grandparents, and two children. They were all bundled in their wintry garb, replete with knitted scarves and hats and gloves and rosy cheeks. The mom was holding a large brown paper bag and the father was holding a cardboard box that once contained a case of wine.

"Good morning everyone! Please, come in out of the cold," said Hagen.

"Good morning, Hagen! Good morning, Uncle Hagen!" Their voices a mix of Polish and American accents.

Piotr, Krystyna and Piotr's parents, Zelik and Ryfka, emigrated in 1973 to America from Poland. The children, David and SJ, had no Polish accent and spoke perfect English. They went inside and the kids gave their Uncle Hagen hugs. Hagen closed the door to keep the cold out and the heat in. The parents handed the bag to SJ and the box to David, and took turns giving Hagen a big squeeze.

"It is so good to see you again. How is everyone?" asked Hagen.

"We are quite well, thank you. The question is, how are you?" asked Piotr.

"Yes, yes, my dear," said Krystyna, putting her hand to his cheek. "We are so sorry to hear about Sal. We will miss him terribly."

Hagen smiled a brave smile. "I miss him, too. I'll be fine."

"He was a good man, as are you, my friend," said Piotr.

"Yes, yes he was." Krystyna dabbed her eyes with her gloved hand. "He touched a lot of lives and everyone is better for having known him."

Ryfka took Hagen's face in both hands. "*Wir beten für euch beide.*"

(We are praying for both of you.)

Zelik put a hand on Hagen's shoulder. "*Ja, ja, wir werden ein spezielles Gebet für Salvatore im Tempel sagen.*"

(Yes, yes, we will be saying a special prayer for Salvatore in Temple.)

"*Danke. Ich danke Ihnen und meiner Familie dankt Ihnen,*" said Hagen

(Thank you. I thank you and my family thanks you.)

The children stood there, holding the bag and box, listening to the conversation. Emily stood near the elevator watching everything. She could see the genuine affection this family had for Hagen, and for this Sal, and surmised from the conversation that Sal was in the casket.

"Thank you. He loved you all so very much."

Hagen noticed Ryfka's eyes looking over at Emily.

"Oh, where are my manners? Morawski family, this is Emily. Emily, these are the Morawskis, Zelik, Ryfka, Piotr, Krystyna, David, and SJ. Emily is my assistant for our trip home."

Emily smiled and nodded to them. "Nice to meet you all."

In a jumble of Polish and American accents, the Morawskis responded in kind.

"David, SJ," said their mother. "Why don't you take the food upstairs and put it in the kitchen for your uncle?"

"OK, Mama."

"Yes, Mama."

"Emily, would you mind playing elevator operator for them?" asked Hagen.

"I'd love to." Emily followed the Morawski siblings into the elevator and closed the door behind her. Henry Mancini's *Mr. Lucky* serenaded them as they disappeared into the ceiling.

"She seems like a very nice girl," said Krystyna.

"She is indeed. She has already been good company for me. She has a quick sense of humor and has so far been quite amiable."

"Good, that is good," said Piotr. "Is she going to be with you until New Jersey?"

"I only have her in an employee capacity until Philadelphia. I think she is very curious to know more about me, and Sal. I haven't told her about him." He turned and looked in the direction of the cargo hold then back to the Morawskis. "And, she respectfully hasn't asked. I commend her for that, but I may tell her about me, about us." Another glance in the direction of the cargo hold. "I also believe that it might be time for me to write my memoirs. Emily is interested in journalism; and photography, just like Sal. Maybe she's the one to help me, I don't know. What I do know is that I am not comfortable letting one of those greedy, publishing company vultures, with dollar signs for eyes, write my family's story. It should be written by family. *I* need to do it, but I will need help."

Hagen locked eyes with Ryfka. She smiled and nodded. He smiled and nodded back.

"Maybe it is time," said Piotr. "You and Sal have lived amazing lives. If I didn't already know you, I would read your story. Well, I lie, I will read it. I hope you write it. It does feel like the right time."

"Hagen, my dear. I have something I would like for you to give to Sal." Krystyna held out her hand. "Would you mind giving this to him?"

She handed him a small linen napkin with something wrapped inside. He unfolded it a bit to get a peek at what was inside. He choked up a little. "Sal so loved your *chruscikis*. He said that if he had to choose what to have for his last meal, it would be a big plate of your *chruscikis*." A tear formed in each eye and made a trail down his cheeks. Krystyna wiped them away with her gloved hands.

"I will never forget the first time he bit into one of Krystyna's *chruscikis*," said Piotr. "He looked like he had been kissed by an angel."

"Would you like to give them to him?" Hagen asked Krystyna.

"Will you please do it for us? There is not much time remaining before the train starts to move again."

"Yes, I will give them to him."

"Thank you." Krystyna's eyes teared up and it was Hagen who now wiped away tears.

The elevator delivered Emily, David, SJ, and Lawrence Welk back to the lower level. "Wait until you see what new goodies are waiting for you upstairs," said Emily, as she opened the elevator door. "You're definitely not going to go hungry anytime soon."

Hagen looked at Piotr and Krystyna. "What did you do?"

"Oh, nothing really. Just a little of this, a little of that," said Piotr.

"Thank you so much. Here..." He reached around to put his hand in his back pocket.

Krystyna stopped him in mid-reach. "No, no, no; not this time. We love you and it is the least we could do. Please, enjoy the food and the memories it will bring."

"I will. Thank you, all of you."

The engine blew its horn announcing all aboard. They all hugged one another. Krystyna took Hagen's face in her hands and looked him deep in his eyes, "May G-d bless you. Take care, my friend." She kissed him once on each cheek, then looked over at Emily and said, "It was so nice to meet you, my dear. Take good care of our Hagen."

"Yes, ma'am, I will. It was nice meeting all of you."

Ryfka hugged Hagen, holding him for a long minute. When she looked up at him her eyes had welled with new tears and she again held his face in her hands. *"Hagen, mein liebster Engel. Bitte kommen Sie bald wieder, um uns zu sehen. Wir müssen mehr von euch sehen."*

(Hagen, my dearest angel. Please come back to see us, soon. We need to see more of you.)

Hagen held her face in his hands. *"Mein liebster Ryfka, da stimme ich zu, wir sehen uns nicht oft genug. Ich werde Vorkehrungen treffen, um hier für eine Weile auf dem Weg zurück nach Hause zu bleiben."*

(My dearest Ryfka, I agree, we do not see each other often enough. I will make arrangements to stay here for a while on my way back home.)

Ryfka dropped tears onto his hands. He kissed her on both cheeks. Zelik gave Hagen a big hug.

"We had better go before the train takes us with it," said Piotr.

Hagen pressed a button and the entrance door swung open; cold air spilled in at their feet. The Morawskis walked out onto the platform and turned around to wave to Hagen and Emily as the door closed. A few minutes later, the train jerked forward, and then settled into a smooth acceleration. The Morawskis watched as the tail end of Hagen's railcar left the station, then put their arms around each other as they left the platform.

Emily and Hagen went into the elevator. Al Hirt played *Java* on the ride to the upper level. "The Morawskis are really sweet people," said Emily.

"Yes, they are," said Hagen affectionately.

The elevator arrived at the top. Emily opened the door. They talked as they walked to the kitchen.

"Did you really order food, or did they just show up with it?"

"They knew we would be coming through Kansas City. I knew they would want to see me. And I wanted to see them as well. They have been our good friends for many years. They are wonderful bakers. Their bakery is right around the corner from the train station. We always made time to see them when we would come through Kansas City."

They walked into the kitchen and Hagen saw the pastries laid out on a plate. There were fruit danishes, cheese danishes, plain croissants and chocolate croissants. An enormous loaf of freshly baked rye bread, sliced and bagged, sat next to the plate.

"The pastries look amazing." She opened another box. It was full of something she didn't recognize. "But what are these?"

"Oh, she really did outdo herself. Those are *chruscikis*, a traditional Polish Holiday cookie. They are deep-fried and dusted with sugar. Krystyna's are the best. Go ahead, try one."

Emily picked out a small one and bit into it. She savored the flavor, smiling. "Mmmmm, that *is* good."

"I know, and they are addictive, so be careful." He patted his stomach. "OK, let's have some coffee." Hagen reached into a cabinet underneath the espresso machine and pulled out a large, stainless steel coffee press. From the cabinet above, he retrieved a bag of ground, dark roasted coffee.

"Have you ever had French pressed coffee?" asked Hagen.

"No, I've heard of it but never had it."

"How do you like your coffee?"

"I like it dark and strong. You?"

"Me too. This makes a very strong brew."

Emily watched him as he measured out ground coffee and put it into the press, then filled it with hot water from the espresso machine. He put the lid on the press. "Voila, that's it."

"That's it? That easy?"

"Yes, that easy. It will steep for a little while before I press it."

"Where do I find coffee cups?"

Hagen reached into the same cabinet where he found the coffee and pulled out two cups. "Do you take anything in your coffee?"

"Nope, I'm a purist. I take it straight."

"Shall we have our breakfast at the dining room table?"

"Sure." She picked up the plate of pastries and went into the dining area and put it on the table, then went back into the kitchen to wait with Hagen for the coffee to steep.

"Oh, I forgot," she opened the refrigerator door. "Look—more food." She pulled out a large, foil-wrapped Pyrex dish. "David and his sister said these are cabbage rolls."

"Krystyna's *golumpkis* and *chruscikis* all in the same day. There is a God."

"And" —she pointed to six brown, champagne-corked bottles on the door shelf— "beer. David said his father brewed this batch especially for you."

"Piotr's lager *AND golumpkis*! With your permission, we may be dining in again this evening."

"This is about you, not me. Who am I to argue with the boss?"

"You're catching on."

"I just know when to quit losing. Besides, home-cooked food beats restaurant food any day. Someone put love into it, and that always makes it taste better."

He nodded. "Yes, it does."

"By the way," she folded her arms, "your refrigerator is overflowing with love. If you make any more food stops, you'll be eating enchiladas and lasagna for breakfast."

"Don't worry," he chuckled. "That was the only food stop."

She leaned against the counter. "How much longer until you press the coffee?"

"We'll give it another five minutes. Let's take it into the dining room and sit at the table instead of standing in the kitchen."

Hagen pulled two small plates from a cupboard and two linen napkins from a drawer. "If you wouldn't mind, I'll take the press and napkins if you get the rest."

They put everything out on the dining room table. She slid in and sat on the plush, leather bench seat and he sat in the chair across from her.

Emily folded her arms on the table and leaned in as she eyed the plate of pastries, like a six-year-old outside a candy store window. "What's your favorite?"

"Anything the Morawskis make is delicious. But, if I had to pick a favorite, it would be the plain croissant. I am a purist."

"I think I'll try one." She picked one out and put it on her plate.

Hagen picked one for himself and ripped it in half before putting it on his plate. "Time to press." He put one hand over the press, and with his palm, pushed slowly downward until the plunger reached its endpoint. The aroma of fresh, dark roast coffee permeated the air as he poured a cup for each of them.

She sipped her coffee. "Mmm, this is really good."

"The way I like it. Strong enough to wake Sleeping Beauty."

"I'd rather have the kiss." She blushed at her spontaneously blurted comment. "Not that the coffee isn't good."

"Ah, you are a romantic." He looked at her over his cup as he sipped.

"I've never been called that before." She put her cup down and pinched off a piece of the croissant and held it in limbo between the plate and her mouth. She examined her life in a few milliseconds and asked herself if she was a... what Hagen had just called her.

Hagen was watching the micro-changes in her face. "You don't agree?"

"I guess I never thought of myself that way."

"Then you are a closet romantic." He broke off a piece of croissant and put it in his mouth.

"Thanks for outing me. How am I ever going to tell my friends?" Her eyebrows raised, her lips pursed like, *now what?*

"Chances are, they already figured you out and you are the last to know. That's the way it usually goes. Believe me."

She wondered if that was his way of coming out to her, just a little peek from the closet. So far, he's mentioned family—parents, brothers, sisters. But not a wife. Who was Sal? She kinda had a feeling—not the time to ask. She changed the subject and pulled off another piece of her croissant and put it in her mouth. "This is *rrreally* good." A flake of pastry fluttered to the table. She quickly pressed it with a fingertip and kissed it off. "So delicious. It doesn't need anything else."

"Enjoy it, and don't be shy, help yourself." Hagen felt the subject being redirected and went along with it.

"Thanks. I'm not shy when it comes to food." She was relieved the discussion of her romanticism had petered out. Another delving into her past so soon after last night's emotional journey was not something that she felt like having with breakfast.

Thank God he didn't want mimosas this morning.

They sipped and nibbled as the train rolled on, gently rocking occasionally as Missouri passed by outside the window.

"When you take your castle on the road, so to speak, what do you do to entertain yourself?"

"Well, it depends on the situation, the company I am keeping. If guests are with us, we talk, listen to music, play cards. I might read a book, or listen to music if I am alone, which is very rarely."

"Did you bring something to read?" She finished the last bite of her croissant. She was interested in the man who owned his own railcar and hoped he might want to open up a bit to her instead of opening up a book.

"No, I didn't. I don't think I could concentrate on a book right now anyway. I'll probably put on some music and sit by the window and watch the scenery. You are more than welcome to join me."

"Thank you, I'd like that. It'll be a nice change to enjoy the view. And, we could talk… if you want to."

"That would be nice, yes. I would like that very much."

Hagen was pleased to see that Emily was amenable to chatting with this old man. He really did feel it was time to tell his story and was hoping that she might be the one to help him.

She smiled and perused the array of pastries and carefully pulled a cheese danish from under the assortment.

"Wise choice. My second favorite, if I had to choose one." He had finished his croissant by then and had also been eyeing the cheese danish.

"I really don't need to eat a whole one," said Emily. "Want to split it with me?"

He slid his plate in her direction as a way of saying yes. She split the danish and put half on his plate.

"Thank you, dear. I didn't want to have to force a whole one down either." Emily slid his plate back. He pulled off a piece of his half. "What do you say we adjourn to the living room after breakfast? We can bring the coffee with us and have a chat and watch the world go by." He popped the piece of danish into his mouth, then sipped his coffee.

"Sounds good to me."

When their plates were empty, they got up from the dining table and brought the coffee cups and the press with them into the living room and put them on the coffee table that separated two opposing dark brown, leather, love seats; Hagen sat in the aft-facing love seat and Emily sat facing him in the other. She poured more coffee for them.

"Thank you."

"My pleasure." She took a sip from her cup. "OK, so I'm curious. How did you meet the Morawskis?"

That question evoked memories spanning decades and the feelings attached to them hovered just below the surface. He and his family had been through so much over the last century. Over time, he began to believe that the history of the Beckenbauers would be something that people would want to read about. Vanity wasn't the impetus. Nor was it money. Hagen was one of the least vain people you could ever know; and one of the wealthiest. He had never felt that there was a right time to write it all down... until now.

One of the main characters in the play is gone. Recollecting memories is all he had; there were no more memories to create. Yes, this is the time. He isn't young anymore. His hands tire easily. If he is going to publish, he will need an assistant who would type and help edit. Maybe he will not have to search for very long for help. Emily might be the one. She is friendly, sensitive and a closet romantic.

Let's test her curiosity.

"We met them on one of our trips to New Jersey one year for Christmas. But I simplified the answer to your question."

"What is the complex answer?"

"It is part of a much bigger story."

"I'd love to hear it."

"It could be a long story."

"Longer than the ride to Philly?"

"Probably not. But I wouldn't want to bore you." He raised an eyebrow and half smiled.

"I have a feeling that someone who owns his own railcar hasn't led a boring life. I also have a feeling that you want to tell me. And my gut tells me that yours tells you that I want to know."

"You are very astute. And, yes, my life has been far from boring." He put his cup down. "Before I start talking your ear off about me, may I ask you something first?"

"Sure, ask away." She lifted her cup to take another sip.

"Emily, where do you see yourself, in let's say… five years, ten years? What are your plans for the future?"

"Honestly, I have no real plans. Right now, I'm on cruise control, riding along, taking things as they come."

"Is that what you want long-term?"

"I don't know, probably not. I'd like to think that at some point in my life, I'll figure out which direction to go.

Right now, the tracks take me. If you don't mind me asking, why are you so interested in my future?"

"I can understand how it might seem a bit odd this soon after making each other's acquaintance, but I must be honest, I liked you from the moment we met. I feel comfortable in your presence."

"Aren't I a bit young for you?" Her smile told him that her mind didn't go down that strange path again.

"Yes, you are, my dear. But I think by now you know my intentions are sincere."

"I was just joshing you."

"I know. What I would like to discuss with you might have an influence on your future."

"Go on." Emily sat there on the sofa, very still, looking him in his eyes, digesting every word he spoke.

"Emily, over the past thirty or so years, I have been approached countless times by journalists and publishers who were begging me for my permission to publish my memoirs. And I have turned them all down. My life is private; my family's lives are private. Also, I was not keen on the idea that someone wanted my story mainly to sell books and make money. I had not stopped living my life. Telling a story that was ongoing didn't seem logical to me."

"But you are still living your life. Remember you told me, 'the last time I noticed, I was still breathing'?'"

"Yes, I am still breathing. But…"

Someone isn't anymore.

"…I feel that I am now at a turning point. This is the beginning of the next act in my play."

"And you want to put down on paper all the acts in your play, so far."

"Exactly." His posture straightened.

"Then you should write a book, or a play, or an article for a magazine. It must be quite a story for so many people to want your autobiography."

"This is not about only me, but about family, friends, and me. About love, faith, the connections we make along the way."

"Have you already contacted a publisher?"

"Oh, heavens no. I want to write it first, without letting on to any of them that I am doing it. If they caught wind of me even considering it, let alone already having started, I would have to go into seclusion. When it's completed, then I will decide on how to publish it."

"When are you going to begin?"

He smiled slyly, looking right into her eyes. "Right now."

"Right now? Do you have a computer or a typewriter here?"

"No. I am not going to immediately begin the writing process. I will need help doing the typing, though, when it comes to that. My hands are not that comfortable typing more than short letters or emails. I want to find a collaborator, someone to hear what I have to tell. Then when all is told, we will put it on paper and publish it together."

"Are you going to look for someone in New Jersey or wait until you return to New Mexico?"

"I already have someone in mind. I haven't approached them yet." He finished his coffee and put the cup down on the table. "This is why I asked about your future. Emily, I would like you to consider being my collaborator, my assistant on this project."

"Me?" She sat fully upright and forward on the sofa. Her eyes widened. "You don't even know me. We only met yesterday."

"I know you enough. I know you are intelligent and sensitive and respectful."

"How do you know that?" Emily's emotions were being stirred up by his compliments.

"Trust me. I just do. You said you were interested in photojournalism. There might be photo opportunities that could be used in the book. Plus, we would be writing it together, ensuring it is written exactly the way it should be, the way I want it to be. And since you know nothing about me, what I say will be heard by your fresh, unbiased ears. My family and friends and some publishers all know about me. I want objectivity in an assistant."

"This is a lot to think about." She paused a moment. "I can't say I am not intrigued."

"Well, that is good to know." He said nothing after, just looked right into her.

"Do you need an answer right now, like, right at this moment?"

"No, not right at this moment, you have some time. But I will need to know what you decide by the time we reach Philadelphia."

"This doesn't seem like it's going to be a small project that can be completed in a couple of days on a train. When did you think I could do this? I have a job that keeps me constantly on the move."

"This will take more time than we will have on this journey together, yes. You would probably need to take a sabbatical from your present employment. This will be a paid position, of course."

"Pardon me if this comes across as sarcastic, but, you haven't already cleared this with *Warren* too, have you?"

"No," he smiled and shook his head, "I haven't. I didn't know who was going to be assigned to me and I never thought I would find someone this soon."

"That's logical. You could have gotten Eddie. I don't think his spelling is too great." She smirked and raised one eyebrow.

"But I did not get Eddie, or anyone else. I got *you*. Remember my philosophy about people's paths crossing. I believe everything happens for a reason. But, if all that comes of our time together is that we have kept each other company before we part ways, then so be it. I've learned to never force the Universe's hand."

"You said you wanted to tell your story to whomever was going to help you. I have a feeling that you are already pretty sure I'm going to say yes. I have a feeling you're also leading up to spending the rest of the trip telling me your story?"

"I would like to. Like I said, this may take some time."

"Time is all we have right now. Where are you going to start?"

"From the beginning."

He emptied the press into their cups and settled into her seat. "My parents came to America from a little village in Germany called Lampertheim, near Mannheim…"

Beckenbauer Farm
Lampertheim, Germany
1914

Horst Beckenbauer was the twelfth generation to farm the land that his family had owned in Lampertheim since 1637. Their one hundred and ninety acres were prime, fertile land with a half-mile stretch bordering the Rhine. The Beckenbauers grew some of the finest Riesling and Muller-Thurgau grapes for local wineries, and barley and hops for breweries. These wine and beer makers used Beckenbauer farm's produce exclusively because of the exquisite final products they created.

There were dairy cows, chickens for eggs, and sheep for milk and wool. Horst's wife, Ingrid, continued the family tradition of making and selling Handkäse cheese, known for being some of the best in the region. She spun the wool at shearing time to sell and to make sweaters and socks for her husband, and later for her children. People from miles around came to the Beckenbauer farm to buy their fresh eggs, dairy, produce, and hand spun wool.

The property contained a rather large farmhouse, built in 1669, the smaller original farmhouse that was built in 1638, and various outbuildings such as the two barns, two chicken houses, a smokehouse, an oast, a brewhouse and, far out in a stand of trees overlooking the Rhine, the family chapel and cemetery. The chapel was built by Adolphus Beckenbauer's three sons, Ingmar, Karl, and Sigmund, after their father's death in 1688. Adolphus and his wife,

Brunhilde, are buried in the floor, side by side, and are the only family members interred inside the chapel. The rest of the Beckenbauers and their extended families are buried in their hallowed ground by the Rhine.

For generations the Beckenbauer chapel, although not very large, held mass every Sunday for family and neighbors. As the population grew, the locals attended services at the larger church in the village and eventually the Catholic Diocese no longer sanctioned a priest to perform mass at the Beckenbauer chapel. But the family still prayed in their little church, surrounded by their eternally resting Beckenbauer ancestors.

Not all the acreage was farmland. There was a small forested area, about sixty-seven acres, which was the home to several species of local fauna: wild boar, fox, rabbit, deer, and badger, not to mention various species of birds including owl, pheasant, and quail. The Beckenbauers hunted deer and boar for roasts, soups, stews and various *Schinken* and *Wurstwaren*; smoked hams like *Rauchschinken* and *Katenspeck*, and sausages like *Pfalzer Hausmacher*, *Leberwurst*, and *Blutwurst*, all made from generations-old family recipes. They never slaughtered their own livestock for food. The cows, sheep, and chickens were family and were treated as such.

Horst and Ingrid had three children—all boys. Their first boy, Georg, was born in 1895. Just like his father, his hair was the color of corn silk, and his eyes as blue as the sky. Then the twins, Karl and Hagen, were born in 1899. They took after their mother, with auburn hair like a summer sunset, and eyes as green as emeralds.

The farm flourished, and as the boys grew bigger and stronger, they helped work the farm. Horst smoked more meats and started making beer that Ingrid sold in her little stand along with the cheese, eggs, milk, butter, and wool. They acquired more cows and with the extra milk, Ingrid increased her production of Handkäse and butter. The family recipes were taught to the boys and in time, they were able to make the cheese, *schinken*, *wurstwaren*, and beer just like their parents and the generations of Beckenbauers before them.

One spring day in 1912, Georg met a girl, Marta Schlessinger, in school. They were smitten with each other at first sight. She was fifteen and the oldest daughter of Lampertheim's mayor, Oskar Schlessinger, and his wife Louisa. By that fall, they had become engaged to be married but had decided to wait to be wed until Marta was seventeen. The wedding was planned for Sunday, June 14, 1914. The ceremony would be performed in the family chapel and the reception held at the farmhouse. It was an exciting time for everyone. Ingrid and Louisa took charge of the wedding plans while the men worked on refurbishing the original farmhouse. The newlyweds would have their own house to live in and raise the next generation of Beckenbauers.

As the months passed, the Schlessingers and Beckenbauers became very close and as the wedding day drew near, the whole village of Lampertheim rejoiced in the coming nuptials. Family and friends from all over came to Lampertheim and helped fill the little chapel to capacity. The wedding day was perfect; the sun was shining and there was a gentle breeze blowing through the open windows. After the ceremony, the families and local townspeople gathered on the lawn at the main house and enjoyed food prepared by Beckenbauer and Schlessinger women. The local wineries and breweries brought their fare, and everyone ate and drank, sang and danced into the night.

It was an evening which the village of Lampertheim would never forget. It was also the night that Cupid shot two arrows: one into the heart of one of the twins, Hagen, and one into Mathilde Schlessinger, Marta's younger sister. They would become inseparable and even though no official declaration had been made, they wanted to be married, just like Georg and Marta, and spend their lives together.

After their honeymoon at the Schlessinger's chalet in Bavaria, Georg and Marta returned to the farm to begin the rest of their lives together. Georg, along with his father and brothers, managed the farm. Ingrid taught Marta the arts of cheesemaking and of spinning wool. The farm had never seen better days.

It didn't last long.

Less than two months after the wedding, on August 1, 1914, Germany declared war on Russia, and two days later, on France. By the third week of August, Britain had declared war on Germany, and the Beckenbauers' lives were changed forever.

With the declarations of war came Germany's need to increase its military forces. Men of conscription age were called to arms to fight for their country. Horst, although still within the age range to be recalled into service, was not drafted, much to Ingrid's relief, due to a slight disability, a limp from an injury he had sustained whilst in China during the Boxer Revolution. The twins, Hagen and Karl, were only fifteen, and safe from being drawn into the conflict. But Georg, being nineteen, was immediately drafted into service.

Marta was beside herself. Her young husband was leaving to fight a war she didn't understand. Ingrid was frantic. She had been through this before when her husband was sent halfway around the globe to fight an enemy she had never heard of and she had seen first-hand what war can do to men and their families—and to their country. Now, both women were helpless to stop the inevitable. As the family watched Georg leave the village with other local men, their hearts ached. They went home, barely a word said amongst them. Marta moved into the main house, not wanting to be all alone, and every day went to the family chapel with Ingrid to pray for Georg.

Germany and its citizens had expected this to be a quick war, ultimately ending with Germany's victory. The Beckenbauers were depending on, hoping for, praying for a swift end to the conflict and Georg's quick return. What Germany and the soldiers' families had not expected was the addition of so many other nations into the fray, dragging the war deep into 1915, their hopes sinking ever lower as news from the Western and Eastern Fronts delivered reports of the numbers of casualties.

Letters from Georg arrived weekly. His last letter informed his anxious family that he was uninjured and somewhere on the Eastern Front fighting the Russians. What he wasn't telling them were the horrors he witnessed; the blood, the chaos. Men and boys, some not much older than his brothers, died right in front of his eyes, some disappearing completely, disintegrating as bombs exploded. The family always kept their letters to Georg positive, never saying anything that would let on that they were so desperately worried about him.

As May 1916 drew closer, a sense of panic settled over the farm. Georg knew his parents were worried. He knew the horrible tales of the war made it home, fueling the stress and strain of families with boys who were reaching conscription age. The twins would be turning seventeen that month. They had already received a notice from the German military office in Mannheim, informing them that Hagen and Karl were to report there no later than the end of the day, May 29, 1916. They were given two days to enjoy seventeen before they were to be whisked away to parts unknown. There would be no birthday celebration. It was a day of mourning, especially for Ingrid. Her three boys were going to be far away where she would not be able to protect them. Mathilde now understood what Marta had gone through when Georg was sent into battle.

When the day came for Hagen and Karl to report to the German Military office in Mannheim, there wasn't a dry eye amongst the family as they said goodbye. Mayor and Mrs. Schlessinger consoled their daughters and the Beckenbauers as best they could. They stayed at the Beckenbauer farm for a few days. While Oskar and Horst kept each other company with *Kirschwasser* and tales of past military heroics, the women soothed each other's hearts with prayer, and kept themselves busy in the kitchen, cooking and sharing family recipes and planning the welcome home feast for their soldiers.

1917 arrived and letters from all three sons were still being delivered each Monday, relieving the tension that built up in the six days between their arrivals; answering the constant barrage of prayers everyone sent to Heaven. So many stories came from the village and the surrounding areas of fathers, sons, brothers, and husbands returning from battle either horribly wounded, dead, or not coming home at all. But their boys were safe and sound, so far.

Thanks be to God. Amen.

There were rumors that an end to the war might be near.

Please, Lord, let it be so. Amen.

Germany and its allies were losing the war by attrition, its arteries bleeding out by the hundreds of thousands of military dead and wounded. November 4, 1918 saw one of the last battles of the Western Front. On November 11, 1918, the cease fire commenced and the war to end all wars ended. At the Beckenbauer farm there was jubilation.

Letters from all three boys had arrived on October 28:

...I am fine, Marta. It should be over soon.

I love you,

Georg

...Karl and I are alright.

Give my love to Mathilde.

I love you,

Hagen

...Hagen and I are well. Do not worry about us.

We will be home soon.

I love you,

Karl

The family waited for more letters to arrive, telling them when they would be coming home, but there were no more letters after October. The family kept their spirits up by telling themselves that the chaos of ending a war made it difficult for the post to get through.

"Death is a distant rumor to the young"

—Andrew A. Rooney

November 16, 1918

Horst was sitting in his chair by the window, smoking his pipe, whilst Marta and Ingrid were busy knitting sweaters for their men. Although the weather outside was cold and dreary, inside the house the climate was warm and cheery. Even though no more letters had arrived, they were hopefully assumptive that they would be seeing husband and sons very soon.

As Horst puffed on his pipe and listened to the women chat, the sounds of truck engines caught his attention. He heard them before they came into view and stood up and looked out the window. In the distance, two Daimler military transport vehicles grew closer, louder, larger. Horst went onto the porch to get a better look. The women heard the rumble of the transports when Horst opened the door and they put down their knitting and joined him on the porch. Excitement took hold of Ingrid and Marta as they saw the trucks. Their boys were home.

The trucks pulled up in front of the farmhouse. The passenger door of the lead vehicle opened, and Georg slowly stepped out and stood next to the truck, leaning on a crutch with a wound to his left thigh. He hobbled to his waiting family and they ran to him, crying his name, hugging him and kissing his face. There were many questions:

"What happened to you?"

"Why didn't you write to tell us you were coming home?"

"Where are Hagen and Karl?"

Georg stiffened, said nothing. Tears welled in his eyes as he looked over the women at his father and almost imperceptibly shook his head. Horst knew at once what that meant and prepared to brace his wife. While Horst steeled his guts, Mathilde rode up on her bicycle. She dropped it near the trucks and ran to the Beckenbauers and hugged Georg and the others. She echoed the same question that was asked a few moments before:

"Where are Hagen and Karl?"

Georg said nothing, couldn't speak. Horst positioned himself behind Ingrid while his eyes remained locked on Georg's.

Sounds emanated from the trucks; muffled voices and scraping. Men in mud-caked boots and dusty uniforms got out of the backs of both transports. As they hopped out, they dragged two wooden boxes with rope handles with them until they were both clear of the truck beds. Mathilde screamed Hagen's name. Ingrid let out an animalistic, guttural cry-moan that sent shivers through the soldiers. (Those soldiers would never be able to forget the haunting sounds of wailing wives and mothers.) Her knees buckled. Georg dropped his crutch as he caught his mother, wincing and grunting with the pain in his leg as she collapsed into his arms. Horst was a statue, his lips quivering, his nostrils flaring as he tried to remain composed, staring at the two boxes on the soldiers' shoulders. Somewhere in his head, something told him that the boxes didn't look heavy enough.

"Papa!" said Georg.

His father didn't even blink.

"Papa!!"

Horst broke his fixed stare on the boxes that contained what was left of his boys and looked at Georg holding Ingrid. He helped Georg lift her, held her tight.

"Mama," said Georg.

She looked up at Georg and fainted completely, held up by both men now.

Mathilde was on the ground, on her knees, hands balled into fists, punching her thighs, trying to beat away the pain, make some part of her hurt more than her heart did at that moment.

"Marta," said Georg, "help Papa take Mama inside. She does not need to be out here."

Marta took Ingrid's left arm over her shoulder; Horst got the other arm and they carried her into the house and laid her on the sofa in the living room.

"Marta," said Horst, his eyes hot, red, wet. "Stay here with my wife. I must go back to my boys."

"Yes, Papa, go, I will take care of Mama, go."

Outside, the scene hadn't changed. Georg stood there, leaning on the crutch again. Mathilde's punching had ceased. Tears mixed with snot and spittle dripped from her chin onto the ground. She was looking up at the caskets still resting on the soldiers' shoulders; their faces drawn; muddy tears streamed down their dusty cheeks. Horst walked over to Georg and said something softly into his ear. Then Georg turned around and said something to the soldiers. They walked to the backs of the trucks like pallbearers and put the boxes back inside, then climbed in with them. Georg opened the passenger door of the lead truck. Horst got in and sat in the middle.

"Mathilde." She didn't respond. Georg crutched over to her and put one hand on her head. "Mathilde."

She looked up at him, her eyes swollen and red.

"Go inside with Marta and help her with my mother."

She took his offered hand and stood up and wrapped her arms around him. He held her with his one free arm, kissed her on the top of her head. She squeezed hard; didn't want to let go.

"Mathilde, please, go inside and help Marta."

She slowly released him, stood back and looked up into his weary eyes, nodded twice, turned slowly and walked into the house.

Georg hobbled back to the truck and got in next to his father. The trucks' engines were started, and they rode off slowly in the direction of the little family chapel by the Rhine. When they got there, Horst opened the chapel doors and the soldiers carried Hagen and Karl inside and placed them gently on the floor, right over Augustus and Brunhilde. Horst thanked the men for all they had done for their country, and for his sons, and bade them farewell. Georg thanked them also, hugging a few of the men, then said goodbye.

When the rumble of the trucks faded into the distance, Horst stood up straight and looked Georg dead in the face. "What the hell happened? The last time we heard from you, all was well, the war was ending. Your wife, your poor mother, they were expecting you, all three of you, to be coming home, alive. Not... in, in, in boxes!"

Georg's eyes were reddened from tears and fatigue and road dust. "Papa, my last letter didn't lie. I was alright. I was expecting to be going home. Then our commanders sent us to re-enforce a battalion at the Western Front. Many of us questioned why, we knew we were not going to win, but we had orders. When we got there, we realized that our being there was not going to make any real difference; but we had orders; and we fought." Georg closed his eyes, squeezing a tear from each. "I had not seen my brothers since I left all of you, standing there in the village, watching me and the others leave." He opened his eyes and saw his father's fresh tears, then took a deep breath and let it out slowly. "When I arrived at the front, I heard that another battalion was there, and I recognized it as Karl and Hagen's. I searched all over for them. By the time I located them, the battle had gotten bad.

They were manning a machine gun, firing at the enemy. We barely had time to speak. I told them I loved them, to be careful, that we were going home together.

"I had to get back to my regiment. I hugged them then ran back to my post. I had not gotten thirty meters away from them when I heard the loud explosion behind me. I dropped to the ground; shrapnel had hit my leg. As I tried to stand up, the dust cleared, and I couldn't see my brothers anymore. The machine gun was gone. My brothers… were…" he stiffened and stifled the tears, "were…" his voice cracked, "…*gone.*" He cleared his throat. "A shell had exploded one meter away from them. There was nothing but a crater where I last saw them, where I last hugged them, where I last told them I loved them. I found them when the battle was over, what was left of them, scattered ten meters from the crater. Do yourself a favor, Papa. Do Mama the same favor. Do not look in those boxes. Remember Hagen and Karl as you last saw them, alive and beautiful and innocent. Let me be the only one in this family to remember them as I found them."

Horst deflated. His shoulders sank, his head hung down, and he began to sob again, silently. He walked slowly over to his dead sons and knelt beside their caskets. Leaning over and resting an arm on each box, he bowed his head and spoke. "My boys. My sweet, sweet boys. I am so sorry." Then he looked up at Christ on the cross over the altar. "Please, Lord, take good care of them."

Georg looked on, not saying a word. His father needed to speak to his God, uninterrupted. Several silent minutes passed. Horst stood up, composed himself and turned around. "Come, son, let us go take care of your mother. The war may have ended for the rest of the world, but your mother's heart is the new battleground. She is going to need all the reinforcement we can give her. You and I will mourn your brothers another time."

69

They discussed the funeral as they walked through the empty barley field. The women didn't need to hear the details. Gravediggers needed to be hired. The stonemason in Lampertheim had to be contacted. They walked a little further, reverently deep in thought, letting the talk of funeral details sink in as the two enormous holes that Karl and Hagen had occupied when they were alive got bigger, deeper, sadder.

Georg's injured leg, and the necessity of the crutch to walk, had him pausing occasionally to rest. Halfway through the barley field, he realized something. The farm was too quiet. There were no animal sounds—no cows, no chickens, no sheep.

"Papa? Where are the animals?"

Horst turned to Georg, shrugged his shoulders, and sighed. "They are gone."

"Gone? What do you mean, gone?"

"The military showed up one day and confiscated the livestock to help feed their army. Your mother had a breakdown when the reality hit her that they were not planning on milking the cows and sheep and using the chickens for eggs. The thought that they were all going to be slaughtered was too much for her. The only thing that kept her going was the weekly post with letters from you and your brothers."

"Is the military going to reimburse us for what they took?"

"I have no idea. They gave me a receipt. I will try to get reimbursement after we lay your brothers to rest. But who knows how long that will take? Germany is in shambles. The best thing for your mother is to get this farm running again. She will need the distraction, to stay busy with a purpose."

A cow *mooed*. Georg and Horst looked at each other. "They were *generous* enough to leave one cow and two chickens, the bastards!" said Horst.

Georg shook his head and they continued walking to the house. Inside, they found Marta sitting on the sofa, holding her sister, who was still crying over Hagen.

"Marta," said Georg. "Where is Mama?"

"I helped her upstairs to bed. She needed to lie down."

Horst and Mathilde went upstairs to Ingrid. Georg sat on the sofa next to his wife.

"This farm is a mess." He shook his head. "All the livestock is gone. It isn't going to be easy to recover from this war."

"I know." She rested her head on her husband's shoulder. "The country is a disaster. It is not going to be easy for any of us."

"Death is not the worst
that can happen to men."

—Plato

Love and Loss

The day of the funeral arrived. Family and friends came to pay their respects. Ingrid did her best to remain calm and reserved during the service. She collapsed when her two sons were lowered into the ground and had to be carried back to the house and put to bed. This time, Ingrid did not recover. A doctor was summoned, and he informed the family that her heart was failing. Two days after the funeral, Ingrid Beckenbauer died of a broken heart and was laid to rest next to her sons.

This was indeed a sad time for the Beckenbauers. The war cost them so much: sons and brothers, a wife and mother, all the animals. It was difficult for Georg to talk to his father about the next course of action. Whenever he brought up the subject of going into Mannheim to speak with someone at the military office about compensation, his father got quiet. All he could think about was his wife and sons, dead and buried. The helplessness he felt, the inability to protect his family, deepened his depression. He barely ate. He slept fitfully; waking up many times in a night with bad dreams. Georg and Marta didn't move back into their little house but stayed in the main house with Horst. He was in no condition to be left alone.

Christmas came and went with little celebration. There were no decorations, no tree, no glad tidings. Horst, Marta, and Georg went to the Schlessingers' for dinner. The giving of gifts was given up that year. Maybe next year. Maybe not. The holidays were never going to be the same.

1919 arrived and brought all of 1918's pain along with it. There was nothing to be happy about. 'Happy New Year' were empty words uttered by broken hearts.

There wasn't much to do around the farm with only one cow to milk and two chickens. Georg went to the military office in Mannheim once a week to inquire about compensation for his livestock. It was always the same spiel— "we do not know anything yet, Herr Beckenbauer. Berlin is overwhelmed with so much paperwork after the war. Come back next week and maybe we will have some good news for you."

Horst gave up hoping that his farm and his family would ever be the same again. He took to drinking *Kirschwasser* at night to numb his pain and keep the demons at bay. Sleeping in the bed Ingrid and he had shared was too painful. He would go into their room and look at where she had slept beside him for twenty-eight years, then kiss her pillow and go down to the living room to fall asleep on the sofa.

The winter of 1918–19 was not a particularly harsh one in general, but there were some occasional frigid nights. On one of those colder nights in January, Horst was having his usual brandy before bed. But, instead of going to sleep, he just sat in his chair, in the dark, staring out the window at the chapel in the moonlight, thinking. His mind wrestled with thoughts of war and dead sons, dead Ingrid, dead farm. After he was sure that Marta and Georg were asleep, he put on his coat and shoes. He stuffed two small glasses into his coat pocket, picked up his bottle of *Kirschwasser* and went outside, closing the door quietly behind him. The night sky was crystal clear. The moon was full and bright, so bright that he didn't need a lantern. In the distance, he could see his family's chapel and the trees of the cemetery. He pulled the cork out of the bottle and took a sip of the cherry brandy. It warmed him on the inside, and he started off in the direction of the chapel. The frozen ground of the bare barley field crunched under his footsteps.

When he got to the cemetery, he opened the gate and went in. He read some of the names of his ancestors in the cold blue-black light of the moon. He paid respects to his parents and their parents. Then he came to his son's gravestones. He stood there, looking from one to the other. He talked to them, cried to them, apologized to them again for not keeping them safe. Then his eyes drifted to the one headstone he was saving for last; the one he was avoiding but not ignoring. He stopped trying not to look, walked over and stood at her feet.

"Ingrid, my dear wife. I miss you so very much. I do not know how much longer I can go on without you. The farm is ruined. Life is ruined."

He pulled the two glasses out of his pocket, put them on her headstone and filled each one with the brandy. Picking up one of the glasses, he toasted his sons, then his wife, then sipped. He spoke to Ingrid, told her things he was not able to say out loud to Marta or Georg, or even to himself. He talked, and sipped, until he started to get wobbly and drowsy. He sat down on the ground above his wife and leaned back against her headstone and talked, and sipped, as the moon made its way across the sky, the icy shadows cast by the headstones moving like rows of moondials. At around three-thirty in the morning, Horst fell asleep in the shadow of Ingrid's headstone.

The next morning, Marta was up before the sun. Georg was still sound asleep. She quietly put on her housecoat and peeked in Horst and Ingrid's room before heading downstairs. The bed wasn't slept in, but that was not unusual. He was always up early, and she expected to see him where she did every morning, sitting in his chair, smoking his pipe, staring out the window at the remains of his farm, and the cemetery in the distance.

This morning she smelled no pipe smoke wafting up the staircase. There was no Horst on the couch or in the chair, and his coat was not on the hall tree by the door. *Maybe he went to the outhouse.* She looked through the kitchen window to see if he was out there. The outhouse door was wide open. It was empty. She walked through all the downstairs rooms and couldn't find him, then went back upstairs and looked in Hagen and Karl's rooms, but no Horst. Then she finally woke up Georg.

"Georg." She gently shook his shoulder. "Georg wake up. I cannot find Papa."

Georg stirred, rolled onto his back and slowly opened his eyes. "Hmm? What?"

"I went downstairs to make some coffee and say good morning to Papa. He is not downstairs. I looked everywhere, in every room. I cannot find him."

"The outhouse?"

"The door was open. But his coat and shoes are gone."

Georg sat up on the bed and rubbed his eyes. "He must be around somewhere." He put on his robe and slippers and together they went downstairs.

"Papa," he called out. "Papa, are you here?"

Silence. No sound except the winter birds outside chirping their greetings to the rising sun.

Georg got a sick feeling in his stomach. He ran upstairs quickly and put on some clothes, came down and put on his coat and boots, grabbed his field glasses and went out onto the porch. He scanned the farm for any sign of Horst.

Nothing.

He turned his attention to the cemetery in the distance. The sun had just peeked above the horizon and lit up the landscape enough for Georg to see a figure on the ground.

"Oh, God, no! MARTA! MARTA!" He ran down the porch steps through the field towards the cemetery. His recent wound, although healed on the outside, burned in his thigh as he sprinted at full speed. Marta came out onto the porch and saw her husband running away from the house. Then it dawned on her why he was running towards the cemetery. She ran inside, put on her coat and boots, and went outside to follow Georg. By the time Marta got to the cemetery, Georg was already on the ground over his mother's grave, cradling his father. Horst was dead; frozen to death in his sleep.

"Oh, Georg, no!"

"Papa, oh Papa. What did you do?" Georg rocked his father, crying as he spoke to him.

Marta went to her husband and knelt down on the frozen ground beside him. "Oh, Papa." She held Georg and cried as they gently rocked.

Together, they picked up Horst and carried him inside the chapel and placed him on the floor where Hagen and Karl had lain just a couple months before. They were stunned and sharing the same thoughts—*now what?*

"Marta, what are we going to do now?"

"We must go to the village and tell the constabulary about Papa."

"I know that, but then what? It is just us now, you and me, and a dead farm."

"We will go on. We will manage. When Berlin pays us for the animals, we will start over. We can do it. Your parents did it all alone before you and your brothers were born."

"Marta, they did not start from nothing. They *took* over, not *started* over."

"When the money comes, we will not have nothing."

Georg sighed then looked down at his father. "Papa, rest easy now. You are with Mama, and God. Look over us, pray for us."

"Georg, for your parents, for your family, we will recover from this."

"I hope so, Marta, I hope so."

Georg and Marta genuflected and sat in a pew near Horst, knelt and prayed to Christ on the wall behind the little altar. They prayed for help from the Almighty, for guidance, for Horst and Ingrid, Hagen and Karl.

They left the chapel and went to the village to report Horst's death and make plans for his burial. News spread quickly throughout the village about what happened the night before. So many families still suffered from the losses of their own loved ones. The news about Horst only piled more sadness on top of the heap of somber times of the day.

A funeral service was held in the chapel three days later, but since it was the dead of winter and the ground was frozen solid, Horst would have to rest in the chapel until spring, when the ground would thaw enough to allow for a grave to be dug.

Two months later, Horst was finally laid to rest next to his wife and sons, and Georg was still waiting for compensation from the government for the livestock. In the meantime, he and Marta did what they could do to keep the farm going. Georg maintained the vineyard and the crops of barley and hops while Marta did her best to keep her husband's spirits up. Georg's heart just wasn't in it anymore. He missed his family. He missed things that hadn't happened yet—watching his brothers' weddings; his parents becoming grandparents; handing down family traditions to the next generation of Beckenbauers. He felt like he was only existing, without purpose. Marta tried desperately to help her husband, but she knew he was not going to last much longer unless something changed for the better.

August 1, 1919

It was a sunny Friday morning. Georg was out in the vineyard and Marta was upstairs rummaging through Horst's wardrobe, looking for clothing to donate to the veterans and their families. She pulled a shirt from the wardrobe and one of the buttons fell off and onto the floor. When she bent over to pick it up, something caught her eye. Horst's wardrobe was on wheels. *Wheels? Why does a wardrobe need wheels?* She folded the rug that was on the floor out of the way, revealing old wheel marks engraved over the years into the wood. The grooves in the floor were in an arc, like the piece of furniture had been pulled away from the wall on a hinge. She grabbed onto the frame around the open door and pulled. Nothing. It didn't budge. Not even a slight movement; like it was glued in place. She looked inside the wardrobe, felt all along the back. Her hand found three wing nuts, one each near the top and bottom right corners and one half-way in between. They were each twisted onto a bolt that came through the back of the wardrobe from the wall behind.

She turned the top wingnut counter-clockwise. As she did, the top of the wardrobe came slightly away from the wall. When it was all the way unscrewed it fell to the bottom of the wardrobe with a small *thud* of metal on wood. She repeated the process with the remaining two wingnuts—*thud, thud.*

Marta grabbed the frame again and pulled. This time it moved. It swung wide on three wheels: the front two and the right rear; the left rear wheel was a dummy. The wardrobe pivoted on a shaft that bolted into the floor through the wheel.

She moved the wardrobe into a perpendicular position to the wall, revealing the three bolts that had held it in place. They looked as old as the house itself. Part of the wall that was concealed from sight seemed to have a removable section. It was perfectly square, three feet on all sides, the bottom running along the floor. There was no handle to pull, no knob to turn. Marta felt around for a way to get her fingernail in the groove to pull on it. The panel was snug in its place, barely a razor's width in the groove. She pressed on it along its right edge. It budged a bit, depressing inwards but only in the area where she applied direct pressure and went back into place like it was spring loaded. It reacted that way when she pushed on it all along its edges and corners. When she pushed directly in the center, the whole square depressed evenly. The panel slid up by itself on hidden springs, revealing a compartment three feet deep.

Inside, on the floor, was an iron strongbox. It looked ancient and was heavier and larger than the common strong box of the day; more like a small chest. Unable to lift it, she dragged it from inside the hidden compartment by one of its iron handles that hung off of the ends, leaving a trail of scratches in the floor. Marta sat on the bed looking down at it, catching her breath. There was a keyhole in the front, but no apparent key. Curiosity about where the key might be, sent her on a quest to find it.

She searched everywhere; all the drawers in the bedroom, all the drawers in the other rooms. She went downstairs and searched every drawer and cabinet. Giving up for the time being, she went back upstairs to continue rummaging through Horst's old clothing.

But she just could not keep her mind, or her eyes, off of that hidden place in the wall and the iron box sitting on the floor. *Where is that key? I will have to wait for Georg. Maybe he knows something about it.*

She continued her rummaging and pulled an old winter coat from the wardrobe. She did not remember ever seeing Horst wearing it. It was tattered in places; one sleeve coming away from the right shoulder. It looked like it hadn't been worn in years. She took it off the hanger and tossed it with the other items to be thrown away. It hit the floor and made a thud. That caught her attention. She picked it up and felt all the pockets. There was something in the coat, at the bottom, like it had been sewn into the lining. She felt all of the pockets, inside and out. Maybe a pocket lining gave way and the object fell inside the coat; no holes in any of the pockets. Then she remembered the open seam where the right sleeve was coming away from the shoulder. She turned the coat upside down.

Shake, shake, shake, *THUD!*

"Damn!"

A key! A large, old iron key slipped out of the open seam and fell right onto Marta's left instep. She rubbed at the pain in her foot. She bent over, picked up the key and put it into the keyhole on the front of the iron box. It barely went into the hole; something was blocking it. She pushed, pushed, pushed. The key would not go in farther than a quarter of an inch.

She wondered if she should bother Georg. *He is out on the farm somewhere. Leave him be. It's just a box, just a key, just a hidden hole in a wall!* She rubbed her instep where the key struck. A small welt was rising. *That will bruise.*

She examined the surface of the box. The sides were plain, but the top had some ornate artwork cast into it, depicting a three-masted wooden ship in full sail making its way through a choppy sea. She saw no other openings other than the blocked keyhole on the front.

Her curiosity increased from simmer to boil. She examined the key again. It was about three and a half inches long from bow to pin. At the pin was one bit with wards symmetrically cast into it. The bow of the key was wider than a normal key, about three inches. Cast into it were the initials AIB on one side, and a date, 1640, on the other.

That did it—ancient key, ancient box, hidden compartment! She couldn't take it any longer. Out the door she flew, down the stairs and out the front door. Jumping from the porch into a full sprint, she ran towards the barn hoping to find her husband there.

Georg heard Marta calling his name and went to the edge of the vineyard. She was running through the barley towards the barn, calling his name. It was obviously not a call to lunch. He became alarmed. Nothing lately that involved running through the fields screaming someone's name was connected to anything good. He ran towards her, called out to her. She changed direction at the sound of his voice and when they met, Marta was out of breath. In between catching her breath, she managed to get out, "Come... quick... I... found... something."

They walked briskly back to the house and she led him upstairs to his father's bedroom. Pointing to the wardrobe, then the hole in the wall and then the strongbox on the floor, she said, "Look. I found this in the wall behind the wardrobe."

"It's Papa's old iron strong box. I haven't seen it in years. I looked for it after he died but when I could not find it, I assumed he had sold it during the war to help with the expenses."

"Here." She held out her hand, showing him the iron key. "I found this in one of his old coats. I tried to open it, but I could not get the key into the hole. Do you think that it even opens this box?"

He took it from her, held it, felt its weight, turned it over in his hand and saw the engravings. "1640? AIB? Hmm. Augustus Ingmar Beckenbauer."

Georg tried the key in the hole on the front side with no luck; he had the same result as Marta. He knelt down to inspect the box closely. He tried to move it, push it. He wanted to tip it on its side to see what was on the bottom. It was quite heavy, and it took some effort to flip it and wondered how his wife managed to move it. He heaved and turned the box onto its side. A muffled sound of movement came from inside the box. They looked at each other, curiosity building, then examined the bottom. Cast into the iron were a name and a date:

$$\text{Franz Gundelscheim und Söhne,}$$
$$\text{Eisenarbeiter}$$
$$\text{Mannheim, 1640}$$

"Gundelscheim," said Georg. "That family still owns the iron works on the river in Mannheim."

They turned the box upright, back onto its bottom. *CLOMP!* The floorboards vibrated under their feet.

Georg tried the key one more time. Still no luck. While he fiddled with the key in the hole, his other hand that rested on the lid felt something move. He looked at the relief of the three-masted ship. He poked and prodded it with his fingertips. A door that covered one of the cannon windows moved. He plucked it with two fingers from the side of the ship.

"Look, Marta. A hidden keyhole!" He inserted the key in the cannon window; it went in about an inch, a good sign. Their hearts raced. With some effort and both hands, he turned it slowly counter-clockwise. Clicking sounds came from the mechanism inside. The key stopped turning and he slowly lifted the heavy lid. What they saw inside made them both utter mouth-wide-open gasps. Currency—modern currency, quite a bit tied in bundles—lay before them, tossed about by the upturning of the chest. Strewn around the inside with the currency were a hundred-or-so coins—20 Mark, Wilhelm I gold coins from the 1870s—gleaming like ornaments against the paper money. Georg picked up a bundle of money, then another, then another, revealing a very old-looking envelope. He took it out, opened it, and removed the contents: folded papers, legal documents, browned with age. Georg inspected the papers. The writing was in German and English.

"What does it say, Georg?" Marta's voice was excited with curiosity.

He said nothing. He was in a daze and kept reading the same paragraph repeatedly.

"Georg?"

He kept reading.

"Georg!"

Looking up from the documents, "Oh, sorry, Marta." He held up the papers and shook them gently, smiling. "I think this," then pointing the papers at the strongbox, "and that, is the answer you have waited for."

"Answer? To what?"

"Your prayers… to God… to help us; to help you help me. I know you have prayed for me. I know I am not the same *me* you married, and I am sorry for that. You have been so understanding, so caring; the woman I married."

Marta's eyes welled with tears, her lips pursed, and a tear fell down a cheek. "Oh, Georg, I love you so much. I cannot help but worry about you."

"Perhaps now you may stop worrying." He handed her the papers.

Her mouth slowly opened as she read the document, then looked at Georg with astonishment.

What they had just found was the deed to three hundred acres of land in America, in a place called New Jersey. The deed was very old, dating back to 1847. With it was a bank book showing annual transfers of funds for property taxes.

During the potato famine in the 1840s, Johann Beckenbauer, Georg's great-grandfather, emigrated to America with the hope of starting a new farm and eventually bringing all the Beckenbauers there to live new, prosperous lives. His ship docked in New York and, having heard that many Germans had settled in Pennsylvania, he intended to travel there and buy some land. He never made it to Pennsylvania.

As he traveled through New Jersey, he came across a large, fertile piece of land for sale in a town called Beverly, in the County of Burlington, and went no further. He purchased the three-hundred-acre parcel, then hired builders to build a barn and house. All was going as planned. When the barn was completed, Johann set up an area inside as living quarters for himself so he wouldn't have to live in the boarding house any longer and could supervise the building of the house.

He had just moved into the barn when a letter arrived from Germany. His brother, Horst (who Georg's father was named after), had died of influenza. There was no one to run the farm. Johann cancelled the construction of the house, boarded up the barn and went home to Lampertheim. He changed the crops to barley and hops and planted the vineyard of Riesling and Muller-Thurgau grapes. The cows and chickens came a year later. The farm that Georg knew before the Great War was a result of Johann's diligence, perseverance, and hard work. The cows and chickens that

Ingrid had been so fond of, the ones that went to their death to help feed the German army, were all descendants of the original animals Johann Beckenbauer purchased in 1850.

Georg counted the money, then they sat next to each other on the bed in silence. Their minds spun.

"Georg, why would Papa not have told anyone about this?"

"I had heard about my great-grandfather going to America. I knew nothing of the property or this money."

"Maybe Papa was saving this as a last resort."

Georg slid the document back into the envelope. "I do not know what he was waiting for. A last resort was what we needed."

Their minds spun faster.

"Marta, are you thinking what I am thinking?"

"Are you thinking about moving to America?"

"I am. It would be a new start. There is more than enough money here to get us there. The land is ours; it is paid for."

"We don't speak English, Georg. How can we move somewhere and not speak the language?"

"Marta, if we can survive everything that we have endured together, then I am sure we can survive learning a new language."

"We have been through so much, Georg, this is true." She looked down at the money and documents in the chest then back into Georg's eyes. "I will follow you wherever you want to go."

They discussed it over dinner, and late into the night, and decided that they would leave Germany. That Monday, Georg and Marta went to Mannheim to initiate the process of obtaining the required documentation for travel to

America. They also met with a real estate agent who would take charge of the sale of the farm in Lampertheim.

Arranging everything for the move to America took some time. It also took some time to sell the farm. It was eventually purchased by a farmer, Marcus Schumacher, from a nearby village, who had lost everything during the war. Not long after the sale of the farm, Georg received compensation from the government for the livestock that the military had taken during the war, and it added to the bounty that Marta had found in the wall behind the wardrobe.

The Schumachers moved into the Beckenbauer farmhouse in January 1922. Georg and Marta stayed with the Schlessingers as they waited for their travel documents. When everything was in order, Georg and Marta Beckenbauer said goodbye to her parents and Mathilde and left Lampertheim in February. They took the train from Mannheim to Calais, then the boat to Dover and from there another train to Southampton. Waiting there to take her maiden voyage was the elegant, two-funneled RMS *Homeric*.

The voyage was smooth, and as the *Homeric* steamed closer to their new home, Marta and Georg became increasingly more excited and nervous. They made the acquaintances of Jane and Rupert Bannister, a nice young couple from England. The Bannisters were on their way to visit Rupert's brother, Elmer, who had moved to New York before the war. Rupert, also a veteran of the war, spoke some German and was delighted to help Georg and Marta with basic English lessons. Georg and Marta were fast learners, and in the five days at sea they managed to grasp some rudimentary English that would be helpful to them when they arrived in America.

The *Homeric* docked in New York, and after clearing customs and immigration, Georg and Marta boarded a southbound train and arrived in Burlington, New Jersey three hours later. It was late, too late to take a taxi to Beverly and then try to find a hotel, so they decided to stay the night in Burlington, at The Metropolitan Inn on Broad Street, conveniently right across from the train station.

The next morning, a taxi drove them to Beverly to see their farm. They asked the driver to take the dirt road which led into the property. In the distance, they could see the old barn that Johann had built in 1847. Georg and Marta wanted to get a closer look. Instead, they decided that rather than keeping the taxi driver waiting and the meter running whilst they went gallivanting around the barn, they would ask him to take them to the nearest truck seller.

The driver took them to the Sterling Truck dealer, in Camden, where Georg and Marta chose a truck—a real beauty, dark blue, with dual drive wheels with a wooden flatbed and high side panels and gate. After a little friendly haggling back and forth with the salesman, they paid cash and drove off in their first American purchase. After getting slightly lost in Delanco, they found their way back to the farm in Beverly. What they discovered was more than they could have hoped for. Their property was prime land, the soil rich. And apparently Johann, while his barn was being built, had managed to plant peach and apple trees, thirty acres of each fruit. The orchards had become quite overgrown, looking more like small forests and less like orchards since Johann first planted the trees in 1848. Many of the original apple trees still stood, surrounded by some that had sprouted from fallen apples. The original peach trees were long gone. The ones standing now were descendants of the ones Johann had planted.

They drove back to the barn and found it to be sound but enduring seventy-five New Jersey winters had taken its toll on the exterior. Some boards needed replacing, as did a good deal of the roof. When they went inside, they could see that it had never been used, except for the living quarters. The room Johann had made for himself was quite self-contained and functional. Any furniture that he may have had was gone, most likely sold before returning to Lampertheim. But the wood-burning stove still sat in the corner and was in remarkably good shape for its age. Apparently, Johann must have thought he would be returning again and had slathered the stove in axle grease to prevent it from rusting. He did such an outstanding job at weatherproofing the thing that it would require a thorough scouring before lighting it to avoid setting the barn on fire.

On their voyage across the Atlantic, Marta and Georg had discussed what they would do once they arrived at their new home. Georg's idea to build a barn first, then a house, followed his great-grandfather's same line of thinking. Finding an established fruit orchard and a barn, although both were in dire need of a sprucing up, was a sign that leaving their home in Germany to make a new one in America was the right thing to have done.

After finding a room to rent in Beverly (at Ruth McClintock's rooming house on Warren Street), they went to work looking for supplies and tools needed to repair the barn. It took just over two weeks for Georg to repair the walls and roof. Once their temporary home was weatherproofed and habitable, they went to a furniture store to get a few basic things—a bed, a dresser, an armoire, a table and two chairs—and moved into the living quarters on March 3rd.

Now that they had a place to sleep, they put all of their efforts into getting the orchards into shape. It took two and a half months to clear out all of the dead and unwanted trees. Georg used the new Fordson tractor that he had purchased from Van Brunt's Farm and Tractor Company over in Riverside to drag all of the cut and dead fruit trees to a central location. He then took some of the good wood back to the barn and made a woodpile for the wood stove.

Occasionally, one of the locals would drop by to meet their new neighbors. It wasn't easy at first to communicate, but after a few months Marta and Georg were able to speak and understand enough English to effectively converse with their friends and neighbors. They became parishioners of St. Paul Roman Catholic Church in Burlington and met some other German speaking members of the church who also helped them learn English. It didn't take long before Georg and Marta became respected members of the community, acquiring many friends.

Georg hired a company to build their house, and by the end of October, they moved in. He had designed a house for the family he did not yet have and always wanted. He wanted a house that would be spacious and convenient. Although the house in Lampertheim had been large and had electricity, there was no plumbing. They still relied on ice delivery for the refrigerator, and the kitchen sink had a hand pump that drew from the well. And the toilet was—well, the outhouse.

Their new house had running water and to go with it, three full bathrooms; one downstairs and two upstairs. There were four large bedrooms upstairs, and a staircase that went to the large, third-floor attic. Downstairs there was a big living room, dining room, huge eat-in kitchen, laundry room, mud room, a wrap-around porch, and a basement under the house that would double as a root cellar. There was running water in the kitchen and even an electric refrigerator—a very new appliance in that day. Now all they needed to do was make a family to fill their new home.

To celebrate moving into their new house, Georg and Marta invited neighbors and friends from church to a bonfire celebration. All the guests brought food, and a buffet was set up in the barn. It was a chilly October evening, but everyone stayed toasty warm as they sat on blankets around the crackling bonfire of peach and apple woods, breaking bread, and strengthening bonds of friendship.

Hagen's Railcar
Somewhere in Illinois

"And that, my dear, is how my family came to America."

All the while that Hagen relayed the early history of his family in Germany, Emily was totally enthralled, immersed in the tale. She visualized everything he had described—the farm, the cemetery and chapel, his parents and brothers and grandparents. When Hagen described how his father had come home after the war, with his brothers in caskets, she teared up and had to find some tissues.

"Hagen, I had no idea things like this happened in peoples' lives. I *know* people will want to hear it. It's touching, very personal, real and wonderful."

"You understand now why I feel the need to write it?"

"I do. You said that you weren't ready to publish anything, until now; that the time is right to do it. It's because of…" Emily glanced down then at Hagen.

"Yes, Emily, it is. I know you are curious to know about who is in the casket, and you have been remarkably patient and respectful. I am going to tell you. I haven't yet because I didn't know how to tell you. I don't just go around willy-nilly telling everyone my personal business. I wanted to know you better. Yesterday, we were perfect strangers. We have been enlightening each other with personal details about ourselves that has elevated us beyond acquaintances. I wanted you to know a little more about my family, our history, my history."

"I completely understand. Of course, I'm curious about…" Her eyes glanced down briefly again "…you know. I assumed you would tell me, in your own time."

"I have every intention of telling you everything. I want to incorporate it into the story, but I will tell you this much. It is a family member and his name is Salvatore. We called him Sal."

"I deduced that much from hearing you speaking with the Morawskis. Tell me, they're Polish, right?"

"Yes, that is correct. And you want to know why I was speaking in German to Ryfka and Zelik, I assume."

"It did cross my mind."

"In a nutshell, I speak German, not Polish, and they speak better German than English."

"Ah, that makes sense. I assume that how you met them is also part of your story."

"It is. Everything will be explained as the story unfolds."

"I understand. And, for what it's worth, Hagen, I am in no hurry. I'm intrigued."

"I am pleased to hear that. Before I go on, how about a fresh pot of coffee?"

"That's a great idea, and maybe another danish? Digesting your story made me a little hungry."

"I'm feeling a little peckish and thirsty myself. I haven't talked so much in one sitting in quite some time."

"Alright, boss, time for me to earn my wages." Emily got up from the sofa. "You enjoy the view, collect your thoughts, and I'll take care of round two."

"Yes, ma'am. While you are in the kitchen, there is something I need to take care of. I'll meet you back here."

"OK." She picked up the coffee press and the two plates and walked off towards the kitchen.

Hagen sat there, floating on a moment, very content, very peaceful. He was looking out at a little town passing by outside the window and was thinking of how he would continue next with his story. There was so much to say, but it had to be told in just the right order. He thought about Sal, then got up using his cane and went to the elevator, closed the door and pushed the lever down.

Downstairs, he exited the lift and walked over to the laundry room and opened the door. He went inside and found the linen napkin and the *chrusciki* he had stashed in there when everyone was saying goodbye to Emily. He opened another door that led to the cargo hold and went inside. He flipped a switch; lights flickered on and there, strapped securely in place in the far corner was the metal cart supporting the flag-covered casket. He slowly walked over, catching his balance as the train rocked a bit on a curve. He folded the flag back, unlocked the lid and opened it. He gazed upon Sal, dressed in his military dress uniform with all his medals and decorations.

He sighed. "I miss you." He held up the napkin and smiled. "I have something for you from Krystyna."

He tucked the linen napkin with its contents next to the pillow and stood there admiring Sal's pressed uniform, smiling proudly as he ran his fingers over the medals. Memories of when he first saw pictures of Sal in his dress uniform over fifty years ago played on his mind's silver screen. "How handsome you were." Hagen closed his eyes and smiled. Visions of how Sal had looked after the war was over replaced the beautiful ones, and his smile turned to a cringing wince. He opened his eyes again.

"We have been through so much together. No more pain. Rest in peace, oh captain, my captain." Hagen leaned over and kissed Sal's forehead. A tear dropped onto his face. "Oh, *Scheiße*!" He dabbed it with a corner of the linen napkin. He laughed at himself. "Sorry, I hope I didn't ruin your makeup." Then he closed the lid, locked it tightly, replaced the flag, and went back to the elevator. As he rose through the floor, he could see through the window that Emily had returned to the sofa. The elevator stopped, he opened the door and walked back to his place and sat down.

"I see you are a fast barista. You had no trouble finding everything?"

"I had no trouble. I watched you closely the first time. But fast? Not really." She tapped her Timex. "Do you know how long you were gone?"

"Only a few minutes, ten at the most."

"You were down there almost half an hour."

He looked at his watch, puzzled. Then looked up at her. "I am sorry if I kept you waiting. I guess I got lost in the moment."

"Don't apologize. We're in no hurry. Your time is yours to spend however you want to."

Hagen's melancholy smile said thank you and a million other feelings in one brief jiffy of time.

"I brought us each a bottle of water. The coffee has been steeping for a bit. I assume that the longer it steeps the stronger it gets?"

"That is correct. And I see you decided to bring the whole plate of pastries over. Good idea."

"I thought so," she said, then poured their coffees. "Drink some water before you do anything else. You're dehydrating right in front of me." Then she *Spocked* her eyebrows and twisted her smile.

"I like your style, young lady." He twisted the cap off the bottle and took a long, cool drink of water.

They each chose a pastry for themselves, took a bite, sipped some strong brew and then Hagen settled back into the leather sofa and continued with his story.

"During that first winter in their new home, my parents planned how to best use their land. They were going to keep the orchards, but what to grow on the rest of the land had yet to be determined. Using a map of their property that they got from the Mount Holly Courthouse, they designated areas for corn, tomatoes, pumpkins, melons, yellow squash, and zucchini. They also set aside an area for cows, chickens, a coop, and another barn. My father wanted to keep some traditions in the family. He wanted fresh milk and eggs like they had in Germany."

"It all sounds so nice, so simple."

"It was a simpler time. No technologies to complicate anything."

"When did you come onto the scene?"

"Spring 1923 came. My parents cultivated the orchards and sowed seeds, both vegetable and human. I was born, February 19, 1924. It was a cold day; heavy snow had fallen the night before. My mother woke up with the sunrise and the first contraction. My father bundled up my mother, packed some necessities and clothes and put her in the cab of the Sterling—that beast could get through anything—and off they went through the snow to Zurbrugg Hospital in Riverside. I was born ten and a half hours later. I am named after one of my uncles who died in the war."

"I had a feeling, after hearing about your uncles, that that was how you got your name."

"My father and mother had always intended to name any sons after my uncles."

"You said you had sisters and a brother?"

"Yes, I have two sisters, Mathilde and Diana. They were born in 1926."

"And your brother?"

"My brother, Karl, was born in 1932. But before we get to 1932, I would like to lead up to it as my story continues."

"Of course, of course. It's your story."

He took another sip from the bottle of water and thought for a moment how to proceed.

"In 1929, there was a recession in August, and then the Great Depression hit in October. Although my parents didn't lose money when the stock market crashed, prices on everything fell swiftly, including food. My parents still had crops, but they were not earning enough from the sale of their produce and dairy to offset the cost of planting them earlier in the year. My parents were frugal people, as we Germans can be. They would spend only when they knew it was prudent to do so. They had savings, but still they worried about making it through the Depression without having to sell the farm, either in parts or the whole thing. Then one day, in January of 1930, my parents had a visitor at the farm."

Beckenbauer Farm
Beverly, New Jersey
January 3, 1930

It was cold that Friday morning. Snow had fallen during the night. The temperature had dropped into the teens and the wind moved it around, making snow dunes, like a white desert.

Georg was in the barn milking the cows when, at around half-past nine, he heard a car drive past. He went outside and saw a Model T riding up the drive towards the house. He told the cows he'd be back soon, not to fret, and headed on up to the house to see who was paying them a visit.

When he got to the house, he noticed that the Ford was still running but there was no one inside. By the time he opened the front door, Marta had already taken the man's hat, coat, scarf, and gloves and was in the kitchen getting coffee, while the visitor, who was now sitting on the sofa with his hands folded in his lap, listened intently to three-year-old Mathilde as she sang her ABCs. Georg hung his coat next to the visitor's and watched from the doorway; both men were waiting for Mathilde to get to Z.

"W, X, Y, and Z."

Georg entered the living room and joined the visitor in applauding Mathilde.

"That was wonderful, Mathilde. You are a very smart young lady," said the man.

"*Danke.*"

"In English, Mathilde," said Georg.

"Thank you."

"You are very welcome." The visitor stood and turned to greet Georg. He was shorter than Georg by about four inches, in his mid to late thirties, of medium build, with brown hair and gentle, hazel eyes. He wore a black suit and a black shirt with the white collar that denoted his status as that of a clergyman. "Good morning, Mr. Beckenbauer." He held out his hand. "I am the Reverend Samuel Osterman. I am the pastor of the Mount Holly Methodist Church. How are you this morning?"

He shook his hand. "Good morning, Reverend. It is a pleasure to meet you. I am well, how are you?"

"I am as well as can be expected on such a cold day."

Georg pointed in the direction of the front door. "Do you know your engine is still running?"

"Yes, I left *Lizzie* running on purpose." Putting a hand on his low back. "It was enough just to crank her over the one time this morning. I don't plan on shutting her off until I get back to Mount Holly."

"I can understand that, Reverend. It is quite a cold morning."

Marta came in from the kitchen with three cups and a pot of coffee on a tray, with cream, sugar and one spoon, and a glass of milk for Mathilde. She put the tray on the coffee table.

"I see you two have met. Coffee, gentlemen? Please, Reverend, have a seat."

Both men sat next to each other on the sofa. Mathilde sat on the floor at the coffee table and watched her mother pour. Marta handed Mathilde her glass of milk and she took a sip, watching the man on the couch.

"Reverend, what do you take in your coffee?"

"Black is fine, Mrs. Beckenbauer, thank you." He smiled at her and then at Mathilde, who was staring up at him with twinkling eyes and a milk-mustached smile.

Reverend Osterman had just told a lie and crossed his toes in his shoes. He liked his coffee creamy and sweet—half coffee, half sugar, half cream. But in those hard times, he would never impose upon anyone and would politely drink it black. He would ask God later to forgive him for lying to Marta. But that wouldn't be necessary; Marta caught the movement in his shoes. She forgave him before God had the chance.

Marta handed Reverend Osterman his cup and saucer, then handed Georg his. She sat in a chair and watched them sip. Georg sipped his like he always did, enjoying his wife's strong, dark coffee. Reverend Osterman, on the other hand, sipped his coffee respectfully, but only enough to get the taste, like a child eating his despised peas one at a time in front of his watchful mother.

"Now, Reverend," said Marta. "We have cows, the cream is free. And, a couple teaspoons of sugar are not going to send us to the poor house."

Georg watched his wife, smiling at her all-knowing and gracious ways, then turned his eyes to the reverend, who now sported a sheepish grin and blushed cheeks. Georg liked this man and appreciated the reverend's abstaining from the accoutrements on their behalf.

"She knows things, Reverend. She knows things about me that I do not know about myself. There is no sense in pretending."

"In that case, cream and sugar, please," said the reverend, handing his cup and saucer back to Marta.

Marta took his cup from him and put a good dousing of cream and two healthy spoons of sugar into his coffee. She gave it a stir and handed it back to him. His next sip was big, as was his smile.

"Thank you, Mrs. Beckenbauer, you are very kind."

"It is my pleasure, Reverend. And please, call me Marta, and my husband is Georg."

"Alright, thank you, Marta. Do you have any other children?"

"Yes, a boy, Hagen. He will be six next month. He is at school today."

"*Mein Bruder geht an die Shedaker Schule*," chimed Mathilde.

Marta tilted her head. "In English, Mathilde."

"My brother goes to Shedaker school."

"Ah, Shedaker. A good school. Mrs. Donald is a very good teacher."

"Yes, she is," said Marta. "Hagen is learning quite a lot there."

They all sipped from their cups. Mathilde drank from her glass at the same time. She only sipped when they sipped.

Georg put his cup down. "So, Reverend, what brings you all the way to Beverly on this cold and windy morning?"

Reverend Osterman finished another sip and placed the cup gently down on the saucer. "Yes, first, I do apologize for coming here unannounced. Normally, I would have requested a meeting instead of just showing up. But this was very spur of the moment. I had an idea and I felt the need to not delay."

"Is there something wrong, Reverend?" asked Marta.

"Nothing is wrong, *per se*. Well, with this depression not a lot seems right, you see."

"Yes," Georg nodded, "it has been difficult with the falling prices and so many people without jobs."

"I cannot think that there are many families who have not been affected by these hard times, including yours. The church depends upon donations, as most do, and so does our orphanage. We are struggling right along with everyone else."

Georg's posture changed, stiffened a little. Marta looked over at her husband, knowing he was thinking the same thing that she was thinking; that Reverend Osterman was looking for donations.

The reverend saw Marta looking over at her husband. "Let me get to the point. I would like to discuss a deal."

"A deal?" asked Georg, his posture relaxing slightly.

"Yes, a deal. The church, and more specifically the orphanage, are reaching out to local farmers. We know it has been difficult for all of you to sell your produce, let alone make a profit. And you can only barter so much. Our orphanage, and others all around the country have been receiving more and more children. We do not only offer a home to orphans, you see, but families who are struggling in these hard times are taking advantage of the option to leave their children in our care as well, until they can recover financially."

Marta looked upon her little girl and shuddered at the thought of losing her children. She took a deep breath, clutched the rosary in her apron pocket, closed her eyes and said a quick, yet efficient, silent prayer.

"The Methodist Church has authorized me to reach out to local farmers to offer to buy exclusively from them. We cannot pay pre-depression prices, but we can help you stay afloat and make it through this depression while at the same time help us feed the children."

"What have the other farmers said?" asked Georg.

"I haven't met with any of them, yet. Please don't repeat this," he put the saucer and cup on the coffee table, looked

103

back and forth from Marta to Georg to Marta again, his voice lowered, "but since you came to Burlington County, you have gained a reputation for your top-notch produce and dairy. That's why I came to you first. If you could be our dairy supplier, then I could also buy produce from you throughout the year, and what you don't grow, I can find at another farm."

Georg looked at Marta. Marta looked at him, gave a little shrug. Being modest, they didn't acknowledge the compliment.

"We should discuss this before we decide," said Georg to the reverend.

"I completely understand. Please, talk it over and get back to me as soon as you have made a decision. I won't approach any of the other farmers until I hear from you."

"We will have a decision for you tomorrow," said Marta.

Georg nodded in affirmation.

"Very good then." He finished his coffee. "Thank you for your gracious hospitality and the coffee," he smiled, "and the cream and sugar." He stood up and Marta went to get his coat and hat. He shook Georg's hand. "It was very nice meeting you both."

"It was a pleasure to meet you, Reverend," said Marta.

"The pleasure was all mine." He bent over and extended his hand. "It was nice meeting you, Mathilde." She still had her hands full, holding her half-full glass of milk with both of them. She handed the reverend her glass. He took it with his left hand and again held out his right. Mathilde shook it with her left hand, as young children often don't know the difference.

"What do you say, Mathilde?" asked her mother.

"*Danke*."

"In English," said Georg.

"Thank you."

"You are very welcome." He released her hand and returned her glass of milk. Marta helped him with his coat then handed him his hat, gloves, and scarf.

"Thank you for coming to talk to us," said Georg.

After putting on his coat and hat, he shook Marta's hand. Halfway out the door, he turned. "Happy New Year."

"Happy New Year to you, Reverend," said Marta.

The reverend smiled with a good feeling in his heart as he walked back to his idling Model T and drove off down the long dirt drive to Perkins Lane.

Marta closed the door, then turned to her husband. "Georg, what do you think about all of this?"

"I do not know. It does not sound bad. What do you think?"

"I think we should at least consider it. Sold produce is better than rotting produce. I can only fit so much in the cellar."

"I do have to agree."

They went about the rest of the day pretty much with their minds made up to accept the reverend's offer. Over dinner, they discussed how they both felt, and decided to go to the orphanage the next day to see Reverend Osterman.

January 4, 1930

The morning was cold and bright. After breakfast, the Beckenbauer family prepared for their trip to Mount Holly to see Reverend Osterman. As they walked to the Sterling, they squinted at the bright sunlight radiating from the sky and reflecting off the snow. Marta and Georg were excited about the meeting with the reverend. Hagen and Mathilde were the opposite of excited; bored and wanting to go play in the snow. It was Saturday, no school for Hagen, and his sister wanted him to help her make a snowman. Spending precious play time doing boring stuff with their parents simply annoyed them, and their faces and folded arms didn't hide what they felt and thought.

The family arrived at the orphanage near eleven o'clock. When they got out of the truck, they heard the reverend's voice calling to them from the porch.

"Hello."

"Good morning, Reverend Osterman," said Georg, waving. They walked up the porch steps to the open door where he was standing.

"Come inside, please," said the reverend.

They went into the warmth of the lobby and the reverend closed the door behind them. "Good morning Georg, Marta." They shook hands. Reverend Osterman bent over to greet the children and extended his hand. "Hello Mathilde, it is good to see you again." She shook his hand; this time she got it right and used the correct hand. He turned to their son. "And you must be Hagen."

"Yes, sir," said young Hagen. "It is a pleasure to meet you." This time it was the child who initiated the handshake, holding out his right hand, his smile revealing the space that awaited the arrival of two new front teeth.

"My, my, what a gentleman you are, young man," taking Hagen's offered hand.

"Thank you, sir."

"And so polite. You do your parents great credit, both of you."

"Thank you, Reverend," said Marta. "Respect is very important to us, and we do our best to teach that to them."

"It is quite apparent. We do our best to instill that in the children here as well. Come, let's walk to my office so we can talk."

He led the way down a short hallway to his office; a cozy room with a desk and chair, filing cabinets, two wingback chairs and a small sofa under a window that looked out onto a courtyard. The reverend took everyone's coats and hung them on hangers in a closet, then asked everyone to have a seat. Georg and Marta sat in the two wingback chairs that were on the other side of the desk from the reverend. Hagen and Mathilde sat next to each other on the sofa under the window.

While the adults began their business discussion, Hagen and Mathilde listened apathetically, bored, getting fidgety. But their attention did not remain on the adults for very long. From outside, heard through the window behind them, were the sounds of children playing in the courtyard. Hagen and Mathilde turned around, on their knees, and watched as children played on swings and seesaws, a merry-go-round, and in the snow. They were having so much fun despite the cold.

Marta and Georg were unaware of their children silently looking out of the window. Reverend Osterman gave a little nod to Georg and Marta and nudged his chin in the direction of the sofa. They turned around. "Mathilde, Hagen, do not kneel on the reverend's nice furniture," said their mother. They immediately spun around, sat down, heads lowered in shame, hands folded in their laps.

"I am sorry, Reverend," said Hagen.

"*Ich auch*, Reverend" said Mathilde.

"In English, Mathilde," said her brother, giving her a little elbow nudge.

"Me too, Reverend," said Mathilde.

All three grown-ups bit their lips to keep from laughing.

"I'm not worried about the sofa," said Reverend Osterman. "There are children crawling on it all the time. I was more interested in Hagen and Mathilde watching the children outside."

"I understand," said Georg. "But they should not be kneeling on the furniture."

"Well then, how about letting them go outside to play with the others?" asked the reverend. "They are all very nice children and a couple of new faces might be good for everyone."

Georg looked at Marta and shrugged. "What could it hurt?"

"I guess it would be alright," said Marta. "Mathilde does not get to play with other children often."

"Hagen, Mathilde," said the reverend. "Would you like to go outside and play with the other children?"

Their bowed heads sprung up, eyes widened, pursed lips hiding the smiles that were about to explode from their faces.

"Oh, yes please," said Hagen.

Mathilde, barely able to control her excitement, just nodded her head up and down like it was on a spring.

Marta retrieved their coats from the closet and helped Mathilde put hers on while Hagen, in his excitement, turned himself into a pretzel trying to get into his. While Marta helped Mathilde with her hat, mittens, and scarf, Reverend Osterman helped Hagen with his predicament. Once they were all bundled up, the reverend walked them down the hallway to a door that led out to the courtyard. He opened the door and out they sprang like horses from the gate. Georg and Marta watched from the window as their children zeroed in on their targets of play. Mathilde found the girls who she'd seen from the window playing in the snow. They were around her age and they took to her immediately.

Hagen went right for a boy on a swing. He was around Hagen's age, sitting there alone, not swinging, digging his heels into the ground. From a very young age, Georg and Marta had felt that their son was an old soul. He seemed too wise, like he had already lived a life before he entered into this one. Ever since he was able to convey his feelings, Hagen was always sympathetic—no, empathetic to someone near him who was suffering. While they watched the children, Marta recalled a memory…

St. Paul Roman Catholic Church
Burlington, New Jersey
May 13, 1928

The Beckenbauers sat high up in the balcony that Sunday, at Hagen's request, because he loved to sit near the organ. He paid more attention to the organist than the priest, anyway. His English wasn't as good as his German, and he loved watching the organist's fingers move over the keys and his feet dance on the pedals. Hagen would sit when his parents sat, kneel when they knelt, and stand when they stood. At four, he was old enough to quietly stay behind while his parents made their way to the altar, Georg holding little Mathilde, to get the *cracker* that the priest puts in their mouths. It took a little longer this time to get into line because Marta and Georg had to go down a flight of stairs with the rest of the people from the balcony. This gave Hagen more time to observe the people down below. With the balcony now vacant, just the organist and him, he went up to the front and gazed out over the entire nave to watch the parishioners as they stood in line to receive the Host. From high on his perch, he scanned the pews and the people in line. His attention was soon drawn to a man and his wife, sitting next to each other, just below him, in the last pew in the back of the church. The man was leaning in close to the woman, saying something softly to her. She was dressed all in black and was wearing a black hat with a mesh veil. Her bowed head gently shook back and forth. The man put his hand on her shoulder, then got up and made his way through the pew and stood in the communion line.

The Lady in Black pulled the kneeler down on its hinge and knelt, clasping her hands in front of her in prayer, her black rosary dangling from her fingers, neck arched up to look at Jesus on the cross overseeing the ceremony. Hagen couldn't take his eyes off of her and hadn't noticed that his parents had received communion and were returning up the side aisle. Marta looked up and saw her son standing at the edge of the balcony, hands on the ledge, looking down. She followed his gaze to the Lady in Black, sitting in prayer alone in the last pew. Marta saw the veil of mourning covering her face and said a little prayer. She said *Amen,* swallowed the last bit of melted communion wafer, then looked back up at the balcony to find that her son was now watching *her.* He stared down into his mother's eyes, his expression like the statue of Christ looking down on the candle lighters, with sympathetic eyes and a compassionate smile. Goosebumps spread from Marta's nose to her toes. She looked back over at the woman; whose husband had returned. She was sitting back in the pew next to him. When Marta looked up at the balcony, her son was gone.

Hagen's parents returned to the balcony to find their son where they had left him, in his seat watching the organist. Marta sat down and gazed upon her Hagen, sitting there so beautiful, a mini version of her handsome husband—her angel. She leaned over and kissed the top of his head. He turned and looked up at her, gave her a smile, and said, "*Ich liebe dich, Mama.*"

If she could have loved him any more than she already did, it was at that moment, and she didn't have the heart to tell him to say it in English and instead responded, "*Ich liebe dich auch, mein Liebling.*"

Mass ended and Father Kelly exited towards the front doors of the church as the parishioners followed behind. The Beckenbauers left the balcony and made their way down the stairs and into the rivulet of people trickling to the exit where Father Kelly stood on the porch, chatting with the parishioners as they left. Outside, the sun shone warm in a bright blue sky as sparse, cottony puffs of clouds floated high overhead, tickling the belly of Heaven. A dogwood tree in the corner by the sidewalk was in full, glorious bloom. Two enormous, full stands of forsythias, blazing in all their golden-yellow splendor, stood like sentries at each side of the gate. So much color on this beautiful day; so peaceful and inviting that the parishioners lingered longer than usual as they discussed their plans for the rest of the weekend. There was talk of driving to the shore, and of picnics with relatives in nearby towns. Georg discussed fruit trees with another farmer from out in Florence. Meanwhile, Mathilde toddled in the grass with some of the other children as Marta chatted with a woman who was holding her own baby girl.

Hagen, well, he was aware of the trees and the flowers and the people and the little ones playing on the lawn. But that was all background noise. In the foreground of his thoughts was the Lady in Black, who now stood with her husband, his arm around her waist, on the porch near the big, Gothic-arched wooden doors talking to Father Kelly. The priest looked very serious and sympathetic; no smile, his head tilting as he spoke. The lady's hat moved up and down, ever so minimally, nodding in acknowledgment to the serious priest's words. The husband nodded, occasionally looking at his wife, then back to Father Kelly. The priest took the lady's right hand in both of his and held it as he spoke, smiling compassionately, like Hagen had smiled at his mother from the balcony. Then he took hold of the husband's right hand in both of his, shook it, saying something, again with a compassionate smile. He blessed them both with the sign of the cross, then the Lady in Black and her husband walked down the granite steps and met with some of the other parishioners. The husband began talking to an older gentleman with a great moustache and wire-rimmed, round glasses. They shook hands and the older man greeted the Lady in Black. She said something to her husband; he smiled and nodded. Hagen could read the *OK* on his lips. She left the two men to talk and sat by herself on a wrought iron bench under a magnificently blooming magnolia tree, looking out onto the lawn that separated the rectory from the church; so still, one might have mistaken her for a statue.

Hagen had been feigning interest in the forsythias, trying to blend in with them, while he watched the lady walk to the bench and sit. He looked over at her husband, whose eyes followed his wife, and the mustachioed man, who watched the husband with concern on his face. The husband sighed. The mustachioed man put a hand on his shoulder, consolingly. The husband, now on the verge of weeping, took a deep breath, closed his eyes tightly, and squeezed out a trail of tears as he shook his head and exhaled. Hagen turned his attention again to the Lady in Black and walked over to the magnolia tree, climbed onto the bench and sat to her left and looked straight ahead. They were now two statues, both staring off into the nothing.

The Lady in Black had been so deep in her thoughts that a few moments passed before she realized someone was sharing the bench with her. She looked down at this beautiful little boy and could see that there were tears running down his cheeks.

Her concern diverted her mind for a moment. "Little boy. What is the matter?" The lady looked around for any sign of distressed parents who might be searching for their child. "Are you lost?"

Hagen didn't answer her. He turned his head towards her and looked up through the mesh veil into her eyes. Hagen's stunningly blue eyes, like little pieces of sky, had a look of depth, age, understanding that you would not expect in one so young, and the Lady in Black caught her breath.

Hagen looked forward again into the nothing, without speaking, and slid very close to her, resting his head against her arm.

The Lady in Black was baffled, her concern increasing. "Little boy, what *is* the matter? Where are your mommy and daddy?"

Hagen took a breath, deep and slow, then let out a sigh. He sat up straight, slid off of the bench and stood directly in front of her, very close; so close that he reached up and put a hand on each side of her face. He pulled her closer to him, lifted her veil, and kissed her gently on the forehead. As he let her face go, she sat back, mesmerized by those blue eyes and angelic smile. A Viceroy butterfly landed on his head and sat there, slowly waving its wings up, and down; up, and down. Hagen stood very still, seemingly unaware of the butterfly on his head, looking deeply into the lady's eyes as she stared in amazement at the appearance of this creature on this little boy's head.

Georg and Marta were now looking around for their children. They found Mathilde, sitting in the grass plucking and sniffing clover flowers. Marta picked her up and the two parents searched for their son. Georg spied Hagen and the Lady in Black and pointed. "Look, over there under the magnolia tree."

As they approached their son and the Lady in Black, the butterfly lighted on Hagen's head and Marta stopped, wide-eyed.

"Georg, do you see that?"

They watched their son, the lady, and the butterfly; speechless and frozen to the spot where they stood.

With a quick flap of its wings, the butterfly took flight. It flew around the lady and landed on her left wrist. She held up her arm. The butterfly didn't startle at her movement but instead did something very odd. It walked from her wrist to her ring finger and stopped on her wedding band. It did some more slow flapping, then turned in place three times on her ring; one, two, three, then stopped, facing her, seeming to look right into her eyes. It raised its wings high, bringing them together, holding them there like hands in prayer, then with another quick wing-flap, it flew off.

The lady, Georg, and Marta watched the butterfly fly right over the lady's husband's head as he walked across the lawn in the direction of the magnolia tree, then disappear into the blue heavens.

The Lady in Black stood as her husband approached and turned to him, and she smiled. He could see she had been crying, and he put his hands on her arms, his face quizzical. "Are you alright, Abigail?"

She blinked. A tear fell from each eye and trickled down her cheeks. "Yes, Stephen, I'm alright, quite alright, actually."

He took his handkerchief out of his pocket and caught her tears before they could fall from her chin. "Forgive me, but I haven't seen you smile since..." and he looked down as if afraid to say any more and cry again himself.

She lifted his chin up to look into his cry-reddened eyes. "I know, dear. I haven't been able to. I'm so sorry for making you suffer my disposition along with everything else."

"There is nothing to be sorry for, darling." His eyes glistened with new tears on the rise.

The lady unpinned the mesh veil from her hat and tucked it into her pocketbook. She kissed her husband on each cheek, wiped away his tears with her fingers and turned to look down at Hagen, who had now been joined by the rest of his family.

"I am sorry if my son was bothering you," said Marta. "Hagen, why are you bothering this nice lady?"

"Oh, he wasn't bothering me at all," said the Lady in Black. "He sat with me while my husband chatted with his boss."

"Are you sure?" asked Georg.

"Absolutely." Looking down at Hagen, "Hagen? That is your name?"

Hagen nodded.

"It is so very nice to meet you, Hagen. Thank you for…" What could she really say?

"… keeping me company."

He wrapped his arms around her legs and squeezed. The Lady in Black put one hand on his head, caressing his blonde hair, the other hand to her mouth as fresh tears fell from her eyes.

He released his grip, stepped back, looked up into her eyes and smiled a different smile—not compassionate, but content. Then he turned his eyes up at his parents, who had no idea what to make of everything, and their faces showed it.

Georg took Mathilde from his wife. "Come, Marta," still looking at Hagen. "I want to get home and check the orchards before lunch."

"Hmm?" Marta nodded as she stared in wonderment at her son. "Oh, yes, orchards, lunch."

Georg turned back to the Lady in Black and her husband, who were now in a tight embrace, her back to the Beckenbauers. As Georg was about to say goodbye, the

Lady in Black's husband opened his crying eyes, looked at Hagen and his family, lifted his face from his wife's shoulder and mouthed *thank you*. Hagen flickered a smile. All Georg could do was nod then turn to leave.

The Beckenbauers walked to the Sterling in silence. When they were all seated in the cab of the truck, Marta asked her son, "What was that all about, with that lady?"

Hagen looked up into her eyes and simply said, "*Die Dame war sehr traurig*. Sorry Mama, I know, in English. The lady was very sad."

Marta and Georg were dumbfounded by their profound four-year-old little man.

"Why is she sad?" asked his father.

"I do not know, Papa. I know she was sad."

Georg and Marta looked over at each other with puzzled looks and shrugged.

Another thing that Hagen didn't know was that his parents *did know* why the Lady in Black and her husband were sad. They knew—the whole congregation knew—that Stephen and Abigail Gilchrist had lost their little Elizabeth, five-and-a-half-years old, to influenza three months before. Stephen was of course devastated, still grieving intensely, but mostly on the inside. He cried when he was alone, for Abigail's sake, because she was losing her battle with depression. The loss of their only child was too much for her to bear. She had stood by helplessly, watching her little girl take her last breath and slip away to Heaven. Her faith in God, her religion, herself as a mother flew away with her daughter's spirit.

Something else that nobody knew, except for God and Abigail herself, was that she was planning to get up in the middle of the night, that very night, when Stephen was fast asleep, and sneak downstairs to her husband's office and take his WWI revolver from his desk drawer, walk far out to

117

the edge of their property, put the barrel in her mouth and end the pain.

What happened that warm, spring Sunday under the magnolia tree was the miracle that she needed to restore her faith in God, and in life.

You see, when Hagen saw the Lady in Black sitting all by herself, kneeling in prayer while her husband was receiving the Host, she was praying to God to forgive her for the sin she was planning to commit that evening. If burning in Hell for all eternity was to be her punishment, then so be it. Nothing could compare with the living Hell she existed in since she lost her baby girl.

God's response was Hagen. When Hagen gazed up into her eyes, a sense of peace had come over her. The pain of loss was there, it would be forever present, but no longer despairingly. Her little girl, Elizabeth, had loved butterflies and her favorite was the brightly colored Viceroy. When one landed on Hagen's head it was, to Abigail, a sign from God—and Elizabeth. When the butterfly landed on her hand and twirled on her wedding band, it was God telling her that there was more to live for than to die for, and she smiled at her husband for the first time in three months, and all thoughts of suicide flew away into the sky with the butterfly.

But there was one more thing that no one that day knew—not the Lady in Black, not her husband, not Hagen. The most amazing thing, that only God knew that day, was that in eight months, Abigail Gilchrist would be giving her husband a son—a boy they would name Hagen.

"Souls recognize each other by vibes, not appearances."

—Unknown

The Courtyard

The boy on the swing was Hagen's opposite; dark brown, almost black hair; big, deep brown eyes and light, olive-toned skin of someone with Mediterranean heritage. He was so lost in his own thoughts that he was unaware of Hagen's approach and occupation of the swing to his left.

Hagen stared down at the ground, mimicking the dark-haired boy. He waited. The dark-haired boy still did not move. Then, Hagen raised his gaze to the sky and began to swing. It was gradual at first; he didn't use his feet on the ground, just the back and forth momentum of his body and swinging of his feet while he held tightly to the ropes. The dark-haired boy came back from wherever his mind had been and took notice of Hagen after he had achieved a fairly decent arc. Hagen didn't say anything, didn't smile, never looked anywhere but straight ahead. The other boy watched him go higher and higher until on his highest forward swing, Hagen let go of the ropes and flew off of his seat, seeming to hover in mid-air, almost in slow motion as if the air had become viscous, then landed on his feet. The dark-haired boy watched this stranger, but said nothing, his head cocked a little to the left, his mouth opened a little, more in awe of the jump than in an attempt to say something.

Hagen turned around, walked right up to him, looked him right in the eye, yanked off his right mitten, held out his hand, smiled, and said, "Hello, my name is Hagen. What's yours?"

The boy on the swing looked right back into Hagen's sky-blue eyes, mouth still slightly open. Whatever had occupied his thoughts earlier, that had him wallowing in distant loneliness just moments before, was kicked aside. None of the other little boys at the orphanage played with him. They tried once, maybe twice, but gave up when this boy was not at all receptive to their advances of friendship. Something about Hagen, though, marched right through this dark-haired boy's gloom with Hope's blazing torch.

The boy on the swing blinked once but never averted his eyes from Hagen's. He slowly pulled off his mitten, held out his right hand and said, as Hagen grabbed it and shook it like a man who had just sold a car, "Hi, my name is Salvatore." Hagen's hand was warm, very warm, almost too warm even with a mitten, and with that touching of flesh the feeling of Hagen's warmth spread up Salvatore's arm into his chest, heart, soul, and head, into his limbs right to the ends of his toes and fingers. It was… euphoric.

At that moment, something happened to both of them. Not being old enough, this-life experienced enough, they didn't know that it was love at first sight. Their souls met, they recognized each other, they smiled and danced. Angels sang jubilantly as God smiled proudly. (Pride is not a sin, by the way, and He never understood why humans put those words in His mouth.) God smiled the smile of someone who was happy with His own work.

"Nice to meet you, Salvatore." He released Salvatore's hand, leaving the warmth behind. "Want me to push you on the swing?"

Hagen didn't wait for an answer. He slipped his mitten back on as he marched right around behind Salvatore. Grabbing the ropes close to the seat — "put your mitten back on, Salvatore" —and he pulled, walking backward while Salvatore quickly put on his mitten and held on tightly to the ropes. Salvatore's eyes widened. Hagen was a strong almost-six-year-old and he pulled his soulmate back as far as he could, then pushed hard, sending Salvatore on his way forward and up. Hagen's hands met him on the backswing, flat on Salvatore's lower back and pushed again, sending him higher. The feeling of Hagen's touch was comforting, even through the mittens and coat. Each back swing met Hagen's touch. Each push shoved the doldrums away and allowed the sun to shine again on his soul.

Salvatore was having fun. It had been a long while since he'd had any fun. After a few more pushes, Hagen released him, and Salvatore took over and continued to swing on his own. Hagen returned to his seat and started swinging faster, higher until he was in sync with Salvatore. Back and forth they went. Hagen looked over at Salvatore, who was smiling for the first time since arriving at the orphanage, missing the same two front teeth as Hagen. Hagen ear-to-ear grinned, his soul flying higher and higher, taking Salvatore's with him, and looked straight ahead as he swung alongside his new friend. He was gearing up to do another jump.

"Salvatore."

"Yes, Hagen?"

"I bet I can jump farther than you!"

"I betchu can't!"

"Jump with me." Hagen counted, "One… two… three!"

On the third swing they released their grip on the ropes; their bottoms left their seats. Their hands met briefly in mid-air—a forever moment; angels sang. Salvatore landed two feet farther away from the swing set than Hagen.

"Wow," said Hagen. "That was high."

"I told you I could jump farther."

Hagen had known he could.

Marta, Georg, and Reverend Osterman observed through the window as Hagen and Mathilde played. They watched as Mathilde blended right in with the other little girls, and when the parents were satisfied all was going well with their daughter, they turned their eyes to their son. By then, Hagen was sitting on the swing, as still as the other boy.

"What are they doing?" asked Georg.

"They are just sitting there," said Marta.

"Are they talking to each other?" asked Georg.

"No," said the reverend. "They aren't speaking."

Then Hagen began to swing.

They watched him swing higher and higher.

"Why is the other boy just sitting there? He doesn't seem to notice Hagen at all," said Georg.

"Salvatore is a very sad little boy," said the reverend. "He has not adjusted well to living here at the orphanage since he and his sister arrived three months ago. We have had a difficult time getting him to eat. He won't play with anyone, doesn't say much at all."

"Does he have any family, besides his sister?" asked Marta.

"None, no family. Remember that accident last September when the trolley went off the tracks and fell into the Assiscunk Creek?"

"Yes, terrible thing that was," said Marta.

"Both their parents died in that accident."

"Oh, my, so awful, poor thing. It is no wonder he looks so sad," said Marta.

"His sister has her moments too, but she is adjusting better than her brother. See that little girl in the red coat playing with Mathilde? That's Salvatore's sister, Diana. They seem to have hit it off."

Just then, Hagen jumped off the swing and landed on his feet.

Marta gasped. "Did you see that? He is going to hurt himself."

"He will be fine, Marta, our Hagen is a strong boy." A hint of pride came through in his words.

Then they saw Hagen introduce himself to Salvatore and Salvatore shake his hand.

"This is very interesting," said the reverend.

They watched the scene between the two new acquaintances play out. When the reverend saw Salvatore smile, he exclaimed, "Thank you, God! There is hope for him yet."

Then when both boys jumped from their swings together all three adults gasped, and the reverend clapped his hands together in prayer at his chin. "I can't believe I am seeing this. Salvatore has found a friend!"

"It seems our son has as well," said Marta, watching the two boys scrambling to get back on the swing.

"What will happen when we go home?" asked Georg.

"I have no idea," said the reverend. "They do seem very happy together. Salvatore will probably sulk and go back to his depressed state." He paused in thought. "Unless…"

"Unless?" said Georg.

"Unless Salvatore had something to look forward to, perhaps another visit from his new friend? If he knew this was not a one-time occasion it might keep his spirits up."

"Hagen has school during the week," said Marta. "He would have to wait until summer vacation to come with Georg on one of his deliveries."

"Unless…" said the reverend.

"Unless?" said Marta.

"Unless you bring Hagen and Mathilde back before summer vacation. Maybe a not-too-distant Saturday?" Reverend Osterman grinned like a child asking his parents for a puppy for Christmas. "Maybe, next Saturday?"

"I do not see why we could not return sooner," said Georg. "Look how happy they are."

"I am fine with it, Georg," said Marta. "We cannot ignore a child's happiness."

"We should ask Hagen and Mathilde first before we make any promises to the other two," said the reverend.

"That is a good idea," said Marta. "But, from what we see out this window I do not think there will be any objections."

Back on the playground Salvatore and Hagen continued swinging and jumping. Mathilde played with Diana, getting along quite nicely.

The adults returned to their chairs and discussed the details of their new arrangement, coming to a mutually beneficial agreement. Their farm will supply dairy and eggs throughout the year and produce seasonally. Georg will plant potatoes, cucumbers, spinach, and string beans in addition to what they already grew. What they could not supply, the orphanage would acquire from other farmers and together they would survive the depression.

After about an hour, playtime was over, time for lunch, and the children were brought inside. The reverend went to retrieve the two little Beckenbauers and returned with four children in tow.

"Children, did you have fun outside?" asked Marta.

"Oh, yes Mama," said Mathilde.

"Salvatore and I jumped off the swing," said Hagen, his face beaming.

"We know," said the reverend. "We saw you. Did you have fun, Salvatore?"

"Yes, sir," he said. Hagen and Salvatore looked at each other and smiled wide, toothless smiles. The reverend had never seen Salvatore so happy; a completely different child.

"Salvatore, Diana," said the reverend. "This is Mr. and Mrs. Beckenbauer—Hagen and Mathilde's mommy and daddy."

"Hello, Salvatore and Diana," said Marta. "It is a pleasure to meet both of you."

"Hello," said Salvatore, his eyes darting back and forth from Marta to Hagen.

"Hello," said Diana as she and Mathilde held hands.

"Hagen and his sister have to go home with their mommy and daddy now," said the reverend.

Both boys' toothless smiles melted into frowns. Hagen looked at his parents, a forlorn look on his face. "Can I stay here with Salvatore?"

Marta looked at Georg then the reverend then back to her son. "I am sorry, *Liebchen*. We must go home. Would you like it if your Papa brought you and your sister back here to play with Salvatore and Diana next Saturday?"

Salvatore's toothless smile came back; not in full, but it was a smile. The thought of seeing his new friend next Saturday lifted his spirit up again. He nodded to Hagen.

"I guess," said Hagen, like he had just been grounded.

"We will be back next Saturday, I promise," said Georg to Salvatore and Diana.

Salvatore ran to Georg, slammed into him at full speed and hugged him around his legs. Georg looked over at his wife and saw the tears in her eyes. Watching this parent-less child grasping onto to the father of her children plucked at her heartstrings. Diana and Mathilde were hugging. The reverend was smiling like a proud parent. Hagen smiled a little as his soul conjured up an idea.

"We have to go home now," said Georg. "Hagen, Mathilde, say goodbye to your new friends."

Mathilde and Diana hugged once more, kissing each other on the cheeks.

"Bye, Salvatore," Hagen said, pouty faced, holding out his hand. Salvatore released his grip on Georg and ran the four steps to Hagen, bypassing the handshake and threw both arms around him, holding on so tightly, like he wasn't going to see him ever again. Hagen put his arms around him slowly and gently held him as Salvatore squeezed harder.

Now, it was the reverend who had tears in his eyes. It always hurt his heart to see a child suffer. The sight of Salvatore's reformation was inspiring and touching. He pulled a handkerchief from his inside coat pocket and dabbed at his eyes. "Well, now," he sniffled then continued, "we will see all of you next Saturday. I'll walk you to the door."

Salvatore and Diana followed closely behind the Beckenbauers as Reverend Osterman led the way. Salvatore's eyes never strayed from his savior as he and his family walked to their truck.

As the Sterling rode away, Hagen turned around on his knees to look out the back window as Salvatore, Diana, and Reverend Osterman waved from the porch. Hagen couldn't sit back down on the seat until Salvatore was out of sight. Salvatore stayed glued to his spot on the porch until the Beckenbauer's truck disappeared around a corner.

On Monday morning, Georg made his first delivery as planned. When the Sterling pulled up to the orphanage, Salvatore heard the engine, and was at the classroom window, forehead against the pane, heart racing, waiting to see his friend. Logic isn't part of a five-and-a-half-year-old's thought process; it being Monday, and a school day, didn't occur to him. When he realized Georg was alone, Salvatore returned to his desk, deflated.

When Hagen returned home from school that afternoon, his mood was quite different than it had been at the orphanage two days before. He knew he would be seeing Salvatore on Saturday. He also knew Salvatore was anxiously waiting for their reunion. He couldn't wait to get home and give his mother something he had safely tucked into one of his books. He showed it to his mother and asked her to give it to his father to give to Salvatore on Wednesday. When she showed it to Georg, he looked at it and shook his head with a smile. What he saw was this:

Their young son had drawn an incredibly detailed picture, in crayon, of two boys and two little girls. They were unmistakably Hagen and Salvatore, Diana and Mathilde; right down to hair color, eye color, and missing teeth. Both boys were swinging together, and they had just made the leap from their seats. They were in mid-air, laughing, arms stretched out to their sides like wings, their hands touching. Mathilde and Diana were playing with dolls and a tea set at a picnic table. A brilliant sun shone in a bright, cloudless, blue sky. There were some significant differences, though, between the scene in the picture and last Saturday. The season and the landscape had changed. It was summer, not winter. There were no snow dunes on the ground. They were not in the orphanage's courtyard but on a lush, green lawn, and in the background, in the distance, was a cornfield. Georg was riding his Fordson tractor near a barn and his mother was standing on the porch waving.

"What do you make of it?" asked Georg.

"Well, it is quite obvious that our son has drawn, and very well I might add" —Marta's pride this time— "our farm, with all of them playing together. And if I did not know better, I would say this is Hagen's way of telling us that he wants Salvatore and Diana to come live with us."

"Do you think that it would be possible? Times are difficult enough now, with this depression and two of our own."

"I know, *mein Schatz*." She looked into her husband's heart through his eyes. "Those two children just lost their parents. Many of the other children living at that orphanage still have parents, somewhere, who will one day come back.

for them when this awful depression is over. Who is going to take care of Salvatore and Diana? Who, in these times, would be able to take both of them?"

"You have a big heart, Marta. I am so happy you are my wife, and the mother of our children."

They hugged each other, then kissed, just a brief kiss as their small children, who had big ears and eyes, were lurking about somewhere.

"Do you think they are Catholic?" asked Georg. "I think they are Italian, probably Catholic. It would be the Catholic thing to do, to take them in."

"Yes, it would be the Catholic thing to do. Moreover, it would be the human thing to do."

"You are right, again. When I go to the orphanage this Wednesday, I will give Salvatore this picture and have a chat with Reverend Osterman."

"*Ich liebe dich, Georg.*"

"I know." He kissed his wife, and throwing caution to the wind, a little longer this time.

On Wednesday, Georg made his delivery and asked the reverend if he could talk to Salvatore. The reverend escorted him to the classroom where Salvatore was diligently practicing writing the capital letter Q—*Q* (Why that letter had to look like the number 2, I never understood.)

When he saw the two men in the doorway, his face lit up and beamed that toothless smile he shared with Hagen.

"Salvatore," said the reverend, "will you come into the hallway, please?"

Salvatore shot from his seat to meet them in the hallway, expectancy all over his face.

"Hello, Salvatore," said Georg.

"Hello, Mr. Beckenbauer," said Salvatore, peeking around Georg's legs. Maybe Hagen was playing hide and seek. "Is Hagen here?"

"No, Salvatore, he is in school."

A frown smeared hope from his face.

"But I do have something for you, from Hagen. He made this in school and asked me to give it to you today."

Georg handed the picture to Salvatore. He looked at it, eyes widening, pushing the frown back to where it came from. "WOW! Hagen made this for me?"

"Yes Salvatore, for you," said the reverend.

Salvatore saw the grass, the corn, the swing, he and Hagen flying through the air together.

Together.

He repeated Saturday's performance and flung his arms around Georg's legs and squeezed as hard as he could.

"Thank you, Mr. Beckenbauer."

"You are welcome, Salvatore. We will see you Saturday morning, OK? Tell Diana that Mathilde is coming, too."

He released Georg's legs and looked up into the eyes of his savior's father, "Yes, sir," then back at what he was holding. Salvatore could not stop staring at Hagen's drawing. It would become his *Saturday at the Farm with Hagen,* and priceless.

The reverend patted him on the head. "OK, Salvatore, go back to your desk and finish practicing your penmanship."

Salvatore walked back to his desk, head held high, smiling from ear to ear, holding Hagen's gift like a holy relic.

"That was very nice of Hagen to do that for Salvatore. It is very thoughtful and well done. You might have a young artist in your house."

"Hagen has always been artistic. Since he could hold a pencil, he would draw things that seemed beyond what a child his age could do."

"I don't think Salvatore would have cared if it were stick figures. You made his day. He has made a complete turn-around since Saturday. He is eating better and smiles now. He can't stop talking about Hagen."

"Hagen and Mathilde are excited to be coming back on Saturday."

"That's wonderful. I'm happy for them, all of them."

"So are we. Reverend, did you take a good look at that picture?"

"Oh, yes, I did indeed. Besides the fact that it was very detailed, the children in that picture were not here at the orphanage."

"This might seem premature and presumptuous, but…"

The reverend interrupted Georg in mid-sentence. "You are thinking about bringing Diana and Salvatore home to live with you, aren't you?"

"Yes, we, Marta and I, talked it over. It might stretch us a bit, but we cannot ignore the happiness and welfare of children."

"You and your wife are true Christians, Georg."

"Thank you, we try. So, Reverend, where would we go from here?"

"Well, I think the first step is for me to contact my superiors in the church. They would have to approve of Salvatore and Diana living with you. If they do approve, then we ask the children what they want. I think you and I both know what they will say."

"I think we do, Reverend. When would we know anything?"

"I will make a call to the bishop today. We should know something, one way or the other, by Friday I should think."

131

"Thank you, Reverend."

"No, Georg, thank you."

They walked to the door together, shook hands and bade each other goodbye.

Back in the classroom, Salvatore's heart beat faster. He smiled all the rest of the day; even when the teacher gave them homework. When classes were over, he asked the reverend to help him hang the picture, and together they thumb-tacked Hagen's gift to the wall above Salvatore's bed.

Friday morning was like Monday and Wednesday; Georg milked the cows, gathered eggs and packaged butter that Marta had churned the day before. He loaded the goods into the back of the Sterling and started his drive to the orphanage.

Georg was nervous as he drove to Mount Holly, his palms sweaty on the steering wheel. He was nervous about the thought of adding two more children to the household; not just the additional cost, but the responsibility for the care and upbringing of two more lives. He wanted to help Salvatore and Diana; he really did. And so did Marta. They knew that countless children all over the country were living in orphanages; real orphans, not deposited for safekeeping until their parents returned for them once times improved. If they could make a difference in the lives of one child, or two… but he was putting the cart before the horse. What if the reverend were to tell him that the church would not allow Georg and Marta to take Salvatore and Diana home to live with them? Only the adults would feel the disappointment and loss of what might have been.

Georg pulled into the driveway and drove around to the back of the orphanage to the kitchen door to deliver the milk, eggs, and butter. He was in the kitchen helping Mrs.

Winklespecht, the cook, check everything in when Reverend Osterman poked his head through the door.

"*Guten Morgen, Georg.*"

"*Ah, das war sehr gut, Reverend. Sprechen Sie Deutsch?*"

"No, that was the extent of my German. I have been practicing those two words since I woke up this morning."

"I do appreciate the effort." Georg noticed the reverend's upbeat attitude and had to ask. "You are very happy today, Reverend. Is there any *particular* reason for your good humor?"

Reverend Osterman's ear-to-ear smile and tears of joy welling in his eyes told Georg the answer to his question.

"Really?" Georg's waterworks and smile mirrored those of the reverend, and he spread his arms wide and engulfed Reverend Osterman in a bear hug to rival any grizzly's.

"Yes… Georg… really," said the reverend with the remaining air in his lungs.

Georg released him so he could breathe normally. "When will we be able to bring them home?"

"First, we have to ask them what *they* want to do. We have a feeling what they will say but we can't assume anything. Children are funny creatures and can be very unpredictable. I don't know whether we should ask them before you come tomorrow with your family or ask the children all at once how they feel."

"I am going to, how do you say, go out on a limb here, Reverend and bet on the second option. Tomorrow we will let them play outside, to see if they still seem the same way around each other as they did last Saturday. And I will go even further out on that limb and say that it will be even better than last Saturday."

"I feel quite safe sitting out on that limb with you, Georg. What time should we expect you tomorrow?"

"After breakfast and chores. Let's say... eleven o'clock?"

"Excellent." He clapped his hands together. "Oh, Georg, I am very excited."

"So are we. Marta and I were up all night last night talking about it. I had better get home and tell her the news. We will see you tomorrow at eleven."

"Yes, see you then."

Georg was almost out the door when he turned around. "Oh, Reverend, do you have any children?"

"Yes, my wife and I have three of our own; two boys and a girl."

"And you still have time and compassion for these children. I commend you, my friend."

Georg left the kitchen and walked to his truck. He got in behind the wheel, started the Sterling's engine, and sat there for a moment, saying a silent prayer asking God for guidance and strength for his wife and himself, and to help them to be good providers for the children.

January 11, 1930

Hagen and Mathilde woke up with ants in their pants. Georg was up early, as usual, tending to the cows and chickens. There was no food delivery that day. The trip to Mount Holly on that bright, sunny Saturday was to deliver two children and hopefully return home with four; all adults' fingers and toes crossed.

After finishing up in the barn, Georg came into the house and cleaned up. Marta was preparing breakfast and the children were getting dressed. When they all sat down to eat, Marta asked Hagen if he would like to say grace, in English.

Hagen began, "Bless us, O Lord, and these, thy gifts, which we are about to receive from Thy bounty, through Christ, our Lord…" and before anyone could say *Amen*, he continued, "…and bless Salvatore and Diana and Reverend Osterman. Amen."

"Amen," said the rest.

"That was very nice of you, *Liebchen*, to include Salvatore, Diana, and Reverend Osterman," said Marta.

"Yes," said Georg, "very nice, indeed."

Hagen smiled. His parents took it as a response to their compliments, but he was really smiling because he was thinking about seeing Salvatore again.

After they finished their breakfast, the children helped their mother with the dishes. Georg went upstairs to get some blankets for the ride home. *If Salvatore and Diana come home with us today, there won't be room enough for everyone in the front. Someone will have to ride in the back, most likely the boys, and they will need something more than coats to keep them warm.* While he was outside that morning, he also threw a large pile of hay in the back of the Sterling for insulation against the cold wood of the truck bed; and a crate with two quarts of fresh milk, a quart of fresh cream, and two dozen eggs.

When it was time to leave for the orphanage, everyone put on their coats and hats. Antsy-pantsy, contorting children take longer to get ready than calm children. If they knew that, they might try to sedate the ants long enough to get dressed. Logic and young children don't usually make acquaintances until they reach the age of *have to go to work to pay the bills*. So, for now, the ants were in charge.

When all were bundled up for the weather, they got in the truck. Now, not only were Mathilde and Hagen suffering from *antsinpantsitis,* but their parents caught g*astrobutterflyosis*. Marta and Georg glanced occasionally over the children at each other, biting their lips to keep from giggling. This felt more exciting than secretly hiding Christmas presents.

When the Sterling turned left onto Brainerd Street in Mount Holly, the orphanage came into view and the children's fidgeting intensified. They sat forward, leaned on the dashboard, and looked out of the front window for any sign of their friends. As they got closer, they could see Salvatore and Diana waiting on the porch, wagging imaginary tails like puppies. Apparently, there was an *antsinpantsitis* epidemic. The reverend stood between them, each hand on the shoulder of a jiggling child.

Georg parked the truck in front of the orphanage. Turning off the engine turned up Hagen and Mathilde's fidgeting, and Georg found it necessary to have that talk. You know, *THAT* talk. The one about what might happen when certain children are not behaving; like turning around and going home. *Turning around and going home? Oh no!* All fidgeting ceased and the children sat up straight and still.

"That is better," said Marta. "We have to be good examples for Salvatore and Diana."

"Yes, Mama," they said, hands folded, heads bowed, biting their lower lips to keep from giggling. They knew this routine. And they knew if they held onto their composure long enough to satisfy Mama then they would get what they wanted.

"Good, we would not want your friends to…" Marta almost let the cat out of the bag. She almost said, *not want to come home with us,* but recovered with, "…to think you were raised by wild animals, would we?"

Georg smiled at his wife; he saw her almost give away the secret.

"No, Mama," said the children, *and* Georg.

Marta looked at Georg with loving, smiling eyes and mouthed, *Ich liebe Dich.*

Ich liebe Dich, he mouthed back, then blew a kiss. "Are you ready, *Schatzi*?"

She nodded back at him and prepared for the onslaught.

"Let's go see your friends," said Georg. "Before they go back inside and lock the door."

Well, that started the children up again. This time Marta and Georg just opened the doors and got out. Georg helped Hagen down. He hit the ground running. Marta helped Mathilde out of the truck, and she followed her brother. They ran towards Salvatore and Diana, who had already come down from the porch and were running full steam ahead towards the truck.

The children met halfway, and the boys hugged, and the girls hugged and then they group-hugged. Georg and Marta looked up at Reverend Osterman, who was looking down from the porch at the four hugging and jumping children. He looked over at Georg and Marta, smiled, put his prayer-clasped hands to his chin and nodded.

"Alright children, why don't we take this into the courtyard?" said the reverend.

He opened the door and in ran the children. "Walk, don't run! We know the rules, right, Salvatore?"

"Yes, sir," he said. "We have to walk in the hallway," he told Hagen and Mathilde, and led them in single file. The adults couldn't help but giggle at the sight as they joined the parade to the courtyard. Reverend Osterman held the door open and one by one, like bullets, they shot out into the open air and paired off; Hagen and Salvatore went to the swing set, their sisters to the seesaw.

"Well," said the reverend. "Let's go to my office. We can watch them from the window and talk about what happens next."

He led the way to his office. Instead of sitting at his desk, he offered them the sofa under the window and pulled one of the wingback chairs over to face them, then sat down. Between them, on the floor, was a steamer trunk, with the lock facing the sofa.

"Georg, Marta, from the looks of what we just witnessed, I believe that you will be sharing your home tonight with two more little people. I need to hear, from both of you, that you are aware of what this entails, and that you are willing to take this responsibility seriously."

They both looked at him incredulously, then at each other and back again.

"Reverend Osterman, do you doubt our commitment or our capability?" asked Marta.

"I don't doubt you in the least, Marta. From what I have seen of you and your family, I know you are wonderful parents. I want you to be sure that you do not doubt yourselves."

"Ah," said Georg, "you want us to be absolutely sure before we sign on the dotted line."

"So to speak, although there is nothing to sign, physically. The dotted line gets signed when we tell the children."

"We are aware of the responsibility," said Marta. "We do not take this lightly."

"Good," said the reverend. "Before we get to the good part, I think I should tell you a little about the Cristoforos."

"Cristoforos?" said Georg. "Oh, their last name! We never even asked who these children are, or where they came from."

"I know," said the reverend. "We were so caught up in the joy of what was happening that we forgot about the sorrow that brought us together."

"I am so sorry that we did not ask about their parents," said Marta.

"Don't be sorry," said the reverend. "We are only human. God watches over us all and it is He who brought us together."

"Quite right, Reverend," said Georg. "Please, tell us about the Cristoforos."

The reverend began. "After Salvatore and Diana's parents passed, all of their family possessions were put into this trunk." He laid his hand gently on the lid of the steamer trunk. "And it came here with them. This trunk, their clothes, and the few personal items they have received since arriving at the orphanage, are all that Salvatore and Diana Cristoforo have to their name."

Georg and Marta looked down at the trunk. Marta put her hand on it reverently, like she was touching something sacred. She closed her eyes as a silent prayer went up to Heaven.

"Please, open it," said the reverend.

Georg and Marta looked at the reverend as if he had just asked them to open the Ark of the Covenant. Then they looked at each other, each saying with their eyes and expressions: *You do it! No, you do it!*

Marta got up the courage and turned the key in the lock and, with Georg, slowly opened the lid. The contents barely filled one half of the trunk's space. There were a few items of clothing—baby clothes, shoes, a woman's house dress and apron. Under the clothing, was a photograph album. Georg pulled it out, put it on his lap and slowly opened it. On the first page was a photo with scalloped edges that took up the whole page and was held in place by four corner adhesive mounts.

"Meet Giuseppe and Anna-Maria Cristoforo," said Reverend Osterman.

The Cristoforos were standing in front of an ornate sanctuary as Jesus looked down upon them from the large wooden crucifix on the wall behind them. Candles burned on either side of the altar. The woman was beautiful, her face like a Roman goddess. She wore a white wedding dress, the train pulled around on her left side and flowing down the steps in front of the altar. With both hands in front of her bodice, she held a large bouquet of white flowers. On her head was a crown of the same flowers, haloed by her pulled back veil. A three-stranded pearl necklace adorned her neckline. It matched the bracelet on her left wrist.

The groom, as beautiful as his bride, with his Greco-Roman nose that led from his large, dark eyes to his Michaelangeloesque mouth, wore a black dress suit with satin lapels and a white shirt with a high collar and a white bow tie. A single rose was pinned to his lapel. He wore white gloves and stood to his bride's right with his left arm around her waist and his right hand resting on her right arm. Neither was smiling, which was typical for the era. They were in love but could not show it outwardly. Even without a smile, the man cut a handsome figure. There was an air of confidence about him; he was a man who knew his destiny. His stoic demeanor couldn't hide the love that he had for Anna-Maria. His bride, just as serious as her groom, looked like the photograph had been taken when she had just controlled a giggle. Looking at this photo, you could sense the excitement; you could imagine being in that church when the last photograph was taken and the statues unfroze, and laughed, and kissed. And it was not difficult to see the resemblance of the two children the Beckenbauers were about to bring home, to the newlyweds in the photograph.

"Oh my, they were so beautiful," said Marta.

Georg turned the page, revealing more photos of the couple—some of just the two of them, some with family. They turned another page and there was Giuseppe, standing dressed in a WWI Italian military uniform, holding a rifle, butt on the ground, bayonet pointing to the sky. His boots were shined and black. His hat was wide-brimmed, round, with a leather chin strap and a large plume of black feathers flowing off to the right.

"He was a *Bersaglieri*," said Georg.

"What's that?" asked the reverend.

"A sharpshooter in the Italian Army during the war," said Georg. "Very prestigious."

As Georg turned the pages, time progressed in the lives of the Cristoforos. Another turn of a page and they saw a photo of two men, a father and son by the resemblances. They were standing side by side, sporting wide smiles, arms over each other's shoulders in front of a storefront. The sign above them on the building said:

Cristoforo e Figlio, Cappellai

Men's hats displayed in the windows told Marta and Georg that Sal and Diana's father and grandfather were milliners in Italy.

Georg turned the page, and both he and Marta gasped in amazement. Affixed to the page was a flier for steamship travel to America. Below it was a postcard depicting a steamship in all its majestic glory.

When Georg and Marta saw it, they stared, wide-eyed, mouths agape.

"What's wrong?" asked the reverend.

"We came to America on that same ship," said Georg.

"Well, now, that sure is a coincidence," said the reverend.

Poking out from behind the postcard were two ticket stubs from their voyage. Marta pulled them out and began to cry.

"What's the matter?" asked Georg.

She handed him one of the stubs. He looked at it and covered his open mouth with the other hand.

The reverend was looking at them quizzically. "What's wrong?"

"The Cristoforos took the same ship, yes," said Georg, "but we were on it at the same time. We came to America, together!"

"The Lord again in all His mystery," said the reverend as the three of them were covered in goosebumps.

As the pages were turned, the timeline progressed to pictures in America; Anna-Maria and Giuseppe standing in front of their new car; one in front of a small house. There was one of Giuseppe in front of his storefront, smiling, arms stretched widely. Carrying on the family tradition, the sign above the door said:

CRISTOFORO & SON, MILLINERS

Georg closed the photo album and placed it next to him on the sofa, then reached in the trunk. A linen bag lay there, fluffy with its contents. When he pulled the bag out of the trunk and opened it, a billowy, white fabric issued from inside. It was the same fabric that they had just seen in the wedding photo. It was Anna-Maria's wedding dress, and it was as beautiful in person as it was in the picture. Something was nestled in the fabric, something not fluffy. It was a King James Bible; hardcovered and bound in rich, mahogany brown leather. Marta opened it and they saw writing on the first page, a dedication page. This was their wedding bible. The writing was in Italian, but they didn't need a translator to understand the information in front of them:

The groom's name—Giuseppe Giovanni Girolamo Cristoforo; the bride's name—Anna-Maria Caterina Francesca Battaglini.

The date—23 May 1914. The Church—Basilica di San Francesco d'Assisi, Palermo. Pressed inside the book were a single rose and some of the flowers from Anna-Maria's bouquet.

Her flowers were pressed into Psalms.

Psalm 143:8 was circled.

"Let the morning bring me word of your unfailing love, for I have put my trust in you. Show me the way I should go, for to you I entrust my life."

Giuseppe's rose was pressed into Song of Solomon. Verse 4:9 was circled.

"You have captivated my heart, my sister, my bride; you have captivated my heart with one glance of your eyes, with one jewel of your necklace."

"Oh, Georg, they were so in love," said Marta. "I wish we could have known them."

"It is possible that you almost met them," said the reverend. "You were on the same ship together. You may

143

have even seen them in passing. The day they were killed in the trolley accident, they were looking for work."

"Looking for work?" asked Georg. "What about his business?"

"From what information I could gather, Giuseppe's business had failed before the Depression began. So many people were losing everything. People were struggling to survive; buying a new hat was not a priority. Giuseppe and Anna-Maria found work where they could, including migrant farm work. They did what they could do to survive, to take care of their family."

"And they were in our area when they died," said Marta. "If the accident hadn't happened, they may have come to our farm for work. Oh, Georg, we were looking for help with the harvest at that time."

"God connected all of us for a reason, Marta," said Georg. "I wish He had put us *all* together, not just the children."

Marta nodded, wiping more tears from her cheeks.

"There are a few more things in the trunk," said the reverend.

Georg reached in and found two small boxes, something wrapped in linen, and a hat box. The two small boxes contained baby shoes, bronzed and mounted on little wooden stands. On each stand was screwed a metal plate with *Salvatore Giuseppe Cristoforo* engraved into one and *Diana Luisa Cristoforo* into the other. Wrapped in the linen were two silver candlesticks—probably the only valuable possessions they had left.

On the hatbox lid was written:

Cristoforo & Son, Milliners
201 Washington Street
Hoboken, New Jersey
Phone: Hoboken-3361

Georg lifted the lid off the hatbox and pulled out a black, rabbit hair Homburg. "This is a beautiful hat, and very well made." Inside the hat, the label read:

Giuseppe Cristoforo & Son, Hoboken, NJ.

"Giuseppe was a very talented man," said the reverend. "When I first looked through this trunk and saw this hat, something seemed familiar. Then I went home, and I examined my hats. One of them was given to me as a gift from my brother-in-law and his wife for Christmas, 1927. It is a Homburg, just like this one, and with the same label inside. It gave me goosebumps."

Georg put the hat back in its box, put the lid on and placed it back in the trunk. Marta put the rest of the Cristoforos' belongings inside just as they were found, and together she and Georg lowered the trunk lid.

"Reverend, when the time is right, when Diana and Salvatore are old enough to understand what these things mean to them and to their parents, we will be sure they get them," said Georg.

"In the meantime," said Marta. "We will keep this quite safe."

"Thank you. I know you will." He patted the trunk one more time. "Now, before we talk to the children, there is one more thing I would like to discuss. When I spoke with Bishop Hartwell about the Cristoforos going to live with you, he had some concern about the cost of adding two more mouths to feed, and wanted me to offer you a monthly stipend to help offset any financial strain this may cause your family."

Georg and Marta looked at each other. At the same time, they shook their heads *no*.

"That will not be necessary, Reverend," said Georg. "We will make do."

"Salvatore is smaller than Hagen," said Marta. "He might be able to wear some of Hagen's older clothes."

"And Reverend," said Georg. "I am sure you will be receiving more children to fill their places."

"We will most likely fill their spots, this is true."

"Then, Reverend, we will be just fine," said Georg

"If you are both sure, I do appreciate it. I had to make the offer, though. If at any time you need assistance, please, talk to me."

"We will, and thank you," said Marta.

"Very good, well, now," said Reverend Osterman, standing up. "I don't think that there is anything left to do except talk to the children."

"Before we do that," said Georg. "We should put the trunk in the back of the truck."

"Good idea," said the reverend.

Georg and Reverend Osterman each took an end and lifted the trunk by its handles. They carried it out of the office into the hallway and made their way to the front door and out to the truck. Once the trunk was secured in the back, Georg grabbed the wooden crate with the milk, cream, and eggs and handed it to the reverend.

"What is this for?" asked the reverend.

"This is for your family."

"Thank you, but this isn't necessary."

"Reverend, please take it. No one is immune to this depression."

"This is very kind of you, Georg, thank you. My wife and family will very much appreciate this."

"Our pleasure, Reverend. Now, let's go excite some children."

They walked back to the office and found Marta kneeling on the sofa, looking out the window at the playing children.

"Ahem," said Georg. "Kneeling on the sofa?"

She spun around and sat down, hands clasped in her lap, head bowed with a made-up frown. She looked up at the two smiling men. "How could I not watch them?"

Georg walked over, knelt next to his wife and leaned on the back of the sofa, his chin resting on his forearm, and watched the children. Marta turned around and leaned on the back of the sofa, mimicking Georg. The reverend knelt next to Marta and followed suit; three big kids remembering their childhoods. Inside each of them, there was a child wanting to go swing on a swing and play in the snow.

"I see what you mean," said Georg.

"We had better go get them before I want to keep all four of them," said the reverend.

"Hmm," said Marta, turning to look at her husband. "What do you think about leaving them here and we run away for a while?"

"I like that idea very much," said Georg, as fake straight-faced as he could be. "Let's leave before the reverend changes his mind."

Marta and Georg looked over at the Reverend Osterman's sarcastic smirk.

"Very funny, you two."

The three of them got up from the sofa, paused, and stood there, hearts racing.

"Are you ready?" asked the reverend.

Georg and Marta both took deep, long breaths, then nodded once. They left the office and went down the hallway to the courtyard. "Are you sure?" asked the reverend, one hand on the doorknob.

"Very, very sure," said Marta as Georg nodded in agreement.

The reverend opened the door slowly, like Dorothy opening the door after her house landed in Oz. When they walked outside, the sky seemed bluer, the sun brighter, like God was smiling down on a happier day. Hagen and Salvatore were swinging and laughing. Diana and Mathilde were playing with some of the other little girls in the snow.

"Hagen, Mathilde," called Georg.

"Salvatore, Diana," called Reverend Osterman.

The girls looked up from their snowman. The boys skidded their heels into the ground, abruptly ending their swinging. They stared at the adults waving them over. They knew their time was up. Time for Hagen and Mathilde to go home, *again.* Time for Salvatore and Diana to say goodbye, *again.* Time to begin the long wait for next Saturday to come, *again.* They remained there, unmoving, like cute woodland creatures who hide in plain sight by remaining... completely...... still.

"Come, children, come inside now," said Marta.

"Oh, Mama," said Hagen. "Just a little longer, please?"

"No, *Liebchen*, you must come inside now, hurry up."

Slowly, the very opposite of hurrying, the children shuffled and scuffed, barely walked, towards the door; Mathilde and Diana were hand in hand; Hagen and Salvatore were bumping shoulders with each sad step.

"If they only knew what was about to happen, they would stampede and run us over to get inside," said the reverend.

"They look so dramatic, so sad. I feel sinful finding it humorous," said Marta.

"Enjoy the slowness, Marta," said her husband. "In a few minutes, it will become fast and stay that way until we marry them off."

All three of them giggled.

The children walked through the door as Georg held it open for everyone. Once inside, Reverend Osterman went to the front of the pack and led the way. But he didn't go back to his office. Instead, he led everyone to a staircase that went up to the dormitories.

"Normally we keep the boys and the girls separated by gender and age groups," said the reverend as they climbed the stairs. "Salvatore and Diana were allowed to stay with each other in a room meant for new arrivals and younger siblings."

They walked to a door at the end of a hallway. He opened the door and they followed him inside. The Beckenbauers looked around at the room that the Cristoforo children had called home for the last three months. It wasn't large—twelve beds, six on each side, a walkway down the middle. At the far wall were two large windows that looked out onto the neighborhood below. In between the beds were little night tables, with little lamps and some personal items belonging to the child who occupied the bed next to it.

"Salvatore, Diana," said the reverend. "Why don't you show Hagen and Mathilde where you sleep."

The Beckenbauers followed them to the last bed on the left, the one with Hagen's picture pinned to the wall above. Salvatore pointed to it. "This is my bed." Then he pointed to the bed next to his. "That is Diana's bed."

On each bed was a suitcase. Salvatore looked at the one on his bed like an out-of-place foreign object, then looked up at Reverend Osterman questioningly.

"I took the liberty of going way out on that limb that Georg and I climbed onto a few days ago," he elbowed Georg in the ribs, "and had their suitcases packed and ready to go."

Salvatore opened his suitcase. Inside were his clothes, a few books, some things he made in art class. There were also a new pair of pants, a new shirt, and new shoes; for a new beginning. When Diana opened the suitcase on her bed, she found it contained her belongings, as well as a new dress, new shoes and a hat.

"Children," said Reverend Osterman. "I want you to all come and sit next to each other here." He patted Salvatore's bed. All four of them climbed up and sat next to each other, their faces a mish-mosh of confused expressions.

The reverend sat across from them on Diana's bed and continued. "Salvatore, Diana, it's time for Hagen and Mathilde to go home now."

Again, with the pouting faces. Georg and Marta were just about ready to burst.

"Mr. and Mrs. Beckenbauer would like you to go live with them," said the reverend.

Well, that took them so by surprise that it kept them frozen in a stare.

"Would you like to come live with us?" asked Marta, relieved that the cat was out of the bag.

"YES! YES! YESYESYES!" shouted Hagen.

"Now, Hagen," said his father, "let Salvatore and Diana answer for themselves. Salvatore, Diana, would you like to come live with us?"

"YES! YES! YESYESYES!" they both shouted, echoing Hagen verbatim.

All four children were now bouncing on the bed on their bottoms like they were sitting on a hot griddle.

"Alright then," said the reverend with a giggle. "I had a feeling that you would react this way, so while you were outside playing, Mrs. Schnibbe packed your suitcases for you. Salvatore, I asked her to leave your picture on the wall. I thought you might want to take it down yourself."

Salvatore looked up at Hagen's masterpiece on the wall over his pillow. He crawled on the bed, around Hagen, got on his knees and pulled the thumbtacks out of the wall, ever so gently, one by one, like an archaeologist uncovering a sacred parchment. He had been so careful not to damage Hagen's gift when he and the reverend pinned it up, that he didn't stab the pins through the paper, but next to the edges, so the pressure of the flat heads of the thumbtacks held it in place.

He handed the unscathed artwork to Marta. "Mrs. Beckenbauer, will you keep this safe?"

"Of course, *Liebchen*," she said.

Salvatore looked at Mrs. Beckenbauer very confusedly, then at Hagen.

"It is German, Salvatore," said Hagen. "In English, Mama."

Marta looked over at her husband who was doing his darnedest not to laugh, then back to Salvatore. "I am sorry. Of course, *dear*."

"Thank you, Mrs. Beckenbauer."

"You are very welcome."

"Salvatore?" said the reverend.

"Yes, sir?"

"Why don't you carry your suitcase, and if Hagen wouldn't mind being a gentleman, he might carry Diana's for her?"

"Yes, sir," said Hagen, then he and Salvatore grabbed the suitcases, pulled them off the bed and headed for the door.

"I guess now we are leaving," said Marta.

"I guess so," giggled the reverend.

Diana and Mathilde hopped down off the bed and ran to catch up with their brothers. The adults brought up the rear as Hagen and Salvatore *thump*, *thump*, *thumped* the suitcases down the stairs and hurried to the main entrance.

"You go ahead, and I'll meet you outside," said the reverend to Marta and Georg. "I have to go to my office really quick."

The Beckenbauers plus two continued their march to the truck with the boys leading the way. *Thump, thump, thump* went the suitcases down the porch steps as the boys walked as fast as they could to the back of the Sterling. Marta helped the girls get into the front seat of the truck. Georg put the suitcases up in the back and then lifted Salvatore, then Hagen up into the back with the suitcases and the steamer trunk.

Marta retrieved the two blankets from the front and brought them to the back of the truck. "Hagen, Salvatore, here, take these blankets and bundle up," she said.

"Sit on the hay, it will help keep you warm," said Georg.

"Yes sir, Papa," said Hagen. He walked to the far inside of the truck bed, Salvatore close behind like a puppy, and flopped, bottom first into the hay then pulled a blanket over himself. He patted the hay next to him. "Sit next to me, Salvatore."

Salvatore turned around and flopped into the soft hay right next to Hagen and let out a little giggle, then pulled his blanket over himself.

Hagen smiled at Salvatore. "We are brothers, now."

"Brothers and best friends," said Salvatore. Their grins widened like contestants in a missing-tooth smiling contest.

Reverend Osterman came down the porch steps holding something in his hand. It was an envelope; one of those big, brown, thick, manila things that was held closed by a string figure-eighting around two round buttons. He met Georg and Marta in front of the truck.

"Here," he said handing Georg the envelope. "These are Salvatore and Diana's documents: birth certificates, baptism certificates, and records from their stay here with us at the orphanage. I forgot to put them in the trunk with the rest of their belongings."

"Thank you, Reverend," said Marta. "We will take good care of these, too. Please, don't be a stranger. Stop by anytime." She gave him a hug and a kiss on each cheek.

"Yes, Reverend, please visit," said Georg. "You are family now." He extended his hand and the reverend grasped it in his. Georg pulled him in for another one of his grizzly bear hugs. The reverend did his best to match Georg. Close, a good effort, but nothing matched Georg's grizzlies.

"Thank you... for everything," said the reverend as Georg squeezed him breathless.

Georg released him, held him at arm's length, a hand on each shoulder. "No, Reverend, thank *you*."

Marta and Georg got into the truck and made a Diana-Mathilde sandwich. Georg fired up the Sterling's engine and put it in gear. As the truck began to move, the boys in the back leaned forward with the negative G-force and then back into the hay, giggling and smiling at each other. Dreams were coming true.

Reverend Osterman waved as they pulled away. He watched the two boys sitting in the back of the truck, just their heads poking out from under their blankets, and missed the carefreeness of boyhood. No worries. No stress. Just eat, play, school, sleep, repeat. Hagen waved back at him, his fingers jiggling the blanket as Salvatore gazed at his new brother and best friend. When the truck turned a corner and was out of sight, the reverend went back inside into the warmth of his office. He poured a cup of coffee from the thermos on his desk and looked at the crate Georg had given him with the milk, cream, and eggs. He drank his coffee black that morning, saving the gift from the Beckenbauers for his family.

Back in the truck, Marta listened to the girls giggling, talking about dolls, and favorite foods, and yucky foods. Georg's mind spun with thoughts of responsibility and crops and cows, beds for Diana and Salvatore, a car that will fit everyone *inside* so no one has to ride in the back under blankets in hay piles.

In the back, the boys jiggled and jostled along with the moving truck. Salvatore looked cold. "Here," said Hagen as he lifted his blanket. "Get under with me. I will keep you warm."

Salvatore slid under the blanket with Hagen, then pulled his blanket under with him, and they sat next to each other, holding the blankets close. Hagen wriggled in the hay, nestling his bottom deeper into it, pushing some of it away so Salvatore could sink in with him. Now they were covered by hay on their sides and two blankets on top. They were shoulder to shoulder, elbow to elbow, leg to leg, snug as two bugs in a rug.

Although technically not a true hayride, this was Salvatore's first time riding in a pile of hay in the back of a truck. It was also the first time that he experienced the feeling that he had a real friend. A good—no—a best friend. He had played with some of the other little boys in the neighborhood in Hoboken. But they never affected his spirit like the boy sitting next to him in the hay. He had only known Hagen for a week and a day, but if he had known the definition of the word *savior,* then that is what he would have called him; his new brother, best friend, and savior; Saint Hagen.

Last Saturday, if you could have asked God to point out the saddest boy, the bluest, the most down-in-the-dumpiest little five-and-a-half-year-old boy in New Jersey, then God's Holy Finger would have come down from Heaven above and pointed to Salvatore Cristoforo, son of Giuseppe and Anna-Maria Cristoforo, sitting on a swing in the courtyard of The Methodist Orphanage in Mount Holly, New Jersey.

Then, as if God was answering Salvatore's unthought prayer, here comes Saint Hagen, patron saint of sad little boys on swings, to wash away the blues and revive his soul with seven words, a smile, and a handshake. The moment that Hagen walked into his life will be forever remembered by Salvatore as one of the two best in his life.

The other one? That one comes later.

The boys sat there all snugglybugglywuggly as the truck rocked and rolled through the streets, the wind whipping around them, kissing their noses and pinching their cheeks. The blankets puffed up and down. Small pieces of hay whirled around in mini vortexes of cold winter air on the wooden truck bed. They were warm under the blanket. But their faces were cold with rosy cheeks, and noses waxing crimson. Hagen could see Salvatore's lips beginning to quiver as the shivers began. Hagen lifted the blankets up and over their heads, shutting out the windy pinches and kisses. Their noses slowly un-numbed. Quivering lips calmed. The truck's engine sound was muffled. They couldn't see each other now, but they could hear each other better.

"Hagen?"

"Yes, Salvatore?"

"Where do you live?"

"In Beverly."

"Hagen?"

"Yes, Salvatore?"

"How long will I live with you?"

"Forever."

There were no more Salvatore inquiries, for now.

In the darkness under the blankets, in the hay, Hagen couldn't see Salvatore's lips quivering again. It wasn't the cold this time. It was joy, and relief, and release. Salvatore was about to cry. He was happy. Even at five-and-a-half years old, little Catholic boys know how to pray. They pray for everything. They pray for a toy fire engine at Christmas. And lots and lots of snow to play in. They pray at night before bed for God to bless Mommy and Daddy and sisters and brothers and their teachers and friends and the cat and the dog.

They also pray for help from God—*Dear God, please help Papa find work so we can eat, and Mama will stop crying.*

And they pray for miracles—*Dear God, please bring back Mama and Papa like you brought back your son Jesus.*

And they pray to give thanks—*Dear God, thank you for this food, this house, my toy truck. And my new best friend, Saint Hagen.*

We hear the words *The Lord works in mysterious ways* said oftentimes when there is no logical way to explain the reasons why something bad or good has happened. Some less religiously inclined persons amongst us call it fate or kismet or just plain luck. Some little five-and-a-half-year-old orphaned Catholic boys believe that God makes it happen. God makes *everything* happen. He makes the Sun rise and birds sing and the flowers bloom and Mama and Papa go to Heaven and angels come to you in your darkest hour and rescue your soul.

Under the blankets, in the hay, Salvatore Cristoforo thanked God for Hagen and his family and forgave Him for taking Mama and Papa away to Heaven. He knew in his big little heart that his parents had something to do with their new-found family. They wanted him and his sister to be happy. Giuseppe and Anna-Maria asked God to send Hagen's family to him and Diana. *The Lord works in mysterious ways, with a little nudging from Mama.*

Salvatore leaned a little more against Hagen. Hagen put his left arm around him and pulled him closer. Warm tears fell from Salvatore's cold cheeks onto Saint Hagen's coat.

Hagen's spirit spoke to Salvatore's: *you are home now, you are safe.*

The truck rumbled down Mount Holly Road as its passengers bonded with each other. Georg said something to Marta about new beds. Marta said something about church the next day. The girls were talking about how they liked puppies. Marta and Georg looked at each and rolled their eyes when they heard the word *puppies.*

In the back of the truck, all was quiet for a while. Hagen was thinking about how much fun it was going to be to have a brother to do things with. Mathilde was too little, *and* she was a girl. She didn't do boy stuff like jump off swings. Although, she did play hide-and-seek well. She was very good at hiding.

Salvatore was wondering what it was going to be like to live on a farm. He had never seen a farm up close until his Mama and Papa started to work on them, picking fruits and vegetables and digging in the dirt. Sometimes he and his sister would go with their parents when they went to these places to look for work. He remembered seeing fields of corn and green things growing and trees with fruit hanging low on their branches. But he never lived at any of these places. He never even saw the inside of one of the barns. He always wanted to pet one of the animals.

He lifted his head off of Hagen's shoulder.

"Hagen?"

"Yes?"

"Do you have a barn?" he asked.

"I have two barns," said Hagen.

"Two barns?"

"Uh-huh. One for the tractor and other stuff and one for the cows."

"You have cows?" asked Salvatore enthusiastically.

"Uh-huh, and chickens, too. But they have their own barn, it's called a coop."

"A coop?"

"Uh-huh, it's like a little barn. They sleep in it at night and when they wake up, they lay eggs and go outside to play all day, then Mama goes in the back door and takes the eggs and we eat them."

"Can I pet a chicken?" asked Salvatore.

"Sure, if you can catch one. They run fast."

"Do cows run fast, too?"

"No, they stand around outside and eat, then come inside and stand around while Papa milks them."

"Can I pet a cow?" asked Salvatore.

"Sure, I do it all the time. You can milk one, too, if you want."

"Wow!" then a pause, then, "Hagen?"

"Yes?"

"Do you have a puppy?"

"No. I want a puppy. I asked for a puppy when I was littler, but Mama and Papa said I need to grow bigger before I could have one."

"Are you bigger now?"

"Much bigger. I'm going to be six next month."

"Big enough for a puppy?"

"Do you want a puppy?"

"Oh, yes, I always wanted a puppy but Mama and Papa..."

Hagen could feel Salvatore's weight shift as his shoulders sank and his head lowered. He waited for Salvatore to say something.

Nothing.

Salvatore's shoulders shook as he sobbed hard. Deeply hard, breath-sucking hard. The only one in the world that heard him was Saint Hagen. The blankets and hay kept everything a secret between them; a makeshift confessional. Everything that was inside him was now, for the first time since he became an orphan, spewing from his soul. Innocent talk of puppies seeded a storm that now blew hard and was unstoppable.

"I... miss... my... Ma-huhma... and... Pa-huhpa...!" His head fell onto Hagen's chest, re-wetting his coat with fresh tears. Hagen put both arms around him and hugged him and rubbed his back like his Mama did when Mathilde cried.

The truck slowed down and made the turn off of Perkins Lane onto the long dirt drive that led to the farmhouse. Hagen knew they were home now by the way the truck felt on the earth. Salvatore's sobbing had ebbed. He was just sitting there, very still, in Hagen's embrace, thinking everything and nothing all at once.

"Salvatore?"

He lifted his head off of Hagen, sniffled and wiped his eyes. "Yes?"

"We're home."

Hagen pulled the blankets down off of their heads; the blast of sunlight in the bright, winter sky made them squint. Through the wooden slats of the side rails, Salvatore's squinting red-from-crying-eyes saw the wide, empty, winter fields. He saw a barn passing by on the left, and the meandering cows, chewing their cud. He could smell the farm smells: hay, and dirt and cow poo; faint now in the winter's cold. In the summer, Salvatore would experience them in full bloom along with fields of corn and tomatoes and all the other fruits and vegetables the Beckenbauer farm produced.

Hagen watched Salvatore taking everything in; a good distraction from the emotional ride home. Hagen didn't know what happened to Salvatore and Diana's Mama and Papa. He knew they died. He knew *died* meant they are angels in Heaven with God and Jesus and Mary. But the bad part of it—the not having a parent to take care of you when you're sick or bake a cake for you on your birthday or put you on their shoulder so you can see high above the corn stalks or sing you to sleep—does not occur to a child until Mama and Papa are taken away and missed; until it's kicked into their psyche that they *died* and are angels in Heaven with God and Jesus and Mary.

And there are no more Mama's cakes or Papa's shoulders.

And no more songs at bedtime.

And your spirit stops singing.

Georg steered the Sterling up to the front of the house. He got out and walked to the back of the truck to help the boys. Marta lifted the girls out of the cab, and Diana looked up at the large, three-storied farmhouse with its deep, wraparound porch with a swing and rocking chairs. Then she turned to look at the barns and the cows she had seen through the windows. Georg deposited the boys on the ground and then retrieved the two suitcases. Salvatore stood there like his sister and gawked open-mouthed at the house and the barns and the cows.

Georg and the boys walked to where Marta and the girls were standing.

"Did you see the cows?" Diana asked her brother.

"I did, and the chickens, too!"

Georg got Marta's attention and blinked two times, then nudged his chin in Salvatore's direction.

She understood his meaning when she saw the remnants of Salvatore's emotional moment—his red eyes, the round wet spot on Hagen's coat. *That poor boy. And my gentle son; ever the consoler.* Thoughts of that day in front of the church fluttered like butterfly wings at her soul.

"Maybe we should go inside and get settled in, and then I will make hot chocolate," said Marta.

"Hot chocolate?" asked Diana, looking at Mathilde then Georg then Marta.

Even red-eyed Salvatore smiled as cows and chickens, barns and hot chocolate, soothed the pain that had him crying moments before.

"My wife makes the best hot chocolate in New Jersey," said Georg, matter-of-factly.

Marta looked at him and smiled. "Let's go inside and get those coats off and get warm. Papa, if you take the suitcases upstairs, I will take the children with me into the kitchen."

"Yes, Mama," said Georg, then led the way up the porch steps and waited for Marta to open the door, then went inside and upstairs with the suitcases. Once inside, Marta helped the children remove their hats and coats and put them on the hall tree next to the front door. The new arrivals looked around at the living room with the two big sofas and two chairs and a fireplace big enough for a whole tree trunk.

And a *RADIO!*

On a table next to the fireplace was the Zenith Tombstone radio. It will become the family's nightly focal point for years to come. It will entertain them with broadcasts of Amos and Andy, The Lux Radio Hour, Little Orphan Annie, and The Lone Ranger. And it will captivate them with newscasts and presidents' speeches and the announcement of another World War. It will be their friend and companion for the good times and the terrible.

Salvatore walked over to the Zenith and gently ran his fingers from the curved apex down its side, feeling the smooth wood, petting it like he was touching one of the cows for the first time. He turned to see Marta smiling, watching him, and he pulled his hand away.

"It's alright to touch it. Papa..."

She caught herself too late. She said *Papa.* She had no idea how these two new members of the family would refer to her and her husband. *Mr. Beckenbauer? Mrs. Beckenbauer? Aunt Marta? Papa and Mama?* She never presumed that she and Georg would replace Giuseppe and Anna-Maria. She had no idea how she would introduce Salvatore and Diana to other people tomorrow when they go to church. *'Good afternoon, Mr. and Mrs. So-and-so, these are our children, Hagen and Mathilde, and their orphan friends who live with us?' Is exclusion better than inclusion? Dare we refer to them as our children? Do we dare ask them what* THEY *want? And when will it be a good time to do that? After a day, a week, a year?*

Marta finished the sentence; it had already begun.

"...will show you how to tune in the stations."

"Papa lets us listen to the radio after dinner and chores," said Hagen.

Thank you, Liebchen, Marta said to herself. *To the rescue again.*

"Alright, who wants to help me make the hot chocolate?"

"Meee, meee, meee," sang the newly formed Beckenbauer-Cristoforo Children's Choir as they followed her into the kitchen.

Upstairs, Georg put Diana's suitcase on Mathilde's bed and Salvatore's on Hagen's. He looked around at each room, arranging furniture in his head, imagining two beds in each. He heard the chorus of *meees* coming from downstairs and put the furniture arranging to the back of his mind for now and went down to join everyone in the kitchen. Georg loved his wife's hot chocolate, too.

Marta warmed milk on the stove while the children watched. Diana and Salvatore hadn't had hot chocolate since they lived in their own house when Giuseppe still had his hat making business. Diana didn't have any clear memories of her mother making the hot chocolate, just vague remembrances of tasting it. Salvatore, on the other hand, remembered vividly his mother in the kitchen pouring her hot chocolate into little cups for him and his sister. The smell of it, chocolate mixed with hints of cinnamon and cardamom, would always waft through his memories. Anna-Maria's was thick, like hot pudding, and there were homemade biscotti for dipping. Watching Hagen's mother standing at the stove stirring a pot of steaming chocolate deliciousness also stirred a pot of melancholia. Marta saw his empty stare. He was somewhere else, she could see that, and wondered where his mind had run off to.

When the hot chocolate was ready, she poured it into cups and topped each with a fat dollop of whipped cream. "Alright children, go have a seat at the table."

...Before we go any further, the use of the word *table* here needs a little clarification. It is a simple word with multiple uses both as a noun and a verb. When Marta tells everyone to have a seat at the table, it is used as a noun because a table is a thing. The Inuit people have fifty different words for snow, each one describing the type, texture, color, etc. And if they had fifty different words for *table,* and Marta could use one of them here, it would describe the size, weight, type of wood, and how many elephants it could hold on its back. The word *table* was just the general term for the gargantuan slab of oak, five feet by ten feet, drawbridge-across-the-moat big table that sat in the middle of her kitchen. This is how it came to be:

Georg had always wanted to work with wood. When he and Marta had first arrived at their farm almost nine years before, he didn't think of repairing the barn as work, or a chore. Yes, it had to be done, but he loved the feeling of the wood, the cutting of the planks and making them fit just right before nailing them into place. In Germany, his father dabbled in making small pieces of furniture: a small side table, a coat rack, and even a chair. When he and Marta built their new house in New Jersey, they wanted it to be roomy, able to accommodate gatherings of family and friends without cramming them together like sardines in a can. The best place to gather was in a large kitchen around a big table with lots of food, and laughter, and love.

After he and his wife left the barn to live in their newly built house, Georg turned the living quarters in the barn into a woodworking shop. He told his wife that he was intending to build a table for her kitchen and for the family and friends they were going to make. She had no idea what he had in mind.

At the edge of the farm, alongside the railroad tracks that bordered the western edge of their land, was a stand of white oak trees, about thirty large ones that had been there since before New Jersey was New Jersey. They were spared the fate of whatever was standing directly to the west where the railroad had come through. Georg enlisted the help of a local sawmill, and in exchange for helping him cut down some of the trees and milling some of them into enough wood to make his table, he allowed them to keep some of the wood for themselves to sell as lumber. Marta had no idea any of this was going on. The tree cutting happened when they were at church one Sunday. When it was ready, again when the Beckenbauers were at church, men from the sawmill delivered the lumber directly to Georg's wood shop, and Marta was never the wiser.

At first, he thought he had bitten off more than he could chew. But as he got deeper into the project, the table seemed to create itself. The wood *spoke* to him and choreographed its own evolution. The chrysalis of white oak transformed into a stunning work of artistic beauty; four inches thick, with six beautifully turned legs, one at each corner and two supporting the centerline. The wood grain blossomed under the stain and perfectly smooth shellac finish. After it was completed and dry, he stood there admiring his handiwork, gazing at it like it was his firstborn child.

As he felt around the edges—just one final inspection; a little quality control and pride mixed together to make sure it was smooth, splinter-free and ready—it dawned on him that surprising his wife was not going to be easy. He couldn't simply carry it into her kitchen in the middle of the night while she was upstairs asleep. Even Santa Claus would have needed help delivering this present; lots of elves and most likely more than eight tiny reindeer.

First, he had to find a way for Marta to be somewhere else and coordinate her absence with the arrival of at least six strong men to help him move it from the barn to the kitchen.

Lorraine Varsaci, the wife of one of the neighboring farmers who was enlisted to help move the table, asked Marta to come for lunch one Saturday, to get better acquainted. *Wink, wink.* Georg dropped Marta off at the Varsacis' and hurried home to meet his helpers—Lorraine's husband Luigi, his three brothers Francis, Vincent, and Anthony, and two of their cousins, Lorenzo and another Anthony. When Georg returned home, they were gathered and waiting by the barn.

Georg opened the door to the workshop and the Varsacis whistled in amazement. One look at the fifty square feet of six-legged, four-inch thick solid oak told them their work was cut out for them. By the time the table was loaded into the back of the Sterling, they were ready for a break. And that was the easy part. Even the Sterling lost a couple of inches in height, its springs tested under the weight of Georg's masterpiece. The hardest part was going to be carrying it up the porch steps, through the living room, and into the kitchen.

After lots of grunts, groans and adult-only expletives, the table was in place, and seven very overworked men sat on the porch, recovering with Georg's homemade Beckenbauer beer. (Father Kelly's confessional was going to be very popular the following Saturday as all seven men would be entertaining him with the story about moving a table bigger than the one Jesus sat at with his disciples, and requests for forgiveness for taking the Lord's name in vain. *That was one heavy table, Father*).

After the Varsacis rested enough to get up off their bottoms and drive home, Georg got in the truck and went to pick up his wife. On the ride home, Marta asked what he'd done for entertainment while he had the farm all to himself.

"Oh, nothing much, relaxed, rode one of the cows around a while, juggled some chickens. I think you are going to get scrambled eggs in the morning. And we might think about getting a horse, the cow was not very happy, or comfortable." He scrunched his face and rubbed his bottom.

"Very funny." She gave him a little punch on the arm.

"Did you have a nice time with Lorraine?"

"Very nice. We had lunch with some of her sisters-in-law. We talked about church and the school their children go to. The same one ours will go to one day." She looked over at him, leaned in and gave him a kiss and smelled the alcohol on his breath. "Ah-ha! Beer! Now I know why you were riding the cows and juggling my chickens."

They laughed and she scooted close to him for the rest of the ride home. When they arrived at the house, Georg parked right in front and ran around to open the door for his wife.

"OK, what's wrong? What did you *really* do while I was gone that has you opening the door for me?"

"Nothing, *Schatzi*." Georg was just about busting at the seams trying to contain his excitement. "Just beer, cow riding and chicken juggling, nothing else."

They walked into the house with Georg holding the door for a suspicious Marta. He took her coat and hung it on the hall tree. She looked around the living room. Nothing seemed out of place. But there was a smell, a new smell. Wood and varnish. He saw her sniffing the air. He smelled it, too.

"Close your eyes."

"I *knew* you were up to something."

"Just… close your eyes, please."

She closed her eyes and he led her into the kitchen. As they got closer, the smell became stronger, not bad, just stronger, like new...

"Open your eyes."

...furniture.

She had no sentences. Just sounds—gasps, giggles, single words.

"How? When?"

"I had a lot of help today. We owe six men and their wives dinner."

"Well, I think we could feed all of them at the same time." She walked around it, "This is a very... big... table, Georg," running her fingers over it, under it, looking underneath it at the two mid-line support legs, leaning down on it and feeling the sturdiness of this *Tableosaurus Rex*. Oh, it was sturdy, alright. Sturdy was an understatement, just like the word table. "Now I know why you were spending so much time in the barn. But, honey, are we going to sit at it or stand around it?" She looked at him with a smirk, pretending to be critical of the lack of chairs.

"Oh *Schatzi*, I am sorry. I wanted to make chairs, but I do not think that I could have waited that long to give you the table."

"Georg, sweetheart, I was joking."

"I would really like to make chairs, at least one just to say I did; more if the first one turns out well."

"You can do whatever you want. And, I forgot to tell you that I love this table… and I love you. Thank you." She put her arms around him, kissed him on the lips and hugged him tightly. Then she released him and stepped back to bask in the love she always felt when she looked into his blue eyes.

"I am so glad you like it. I was afraid you might think it is too big."

"It is perfect. We can still use the two chairs we used in the barn in the meantime until you make one, or two." Marta giggled. "Or twelve."

He wrapped his arms around her and gave her one of his big Georg hugs.

Now, that may have sounded like a lot of explanation for just a table—a piece of household furniture. But that twelve-hundred-pound Brobdingnagian slab of oak on six legs became another member of the family—a stable, solid sentinel like the Zenith in the living room. It would support countless family meals, holiday gatherings, and celebrations, and would remain with the family for generations. Oh, and Georg did make chairs. The first one was perfect, and over the course of a year he delivered one a month—and Marta, and *Tableosaurus Rex*, got their twelve chairs.

Generations one and two sat down with their cups of hot chocolate. Hagen and Salvatore on one side, Marta and the girls across from them. Georg sat next to Salvatore. They sipped carefully the sweet, hot, creamy deliciousness.

"How is it?" Georg asked.

"It's yummy," said Diana.

"Thank you, Diana," said Marta.

"It's really good," said Salvatore.

"Thank you, Salvatore."

"Mama and Papa call him Sali," said Diana.

Georg and Marta looked at Diana, then at each other, then at Salvatore.

"Is that what they called... call you, Salvatore?" asked Marta.

"Yes, ma'am, and they called me Sal, too," he said, a dab of whipped cream on the end of his nose. "You can call me Sal if you want."

"Alright, Sal," she said, holding back a giggle.

"Or Sali," said his sister.

Salvatore looked across the table at Diana distastefully.

"What do you want us to call you?" asked Georg.

"I like Sal," he said. "Sally is a girl's name."

Diana and Mathilde giggled.

"OK, Sal it is," said Georg.

They enjoyed the rest of their hot chocolate together and talked about the rest of the day; what they wanted for dinner, the radio, bedtimes on school nights and weekends. Then the men went up to Hagen's room and the women to Mathilde's room. The adults helped the children empty their suitcases and put away clothes in drawers and closets. Hagen helped Sal hang the picture on the wall above the bed; no holes in the artwork. Hagen loved that Sal took such good care of his present.

They ate their first family dinner together that night. Marta made a wonderful venison stew with vegetables from their farm and homemade biscuits. There was laughter and smiles and talk about school and the summer and cows and chickens and fields of corn so tall that you could hide in it.

And puppies. Oh yes, puppies. The puppy subject came up again.

And the subject of a puppy was put to rest.

It just so happened that one of their neighbors, Mr. Farias, had puppies two months ago. Well, his German Shepherd had puppies two months ago. The following Saturday morning the whole, new family would go to see Mr. Farias's puppies and bring home the seventh family member—a girl they named Heidi. And truth be told, Georg and Marta had always wanted a dog. It didn't take a lot of children's *pleeeeeases* to get them to say yes. They just didn't want to seem like easy pushovers and set a precedent.

After dinner, they had milk and peach pie, made with canned peaches from their orchard. Little Orphan Annie from the Zenith radio captivated little ears as the fireplace blazed warmth into the room. Georg and Marta paid more attention to the children staring at the radio than to the show. Full bellies were making eyelids heavy and necks rubbery, but God help them if they missed one moment of Annie's escapades. After the announcer told everyone when to tune in again to hear more about Little Orphan Annie, it was time for bed. Marta took charge of the girls, and Georg the boys. The children would have to sleep in the same beds until they could get two more for Sal and Diana. No one cared.

Mathilde and Diana were tucked in nicely, each holding a doll. The exciting activities of that day had them asleep seventy-seven seconds after Marta and Georg kissed them goodnight.

Hagen and Sal, on the other hand, didn't fall asleep as quickly as their sisters. They giggled and talked. Hagen answered more questions: Do cows sleep? What is your school like? Do you play with any other kids around here? Then Sal asked Hagen something that both would remember for the rest of their days.

"Hagen?"

"Yes, Sal?"

"Am I still an orphan?"

"No. You have me."

Sal rolled onto his side and snuggled close to Hagen. Hagen put his arm over his new brother, and they fell asleep, but not before both dropped a few tears onto their pillows. That night Sal had no bad dreams, just dreams of puppies and cows, corn fields and swings, radios and Little Orphan Annie. And his new family and best friend.

After all the children were left in the care of Mr. Sandman, Georg and Marta relaxed on the couch as WCAU broadcast music from Philadelphia.

"All in all, it was a good day," said Georg.

"Yes, dear, I think so too," said Marta as Georg put an arm around her. "Although it looked like Sal might have had a good cry on the way home."

"And from the look of the wet spot on Hagen's coat, I would say that our little angel took good care of him."

"He is very good at that." Marta sounded like the proud mother. "He always seems to know when you are blue and what to do to make you feel better."

"Like that lady at the church. I still have no idea what happened that day."

"The Lord working in His mysterious ways— sometimes, I think, through our son."

Georg got up and went to the rolltop desk where he had stashed the envelope that Reverend Osterman had given to them. He opened it as he walked back to the sofa and sat back down next to his wife. He pulled all the papers out, and together they examined them. They were arranged by child; a small stack for Sal and one for Diana. They went through Sal's papers first. On top was his birth certificate. Salvatore Giuseppe Cristoforo was born on September 12, 1924, at St.

171

Mary's Hospital in Hoboken. He was baptized at The Church of Saints Peter and Paul on Hudson Street, also in Hoboken. The other paperwork was just transfer papers from Hoboken Children's Home to the Methodist Orphanage. HCH was overflowing and had reached out to other orphanages for help with their overabundance of children. That's how Sal and Diana came to be with Reverend Osterman.

Diana's documentation was like Sal's. Birth certificate, baptism certificate, and transfer papers. Diana Luisa Cristoforo was born...

Marta gasped when she saw the date. They looked at each other as goose bumps raised every hair. Diana and Mathilde were born in the same year, on the same day— December 7, 1926!

"How many more coincidences can there be?" asked Marta.

"Wait until the reverend hears this." Georg shook his head in disbelief.

"Wait until the girls find out they have the same birthday. Double birthday parties! Double presents! Double cakes! That kitchen table might not be large enough."

"Pfff! It will have to be! I am *not* putting the Varsacis' backs through *that* again, or mine for that matter."

They laughed. He put his arm around her again and they sat on the couch a while longer listening to Bix Beiderbecke's *In a Mist* playing from the Zenith, their minds spinning with thoughts of the future.

Marta felt the effects of the busy day; the *tiredness* was settling in. She got up.

"I don't want to wake up to a sink full of dirty dishes. Come, husband, help me." She extended her arm and he grabbed her hand and she helped pull him up off the couch. They cleaned the dishes and put them away; Zenith off, lights out, and climbed the stairs to go meet Mr. Sandman themselves.

The next day, Sunday, Georg and Marta, with four children in tow, walked into St. Paul Church. Eyes were watching as the Beckenbauers-plus-two sat in the pew. There were some quiet introductions and quick explanations to the nearby parishioners. After Mass, the Cristoforos were introduced to Father Kelly on the steps outside, and he welcomed Sal and Diana into the church. It was now official—Sal and Diana were now part of the Beckenbauers' *and* St. Paul's family.

The following year Hagen and Sal made their first Holy Communions together. The celebration at home included other children who had made their first Communion, their families, Father Kelly, and Reverend Osterman and his family. *Tableosaurus Rex* was put to good use. Several comments were made praising Georg's workmanship. Father Kelly commented to himself on the object of seven men's confessions as he gently tried to lift one of the corners. *They weren't kidding! This is a heavy table. Jesus and the Apostles could easily have had the last supper around this.*

That day, after all the guests had departed and everything was cleaned up, Marta and Georg were sitting on the porch swing, bushed from the day, his head leaning on her shoulder. "Georg, honey?"

"Mhmm?"

"I have something to tell you."

"I love you, too."

She kissed him on the top of his head. "Always thinking you can read my mind, but no—yes, I love you—but no, something else."

"Oh? What is it?"

"I am going to help you fill another chair at the table."

"Hm?" He still sat crooked with his head on her shoulder until the curiousness of her last statement had him sit up and turn his head. He looked at her with a *what are you talking about* look on his face. "Huh?" She stared back at him wide-eyed, her expression saying *Really? You can't figure it out?*

She looked down at her belly then back at him again with a *do you get it now?* Look.

"You are having a baby? You are having a baby! HA!" He jumped up and knelt in front of her and wrapped his arms around her, burying his face into her belly.

"Oh, honey," she started to laugh-cry. "I am so happy you are not upset!" She leaned over and kissed the top of his head and wrapped her arms around his neck.

He looked up at her tear-wetted, ear-to-ear grinning face. "Upset? Are you kidding?"

"We are already feeding four children. Can we manage five?"

"I know we can. President Hoover said this depression will be over soon. We are managing fine now. We can manage. We *will* manage."

She looked down into those happy, tear-filled, blue eyes of his. Oh, how she loved this man; this man who had experienced in his short time more than most men do in three times his years in this world; the horrors he'd seen in the war; his brothers dying right in front of him and his parents dying from the loss and grief; a journey half-way around the world to start a new life and family. After all that he'd been through, this man still had the heart to love, to be kind, to be generous, and to be a wonderful father and husband. God surely made Georg in His image.

She leaned down and kissed him on his forehead. "I love you, husband."

"I love you, wife."

September turned into October. Leaves on the trees changed. The pumpkins in the patch grew large. And the little Beckenbauer inside Marta began to show. The children were looking forward to meeting their new sibling. Of course, the boys wanted a brother and the girls wanted a sister. Georg didn't care. He was busy in his wood shop creating another masterpiece: a crib. He wondered why he hadn't thought about making one for Hagen or Mathilde. He had already made *Tableosaurus Rex* and twelve chairs. He figured better late than never.

March 9, 1932

A new year had come and brought the same old Depression with it. But the Beckenbauer family was surviving. All four children were at Shedaker School. Georg was out in one of the fields somewhere on the Fordson while Marta was in the kitchen making bread.

Then the pain hit!

Like a mule-kick in the stomach followed by searing pain. If she didn't know she was alone, she would have thought that someone was sliding a hot knife into her belly.

Down to the floor she fell, collapsing onto her knees. Something was awfully wrong. The pain was horribly different from what she had experienced with Hagen and Mathilde. She could not move and fell over onto her side in a fetal position.

Pain. Fear. Alone. Water breaking. Blood. So much blood. She screamed. "GEORG! GEORG!" Consciousness faded as the pain, the shock, the blood loss took over. She felt her baby moving.

"Oh no, God help me!" She prayed. "Our Father, who art in Heaven, hallowed be Thy name..."

She Hail Maryed. She Lord is My Shepherded.

Heidi was outside having a fit by the back door; yipping, yelping, and barking. She heard, she smelled that something was wrong. Marta heard her and cried out, "Heidi, get Papa, get Papa!"

Heidi heard Marta's plea and ran way out to the far side of the farm where Georg was riding the tractor, turning the soil in the corn field. He saw her in the distance running at him at full speed. Flashbacks of himself running through the field to the cemetery in Lampertheim flashed in his mind. When Heidi reached him, she behaved unlike any way he had ever seen her behave. She was frantic; barking and yipping, then running back in the direction of the house, then at Georg. She sprinted towards the house ten feet, and then back to him. Something was wrong. He felt it.

He turned off the tractor's engine, hopped down and ran as fast as he could through the soft, newly-turned soil. Heidi ran alongside him; little yips escaped her mouth with each gallop. He reached the front porch steps and took them two at a time, ran inside and called to his wife. Heidi waited outside and ran to the back door and sniffed at it, pacing in between sniffs.

"Marta!" No answer. No response or sounds of her movement. Then he heard a raspy *Georg,* and Heidi begin barking wildly through the back door. He followed the sound into the kitchen and found Marta on the floor, her blood pooling, spreading out around her.

He screamed, "OH MY GOD, MARTA, MARTA!" and ran to her, fell to his knees beside her and lifted her up. She groaned; barely conscious; alive, barely.

His mind screamed. *WHAT DO I DO? WHAT DO I DO? Get her to a doctor, a hospital!* He laid her down gently and ran through the mudroom out the back door to the truck parked out by the cow barn. Heidi stayed behind by the kitchen door, sniffing at it, turning in circles anxiously. Georg started up the Sterling and drove onto the lawn up to the side of the porch near the kitchen. Leaving it idling, he ran up the steps and into the house. He was panting with terror. Sweat was pouring from his face. He lifted his limp wife gently, carried her outside, and put her into the passenger side of the truck. Her blood trailed from the grass

177

back up the steps through the mudroom into the kitchen where a large clotted puddle sat soaking into the floor. Heidi sniffed the blood trail and howled mournfully.

Georg got behind the wheel and drove as fast as the truck could go, one hand on the wheel and one on his wife. Heidi went up onto the porch by the front door and lay there, whimpering as the Sterling and her family drove out of sight.

"Marta! MARTA! Say something! Stay with me! OH GODDAMMIT!" He turned onto Perkins Lane, never stopping, then onto Delanco Road, as fast as the Sterling would go, then onto Burlington Avenue, barely slowing down at intersections. He made it to the bridge over Rancocas Creek.

"*FICKEN! FICKEN! FICKEN!*"

The bridge was open. A boat mast was gliding across the horizon. There was nothing he could do but wait.

"*GOTT VERDAMMT!*"

He pulled out of line and drove around the other waiting vehicles and cut in front of the first car. Angry drivers honked horns. He had to stop for the open bridge, but he wanted to be first to cross and not be stuck behind slow traffic. Horns kept honking. The driver of the car Georg cut off got out and walked towards his truck. Georg's window was down. From ten feet away, the disgruntled, cut-off driver could see the panic on the face of the man who cut him off.

"Hello, sir? Is everything alright?"

The man saw Georg's anguished terror. Georg began to cry. Then scream. "*MEINE FRAU!* MY WIFE!"

The man approached the truck and looked in the driver's window past Georg at Marta slumped on the seat, leaning on Georg, her belly swollen with child, her no-longer-yellow dress now soaked with her blood.

"Dear God!" said the man and ran to the other side and opened the passenger door. "Sir, my name is Dr. Alexander Small." He checked Marta for a pulse, first at her wrist, then her jugular. Her pulse was thready. He looked back at his car and waved at the woman in the front seat.

She opened the door and got out. "What is it, Alex?"

"Barbara, quick, bring me my bag!"

Barbara retrieved his bag from the back seat and brought it to the doctor. One look at the woman in the seat and Barbara understood the urgency.

"She's lost a lot of blood," the doctor told Barbara. "What is your name?" he asked Georg.

Georg was focused on his motionless wife.

"HELLO, SIR!" said the doctor. Georg looked up at him. "What is your name?"

"Georg Beckenbauer."

"What is your wife's name?"

Georg looked down at his wife's face. "Marta." His lips quivered.

"Listen, Mr. Beckenbauer, your wife has lost a lot of blood. The baby must come out now. Do you understand what I am saying?"

Georg sat there stunned, in shock, staring at his limp wife.

"Mr. Beckenbauer, please, you must listen to me. I need you to get out of your truck and help me. Your wife needs to lie down on the seat."

Georg got out of the truck and stood there, never taking his eyes off Marta.

"Barbara," said the doctor, "go around to the other side and hold her head. Mr. Beckenbauer, I need you to go ask the other drivers if they have any blankets." Georg was like a deer in headlights. "MR. BECKENBAUER!" He looked over his wife at the doctor. "This is my wife, Barbara. She is a nurse. We are going to do our best to help your wife and your baby, but I need you to help us. Go find blankets, NOW!"

Georg hesitantly walked away from his wife towards the line of cars.

"Alex, we have blankets in the car," said Barbara from the driver's side as she held Marta's head.

"I know. I need him to be occupied elsewhere." He palpated Marta's belly from the passenger side. He looked over Marta's swollen abdomen at Barbara. "His wife died sixty seconds ago and if I don't get that baby out of her right now it will die, too. I did not want him to know that. I can still feel movement and I do NOT want him to witness this."

"Oh, dear God, Alex. That poor man," said Barbara as she turned to watch Georg walking away.

"Right now, Barbara, I am more concerned about this poor infant."

Georg approached the first car. The driver was a woman, by herself, in her late twenties. Georg's pained facial expression and Marta's blood all over his clothes gave her a fright. She started to roll up her window but stopped when Georg spoke.

"Please, ma'am, do you have any blankets? My wife is having a baby and the doctor asked me to find blankets."

There was too much blood on Georg's clothes. The woman knew from experience that there should not be that much blood, that something was wrong and that the man looking for blankets was in shock. She got out of her car and opened the back door and retrieved a plaid, woolen blanket and handed it to Georg. That's when Georg could see that the woman was also swollen with child. He stared at her belly then into her eyes; eyes that were no longer frightened, but concerned, compassionate.

"Oh, ma'am, I am so sorry if I upset you. It is just, my Marta is bleeding a lot and she… she..." Then he lost it, and hit the ground on his knees, hugging the blanket, burying his face deeply into it, muffling his cries. The kind woman put one hand on her belly and one hand on Georg's shoulder and felt the convulsions of the storm blowing in the man's soul.

Curious drivers and passengers had gotten out of their cars and walked towards the scene unfolding at the front of the line. It seemed like the bridge was up forever. There was a line of boats making their way down the creek, and a small audience was now gathered near the back of Georg's truck.

Dr. Small saw the boats coming down the creek, and the people watching from the end of the truck. He called to one of the men. "You there, sir—yes, you," he said pointing with a bloody hand to one of the bystanders. "Get that bridge tender to bring that bridge down, NOW! It is a matter of life or death here!"

The man, reacting to the doctor's words and bloody hand, ran alongside the roadway to the edge of the creek and shouted up at the bridge tender in the booth. "HEY, HEY, HEY!" The tender couldn't hear him. Then the man, who happened to be a private investigator, pulled his concealed pistol from its holster and fired three shots into the air. That got the tender's attention. He slid open the window and looked down at the man with the gun. "What the hell do you think you're doing?" he yelled down from his perch high above the water.

"BRING... THAT... BRIDGE... DOWN... NOW!"

"I can't do that with boats approaching."

"We have a situation down here, a matter of life or death. BRING IT DOWN NOW!!" He pointed his pistol up at the booth.

"Alright, alright, alright." The operator sounded the horn signaling an alert to all vessels of the emergency

181

closure. A few moments later the bridge began its slow descent.

The crowd heard the shots and looked in the direction of the man with the gun then returned their attention to the goings-on in the truck.

While the man with the gun was dealing with the tender, Dr. Small had reached into his bag and retrieved a scalpel and scissors. Using the scissors, he cut Marta's dress up the mid-line from the hem to her chest and exposed her belly. Then with the scalpel, he made the deep, vertical incision in her abdomen. "Barbara, go get a blanket, please."

Barbara said a prayer as she walked back to their car. When she returned, the doctor had completed the Caesarean, and was removing the baby from Marta's womb. He cut and clamped the umbilical cord.

"Put the blanket over Marta, please."

Barbara covered her from head to ankles and said another prayer.

Still on the ground on his knees, Georg heard the shots. The sound of gunfire hearkened back to his days on the battlefield and brought him closer to his senses. He stood up. "Thank you for the blanket, ma'am." He walked quickly back to his truck and saw Barbara getting a blanket from her car. That's when it struck him that the doctor had wanted him somewhere else. Something was not right. His walk turned into a sprint.

By then the word had made it around the small crowd of onlookers that someone was having a baby. Everyone understood that giving birth was a painful experience and that meant cries and screams of pain. This scene was eerily quiet. No cries. No screams. No coaching by a nurse or midwife to *push, push.*

The baby wasn't moving. The doctor held it up by its ankles and gave it a light smack on its bottom.

Nothing.

Not even a twitch.

Then he sat on the running board, putting the infant on his lap face up and started to massage the baby's chest with light compressions.

Nothing.

Then he turned the baby over onto its stomach and continued compressions and light tapping on its back. It coughed. Amniotic fluid drained from its lungs. It started to breathe, then cry, then scream.

Georg was now standing at the open driver's side door staring across the seat at Marta's feet, the only part of her not covered by the blanket. Deep in his gut, the whole way in the truck with his unconscious wife, he knew he was losing her. So much blood in the kitchen. So much blood on the floorboard. He knew that a body can only bleed so much before it cannot bleed anymore. The horrors of war make average men privy to such anatomical trivia.

But he had hoped for a miracle. He prayed for one. Then he heard his baby cry. He looked up from the figure of his blanketed, lifeless Marta. On the other side of the truck, standing in the open passenger door was Dr. Small, holding the crying, new-born infant.

"Mr. Beckenbauer," he said loudly over the baby's cries. "I am so sorry about your wife."

Barbara went back over to the driver's side and put her arm around Georg's waist and walked him to the other side. She took the blanket from him and together she and the doctor wrapped the new little Beckenbauer nice and snug, then she handed the baby to its father. The baby quieted down.

"You have a son," said Dr. Small.

Georg held his new son close. He kissed him on the forehead. "My God, you look just like your Mama."

This is supposed to be a joyful time in someone's life. A time to welcome a new life into the family and into the world, surrounded by loved ones. *And indoors*. Not to mourn the loss of your wife by the side of the road surrounded by strangers and, *oh, by the way, here's your new son, congratulations*. How do you congratulate someone on the birth of their child when it coincided with the death of their wife? You just don't do it. Even the onlookers felt confused, like clowns at a funeral. A new life should bring joy. No one felt any joy that day on the side of Burlington Avenue.

The bridge touched down. The crowd dispersed and walked solemnly back to their vehicles. Cars from the other side began to make their way across. But the cars on this side didn't move. No one wanted to get out of line and go around the Sterling. They waited respectfully.

"Barbara," said the doctor. "I would like you to take Mr. Beckenbauer and his son to the hospital in our car. I will drive his truck."

"Alright dear," said Barbara. She could hardly speak, being on the verge of tears herself.

"Mr. Beckenbauer," said the doctor. "I want you to go with my wife in our car. I will drive your truck. We are going to Zurbrugg Hospital in Riverside. That is where my wife and I work."

"I do not want to leave Marta," said Georg.

"Don't worry," said the doctor. "I will take good care of your wife. Please, you and your son, go in my car."

Barbara led Georg with her arm around his waist to her car. She opened the back door and Georg sank into the back seat holding his son closely. Barbara got behind the wheel and started the engine.

The doctor closed the passenger door of the truck, then went around to the driver's side. He had to lift Marta's head to sit behind the wheel, and then let it rest on his leg. Dr.

Alexander Small was no amateur when it came to death. Before becoming a private physician, he had been a surgeon in the war. He saw his fair share of horrific injuries and unholy mutilations. Nothing prepares you—nothing can steel your heart—for what he had just witnessed.

He started the Sterling's engine, turned on the headlights, put it in gear and cried all the way to the hospital. Barbara turned on her headlights, and everyone in line behind her did the same. Everyone followed Marta. The people waiting to cross the bridge that day became a procession to the hospital, and only then did the bystanders drive on to their original destinations.

As they rode to the hospital, Georg sat in silence. His new son looked up at him through hazy, new-born eyes. Georg leaned down and kissed him again, baptizing him with his tears of love and pain. Barbara saw this in the rear-view mirror and, like her husband, cried all the way to the hospital.

When they arrived at Zurbrugg Hospital, the doctor rushed inside to get assistance. First, they needed to get Georg and the baby inside. Then they would take Marta on a stretcher to the operating room until a mortician could be contacted.

It was now after one in the afternoon. Georg was stunned into shock just like when an animal runs out in front of a car and gets hit. It looks dead, but then somehow stands up, shakes it off, looks at the driver and runs off into the woods.

Georg was just run over by Death; and Life. In the forefront of his mind was the sight of his wife on the kitchen floor in a pool of her own blood, like a swarm of wasps stinging and stinging and stinging, each sting keeping alive the vision of his dying wife. In the background, making their way through the swarm, were his children.

185

Oh, God, how am I going to be able to do this? How do I tell them they will never see their mother again?

Then it dawned on him that if they take the school bus home and no one is there to meet them...

Oh, God! The blood.

Barbara hadn't left his side since they arrived at the hospital.

This poor man is going to need help.

"Nurse, my children are at Shedaker School on Beverly Road. I do not want them to go home and find..."

...their mother's blood soaking into the kitchen floor...

He looked up to the heavens, holding back the tears.

"...an empty house. I need to pick them up before they get on the bus at three o'clock."

"Mr. Beckenbauer, is there anyone we can contact? Someone we can call for you?"

He looked at her kind face. Then he looked down at himself and realized that he could not simply drive the truck, with the blood-soaked seat, to the school, covered in his wife's blood. *The seat is going to have to be replaced. Cannot get blood stains out of fabric.* The thoughts that go through the minds of people in crisis would amaze the most seasoned psychologist.

"Would you please call Reverend Samuel Osterman at the Methodist Orphanage in Mount Holly? Ask him to go to the school and get my children, and if he could take them to his house, I would appreciate it."

"Of course," she said. "I'll call him right now." Barbara left him alone while she went to place the call to the orphanage. A few minutes later Dr. Small came into the room.

"Mr. Beckenbauer," he said. "We bathed your son and I examined him. He is healthy and strong."

Georg looked at Dr. Small and saw his eyes, still red from crying.

"Mr. Beckenbauer, I cannot begin to imagine what you are feeling right now. I am doing my level best to act professionally, and I will admit that I am not doing well with it."

Georg saw the soft side of the doctor. Doctors were supposed to be strong and without emotion. This one did not fit the mold. He was human. Humanity is more beautiful than professionalism.

"Please, Doctor, call me Georg. If you are going to mourn my wife with me, then you call me by my first name."

"Alright, Georg, and you call me Alex," he said. "Georg, my wife tells me you have children in school."

"Yes, four children," he said. "Your wife is calling my friend Samuel to pick them up."

Barbara walked into the room. "Mr. Beckenbauer, I just spoke to Reverend Osterman. He is on his way to get your children now. He is going to take them to his house, and then come here to get you. I asked him to go to your house and get you some clean clothes."

"Thank you, very much," he said. "That was kind of you to think about that. I cannot let my children see me this way."

"Georg," said the doctor. "I want you to rest a little bit before your friend arrives. We are going to take you to one of the rooms and I want you to lie down for a while. I will bring your friend to you when he gets here."

Barbara and the doctor walked him to a nearby empty room, and he lay down on the bed, facing the window. Then, they walked back to the doctor's office and waited.

At half-past three, Reverend Osterman arrived at Zurbrugg Hospital. He was carrying a suitcase with Georg's clean clothes inside. Barbara told the reverend that Georg was going to need a change of everything. She didn't go into details over the phone, but Reverend Osterman understood the urgency. Barbara met him at the door and led him to her husband's office.

"If you wouldn't mind waiting here for a moment," she said. "My husband wants to talk to you before you see Mr. Beckenbauer." She left to go fetch her husband. Reverend Osterman started to worry. The nurse seemed nervous, and she'd been crying. Something was wrong, he felt it.

A few minutes later, Dr. Small walked in. His eyes were still red, too. He extended his hand. "Hello, I am Dr. Alexander Small."

They shook hands. "Hello, Doctor, I am Reverend Samuel Osterman. Please, what is going on?"

"Reverend, there is no easy way to say this." He took a deep breath. "Georg's wife went into labor today and something went terribly wrong. He was bringing her here and was stopped on Burlington Avenue at a bridge opening. I was waiting for the bridge, too, and that is where I met him, in a panic, with his wife unconscious on the seat next to him. She had lost a lot of blood. A few minutes later, she passed away, and I performed an emergency Caesarean to save the baby."

"Marta... is dead?" Oh, the horror of those words; the shock almost bowled Reverend Osterman over, and he had to catch his balance on the back of a chair.

"I am sorry, Reverend, but yes, Marta is gone. Georg is going to need friends and help right now. He now has five children, has lost his wife, and is in a state of shock."

"Dear God, what happened?" asked the reverend.

"After we brought her here, I performed an exploratory examination on Marta. I knew there would be questions and I wanted to have answers for the family. Marta suffered severe hemorrhaging from a partial placental abruption."

The reverend looked puzzled.

"In layman's terms, her placenta prematurely detached, causing severe bleeding."

"Oh, dear God." He looked down at the floor and shook his head, then looked back at the doctor. "And the baby?"

"The baby is fine. A boy. A healthy eight pounds and thirteen ounces."

"A boy," said the reverend. "They were hoping for a boy. They named their son, Hagen, after one of Georg's brothers who died in the war. He wanted another boy so he could honor the other brother."

"This man lost two brothers?" asked the doctor in disbelief.

"Yes, twins, and at the same time, right in front of him. Then his mother died of grief, and not long after that, his father died."

"And now he loses his wife," said the doctor. "I can't imagine what this man is feeling."

"Dr. Small, Georg Beckenbauer is one of the kindest and most sensitive men I have ever known. If I know him, he is in agony over Marta, but he is worried about his children—how he's going to manage without her and how he's going to tell them that she is gone."

"Let me take you to him," said the doctor. "He needs his minister and friend now."

"Doctor, I am his friend, but I am Methodist, and Georg is Catholic. Not that it matters to me, a friend is a minister of a sort. I will call Father Kelly when we get to my house. It's too late for last rites, but I am sure the service will be Catholic."

"I see. Well, Reverend, Georg is lucky to have you as a friend."

Dr. Small led him to where Georg was resting. When they walked in, Georg sat up on the bed. "Oh, Samuel, she is gone, my Marta is gone." His eyes were puffy. He hadn't rested at all. The pillow where he had lain was soaked. "What do I do now?"

The doctor left the room to give them privacy.

"Oh, my dear Georg." Samuel sat beside his friend and put his arm around him. Georg turned and put his face into his chest and cried so deeply, breath-sucking hard, like when Sal cried on Hagen on the ride home from the orphanage.

"I am so sorry. I'm here for you and your children and I know that your friends and neighbors will also help you get through this."

Georg's shaking sobs calmed. He sat up and wiped his eyes and runny nose with his handkerchief and looked at his friend. "Thank you, Samuel. How are my children? Do they know?"

"They're fine. They only know what I knew; that you were at the hospital with Marta. I didn't find out what happened until I got here. They're with my family. Ethel is watching them. You should change and get cleaned up." Samuel stood up and walked towards the door. "I'm going to step outside. Open the door when you're ready."

Samuel left Georg alone to change and walked down the hallway in search of the nurse or the doctor. He found Barbara at the nurse's desk. "Nurse, may I see Georg's son?"

"Of course, Reverend, right this way."

He followed her down a different hall to the nursery. She opened the door and allowed him to go inside.

"If there were other babies in here, I wouldn't be able to let you in," she said. "But since he's the only one in here, and you are a family friend, I don't see the harm." She picked up the new Beckenbauer boy and handed him to the reverend.

"Hello, little one," he said. "I'm your Uncle Samuel." He stared down at the face of that new life. "Oh my, you look just like your mother." His eyes welled up.

"I thought so too," said Barbara. "Oh, Reverend, I feel so terrible about what happened today."

"We all do." He took a deep breath and, on the exhale, "Oh, dear God, I am going to miss that woman. She and her husband are such good people. They don't deserve this." He started to hand the boy back to Barbara. "I should go back to see if Georg is ready. I left him alone to get cleaned up."

"Why don't you hold on to the baby, and we can walk back together? Mr. Beckenbauer hasn't seen his son since..." She choked up.

Samuel was touched by Barbara's sensitivity. She and her husband made a great team.

The reverend and Barbara walked back to see Georg, who had washed and changed into the clean clothes. The door was open, and he was sitting on the edge of the bed staring out of the window. It was spring and the trees were beginning to bud. Hyacinths were blooming in the soil around an oak tree in the yard across the street. The world was coming alive again, and Georg felt dead inside.

The reverend knocked on the open door and walked in with Barbara.

Georg turned his head to look at them, and his baby.

"Georg," said Samuel. "I just met your son. He's beautiful."

Georg stood and went to the other side of the bed. Samuel held out the baby and Georg slowly took him into his arms and looked down at his sleeping face. "He is beautiful, isn't he? He looks just like Marta." Something inside him stirred, like the crocus bulbs at the end of winter. At that moment, the love for this new life put a salve on his third-degree-burnt soul.

"We both think he looks like his mother," said Barbara.

Georg looked up from his new son at Samuel. "How do I tell them about Marta?"

"We will do it together." Samuel put a hand on Georg's shoulder. "We *will* get through this, *together*."

"Thank you, Samuel." He looked over at Barbara, "Nurse?"

"Please, call me Barbara."

"Barbara, when may I take my son home?"

"In most instances, the child and mother would go home together in three days or so, if there are no concerns." It stung for Barbara to say that; mother and child would *not* be going home together. "I'm sorry, Mr. Beckenbauer," she said, lowering her gaze to the floor.

"Barbara, please call me Georg."

"Georg, I am… *so* sorry. I haven't had much experience with this kind of situation."

"Don't be sorry." He could see she'd been crying as well. "You and your husband did what you could to save her. And I thank you for everything you did. Your husband saved my son and I will never forget that."

Barbara quivered a pursed smile. "I'm going to go find my husband so he can talk to you." She left the two men and the baby and went to find her husband.

"Samuel?"

"Yes, Georg."

"How am I going to be able to take care of the farm and the children? I can't hire anyone. We barely get by as it is."

"Let's not worry about that right now. We need to take care of other things first. Tonight is going to be difficult. Together we will tell your children about Marta. Then tomorrow we will talk about funeral arrangements." He closed his eyes. "My God, it hurts to say those words."

"It hurts to even think them, Samuel, but I know it must be said."

Dr. Small and Barbara knocked on the door and entered the room just then. "Georg," said the doctor. "Barbara said you wanted to know when you can take your son home. He is healthy, but it would be prudent for you to leave him in our care for another couple of days. We have bottles and formula. And you have a lot on your plate right now."

"He's right, Georg," said Samuel. "The next few days are going to be very stressful."

"I know you are right," said Georg to the doctor. "But it feels… I cannot think of the words to describe how it feels."

The doctor put a hand on Georg's shoulder. "I don't think there are words."

The baby stirred a little in his swaddling blanket. He yawned a big long yawn.

"What are you going to name him?" asked Samuel.

"Karl Martin Beckenbauer. Marta and I had agreed to name our first two boys after my brothers. We were going to give him the middle name Horst, after my father, but I am changing that to Martin, for Marta."

"That's perfect," said Samuel, wiping a tear from his cheek.

"Georg, Karl will be safe with us. Just a couple of days to make sure there are no complications," said the doctor. "And to give you time to do what you need to do for Marta."

"Thank you," said Georg. "Samuel, we should go now. I need to see my children."

"Alright, Georg," said Samuel. "Doctor, Barbara, thank you for everything you've done today. May God bless you both."

"Thank you, Reverend," said Barbara.

"Thank you," said Dr. Small. "Take care of Georg and we will take good care of Karl. Please, don't hesitate to call if we can help with anything."

"Thank you," said Georg.

The men all shook hands. Barbara gave the reverend a hug then Georg. She held him, probably a bit longer than a modest woman in her position would hold a stranger, but protocol flew out the window when Marta's soul flew away in front of them. They shared something very personal together that day on the side of the road. A bond had formed. Alexander and Barbara Small, although due to the most awful of circumstances, were now a part of Georg's circle of family friends.

Georg placed Karl into Barbara's arms and then kissed him on the forehead. He stirred again, wriggling inside the cocoon of the blanket. His eyes opened slightly then closed again. Then the two men walked to Samuel's car and as they drove away from the hospital, Samuel had the forethought to take a different route to his house in Lumberton, just a little south of Mount Holly and the orphanage. No one needed to cross *that* bridge and pass the spot where so many lives changed—and one ended.

They rode together in silence; so much in their heads they wanted to say, but where to begin? Samuel broke the silence.

"Georg, before we get to my house, we should talk about how to tell everyone about Marta. Ethel doesn't know yet. I will take her aside and tell her so she will be on board with us when we sit your children down."

Georg nodded. His mouth was dry, his throat sore from crying. Samuel continued as he took Georg's silent nodding as agreement.

"We will send my children to the neighbors for a while. Then together we will do what we have to do."

Georg nodded again. This time he spoke. "Samuel, I cannot take my children home tonight. I do not know how I am going to do it, but I need to clean the floor in the kitchen."

Samuel realized what Georg meant by clean the floor. An image of the Beckenbauer kitchen with a pool of Marta's blood on the floor slammed through his mind and branded his soul with more pain.

"I don't think that *you* should do it, do you? We can find someone to help. Maybe Dr. Small will know someone."

Georg bowed his head. He did not want to be the one to get on his knees, his face inches away from what was left of his wife, and then scrub her away with detergent. He looked into Samuel's eyes. "OK, Samuel, I would appreciate it if you could call him. And my truck, it is also full of..."

Marta.

Georg's head lowered as tears dripped from his chin onto his shirt.

Samuel put his hand on Georg's shoulder. "We will deal with that together as well, my friend."

As they pulled into the Osterman's driveway, both men's hearts raced. For Georg, the feeling was reminiscent of heading into a battle. You don't want to do it. You're scared to death; but you can't avoid it. For Samuel, it brought back the memories of consoling dying soldiers or comrades of the fallen; also something you dread doing, but must.

Inside the Osterman house, Ethel and the seven children heard the car pull up and had piled out onto the porch before the engine stopped. All the children's faces wore smiles. Ethel Osterman was glad to see the two men. She really liked Georg Beckenbauer. His love for his family was remarkable. His generous heart and kind spirit always made him a pleasure to be with. But when the men emerged from the Osterman's Chevrolet, Ethel's smile made an about face. Georg and Samuel were forcing semi-smiles in front of their children, who were now bounding down the porch steps towards their respective fathers. Both men knelt and embraced their children, squeezing tightly, accepting as much squeeze as they could get in return.

Ethel watched from the porch. She never took her eyes off her husband, waiting for him to look up from nuzzling their children and give her a sign.

There it was! He looked up into her waiting gaze. His nose flared, his lips pursed, his head shook gently. Ethel's heart dropped into her gut like an anvil, the impact causing her to grab her stomach with one hand and the porch railing with the other.

The men stood up and walked up the porch steps with the children close behind. Ethel embraced them—first Samuel, then Georg. She held Georg a little longer than the regular how-do-you-do hug. She knew how he was doing, and he knew she knew.

Once everyone was inside, Georg sat on the sofa surrounded by seven children who were asking questions that he was not ready to answer. Samuel took his wife into the kitchen so he could fill her in on the accounts of the day. Although the look she got from him while she watched from the porch basically told the bad news, what he told her was unimaginable—the bridge; the truck; Dr. Small; how Marta died.

And what still needed to be done.

Blood in the kitchen!

Blood in the truck!

"We need to send our children upstairs or to the neighbors," said Samuel. "What is about to happen should be between Georg and his children."

"I will call Carole and tell them our three are coming over for a while. I'll let her know it's an emergency."

Ethel and Samuel went back into the living room. Ethel went to the telephone table by the stairs and called Carol Smithson, whose children played with the Osterman children, and asked her to watch their Muriel, Joey and Sam Jr. She briefly explained the situation. Carole knew Georg and his family through the Ostermans. She was shocked to hear about Marta and offered any help she could.

"Send yours over here. I'll keep them as long as you need me to," said Carole.

Ethel thanked her and hung up the phone. She looked over at the two fathers in the living room. She caught her husband's eye and nodded.

"Alright, Sam, Muriel, Joey," said their father. "Run on over to the Smithsons' for a while."

"Why?" asked Joey, their youngest.

"Uncle Georg and your mother and I need to talk to their children."

Hagen, always the sensitive one, had already felt that Papa and Uncle Samuel were somewhat off, that something was not right. He could tell when he and the other children went out to greet them that they were not their usual selves. Sending the Osterman children to the Smithson's made him pay even closer attention to his father. He could see that he was changing, gearing up for something. The air in the room became viscous as the tension rose.

"Run along now," said Ethel.

The Osterman children—Sam Jr, ten; Muriel, seven; and Joey, five—reluctantly walked out the front door, across the street and down a few houses to where Carole Smithson was waiting for them on the porch with her children, lemonade and shortbread cookies. She was going to do her best to keep everyone entertained long enough to give Georg time to do what he had to do. Carole did not need to know specifics. Georg's wife had died, and he had to tell his children. Her heart ached and she said a prayer while she watched Ethel's children come walking up the sidewalk.

Back in the Osterman living room, the adults braced themselves for the task ahead.

Georg began. "Sal, Hagen, Diana, Mathilde... this morning I had to take Mama to the hospital."

"Do we have a brother?" asked Sal.

"Or a sister?" asked Mathilde.

"You have a new brother," said Georg.

Smiles broke out on the boys' faces, frowns on the girls'. Sal's smile was more exuberant than Hagen's; he did not sense the off-ness of their father like Hagen was feeling.

All the while, Samuel and Ethel were watching Georg, waiting for cues from him to chime in and help. For now, he was flying solo. They also were watching the children looking at their father.

"What is the baby's name, Papa?" asked Mathilde.

"Can we name him Fibber McGee?" asked Sal, with a hopeful smile and a nod of encouragement to help his papa say yes.

The girls giggled at the thought of a brother named Fibber McGee. Georg briefly smiled (from the mouths of babes), then it disappeared. Hagen barely smiled as he watched every nuance of his father's expressions.

"His name is Karl," said Georg.

"When are Karl and Mama coming home?" asked Hagen, getting straight to the point.

Georg hesitated. He forced a smile. He looked up at Ethel and Samuel with a *what-do-I-do-now* look.

The children were lined up next to each other on the couch, the girls on the ends, with their father on a chair in front of them. The Ostermans came over and each sat on an arm of the sofa to catch the fallout of the impending explosion.

"*Meine Lieben*," he started. "Mama..." He cleared his throat. "Mama is not coming home."

They looked at him with such curiosity, like he said something in a completely foreign language.

"Mama went to Heaven today," said their papa.

They all knew what that meant.

Going to Heaven meant gone forever!

Never to be seen again!

Dead!

All the looks on their faces were different, unique to each child, yet all conveyed the same emotions—terror mixed with despair and confusion and a little hope that they had heard him wrong.

"Mama... is... dead?" asked Hagen.

The girls began to cry. Sal sat there, very still, staring through Georg, through the wall behind him, as far as his soul could run. Although Marta wasn't his or Diana's biological mother, she had treated them as her own from the day they had come home to live with them, and Sal and Diana had soon found themselves calling Georg and Marta, Papa and Mama. Now, Sal and his sister had lost two mamas. And he couldn't move.

The Ostermans knelt on the floor in front of the couch, each holding one of the girls. Hagen looked over at Sal and saw the look on his face. He had never seen him like this. He was probably like this when he was told *his* parents had gone to Heaven. Georg got on his knees in front of the boys. He looked from Sal to Hagen and back to Sal. Hagen was unable to control his own emotions and began to cry. Sal was still staring somewhere far into the deep reaches of his galaxy, close enough to turn around and see himself, yet far enough away so the pain was just a twinkle. As Hagen's crying deepened, Sal could feel the shaking of the sofa cushion, and his soul dashed back to the living room. He looked over at his friend, his brother, his hero. And this time it was the saved who consoled the savior. Sal wrapped his arms around him, holding him close. Hagen's face fell onto Sal's chest.

He heaved and shook as Sal's tears streamed down his cheek and onto Hagen's hair.

Georg leaned in and hugged both boys, then pulled the girls in, and together they all cried as the Ostermans looked on.

After the tsunami of emotions receded, Georg spoke again. "We will get through this together. We are still a family. I love you all so very much." They all hugged again. After wave two subsided, Georg released the children and sat back on his knees. "Samuel, may I use your phone?"

"Of course."

"I have to make some calls to friends. I will ask Lorraine if she can take the children for a few days until we can go home again."

"Papa, why can't we go home?" asked Hagen. "I want to go home."

"We cannot right now," said his father. He was at a loss for an explanation why. Samuel took Georg's pregnant pause as his cue.

"When your Papa took your Mama to the hospital," said Uncle Samuel. "Um… he forgot to close the door and one of the cows got inside and made a mess. Your Papa wants to clean it up before you go home."

"That is right," said Georg, looking at Samuel with a wide-eyed *thank you*. "Yes, one of the cows got into the house and made poopoo."

"Eeewww," said the girls.

Hagen and Sal stared at the adults like they had three heads, each. They weren't going to argue. Their Mama was dead—and that was that.

"Georg," said Ethel. "The children can stay here with us. They can squeeze in with ours."

"That's right," said Samuel. "I'll take you home and you can pack some of their clothes and I'll bring them back here."

"Thank you, Samuel." He looked at his watch. "We should go soon so you can get back before it gets too late."

Georg hugged his children again. "*Meine Lieben*, be good for Aunt Ethel. I must go home now. Uncle Samuel will be back soon, and I will be back in the morning."

Georg got up from embracing his children and hugged Ethel.

"God bless you, Georg," she whispered into his ear. He squeezed her a little harder. He thanked her for all she was doing, then walked towards the door, followed by Samuel. Before they got to the door, Hagen ran to his father, grabbed him, put his arms around his legs and squeezed. Georg looked down into Hagen's pleading eyes.

"*Geh nicht, Papa. Bleiben Du bei uns, bitte,*" said Hagen, reverting to German as he did when he was upset. He began to cry, burying his face in Georg's trouser leg.

"I will be back tomorrow, I promise." The other children were watching them, tears dripping from their chins. Georg squatted next to Hagen and put a hand on each shoulder. "I need you and Sal to take good care of your sisters tonight. Will you do that for me?"

"Yes, sir, Papa." Hagen wrapped his arms around Georg's neck and squeezed, burying his face in Georg's shoulder. He could feel his father's broken heart pounding inside his chest, and he hugged even harder. They remained that way for a moment, the entire room silent. Nothing moved except tears raining down to the floor. Georg stood and took in the sight. "*Ich liebe dich, meine Lieben.*"

Georg nodded to Samuel and led the way into the gloaming of the evening. In the Ostermans' Chevrolet, they sat quietly, staring forward for a moment.

"Thank you for coming to my rescue," said Georg. "The girls believed the cow story. But Sal and Hagen... mmm, I do not think so."

"The boys are older, a little wiser. But it was the only thing I could come up with."

"Are you sure it is alright if they stay with you for a couple of days?"

"Of course, Georg, we're family."

Samuel put the car in gear and drove down his driveway and out into the street. They rode in silence for a little bit. Then Georg started talking. "My truck is still at the hospital."

"Do you want to go get it?"

"No, Samuel, the seat is covered in her..." He swallowed hard. "I do not know what to do with it. Should I even keep it?"

"Does it still run well?"

"Yes, it is a good running machine. There is not a thing mechanically wrong with it. It is ten years old, but I never saw the need to replace it. I have the Oldsmobile that we bought when Sal and Diana came to live with us, but I need a truck. I would rather keep the Sterling than throw it away."

Samuel thought for a moment then asked, "Will keeping the truck be difficult? With what happened today?"

"My wife died in it and my son was born in it. I love my wife, but I do not think she would want me to be financially burdened by purchasing another truck."

"Marta was very frugal," said Samuel.

"That she was, Samuel, that she was."

Silence took over again. Talking about his wife in the past tense so soon, only hours after she passed, seemed so unreal. Like he wasn't even saying it. Like someone else, an impostor, had taken his place. There was still so much that needed to be talked about, but both men were simply too tired to think, too tired to speak. They rode the rest of the way to the farm without saying another word.

As they approached the house, they both saw a gap in the hedges. Georg didn't remember running the truck through them when he pulled up to the back door. Neither of them mentioned it.

Heidi was still in the same place where Georg had left her when he had driven off to the hospital hours earlier. Her ears perked up when she heard the return of Samuel's car. When she saw Georg get out of the car, she ran to him, crying and whimpering and rubbing all over him.

"She was in that same spot when I came earlier to get your clothes," said Samuel. "I gave her a pat, but she didn't move."

"She must have waited for me this whole time," said Georg. "She was so upset. She ran out to the field to find me and bring me back to Marta." Georg knelt down and gave Heidi some loving and a good scratch. "Good girl, good girl." He stood up and all three walked up onto the porch and went inside. Georg went straight upstairs to put clothes in suitcases for the kids, with Heidi tagging along. He put the boys' in one and the girls' in another, remembering their teddy bears.

While Georg was upstairs, Samuel stood in the living room staring at the door that led into the kitchen. He didn't want to go in there, but at the same time a part of him needed to see what Georg will have to deal with. If Samuel didn't like what he saw—*of course I'm not going to like what I see*—if it was too horrible, he would keep Georg out of the kitchen.

Samuel reasoned with himself and he felt his feet walking slowly towards the door. He pushed it open and flipped up the switch on the wall inside the door. The lights over *Tableosaurus* lit up. In the far corner on the counter was something *blobular*, shapeless. The table and chairs were blocking the view of the floor in the corner under the *blobular* something. As Samuel walked around the table, the floor came into view. He gasped, putting a hand to his mouth. Marta's blood, an ungodly amount, was smeared on the floor. It was glossy and thick in places like drying, spilled, burnt umber paint. He could see the trail leading to the back door. As he got closer, he could tell that the *blobular* something was bread dough.

Give us this day our daily bread.

It had sat so long, and had risen so much, that part of it had oozed off the counter and plopped into the blood. The smells of yeast and drying, coppery blood invaded his nostrils.

"Oh, no, Georg *cannot* see this."

As he said those words aloud to himself, Georg pushed the door open and walked in with Heidi on his heels.

"Did you say something, Samuel?"

"Georg, turn around and go back into the living room."

"I know, Samuel, there is a lot of blood."

He looked past Samuel and saw the over-risen bread dough oozing off the counter's edge, part of it sitting like an island in a sea of his wife's drying blood. He hadn't seen the dough when he found his wife on the floor. He was focused only on her.

"She was making bread," said Georg, as he choked on the words. Memories of himself coming up behind Marta, slipping his arms under hers and around her as he nuzzled the nape of her neck while she kneaded the dough, flashed across his synaptic silver screen. "Oh my God!" He turned back around and went into the living room and stood there looking up at the ceiling.

"Why? Why her?" His chest heaved as his weeping went into high gear. "WHY?!" His knees buckled and he went to the floor, his face in his hands. Heidi sat next to him and leaned against him.

Samuel knelt on the floor on the other side and held him close. There were no words to say. Words had no place right now.

When the heaving subsided and it felt right to speak, "Georg, you cannot be here now. Go upstairs and get some clothes for yourself, too. You and Heidi are coming home with me."

Georg heaved a big sigh, stood up and wiped his eyes with his cuffs. He went back upstairs to get some clothes. He was not going to argue with his friend. And even if he'd wanted to, he did not have the strength. A few minutes later, he descended the stairs holding an armful of folded clothes and walked right out through the front door with Heidi, without saying a word.

They drove back to Lumberton this time without speaking at all. When they arrived, Samuel didn't remember the ride. They walked into the house. The Osterman children had come home. The girls and Ethel were sitting on the couch while the boys were lying on the floor. The radio was on and everyone was hearing; but not listening. When the door opened and Georg walked in with Heidi and Samuel, everyone got up and ran to them.

"Oh, Papa, thank you for coming back. We did not want to stay here without you," said Hagen as he hugged his Papa around the legs.

"Did you clean up the poopoo, Papa?" asked Diana.

Georg couldn't help but smile at her words. "Yes, but I wanted to be with my *Lieblings* tonight."

Sal, Mathilde, and Diana joined Hagen in hugging their Papa while the teary-eyed Ostermans looked on.

That night Georg slept on the Ostermans' living room floor, surrounded by his children and Heidi. A new phase of their lives had begun. It would test their faith in God. It would test their strength as a family.

Hagen's Railcar

Hagen stopped there. He had talked for a long time; a lot longer than his seventy-four-year-old vocal chords were used to. His throat was dry, his mouth parched even though Emily had gotten up once to get more water. The coffee was gone, and its diuretic effects were kicking in.

"I think we should take a break," he said. "I need to use the restroom."

Emily was still riding Hagen's emotional roller coaster. She had gone through almost half a box of tissues. Hagen had a few bunched-up tissues clasped in his hand, as well.

"Me too," she said. "I'll use the downstairs one and meet you back up here."

Emily got up off the sofa. Before walking to the elevator, she pulled a few more tissues out of the box for the elevator trip. Her emotions were not quite off the ride yet, and she cried in the elevator on her way down.

Hagen leaned on the lion head and stood slowly. He was stiff from sitting. His hip ached. His heart hurt. Retelling the story to Emily, hearing the words out loud, stirred his stew of emotions deeper than only thinking them. He could not help crying while he talked; feeding off Emily's emotions added to the pot.

When Hagen returned to the sofa, Emily had already cleared the coffee cups, press, and the pastries. She was in the kitchen putting the cups and plates in the dishwasher. Hagen looked at his watch. It was nearing 1:30 p.m. *I really did talk her ear off.*

Emily came through the door from the kitchen. She saw him sitting there blankly staring out at the passing scenery. "Are you OK, Hagen?"

"Yes, thank you, I'm fine. Talking about it takes a lot out of me. I think that might be part of why I feel the need to put it all on paper, so I won't have to say the words out loud anymore."

"Do you want to go on with it?" she asked.

"I do. I have to. I can't stop there."

The train came to a smooth stop at the Galesburg, Illinois station.

"It's almost lunchtime," she said. "Do you have any thoughts on what to eat?"

"I'm game for anything. You pick."

"Well, I was eyeing that fried chicken in your fridge this morning. How about a simple lunch?"

"That sounds fine to me. We should be in Chicago by dinner time. Amtrak is going to disconnect my car from the train, and another will pick us up and take us to the next disconnect in Pittsburgh. We will have a couple hours to sit in Chicago, and I think that we should have Krystyna's golumpkis and Piotr's beer. We can have dessert on the patio."

"Dessert... on the patio?" she asked, looking at him with that Spock-eyebrowed, smirky look again.

"That's right. You haven't seen it yet. At the end of the car, past my bedroom, is a covered patio."

"I should have known that I haven't seen everything," she said as she shook her head.

"I don't give away all the surprises at once, my dear."

Emily wondered what other *surprises* lay in store for her. "It's a date then. Dinner à la Krystyna and dessert on the patio."

"Good. Now, how about lunch? Talking about it got my stomach interested."

"Sure. Lunch in the kitchen?"

"That's fine with me," he said as he got up off the sofa.

Emily waited for Hagen to get steady on his feet, then led the way into the kitchen. He sat at the table while she went through the refrigerator, pulling out the container of fried chicken and a bowl of potato salad.

"Potato salad OK to go with it?" she asked.

"Absolutely. I forgot Vera put that in there with her fried chicken."

"Do you want your chicken cold or hot?"

"I go either way, but I tend to enjoy it hot when it's fresh and cold when it's leftover. How about you?"

"Same here," she said. "Cold fried chicken and potato salad it is." She set the table with napkins, silverware and plates, then put the bowls of potato salad and fried chicken in the center. "What do you want to drink?"

"I'm in the mood for sweet and bubbly. There are cans of Dr. Pepper somewhere in the fridge. And I don't need a glass. We're *roughing* it with cold fried chicken. We can pretend we are having a picnic."

She opened the refrigerator again and excavated the Dr. Peppers from the back of the bottom shelf, behind a large bowl of cut-up fruit. As she was closing the fridge door, she spied the big squeeze-bottle of Heinz ketchup and grabbed that too. She put the sodas and the ketchup on the table, opened Hagen's Dr. Pepper, then sat down in the banquette.

She stuck a large serving spoon into the potato salad. "Would you like some on your plate?" she asked.

"Please, thank you."

"My pleasure." She plopped a big spoonful of the potato salad on his plate. "More?"

"No, thank you. That's a good start."

"Are you a breast or a leg man?" she asked as she aimed a fork at the mound of cold fried chicken.

"This is the only time that I am a breast man, thank you." He squinted and smiled demurely.

Emily giggled as she stuck the fork into a plump breast and placed it on his plate. "A D-cup for monsieur."

He giggled at her joke. "Thank you."

"My pleasure." She gave herself a scoop of potato salad and two thighs. Then she shook the bottle of ketchup and squeezed a puddle of red tomatoey-ness onto her plate next to the chicken.

"Bon appétit," she said.

"Merçi, mademoiselle." He eyed the bottle of ketchup curiously. "Ketchup on fried chicken," he said as a matter-of-fact statement.

"I know it sounds weird, but ever since I was a kid, I've loved ketchup on cold fried chicken—well, cold meats in general; pot roast, meatloaf, leftover steak…" She poked one of the thighs on her plate with a fork… "and fried chicken. My mom used to laugh, not at *me,* but at the coincidence. She said I got that from my dad. She said he would slather ketchup all over leftover meats, too."

"It doesn't sound weird. It's a matter of taste."

"Have you ever had it?"

"Pass the ketchup, please," he said, then squirted some onto his plate. "Yes, I have."

"Cool," she said. "I don't meet many ketchup and fried chicken connoisseurs."

She picked up a knife and fork and started to cut into her chicken. She managed to remove a nice chunk, then dipped it into the ketchup and put it in her mouth. "Mmm, good fried chicken."

Hagen noticed her awkward cutlery skills as she cut into her chicken. He forked some potato salad.

"Mmm, the potato salad is good, too," he said.

He continued watching Emily's valiant effort at using a knife and fork to dissect her chicken thigh. She got some good pieces off, but everyone knows you need to use your fingers to efficiently eat fried chicken.

"Do you always use a knife and fork to eat fried chicken?" he asked.

"Honestly, uh, no. I figured you did, and I didn't want to look like a heathenish pig in front of you."

Hagen ripped a piece from the breast on his plate, swiped it through his puddle *o'ketchup* and popped it in his mouth. He chewed and swallowed. "Feel better?" he asked.

"Oh God, yes. I never understood eating fried chicken with a knife and fork. Just pick it up and eat it. That's what the napkin is for."

"Or the lips," he said, then quickly finger-licking-goodly sucked each greasy fingertip.

"Or the lips," and she mimicked his finger licking.

They ate their lunch for a bit. Then Emily spoke. "May we continue with your story or would you rather wait until after lunch?"

"You really are interested?"

"You know you don't have to ask that question."

"I know, I just wanted verbal confirmation."

"Consider it confirmed," she said. "May I ask you something?"

"Absolutely."

"You, and Sal... you two were more than brothers, weren't you?"

"Yes, we were. We grew up as brothers, soulmates from the moment we met, and our relationship evolved secretly."

"Wasn't that complicated?"

"For many years it was quite complicated. Our family and friends knew us as brothers. And being gay—there I said the word—being *gay* in the time that we were growing up was unheard of."

"I know," she said. "It wasn't easy for a long time. It's still not easy. Did it ever become less complicated?"

"It did. It got easier when we both moved to Santa Fe. Our family didn't think it strange. We are both artists, me the painter and Sal the photographer. Santa Fe is an artist's Mecca and a very open-minded town. We made friends in our new home and were accepted as a couple."

"I'm glad you two were able to find happiness," she said. "Is that why it took you so long to tell me who Sal was?"

"For the most part, yes. It could take people aback if they think we were incestuous siblings. I wanted you to understand who we were in the beginning before we became who we are."

"I understand. Well, for your information, I am very open-minded. My mother had two really good friends in California who were a couple. We called them the Kens, since both had the same name. I sometimes called them Ken squared."

Hagen giggled. "That is funny. I had a feeling you weren't going to make a fuss. But I have always erred on the side of caution regarding my personal life."

"No need to walk on eggshells around me anymore. OK?"

"Yes, ma'am."

Hagen pulled another chunk of chicken off of his piece. "Do you have any other questions with regards to what you've heard so far?"

"No questions, really," she said. "I am waiting to hear what happened after your mom passed. So, I guess that is sort of a question."

Hagen took another bite of chicken, then a sip of Dr. Pepper and continued...

March 1932

The Depression was in full crappy swing and Marta Beckenbauer was dead. Georg was beside himself and the children were devastated. But there was a new life to love and care for. Karl's birth needed to be celebrated in the wake of his mother's death. Georg was a proud man, a strong man. But he knew he needed help, and it was Samuel to the rescue. The Ostermans and the Beckenbauers had become very close, like family. They had become Samuel and Ethel to Georg and Marta, and Uncle Samuel and Aunt Ethel to the children. When Marta died, it white-knuckle-punched the Ostermans' hearts.

Georg and his children, all five of them and Heidi, stayed with the Ostermans until the funeral. Samuel had conferred with Dr. Small on the awful subject of scouring Marta's blood from the kitchen floor and inside the Sterling. The doctor knew people who did that sort of work. The day after Marta's death, the kitchen was cleaned, and the truck was scoured, and the seat was replaced.

Georg and Samuel went to Yetter's Funeral Home that Friday morning to arrange the service. Georg chose a casket made of walnut with brass handles and peach-colored satin lining. When the funeral director asked where Marta would be laid to rest, Georg said that he wanted his wife to be buried beneath her favorite peach tree. Neither Samuel nor Mr. Yetter were prepared for that response. Georg explained why this was what he wanted.

When Georg and Marta had first arrived in America, they had to adjust to a whole new culture, a whole new way of life, a way of thinking and speaking and eating. Marta cooked some of their familiar German foods, but there were also new foods to discover. When she tasted a peach for the very first time, freshly-picked from one of their trees, it was like tasting heavenly fruit. Never before had something so sweet and juicy passed her lips, and she wondered why Eve hadn't tempted Adam with a peach. And, she had a *whole orchard* of these heavenly nectar fruit trees! Their first summer in New Jersey, Marta and Georg walked out to the orchard and had picnics after church. She chose a large beautiful tree and proclaimed it to be *the family picnic spot*. Marta so loved it under that tree. As the family grew, the children would play under it and pick low-hanging fruit for their Mama. Georg remembered the last time the whole family sat under that tree eating cold fried chicken, and watermelon from their field. And peaches, of course. He was leaning against the trunk of the tree and Marta was lying on the blanket, her head on his lap. Diana and Mathilde were serving high tea to their dollies, who always had an open invitation to the picnic. Hagen and Sal were off climbing one of the trees. The cicadas were sizzling all over the orchard, and a light breeze was moving the scent of earth and fruit through the trees, and the essence of his wife up to Georg's nose. Georg's eyes were closed as Marta and Nature caressed his senses.

Marta was lying there looking up into the branches. "Georg?"

"Hmm?"

"Do you miss home?"

"How could I miss it when we were just there a few hours ago?" He smirked sarcastically; eyes still closed.

"Silly!" She poked him in his ribs. He fidgeted. Georg was very ticklish. "I mean our home in Germany?"

"Do *you* miss it?"

"I asked you first." He got serious, opened his eyes and looked down at his wife's face. "I miss it and I do not miss it." He scrunched his face. "Why are you asking me this?"

"I do not know. I was just thinking about it—the farm, your parents, my parents. The last letter from them made me a bit homesick. We have not seen them since we left Germany."

"Do you wish to go back?" He hoped to God she would say no.

"No, I love it here. I love our farm, our children. I love our friends and neighbors. And I love you."

He leaned down and gave her a tender kiss on the lips.

"Besides, I would miss my peaches," she said.

He chuckled. "I love it here, too. Maybe one day we can go back to visit, or they could come here."

"That would be nice. They might not want to leave once they taste my peach cobbler."

"They can have the barn," he chuckled. "The cows will not mind."

"Ha-ha." Another jab to the ribs and more ticklish fidgeting.

He tickled her back and she sat up to get away from him. He pulled her close, wrapped his arms around her and kissed her on the nape of her neck. That did it. That's the spot. Stops her in her tracks every time.

"Not fair." She pretended to try to get away. "You are using the secret weapon."

"All is fair in love and war, my dear." He nuzzled her nape again, then leaned back against the tree and took her with him. They sat there watching the girls entertain the ladies. Somewhere behind them, they could hear the boys giggling and rustling around in a tree.

"You know what?" she said.

"No, I do not know what. Tell me what." He smiled.

"I could spend forever here, under this tree with you and the children, if that were possible. Maybe we should have built the house out here in the orchard."

"Hindsight is twenty/twenty. Besides, if you saw it day in and day out, it would not be that special."

"You are probably right." Marta sighed. "I hope Heaven is like this."

Every once in a while, he would think about the family cemetery in Lampertheim. When it came up in his reminiscences, he would wax a little melancholy, thinking about what and who they had left behind. Then, he would sweep it back under the rug in his mind. The idea of a family funeral here in America was not consciously thought about. A family funeral should be many years away. He and Marta were young; their children very young. Yet, so were his brothers. So were his parents. But there was no world war raging now, threatening to take anyone away prematurely. Never did Georg imagine on that warm day in the middle of his orchard, underneath Marta's favorite peach tree, that he would be planning her funeral the following Spring.

He never forgot that day, and her words— "*I could spend forever here*."

"My wife loved our home and our land. My family had a private cemetery on our farm in Germany. I know where she would want to be; buried on our land here. She had a favorite place in the peach orchard, her Heaven on Earth. You were there, Samuel, with your family. Marta wanted to be there forever and now I am going to give that to her."

"Georg," said Samuel. "You can't just dig a grave and call it a cemetery. It isn't that simple."

"Alright then Samuel, how is it done?"

"There is a procedure for consecration. A clergyman, usually a bishop, will come to the piece of land and perform a consecration ritual."

"Must it be a clergyman of the same religion as the family?"

"No," said Samuel. "It becomes holy ground no matter who performs the ritual."

"Then I request that you, our dearest friend, perform the ritual. I am speaking for myself and for Marta, my wife, and your sister."

Samuel sat there, looking at Georg, waiting for him to change his mind. Reverend Samuel Osterman had never consecrated ground before. He witnessed it twice as part of the attending clergy, but a bishop always performed the ritual.

"Georg, I am honored that you are asking me to do this for you. But it is highly irregular for someone of my level in the church to perform such a ritual."

"Is it forbidden?"

Mr. Yetter sat there listening to the back and forth. This was a first for him and an interesting sidebar to the usual *pick a casket and put them in the ground, wipe your hands and call it a day.*

"I do not believe that it is forbidden, just unheard of."

"Then as Marta's husband and the owner of my land, I hereby request and insist that you, Reverend Samuel Bernard Osterman, consecrate my family cemetery, not only for me but for my Marta." He said it like a priest pronouncing two people man and wife.

Samuel sighed and looked deeply into his best friend's eyes. He knew Georg was unbudgeable. "Georg, I will call the bishop later today and request approval and permission."

"Thank you, Samuel. This means a lot to me. I love you like a brother, and so did Marta."

Samuel pulled a handkerchief from his inside coat pocket and dabbed his eyes. Even Mr. Yetter sniffled.

Both men thanked Mr. Yetter. They told him that he would be kept abreast of the situation, and then they left to go back to the farm to call Father Kelly.

In the car, Georg continued the conversation. "Thank you, again, Samuel. I hope you do not feel strong-armed into doing this. I know that if it were Marta burying me, she would ask the same of you."

"I am honored that you asked." He took a deep breath, clearing his mind a little. "Will you still be having a Catholic service?"

"I hope that it does not hurt your feelings if I do."

"My feelings… hurt my feelings? Georg, you just asked me to do something that will make a piece of your land sacred for all eternity. You most certainly did not hurt my feelings."

"Thank you, Samuel, because I want you to be one of the pallbearers."

You know how a whole movie or song or even your whole life can zing through your mind in a matter of seconds, completely coherent yet impossible to say out loud? That is what just happened to Reverend Osterman. In a handful of jiffies, he recounted his entire relationship with the man sitting next to him—that cold day in 1930 when they met at the farm, the children on the playground, Sal and Diana becoming part of the Beckenbauer family; the picnics together; the laughter; the tears. It felt like a whole lifetime had passed by in less than two short years.

Samuel wiped a tear from his eye. "I would be honored to be a pallbearer."

Georg put a hand on his shoulder. "Thank you, Samuel."

While that last bit of chat sank into both of them, Samuel thought about the next thing to do, and took another deep breath to compose himself.

"We might want to go see Father Kelly together. It would be the respectful thing to do. He is your priest. He shouldn't have an ego to bruise, but since you asked me to do the ritual, he might want to witness it, especially since he will be performing the first service in the newly hallowed ground."

"That is a good idea. Thank you, Samuel, for helping me think."

They returned to the farm to use the telephone. Samuel called his bishop first. Bishop Hartwell agreed to relinquish the honor to Samuel with the proviso that the bishop himself witness the ceremony. Samuel of course agreed. The thought never occurred to him that he'd be doing it without backup. Then Georg called Father Kelly to make an appointment for him and Samuel to see him at one-thirty that afternoon. After he hung up the phone, he and Samuel went into the kitchen and looked at the place on the floor, *that* place, the one consecrated by Marta's blood; the two-by-three-foot spot that Georg would avoid stepping on for many years.

Men who were sent by Dr. Small had come earlier that morning. They scrubbed away her blood and sanded the wood floor, erasing what was left of Marta. New stain was applied. It was a close match, but not perfect. Georg closed his eyes and spoke to his wife with his heart. When he was finished, the reality of going on took the helm.

"Samuel, I need to tend to the cows and the chickens. They are probably wondering where I've been."

"I'll come with you."

They walked out to the barn, and Georg said hello to each cow. He knew all of them by name. They all responded to his voice and touch like family pets. Georg was a kind and gentle soul, and the cows intuitively knew he cared for them. He milked the cows, then filled eight clean quart bottles and put them in a crate. Then he went out to the chickens, threw down some feed, and collected all the eggs (almost three dozen), and put them in the crate with the milk. When he was finished with the livestock, they walked back to the house. On the way, they stopped and put the milk and eggs in the car, then went into the house and sat on the couch. There was something on both of their minds. A subject that needed to be addressed. They both knew it. Samuel started talking first.

"Georg…"

"I know." He closed his eyes and leaned back in the couch.

"You know *what*?"

"I know what you want to talk about. And what I am avoiding."

"The children."

"Yes, the children."

"And the…"

"…and the farm, I know, I know."

"Georg, you cannot take care of everyone and everything."

Georg winced at the words. "I know. I know."

"I have been thinking a lot about this, and when I talked to Bishop Hartwell about what is happening, we both had the same idea."

Georg opened his eyes and turned to look at Samuel. His temper was poked. "And what, pray tell, might that be?" His tone was sarcastic. As soon as he uttered the words, he knew how horrible they sounded. "I am sorry, Samuel, I didn't mean to come across like that."

"That's OK. You're under a lot of pressure. I'm surprised you haven't snapped sooner."

"Me too. I will probably snap after the funeral. I will ask your forgiveness ahead of time."

"No need. I think God may give you eternal forgiveness."

Georg semi-smiled. He looked so tired. "OK, so what is this idea that you and the bishop have thought up?"

"We think that the children, all of them, should come and stay at the orphanage."

Georg's eyes widened in disbelief. "I cannot send them there."

Those words stung. It came out sounding like the orphanage wasn't a good-enough place. Georg saw the look on his face. "Oh, Samuel, you know what I mean. How can I send my children anywhere? And sending Diana and Sal back to the orphanage would crush their little hearts."

"It really is the best choice to make, Georg. Four young children and an infant? You can't take care of them *and* your farm. I would make sure they are taken care of like family. Your family *is* my family. You would see them often, you know that. And when Sal, Hagen, Diana, and Mathilde are old enough, a little more self-sufficient, they would all come home."

Georg's mind was spinning. He just lost his wife. His children just lost their mother, two of them for the second time. Now to be uprooted from their home to go live somewhere else? How do you tell your children that they have to leave their home because you can't take care of them?

"Georg, I know that deep inside you know that it is the logical thing to do."

"I do know, Samuel. I am more worried about them than my feelings."

"We don't have to say anything now. Let's go see Father Kelly, get through this day and take each as it comes." He looked at his watch. "It's one o'clock. Let's head over there now."

On the ride to St. Paul Church, they talked about the future of the children. "I will be able to see them when I make deliveries?"

"Of course!"

"I want to take them to church every Sunday. That could at least be one constant in our lives."

"I think that is a wonderful idea. Your faith is unwavering, Georg. I admire you for that. I don't know if even I could keep the faith if I were in your shoes."

"Believe me, I have wavered. I waver in my solitude and put on a brave face in front of my children. I guess this is my confession. Forgive me, Samuel, for I have sinned."

"Wavering is not a sin. Nothing you do will ever cause your exclusion from Heaven." He paused a moment. "I envy you sometimes."

"You... envy me?" asked Georg incredulously.

"I don't envy what you are going through; I envy your steadfast resilience. Georg, you have endured so much heartache. Your faith in God and humanity was tested to its limits before we ever met. Yet, you had the strength, the courage, to leave your home, your family's home, a home that was yours for almost three hundred years—and you started over, completely. Then you and Marta had the compassion to take in two more children, during the hardest of times, and love them as your own. And now... *now* you are hit with all of this? If all you have to admit in a confessional is that your faith has wavered, then I may call the Pope himself and ask that you be canonized. And we Methodists don't believe in saints." Another long pause. "I am proud to call you a friend. There, now I have sinned twice in one car ride—envy and pride. Maybe I should confess my sins to Father Kelly. Wouldn't that be a hoot?"

Samuel was trying to gently lighten the mood. A smile briefly flickered on Georg's face, then it blew out as he looked out of the window. They were passing the store where he and Marta had purchased the few pieces of furniture for their stay in the barn until their house was built. Memories. A tear dripped off of his chin.

Fifteen thought-filled minutes later, they pulled up in front of the church on East Union Street and sat for a few moments to collect their thoughts. Georg sat up straight and took a deep breath. "I'm ready when you are."

They got out and climbed the granite steps to the arched doors and went inside. The scent of church greeted them like a butler.

Quiet please, and gentlemen, please remove your hats.

Catholic churches, especially old ones such as St. Paul, had aged gently. The wooden pews, and even the marble columns rising high into the arched ceiling, have been steeped in the smoke of incense and candles for decades, and even on non-service days, the smell is ever-present. It was, in essence, an enormous holy smokehouse.

Father Kelly was sitting in the front pew when he heard the two men come in. He stood up and waved them to come forward. Samuel saw the folded newspaper on the pew where he had been sitting. It was open to the funny papers and he stifled a giggle.

"Hello Georg, Reverend Osterman."

"Good afternoon, Father," said Georg and Samuel. The men then all exchanged handshakes.

"Please, gentlemen, sit," said the priest as he sat back down in the pew.

Georg and Samuel took a seat to the priest's right. As soon as Georg sat down, he realized that he hadn't genuflected and started to get up.

"Eh, eh," said the priest, his right hand motioning him to sit back down. "God isn't going to smite you for that, my son. Even I forget sometimes. We are humans, not saints."

Georg replanted his bottom on the pew. Samuel liked this priest. He had met some stickler Catholic priests before, and he was glad that this one was not wound tightly.

"Georg," said Father Kelly. "I am so very sorry for your loss. Marta will be sorely missed in this church."

"Thank you, Father." He didn't know what to say next. He let Father Kelly lead the conversation.

"I assume that you are here to discuss the service," said the priest.

"Yes, we are." Then Georg turned and looked at Samuel.

"Father," said Samuel. "Georg has requested that his wife be laid to rest on his farm."

"Ah, you have a family cemetery on your farm." He said it matter-of-factly. He wasn't surprised by the notion of a family plot on private property.

"No," said Georg with a sheepish frown. "Not yet."

"You don't intend to bury your wife in unhallowed ground, do you, my son?"

"No," said Georg with the same expression.

"Father," Samuel took over. "Georg has asked me to perform a consecration ritual."

"I see," said the priest. A hint, just a wee tish, of disappointment floated on the surface, then sank again.

"Father," said Georg. "I did not ask Samuel to do this because I do not want you to do it. I asked him because he is my family's best friend; he is family."

He went on to explain why he wanted his wife to sleep eternally in the peach orchard, that he wanted Samuel to be a pallbearer, and that he had every intention of having a Catholic service. Samuel told Father Kelly that the Methodist bishop will still be attending the consecration ritual and that they would be honored if he would attend.

"This isn't a denominational choice," said Georg. "I am still your devoted Catholic servant."

Father Kelly could tell that these two men shared a very strong bond of friendship. He was not about to force his hand and insist on a Catholic ritual of consecration. Their respect for him and the Catholic Church was sincere, and he knew that if he did press the issue that both men would acquiesce, but reluctantly, and it might possibly sour the relationship between Georg and the church.

"Gentlemen, I would be honored to attend the consecration. Let me know when it will be."

"Thank you, Father," said Georg with much relief.

"You are most kind," said Samuel, equally relieved.

All men stood, shook hands and said their goodbyes. As they walked down the granite steps, Georg stopped. "Samuel, I want my son; I want Karl. I want my whole family with me tonight, what remains of it, and I think my children need it."

"I think that's a wonderful idea. Let's go bring Karl home."

Both men's hearts grew lighter on the ride to Zurbrugg Hospital. Karl was the one good thing to come from this awful experience, and neither of them had seen him since Wednesday. He was never off Georg's mind, just frustratingly put aside whilst he and Samuel did what needed to be done. Karl was the last one to touch Marta alive, a living piece of her, and it was time for him to come home.

When they arrived at the hospital, Barbara saw them coming up the walkway and greeted them at the door, with Karl in her arms.

"Hello gentlemen, were your ears ringing? We were just talking about you."

"Like church bells," said Samuel.

"Oh, you were, were you?" said Georg, a smile on his face, his eyes glistening proudly.

"Oh, yes, we were, weren't we," she said looking down into Karl's eyes. A little smile broke out on his face, then a big yawn. Barbara looked up at Samuel and Georg. "We just had lunch. Karl was wondering when he would be going home and *voilà*, here you are walking up the sidewalk." She placed Karl gently into Georg's arms. Samuel could see Georg's whole demeanor reshape into the Georg he had known before Wednesday as the cracks in his broken heart filled with the love for a new life.

"Hello, Karl, my son." He kissed him on the forehead. The soporific effect of Karl's full tummy had him already in a deep doze. "Barbara, may I take him home?"

"Of course. He is very healthy." She stroked Karl's hair. "And so beautiful. Oh, I have something for you. Come inside and I'll go get it."

Samuel and Georg stood inside the front door while Barbara walked off down a hallway. Neither man could take their eyes off of Karl. He really did look like Marta. They were so captivated by the new life before them that they both jumped a bit at Barbara's return. She was holding a large cardboard box.

"Ooh, sorry, didn't mean to scare you," said Barbara. "They are mesmerizing, aren't they? Babies, I mean."

"Yes, they sure are," said Samuel.

She handed the box to Samuel. It had a little heft to it. "What's this?" he asked.

"Just something for Karl—some diapers, bottles and formula, and a baby blanket I knitted a few years back, just to get you started." Then to Georg, "Alex and I knew you were dealing with a lot."

"That is very kind of you," said Georg. "I actually forgot about it, with so much happening. Thank you. Where is your husband, anyway?"

"He's on a house call in Camden. He's going to be sorry he missed you."

"Please, thank him, for everything," said Georg.

"I will." She gave Karl a kiss on the forehead, then Georg one on the cheek. "God bless you, both of you." She turned to Samuel. "You, too, Reverend. And please, don't hesitate to call if you need anything."

"Yes, ma'am," said Samuel. "Thank you."

They walked back to the car, Georg feeling like he was walking on a cloud, a little closer to Heaven, a little closer to Marta. Samuel put the box in the back seat next to the crate of milk and eggs, and they rode back to Lumberton with smiles in their hearts. They were finished running around for the day. Samuel wanted to be near his wife and children, and he was pretty sure that Georg's children were needing a good dose of their father.

When they walked into the house, they were swarmed by children. Samuel handed the crate to Ethel, who came to the rescue. (Not that anyone needs rescuing from a mob of affectionate children, but who needs three dozen eggs splattered all over them?) Georg's children stopped short of tackling their father when they saw who was with him. He knelt down slowly.

"Come, children, and meet your brother."

They slowly gathered around Georg and the baby. The girls thought Karl looked like a doll and wanted to play with him. Sal reached out to touch his head, then pulled back.

"It is alright to touch him," said Georg.

Sal reached out again and gently caressed his head. "His hair is so soft."

The girls joined in and gently touched Karl, the living doll. Hagen watched Sal. He could feel the love emanating from him, and he smiled. Then Hagen reached out and touched his father's face and looked deeply into his eyes. Georg smiled as an overwhelming feeling of peace came over him. Now he knew what the Lady in Black had felt.

That evening the two families broke bread together—or eggs, shall we say. Sometimes breakfast for dinner is a wonderful comfort food. After a dinner of fried eggs and potatoes, Ethel and the children listened to the radio, while the men, with Karl in Georg's arms, went into Samuel's office. Samuel researched the consecration ritual and went over the details with Georg.

"We need to inform the congregation about the consecration," said Samuel. "All should be welcomed to attend as witnesses. It's protocol. If you want anyone from your church to attend, then Father Kelly will have to announce it Sunday during the services. I think we should plan on the consecration for Tuesday afternoon and Marta's service the next day." Georg nodded in agreement. There wasn't much to say. Only to think. And feel.

That Sunday, announcements were made in both the Methodist and Catholic congregations about Tuesday. Samuel and Georg didn't expect too many of the Methodists to attend, as Georg's family wasn't Methodist. And, since Father Kelly wasn't performing the consecration ritual, they didn't think that many of the Catholics would show up, either.

They underestimated their fellow parishioners…

Tuesday

It was a busy morning from the get-go. With all that was happening and going to happen, Georg still had a farm to maintain. Fields needed tending to and the animals weren't going to be fed or milked by themselves. He got up at the crack of dawn and drove to the farm to care for the cows and chickens. He checked on the crops and irrigated the areas needing water. Then he went into the house to shower and get ready for Samuel and the others to arrive.

The consecration was scheduled to begin at two o'clock. Samuel and his family arrived at noon with Georg's children, and the Methodist bishop at twelve forty-five, along with the Methodist diocesan registrar and two churchwardens. Then at around one-thirty, the parishioners began to arrive. They came from both churches. And they kept coming. And coming. Cars were parked here, there, and everywhere. Then at one forty-five, a black Packard Limousine came slowly up the dusty driveway from Perkins Lane. Everyone watched as this long, fancy black car floated by them. Georg recognized Father Kelly in the back seat. He was sitting with two other men. One of them he recognized as (*oh my!*) Bishop Scully. But who was the third man with them? The limousine made its way through the parked cars and found a place near the front of the house. All the parishioners' eyes, Catholic and Methodist, were on the limousine. Georg and Samuel went down the porch steps to greet them.

The driver got out and opened the back door. First out was Father Kelly. Then Bishop Scully. The third man, much older than the priest or bishop, got out with assistance from the driver. His attire gave away his status.

"Good afternoon, Georg, Samuel," said Father Kelly.

"Good afternoon, Father," said both men in unison.

"I would like you to meet Bishop Scully," said the priest.

"Your Excellency," said Georg as he genuflected and kissed the bishop's ring.

Out of respect for the position, Reverend Samuel bowed. "Your Excellency."

"And this is Cardinal Bevilacqua of the Archdiocese of Newark," said the priest.

"Your Eminence," said Georg reverently as he genuflected and kissed his ring.

"Your Eminence," said Reverend Samuel with a respectful bow.

Cardinal Bevilacqua spoke with a heavy Italian accent. "Gentlemen, please pardon our coming unannounced. We are not here to disturb this ritual. We are here to recognize it. Father Kelly has explained all that has happened to you and your family, my son. We have prayed for you, and your wife, and children."

"Thank you, Your Eminence," said Georg.

"Yes," said Bishop Scully, who spoke with an equally thick Irish accent. "A communique was delivered this morning from His Holiness Pope Pius. He will be saying a special prayer tomorrow in Rome that will coincide with your wife's funeral service."

Georg's eyes widened. Almost speechless, the only words he found were, "Please, thank His Holiness."

"As for you, Reverend Osterman," Bishop Scully continued. "We, including His Holiness, want to thank you for taking such good care of our son Georg, and his family."

"I am truly honored, Your Excellency, Your Eminence," said Reverend Osterman.

Bishop Hartwell came out onto the porch, holding Karl in his arms. He was accompanied by the two churchwardens and the registrar. They walked down the steps and joined Samuel, Georg and the Catholic clergymen.

"Good afternoon, Father, Your Excellency, Your Eminence," said Bishop Hartwell.

"Good afternoon, Bishop," the three Catholics responded.

"Who do we have here?" asked Bishop Scully.

"May I introduce Karl Beckenbauer? Georg's son," said Bishop Hartwell.

"He is a beautiful child," said Cardinal Bevilacqua. "When is the baptism to be?"

"Your Eminence," said Father Kelly. "We haven't discussed that yet, in light of the current events."

"Oh, yes, please forgive me, Georg," said the cardinal.

"Nothing to forgive, Your Eminence," said Georg. "I have given it thought. I had intended on talking to Father Kelly next week."

"Would you allow me the honor," said the cardinal, "of baptizing your son?"

All the other men's faces showed some level of surprise. A cardinal performing a baptism? Georg was as speechless as the four men of the cloth.

"Gentlemen, I know what you are thinking," said the cardinal. "But what is the harm in letting an old priest baptize a new member of the church?"

More silence. Father Kelly looked at Bishop Scully. Both gave little *I don't know* shrugs.

"Georg," said the cardinal. "Will you permit me to formally welcome your son into the Catholic church?"

Georg looked at Samuel, then from bishop to bishop to priest. All of their expressions told Georg that something like this doesn't happen often.

"Your Eminence," said Georg. "It would be a great honor."

"Then it is settled," said the cardinal. "Bishop Scully and I will attend this Sunday's service. Afterward, little Karl will be baptized."

Georg's heart was pounding. Why all the high-level fuss over him and his family? And how in the world did the Pope know anything about Marta? And for His Holiness to say a special prayer?

The parishioners kept arriving. They were milling about—a mix of two congregations here to witness a holy event. The talk around the town was of the recent tragedy. It was not gossip. It was community sympathy for a friend and neighbor. They wanted to be there for the Beckenbauer Family, who had been part of the community for ten years. They were family, and there were no religious boundaries when it came to family.

The time to walk out to the peach orchard had come. Ethel came out onto the porch with the Beckenbauer and Osterman children. They walked down the steps and joined Georg and the other men. Bishop Hartwell handed Karl to Georg. Samuel looked around at all of them. He knew he was about to do something very important, for Georg, for Marta, and for the churches and their parishioners. His heart was thumping in his chest.

"Are you ready, Samuel?" asked Bishop Hartwell.

"Yes, Bishop, I am."

"Then let us begin."

Samuel began the walk out to the orchard. He was followed by the bishop, the churchwardens and registrar, the Catholic clergy, then Georg, Ethel, and the children. The parishioners, whose eyes had been on the small gathering in front of the house, joined in the slow walk. Altogether there were ninety-eight people there that day, not including the family.

When they arrived at the tree, Samuel and the others could see the area that Georg had chosen. He had cleared all the debris from under and around it and marked four corners with wooden stakes. An area thirty feet by thirty feet was to be consecrated.

The parishioners gathered around the imaginary boundary. No one spoke. No one needed guidance. Everyone took a place on the perimeter. Then the ritual began.

Georg read aloud the Petition for Consecration and handed it to the registrar. Samuel responded, "I am ready to grant your request. The Lord be with you." A mix of Methodist and Catholic responses, both meaning the same thing, came from the congregation. Samuel said a prayer, then proceeded to the first corner and said a blessing, then walked the perimeter to each corner and repeated the blessing. Returning to the beginning, he proclaimed the ground consecrated and said another prayer.

At this point, a final blessing is supposed to be given by the Bishop, who would normally be performing the ritual. So, Samuel would have been the person giving the blessing. Instead, he leaned over to his Bishop and whispered something. The Bishop nodded.

"Your Eminence," Reverend Osterman said to Cardinal Bevilacqua. "Would you like to say the final blessing?"

This was not only a respectful thing to do, to recognize his high authority, but it also bolstered the bridge of communication and good faith (no pun intended) between the two religions.

"It will be my pleasure," said His Eminence. Then he went to the center of the newly-hallowed ground and beckoned to everyone to step over the boundary and into the cemetery. "Heavenly Father, look down upon this gathering of your servants. Bless them, for they come here today to witness in your name the consecration of the ground we now stand upon. Bless the Beckenbauer family and the souls of their beloved who will rest here eternally.

"*In nomine Patris et Filii et Spiritus Sancti, Amen.*"

"Amen," from everyone.

Hagen could feel the love emanating from everyone in attendance. His spirit was jubilant. He felt his mother smiling down on them.

There was no celebration afterward. It wasn't a party. The gathering dispersed quietly, reverently, as if the whole orchard was now hallowed ground. The parishioners walked back to their vehicles. Ethel and the children went inside the house. Georg and the clergymen gathered in the shade on the porch.

"Reverend Osterman," said Bishop Scully. "A nicely-performed ritual indeed."

"Yes," said Cardinal Bevilacqua. "And thank you for allowing me the final blessing. That was very generous of you."

"It was my pleasure," said Reverend Osterman. "It was Georg's idea. When we were going over the ritual last night, he suggested the last blessing be given by Father Kelly. I mentioned this to Father Kelly just before the ritual and he suggested His Eminence give the final blessing."

His Eminence nodded to Father Kelly and Georg in acknowledgment of their respect. "Thank you, gentlemen."

Ethel came out onto the porch. "Gentlemen," said Ethel. "Would you like to come inside and rest a bit with some tea?"

"We would love to, thank you," said Bishop Scully, "but we must return to St. Paul. Father Kelly has to prepare for tomorrow." He looked over at the parked Packard and waved at the driver. The engine started, and in a moment the car slowly came to a stop in front of the house. The driver got out and opened the back door.

The Catholics said their goodbyes. Rings were kissed again, and one by one they got in the Packard's back seat. The driver closed the door, tipped his cap to Georg and the Methodists, then reclaimed his place behind the wheel and maneuvered the long car through the remaining parked vehicles and rode down the long drive to Perkins Lane.

Georg looked at Samuel. His eyes said, *what was that all about?* Samuel's eyes responded, *How the heck should I know?* Bishop Hartwell saw the ocular exchange and chimed in.

"Samuel, Georg," said the Bishop, "you handled yourselves quite well. I was very impressed."

"Thank you, Bishop," said Samuel.

"And thank you for allowing Samuel to perform the ritual," said Georg.

"It was my pleasure," said the bishop.

What Georg and Samuel didn't know was this:

When Samuel asked Bishop Hartwell for his blessing to perform the consecration ritual, the bishop had no issues with allowing it. He was happy to oblige. His concern, though Samuel didn't know it, was that the Catholics were historically by-the-bookers. He wanted no waves made. So, he contacted the Catholic bishop out of respect for his stature in the church; just in case he wanted to make an equally high Catholic appearance. Bishop Scully appreciated the respect shown.

What Bishop Hartwell didn't know was *this:*

Bishop Scully then contacted Cardinal Bevilacqua to get his thoughts. No one intended to make a stink, he just wanted to give him a holy heads up. His Eminence's interest was piqued when he heard the details surrounding Marta's death and Karl's birth, and the imminent Methodist consecration and Catholic funeral, so he cleared his schedule for the following week. Now, religion is sometimes like politics. Politicians do things in the interest *of* the people, but also so that they look good *to* the people. The same can be said of clergymen. Of course their sincerity is a given, but the church needs to look good as well.

Yes, but what about the Pope, you ask?

Well, it just so happened that Cardinal Bevilacqua and Pope Pius XI grew up in the same place, in a little town called Desio, just north of Milan. The cardinal and the Pope were actually second cousins. The cardinal sent a telegram to His Holiness, who had always wanted the church to shine in the eyes of the world. He truly appreciated the human-interest side of what was happening in a small town forty-five hundred miles away. The aforementioned communique from His Holiness arrived the next day, and it didn't take long for the word to spread that *The Pope Himself* had sent a telegram. Bishop Hartwell had underestimated the Catholics.

The day of the consecration had been a day of getting things done which had to be done. Emotions regarding Marta were suppressed by the necessity of preparing for the inevitable. It was a strange feeling for everyone. They hadn't forgotten Marta. The empty place she left behind was an entity unto itself. It's just, when you have to go on with your life, because you must go on, it naturally consumes your thoughts. The human brain doesn't process grief and logic at the same time. One or the other prevails. On Tuesday, it was logic. Wednesday would be grieving day, and logic would take a back seat.

Wednesday

Georg spent the night before Marta's funeral with his children in their home. The next morning, he got up earlier than usual to tend to the animals and gather the eggs and milk. Then, he went back to the house to take care of the children and make breakfast.

And to wait for the men from the funeral home who were going to dig Marta's grave.

At eight-thirty, four sinewy men pulled up in front of the house in a dented, old 1920-something REO Speed Wagon flatbed truck that had seen better days. Georg asked the boys to watch their sisters and Karl and went out to meet them. It was a family affair. Two brothers in their mid-forties sat in the front, and their two sons, cousins no older than twenty-two or twenty-three, rode in the back. Georg spoke with the men through the passenger window, then grabbed the handle on the side of the truck, stepped up on the running board and guided them through the orchard to Marta's tree. When the truck stopped, Georg hopped off and walked to a place under the tree that he had marked with four stakes. The two older men got out of the truck and followed Georg. The cousins got down from the back and grabbed the shovels, the pick, and the mattock, and joined their fathers. There was little talk. It was pretty self-explanatory.

Dig a deep hole here big enough to swallow a really big box with my wife inside. Oh, the things the mind gets away with!

"This is the spot," Georg said. "Please come back to the house when you are finished."

"Aye, Mr. Beckenbauer," said one of the older men.

On his walk back to the house, Georg stopped at the cow barn and chicken coop. The cows were out grazing in the pasture and the chickens were pecking at the ground around the coop. A few of the cows meandered back towards the barn when they saw Georg. He took the opportunity to get some extra milk and put it into four quart-sized bottles. Then he gathered all the eggs in the coop, put everything in a crate, and carried it back to the house. He finished cleaning up the breakfast dishes while the children listened, or pretended to listen, to the radio. Karl was asleep in the bassinet that Ethel Osterman had given him, handed down from her children. It was on the floor between Heidi and the couch. Two of the children knew what the day had in store. Diana and Sal remembered the last funeral—the only funeral—they had ever attended. It had rained that day. Sal had thought that God was crying for his Mama and Papa. Hagen and Mathilde only knew that today is when their mother officially goes to Heaven.

About two hours later, Georg heard the diggers' truck returning from the orchard, and a few minutes later there was a knock on the front door. When he opened the door, all four men were standing on the porch, dusty and sweaty, holding their hats at their hearts.

"We are finished, Mr. Beckenbauer," one of the older men said in his thick Irish brogue. "Everything is all set for later. We are truly sorry for your loss." The four men put their hats back on and turned around to walk back to their truck.

"Gentlemen," said Georg. They stopped and turned back around as they removed their hats again. Georg reached down to his left and picked up the wooden crate with the four quarts of milk and as many dozen eggs and handed it to the man who had expressed their sympathies for his loss. "Mr.

Ahearn?" He spoke to the man who had been doing all the talking.

"Pádraic, sir," said the man.

"Please, Pádraic, take this. It is the least I can do."

When these men had first arrived earlier that morning, Georg had seen the signs of the less fortunate. The tired old truck, the hungry look of men doing anything they could do to keep their families alive. These men weren't grave-diggers by choice, but out of necessity. The worn-out writing on the Speed Wagon's door proved that—*Ahearn Bros. Construction Company*. He had hoped that their pride was not going to get in the way of accepting his small gift of thanks.

"Mr. Beckenbauer, we cannot take payment from you. Mr. Yetter pays us to do a job, and I don't think he would take too kindly to knowing you paid us as well."

Georg looked at the man right in his eyes. Georg knew Pádraic wanted to take it. His family most likely needed it. All their families did, Georg was certain of it. He could see it in their eyes. It wasn't pride. It was the fear of losing their position.

Georg was sure Mr. Ahearn remembered him. Georg, of course, couldn't forget the Ahearns. He recognized the two older men as Pádraic and Joseph Ahearn. Ahearn Bros. Construction Company had built the Beckenbauer's house ten years before. The two younger men with them were their two oldest boys. Brendan belonged to Joseph, and Pádraic Jr. belonged to Pádraic Sr. Brendan and Pádraic Jr. weren't the only children in their families. The Ahearns lived up to their Irish Catholic heritage and procreated, a lot. Pádraic had five children, and Joseph had seven. Their family business did well until the Depression kicked the economy in the gut, and Ahearn Bros. Construction Company went belly up. Now, Pádraic and Joseph, and their two oldest boys, found work where they could. Today, it was digging Marta Beckenbauer's grave.

"Mr. Ahearn… Pádraic." Georg smiled as best he could under the present circumstances. "This is not a payment; this is a thank you. I do not mean to offend you, but pride is not something any of us can afford in these difficult times. Please, take this to your families. Mr. Yetter does not need to know."

Pádraic put his hat back on and took the crate of eggs and milk. "Thank you, Mr. Beckenbauer. We really do appreciate this." The other three men put on their hats, then all four nodded, turned, and went down the steps. They got back into their truck and drove off down the long dusty drive, their hearts a little bit lighter. Sometimes the smallest acts of kindness can have enormous effects on a weary soul.

The funeral service was scheduled for noon that day. A car from the funeral home arrived at eleven to take Georg and the children to St. Paul Church. When the family arrived, the church was filled with parishioners, friends, and neighbors. The organist, who Hagen always loved to watch, was playing solemn music. Hagen had no desire to sit in the balcony and watch him that day.

The church service didn't stray from the script, although there were a few moments that Father Kelly had to pause for a crying mourner and take a deep breath himself. After it was over, Samuel and five other pallbearers (all Varsaci men), carried Marta out of the church, down the granite steps and put her gently into the hearse. While Georg and the children watched, he was thinking, *I cannot believe she is in there. When will I wake up from this?* He closed his eyes and imagined that at any moment, he would feel a gentle shaking, and it would be Marta telling him to '*get up, Schatzi. I let you sleep in a little today, but the cows aren't going to milk themselves.*' He closed his eyes tighter. He waited. And waited. The back of the hearse was closed with a *thump,* and he opened his eyes, and came back from the universe called Hope.

The ride to the farm was slow and long. The hearse led the way, followed by the car with the pallbearers, then the car with the family, then the Packard with the priest, the bishop and the cardinal, then too many parishioners' cars to count.

At the farm, mourners parked wherever they could find a spot. The hearse drove out to the orchard at a walking speed while everyone else followed on foot. When they arrived at the cemetery, the pallbearers lifted Marta out of the hearse and carried her to the grave site. From a bird's eye view, the new cemetery looked like a big eye, staring up to Heaven; the peach tree like a green pupil, with an iris of people dressed in black with specks of color here and there that radiated out from the center as they surrounded Marta, her family, and Father Kelly as he committed her soul to Heaven.

The graveside service was again by the book, but far from stoic. As Georg looked around, he didn't see a dry eye anywhere. Dr. Small and Barbara were standing arm in arm, holding flowers and dabbing their eyes. And there were the Gilchrists, Abigail and Stephen. She was holding flowers in one hand, and a handkerchief in the other, while her husband held *their* Hagen. Even Father Kelly choked up a smidge. He tried to hold it in, but when you know the person whose soul you are commending to Heaven and are surrounded by so much love, it brings out the human in you.

So many people showed up that day. Even people Georg only made eye contact with at church came to pay their respects. The Beckenbauers had become very well-liked. If not personally, then because they had endeared themselves to the community with their generosity and acts of kindness.

Since the depression began, they never looked the other way when they knew someone was in need. The Beckenbauers weren't financially wealthy themselves, but they farmed, and were able to keep their family fed. Not everyone was a farmer. Instead of throwing away what they couldn't sell, they would give it to families in need, anonymously through St. Paul or Samuel and the Methodist church. It didn't take long for the populace to find out about the Beckenbauers' philanthropy. Georg never admitted to it when asked about it. Everyone's presence there that day was their way of looking after someone who had always looked after *them*.

Afterward, the family and clergy, and the parade of parishioners, walked back to the house to console and commiserate. And eat. Ladies from all over Burlington County brought food—sandwiches, casseroles, soups, stews, pies, and cakes. *Tableosaurus Rex* was camouflaged under a heavy blanketing of dishes, plates, and pots, as was most of the counter space. Fellow mourners shuffled through the kitchen and made plates of food to nibble on as they wandered around inside and outside, chatting with each other.

"*So sad...*"

"*Such a nice family...*"

"*What will they do now...?*"

"*How is Georg going to manage...?*"

"*Five children, one a new-born, and a farm to run...?*"

Hagen was besieged by emotions from every direction. There were so many people, it was impossible to find solitude; sympathetic adults taking turns patting motherless children's heads, telling them how wonderful she was, "*oh, you poor things*". He walked out of the house as he feigned ignorance of the sympathetic voices that were addressing him and talking to each other about his mother in the past tense. Down the porch steps he went and headed in the direction of the cow barn. All the sadness was too much for Hagen. He had his own to deal with. The cows were never sad. On the contrary, they always seemed content to be just where and who they were. The barn was always the perfect place for Hagen to unclutter his thoughts. Sal and the rest of the children, including the Osterman trio, watched Hagen walk out through the front door and rushed to catch up to him.

"Where are you going, Hagen?" asked Mathilde.

"I am going to the barn." He was emotionless on the outside; on the inside his soul was screaming through clenched teeth.

"Can we come with you?" asked Diana.

Hagen could feel that his siblings were overwhelmed by the gaggle of adults invading their home. The Ostermans were just plain bored, but respectfully bored. They weren't pretending like this was some picnic. *Let's go climb trees or swing on the swings.* They were tagging along out of boredom, yes, but also because they loved their Aunt Marta too, and her children.

"Alright, you can come with me."

"Thank you, Hagen," said Mathilde, and gave her brother a hug.

Hugging her back, he scanned the faces of the other children. Diana looked as relieved as Mathilde to be getting out of the house. The Osterman children were watching Mathilde hug Hagen; sad smiles were on all three faces. Sal was looking off in the direction of the orchard, no emotion showing at all.

Hagen kissed Mathilde on the top of her head. She let go of him, and he led them away from the crowded house. Salvatore didn't say a thing. He just followed the others. He had barely spoken three words since the service in the peach orchard. He had been thinking a lot though—of course about Marta, but also about his birth parents and their funeral. The Cristoforos weren't buried in a family cemetery under a peach tree, or under any tree. They were buried on the perimeter of the paupers' section of a Catholic cemetery, somewhere near Hoboken, in graves with simple wooden markers, in simple wooden boxes without any peach satin lining. As emotional as the day had been, Hagen was still sensitive to everyone else's feelings. The other children were quiet, but Sal's silence was the loudest.

When they got to the barn, they followed Hagen up the ladder to the hayloft and they all lay down in the hay. Except for Sal. He stood at the window and looked out at the orchard in the distance.

Hagen sat up. "Sal?"

Sal looked over at Hagen and the rest of them lying there in the hay; his blank-faced stare frightening Hagen.

"Sal? Are you OK?"

Sal shrugged his shoulders a little then looked back out of the window. Hagen got up and walked to Sal's side and leaned against him. Sal leaned back. He needed that, and so did Hagen. They stood there a while, lost in their thoughts, while the other children lay quietly, looking up at the ceiling. No one knew what to do, what to say. After a few more moments of leaning on each other, Hagen led Sal to the hay, and they lay down with the others. One by one, they all dozed off.

While the children napped in the hayloft, Georg milled about, holding little Karl, chatting courteously to the many respect givers as they held plates of food in one hand, and coochiecooed Karl with the other. Georg smiled on the outside, and thanked them for coming, but inside wished everyone would go the hell home. *Dear God, forgive me for thinking that.* He was tired and he had a lot on his mind.

When this part of the day ended, he would have to tell his children that they will be going to live at the orphanage. Every time the thought slinked its way into his mind, while he was feigning gratitude to one of the mourners, he could feel his face making an extra effort not to wince. Some of them asked where the children were, and he would say, *oh, around here somewhere.* He knew where the children had gone. He spied them walking out to the barn and he didn't blame them. He envied them for not having to be responsible for playing host and faking smiles, and he wished that he could go hide out in the barn until he could have his house back.

By around four o'clock, almost everyone had left. When Georg said the last *goodbye and thank you for coming and bringing that casserole,* he headed back to the house. As he was walking up the porch steps with Karl in his arms, he heard a sound coming from the direction of the orchard. It was the Ahearns' truck slowly making its way back from the cemetery. Georg hadn't noticed them going out there after the service. Of course, someone had to put the soil back in and cover his wife, but he hadn't had any spare room in his head for those thoughts. As he stood there watching the truck coming closer, he could see Pádraic Ahearn driving with two women in the seat next to him. Joseph, his son Brendan, and his nephew were riding in the back. Pádraic stopped the truck in front of the house. The three men in the back jumped down while the two women and Pádraic got out of the front. The women led the men towards Georg, who had just come down from the porch.

"Mr. Beckenbauer," said one of the women. She had long dark hair, and wore a simple dress, dark blue with little pink flowers; her blue eyes bluer next to the dress. "I am Catherine Ahearn, Pádraic's wife." She had the same lilting Irish accent as her husband.

"I am Colleen Ahearn, Joseph's wife," said the other woman. Her long, red hair, glowing in the remaining sunlight, contrasted against her black dress; her eyes were the color of rusted iron.

"We are so sorry for your loss, Mr. Beckenbauer," said Catherine. "When our husbands came home today with your gift, we were so very thankful. And when they told us who gave it to them, we felt humbled, and compelled to come back here with them."

"Mr. Beckenbauer," continued Colleen. "Even in this time of sorrow, you still have room in your heart for others. You are a kind man, and we will be forever grateful for your generosity."

Catherine went on, "We hope you don't mind that we came back here with our husbands and sons. We said a prayer at your wife's grave. We prayed to St. Gertrude of Nivelles and put her medallion in with your wife."

Georg stood there, holding Karl, while the Ahearn women spoke. Each word they uttered turned the key that unlocked the gate that held back all of the day's pent-up emotions. He bowed his head as tears clouded his vision, and his shoulders gently shook. He was the one who felt humbled at that moment; ashamed for wanting people to go the hell home. This day wasn't about him. It was about Marta, and all the people to whom he and his family mattered. And now these women, who never knew his wife or him, were praying for her because of his simple act of kindness. He said a silent prayer, asking for forgiveness and looked up at the Ahearns. "Thank you."

Colleen and Catherine both kissed him on the cheek, then Karl on the forehead. "May God bless you, Mr. Beckenbauer," said Catherine. "You and your family are in our prayers." The Ahearn men nodded and put their hats back on, then followed the women back to their truck. The men never spoke. There was no need. Colleen and Catherine said it all. That night, Joseph and Pádraic held their wives very close, and prayed that they would never have to endure Georg's pain.

Georg turned back towards the house and went inside. He put Karl in the bassinet, then found Samuel and Ethel in the kitchen doing dishes.

"Have you seen the children?" asked Ethel.

"They all went to hide in the barn," said Georg, nodding in that direction. "I am going out there to get them. I am sure they haven't eaten anything, and they must be hungry."

"I'm sure they are," said Samuel. "Ethel and I will make plates for them."

"Good, good, thank you. I left Karl in the bassinet in the living room. I will be right back."

Georg called to Heidi, who was lying on the floor in her spot near Karl. She looked tired, too. She wasn't used to having so many people around all at once, either. She gave Karl a sniff, then followed Georg to the barn. It was time for the cows to come in anyway, so Georg and Heidi rounded them up and put them back in the barn for the night.

The commotion of cows and Heidi's barking roused the sleeping children. One by one they got up and stretched and yawned and made their way down the ladder from the hayloft.

"Well hello," said Georg. "Everyone is gone now."

"Good," said Hagen. Georg thought to himself that his son had probably felt the same way he himself had felt earlier, but without the *go the hell home*.

"Are you hungry? There is a lot of food in the kitchen."

"I'm hungry," said Sam Jr.

"Me too," said Joey.

"I thought you might be," said Georg.

His children all shrugged, almost in sync with each other, and with those shrugs, they told their father that food was the last thing on their minds.

"Let's get back to the house now. Aunt Ethel and Uncle Samuel are making plates for all of you."

They walked back to the house quietly. Sal picked up a stick and threw it for Heidi to fetch. She gladly ran after it and brought it back. Sal kept throwing it until they got to the porch.

"Inside, Heidi," said Sal. Georg held the door open. Heidi went in first and they all followed her to the kitchen. She knew food was going to happen.

"There you are," said Samuel to the seven children when they came through the door. "We wondered where you went off to. Come, sit down and eat something."

All the children sat down at the table. While Ethel held Karl, and fed him a bottle, Samuel put plates of food in front of the children. Slowly the Beckenbauers picked at their food. Their bodies were hungry, but their minds were full. Grief is a powerful appetite suppressant. The Ostermans started to eat and eventually, the others followed suit.

While the children were eating, Georg opened a can of Ken-L-Ration. He filled Heidi's bowl, and she ate next to the table, with the rest of her family.

"Georg," said Ethel. "I didn't see *you* eat anything today."

"I have not really thought about food."

"I thought so." She put Karl's bottle on the counter, picked up a plate of food, and placed it at Georg's seat at the head of the table. "Here, sit, eat. You need your strength." Then she resumed feeding Karl his bottle.

"Thank you, Ethel." He sat down and picked at the food a bit before his empty stomach overrode his full mind and commanded him to eat. Samuel and Ethel had already had their fill and sat with the rest of them and watched. Georg knew what Samuel and Ethel were thinking. They knew what was banging around inside his thoughts: the orphanage.

When dinner was over, everyone brought their plates to the sink. Aunt Ethel handed Karl off to Uncle Samuel and enlisted her children's assistance in doing the dishes. This gave Georg the opportunity to take his children into the living room to talk to them privately. He could have put it off until later, but he wanted Samuel and Ethel there for support. He sat them on a couch, then sat on the coffee table so he could be right in front of them.

He didn't know how to begin; what the first words should be. Should he just blurt it out and explain after, or vice versa?

"Children, there is something very important that I must talk about with you." He took a deep breath.

"Papa," said Hagen. "What's wrong?" He knew something was not right, again, but a different not right.

"I want you to know that I love you very much," his voice wavered.

"Papa?" repeated Hagen.

Georg swallowed then continued. "We are a family and that will never change. But… oh God…" then he broke down.

Samuel had been eavesdropping on the other side of the kitchen door, waiting for any sign that Georg needed help. *Oh God* was his cue and he walked in, still holding Karl.

"Papa?" Now Mathilde wanted to know what was going on. They assumed he was crying for their Mama, but Hagen felt it was more than that. They had already had their communal crying sessions. This one felt different.

"Children," said Uncle Samuel as he sat next to Georg on the coffee table. "Your father needs your help." The children looked at him quizzically.

"How can we help, Uncle Samuel?" asked Sal.

"Your mother and father worked together to take care of the farm and you. Your father is going to have to do everything all by himself now."

Georg bowed his head, felt ashamed, tears dripped off of his nose and cheeks onto the woven rug below.

"Papa, we can help you," said Hagen. "Sal and I can pick the apples and peaches and milk the cows and feed the chickens."

Georg looked up from the floor at Hagen. "I know you can help. But you cannot do all of those things and go to school."

"There is also your brother to think about," said Uncle Samuel, looking down at Karl. "He can't do anything for himself. He needs a lot of attention. Your father can't milk cows and feed chickens and pick apples *and* watch over Karl."

Hagen sensed where this was going. "What do you want us to do?"

Uncle Samuel continued, "We think that you should come and stay at the orphanage."

All four of their mouths fell open.

"You don't want us anymore?" asked Sal as tears filled his eyes, staring at Georg.

"Oh, *Liebchen*, no, no. You know how very much I love you. And how much your Mama loves you. Everything we do is for you, so we could be a family and always be together. Your Mama worked hard to help me. She took care of you, and the cooking, and a lot of other things while I took care of the farm, and the crops, and the cows, and the chickens."

The girls cried harder. Sal sat there, numbed by the thought of going back to the orphanage again. Hagen's tears leaked down his cheeks as he looked at his father straight in the eyes. He knew that this was hurting his Papa as much, if not more, than it was hurting him and his siblings. Hagen, at his tender young age of eight, as we know now, was beyond his years. He didn't want to live at the orphanage. He didn't want to leave his father alone. But he knew that his Papa could not do everything. Karl needed feeding, a lot, and poopy diapers needed changing, *a lot*. Adults did those things. Papa was only one adult.

"You guys," said Hagen to his siblings. They looked over to him. The girls' crying had geared down to a sniffle here and there, Sal was still a deer in the headlights. "We will be OK. I will take care of you."

Hagen never ceased to amaze the adults. Georg and Samuel looked at each other, then back at the children.

Uncle Samuel took over. "Thank you, Hagen. Children, your father misses your mother as much as you do. Your Aunt Ethel and I miss her so very much, too. But your father cannot manage your farm alone. If you come to stay at the orphanage..." groans and moans from the girls "...you will see your father very often. You will see him when he makes his deliveries. He will take you to church on Sundays. That will not change. And, your brother Karl needs special attention because he is so little and can't take care of himself. We can do that together, at the orphanage." The next thing Uncle Samuel said kissed Hagen right in the heart. "I love you like you are my own. I will always be there for you. Please, help me help your father."

Hagen stood up and hugged his father. Sal joined him, and then the girls.

"I love you so very much," said Georg. The embrace seemed to go on forever, but not long enough. Then they all let go of each other, and the children sat back on the couch.

"How long do we have to stay there?" asked Sal.

"Probably until Karl is old enough to go to school," said Georg.

Hagen did the math in his head. He was five years old when he started Kindergarten. That meant that he and his brothers and sisters will not be home for… *five years*! The thought nauseated him.

"By then," their father continued, "you will be big enough to really help out here at home. Maybe even drive the tractor."

"But that is five years, Papa," Hagen frowned. When he said *five years* out loud the girls groaned again.

"I know that sounds like an awfully long time, but I promise we will see each other very often. Will you please help me? Hagen, Sal, I need you to be big boys now and watch over your sisters and Karl for me."

Hagen looked at Sal. Sal didn't look as downhearted as he had been when Uncle Samuel first said that they were going back to the orphanage. But he wasn't laughing, either. None of them were feeling all too keen on the idea. Hagen looked at his siblings and said again, "I will take care of you. I promise."

At that point, Samuel felt that Georg, or maybe even Hagen, could handle it from there. He handed Karl to Georg and went back into the kitchen where his wife and children were wrapping waxed paper around the remaining dishes of food and putting what they could into the refrigerator. Ethel looked at her husband with a face that asked, *well, how did it go?* He returned the look with the expression that said, *it's going to be alright,* and then held up two hands with fingers crossed.

After a while Georg and his children went back into the kitchen; all eyes red from another round of hugs and tears. He saw that the kitchen was all tidied up. "Thank you, you two, for cleaning up."

"We helped," said Muriel.

"Yes, they did indeed," said Ethel. "Thank you very much."

"You're welcome, Mommy," said little Joey.

"It's getting late," said Samuel. "We should go. Uncle Georg and his children have had a long day and are probably very tired."

The Ostermans said their goodbyes to the Beckenbauer family minus one. Hugs, hugs, hugs and more hugs. Then they piled into their Chevrolet and drove down the long, dirt drive while Georg and his children watched from the porch.

Sunday came and after Mass, Cardinal Bevilacqua performed Karl's baptism. Uncle Samuel and Aunt Ethel were the Godparents. It was a beautiful ceremony. Emotions were a mix of joy and sadness. Afterward, Georg and his children went home to have dinner together. As he sat at that enormous table, he felt like he was eating his last supper. Not the Biblical last supper, but death row last supper. He had only a few more hours with his family, because that evening would be the first night that his children would sleep at the orphanage and his heart was going to die.

At six o'clock, it was time to go. Their suitcases were packed the night before and were waiting by the door. The children said goodbye to Heidi. Then each of them grabbed their own suitcase and followed Georg to the car, as he carried Karl in the bassinet.

No one felt like talking on the ride to Mount Holly. Hagen tried to remember the good times, like the day he met Sal, and he grabbed his hand and held it tight. Sal was trying to think of something good, but all he could remember was the reason why he and his sister wound up there the first time. The girls were hugging their dolls tightly. They had already told their dollies that they were going to live somewhere where there were lots of other girls with dollies, and they could have tea parties together, and that everything was going to be fine. They were trying to convince themselves more than they were their dolls.

As they pulled into the driveway to the orphanage, Georg's heart slammed hard and fast in his chest, like it was trying to escape. His temples pulsed. His head bobbed slightly with each gunshot of blood through his carotid artery.

He pulled the car up to the front. Uncle Samuel was on the porch waiting for them. The children got out of the car slowly. They waited for their father to hand each of them their suitcase and then get Karl. As they walked from the car, Georg looked up at Samuel. Samuel saw the terror in his eyes. The children climbed the porch steps and got a hug from Uncle Samuel. Georg put Karl down and got a hug, too. Samuel whispered in his ear, "It's OK, my friend, it's going to be alright. It's not forever." The hug ended and Georg mouthed, *thank you,* and wiped a tear away with the heel of his hand.

He knelt and hugged his children, gave them kisses and more kisses, like he was loading them up with enough to tide them over until he saw them again—or maybe, to tide himself over. He stood up, not really knowing what to do next. *Should he follow them inside? Should he say goodbye on the porch?*

"Be good for Uncle Samuel."

"Yes, Papa," said Mathilde.

He turned and walked down the steps and to his car, each footstep feeling heavier than the one before, like he was walking through knee-deep mud. He opened the door and turned to look at them standing there. Hagen had picked up Karl and was holding him closely.

"I will see you tomorrow." He nodded, forcing a smile. The words sounded so strange, like he was casually telling

255

friends to *have a good night, thanks for coming, let's do it again.* To Georg it felt like, *I hate myself, I am a horrible father, GODDAMMITGODDAMMITGODDAMMIT!!*

He got behind the wheel, started the engine and rolled down the window. "I love you."

"We love you, too," said Samuel. He had his hands on Sal's and Hagen's shoulders. He could feel Sal trembling as he tried not to cry.

As Georg drove away, no one on the porch moved or waved. Waving meant goodbye. They didn't want to say goodbye. They waited until the Oldsmobile was out of sight, until they were positive it wasn't just a bad dream, that their Papa wasn't going to stop and turn the car around and they would all wake up and be home. As the car disappeared around a corner, all shoulders sank, even Uncle Samuel's, with the weight of what had just happened. Uncle Samuel took them inside and up to their room. They would all be together, in the same room that Sal and Diana had slept in the first time they stayed there. The crib that Georg had made for Karl was in the corner of the room by Hagen's bed.

That night, the only one who slept alone was Karl in his crib. Diana and Mathilde slept together in one bed, hugging their dolls. In another bed, Hagen slept holding Sal.

Hagen's Railcar
Somewhere in Illinois

Hagen felt that this was a good place to stop and take a break. They'd finished lunch, the Dr. Peppers, and two bottles of water. Emily had used the tissues she'd prepped herself with, plus a handful more. Between the two of them, they'd emptied a box. It had been a while since Hagen had told anyone any part of his history, let alone so much of it all at once. And Emily's sensitivity, her tears and emotions, made it easy for him to let go, too.

Emily blew her nose, then heaved a sigh. "I... I..."

"Don't try to find the words. It isn't necessary."

"Thank you. I didn't want to come off sounding trite."

"I doubt that you would have." He gave her a warm smile. "Do you need to use the restroom?"

"I do, yes."

"Please feel free to use the one up here. I'll go after you."

"Thank you." She got up and started towards the door, then stopped and turned around. "Don't touch anything." She pointed to the dishes like a parent addressing a child. "I'll tidy up when I come back."

"If it makes you feel any better, I have every intention of letting you do all the work today. You're welcome."

"Good, thank you." She turned, left the kitchen, and made her way to the little hallway that led to Hagen's room. She opened the door to the bathroom and found it to be like the one downstairs, except that this one was larger, and there was a jacuzzi tub next to the shower. When she finished and washed her hands, she couldn't resist opening the door that led into Hagen's room. She didn't go in, but just gave a peek. The room smelled like him; like his cologne—citrus, light, elegant. She saw photos and paintings covering the walls, and the door that let out to the patio. Beginning to feel like a peeping Tom, she closed the door and left the bathroom. When she was about to enter the kitchen, she stopped, pushed the door open a little bit and peeked around the corner. Hagen was still in the booth, looking out at the passing terrain. He dabbed his eyes with a tissue. She didn't want to interrupt him. But she didn't want to dilly-dally, either. He'd had just as much coffee, Dr. Pepper, and water today as she.

"OK, your turn," she said as she rounded the corner.

He looked up in her direction, "Right, thank you," and stood with the help of Emily's offered hand; her calming touch quieting his soul. He smiled. "Thank you, my dear," and walked off to the bathroom, gripping the lion's head firmly.

Emily cleared the table and put everything in the sink, grabbed two more bottles of water, and went into the living room. She sat on a sofa and waited for Hagen. When he returned, she could see he looked tired. "Do you want to rest for a while? You look beat."

"I feel beat. But I don't want to waste any time. I have a lot still to go through, and I want you to hear everything."

"Don't worry, we will get to it. But I think you should rest for a while; maybe lie down and close your eyes for a bit."

He knew she was right. His eyes burned; their lids were heavy. "Alright, you win this one. Just for a little while." He lay down, turned onto his side, curled up and used the armrest for a pillow. "Don't let me sleep too long. I still have a lot to get through."

"I won't." She retrieved a crocheted throw from one of the recliners and put it over him.

"Thank you, Emily. You are a dear." He closed his eyes and, in a few minutes, dozed off.

Emily watched him for a little bit. *What is it about this man? He was a complete stranger just two days ago. Now, I feel like I've known him forever. Do I want to be his writing assistant or am I only curious to hear everything about him? How would he know if I would even be good at it?* She went back to the kitchen and put the dishes in the dishwasher, tidied up, and returned to the living room. She sat across from Hagen. He looked so comfy. Watching him sleep had the same effect as seeing someone yawn. *A nap sounds good right about now. Just a short one. Look at me taking a midday nap!* Then she mirrored Hagen and curled up on her sofa and dozed off to the gentle rocking of the train.

When she awoke, it was to gentle rocking, only, it wasn't the train's movement. It was Hagen gently shaking her shoulder while speaking softly. "Wakey, wakey."

She startled awake and bolted upright in a fog as she tried to get her body and brain synchronized. When she could tell up from down, she realized it was dark outside and the train had come to a stop.

"Oh, God, I'm sorry, I'm sorry, are we in Philly already?" She rubbed her eyes.

"No, no, my dear. We are in Chicago. I woke up when they disconnected my car from the main train."

"How long ago?"

"Not long, just a few minutes. You must have been as drained as me."

"I guess I was. I'm sorry. You asked me not to let you sleep too long and we both did."

"It's alright. We both must have needed it."

She got up off the sofa and stretched. "Now what?"

"Well, we have a couple hours until the pickup. Are you hungry?"

"I'm hungry; I could eat."

"Why don't we think about dinner? I dreamed of golumpkis, for some reason, and I woke up thinking you were already warming them up. Then I saw you sleeping. I have to say I was a little disappointed." He grinned and raised an eyebrow.

"Oooookay, I said I was sorry. Don't make me feel any worse than I already do." She frowned and pursed her lips.

"I was... *joshing?* Isn't that how you said it?"

"OK, yeah, but that was mean. You almost made me cry, *again*."

He chuckled, "I'm sorry. I was only having a little fun. Forgive me."

"Nothing to forgive. I'm just sorry if we wasted too much time sleeping."

"Oh, don't worry. We can talk over dinner and make up some time. Since we napped a while, we might be able to stay up a little later this evening."

"Hopefully. I really want to hear more."

"Good... good. I want you to hear it." He *needed* her to hear it. "It has been a while since I said any of it out loud." He opened a bottle of water and took a sip. "Tell me, have you decided whether or not you want to remain with me as my assistant?"

"If I had to give you an answer right now? I would say yes."

He smiled widely, his blue eyes lighting up. "So, do you *need* more time to decide?"

"I don't think so. No. Yes! I do! Oh, who am I kidding? No, I don't. My answer is yes. Yes! You had me at, *Once upon a time…* But what makes you think I'm going to be good at it?"

"Oh, I just have a feeling." He winked and took another sip from the bottle. "Let's eat."

"A feeling, huh?" She folded her arms and cocked her head to the left. "Playing psychic again, are we?"

"No, just going with my gut."

"Well, boss, do you want to feed that gut in the kitchen or dining room?"

"Oh, it makes no difference… kitchen. It is closer to everything. We can still do dessert on the patio."

"The kitchen it is. I'd like to freshen up, first, if that's OK." She brushed her clothes as if to wipe away the wrinkles from napping.

He nodded. "Me too. Let's meet in, let's say… fifteen minutes?"

"I'll see you in fifteen minutes."

They went to their rooms, cleaned up, changed clothes, and met in the kitchen with one minute to spare.

Emily pointed to the booth when Hagen entered. "Sit, relax. I got this."

He knew she did. She opened the fridge and pulled out the covered dish of golumpkis. He directed her to a covered glass dish in a cupboard and she put…

"How many of these can you eat?"

"Oh, don't be stingy. What we don't eat, we can put back."

…eight cabbage rolls and lots of red sauce into the dish, then put it into the microwave oven to heat up.

"You want the beer Piotr made for you, right?"

"Oh, heavens yes. And so do you. You do like beer?"

"I do." She smiled. "And did you notice I didn't argue with you about the *help* drinking on the clock?"

"I did. I'm so proud of you." He smiled.

"Well, I don't feel like I've been on any clock since about three minutes after I met you. This has been the easiest job I've ever had."

"I am pleased that you are feeling comfortable. We are going to be spending a lot of time together."

Emily's life had swiftly changed direction, and the reality of it began to sink in. She took a moment to collect her thoughts, then went on with the dinner prep.

While the cabbage rolls were warming up, she set the table. "Glasses for the beer?"

"In the cabinet to the right of the refrigerator, there are some pilsner glasses."

She set out the glasses. The microwave beeped. Cabbage rolls on the table. Beer bottles opened and glasses filled. "Did I miss anything?"

"The rye bread and butter. I like to dip it in the red sauce."

"Ah, you're a *sopper*, too."

"Indeed I am."

She set the rye bread and butter on the table.

"Anything else?

"I don't believe so. Sit, eat."

Emily forked two cabbage rolls onto each of their plates and spooned some of the red sauce over them.

Hagen watched her take a bite of her *golumpki*. She looked up at him with the same expression as when she tasted the Sassicaia. "Good?" he asked.

"Oh, yes, very." She swallowed and forked another mouthful.

He held his glass up to toast, and she clinked hers against his.

"*Prost*." And they both sipped

She smiled. "Mmm, this is really good, too!"

"I had a feeling you would like it." He took another sip.

"Do you feel like continuing with your story while we eat?" She was giving her plate a good swiping with some rye bread.

"I would like to, but I don't want to talk with my mouth full. I didn't realize how hungry I was."

"Me too!"

They ate and sopped and sipped. "May we talk in between mouthfuls, about what you've already told me so far?"

"Absolutely."

"Did you and your brothers and sisters stay at the orphanage for the whole five years?"

"We did. But the time went by much quicker than expected."

"Really? I'd have thought time would have dragged. How was it adjusting to living at the orphanage?"

"It was not as difficult as you might imagine or as we feared it would be. If my sister and I hadn't had Sal and Diana and Uncle Samuel, then it would have surely been an excruciating time. Although it saddened us to have to leave Shedaker School, and our teachers and friends, there still were children at the orphanage who were there when Sal and Diana had come to live with us. So, it wasn't like we knew no one."

"And you still saw your father occasionally, right?"

"We saw him more than occasionally. He made sure to see us on every delivery day. He never missed a Sunday to take us to church. He never missed a birthday."

"Did you ever go home to visit?"

"After church, we would go home and have dinner together as a family. We missed Heidi, too, and it was good to play with her."

"Oh, Heidi. She must have missed you guys."

"Yes, and we missed her, too. Heidi was my father's companion for the five years he spent alone in the house. He said that when my mother died, Heidi went through a depression. She really loved my mother. My mother took care of that dog like she was her own child. Heidi would always walk with my father out to the peach orchard and lie right over my mother's grave while he sat against the tree."

"What a good dog. I love dogs. But with my job, having a dog isn't really logical."

"Maybe one day you will change your line of work. I didn't think you wanted to work on the railroad *all the live long day* forever."

She laughed. "Thanks, now that song is going to be stuck in my head all the live long day." She hummed the tune to *I've been working on the railroad*... "Oh, jeez, that's really going to stick."

"Sorry about that." He chuckled. "I could sing the first verse from the *Gilligan's Island* or *The Brady Bunch* themes if you want me to change the record in your head."

She bowed her head and palmed her forehead with both hands. "Oh, dear God, no." She looked back up at the smirking Hagen, gave him that *thanks a lot* look. "Gee, thanks, now all three are fighting it out in my head."

"Oops, sorry. Would you like me to sing...?"

She put up a hand, palm facing him as in *STOP!* "NO... no, thank you. I think you've helped the cause enough. Could we just go on? Hopefully, the cacophony will fade."

"Yes, let's go on." He hummed the first few notes of *The Brady Bunch* theme, holding back a giggle, and pursing his lips.

"Evil, just evil." She shook her head, paused a moment to take a breath, then went on. "OK, so you went home after church on Sundays for dinner. Was that the only time you went home? What about holidays?"

"We spent Christmases at home, but my father would spend Thanksgivings at the orphanage with us and the other children."

"What about birthdays?"

"We celebrated our birthdays with the other children at the orphanage as well. It was my father's idea. We wanted to go home for our birthdays, but my father asked us how we would feel if we had no one, or no place to go, and had to watch other children leaving to go home. We were already spending Sundays and Christmases away from the orphanage. There were many children whose parents rarely, if ever, came to see them. When someone would come to visit, it was always heart-breaking when they had to leave. Visitations always ended in tears, and it would put the other children in somber moods. I think it was easier for some of the parents not to come at all, because leaving their child again and again was so difficult. The longer a child was there, the less frequently some parents came to see them."

"The lesser of two evils, sort of?"

"I guess you could put it that way. More like the lesser of two heartaches." Hagen closed his eyes as memories floated through his mind.

Emily saw a pained, worried look come across his face. "Are you alright?" He didn't say anything; his expression remained the same. "Hagen?"

He opened his eyes, his expression softened; his eyes were a little wetter. "I'm here."

"You weren't for a moment. Where did you go?" She put her fork down.

"I was back at the orphanage, remembering some of our friends. Their sadness, their despondency. It really had an effect on me. But I did my best to help them through it."

"How?"

He shrugged slightly, gave her a look that said *I don't really know.* "I would sit with them, talk to them. Put my arm around them. Tell them everything would be alright, that they were safe, they have friends, they have me and Uncle Samuel. I have always been able to make people feel at ease, more comfortable, calm during stressful times."

"I can attest to that." She raised her glass to him and took a sip of beer.

"Yes, I guess you can." He raised his glass and sipped his beer. "We could tell how some of the other children felt when my father came to see us. They weren't jealous, just sad that their family didn't visit them as well. And, of course, there were those who had no parents at all. We were the only children who saw a parent so frequently. We never bragged or rubbed their noses in it." He held up a hand and wagged an index finger. "Mm-mm. We didn't want to do that to our friends. So, on our birthdays my father enlisted the help of Lorraine Varsaci, and some of the other local ladies, to bake enough cakes so everyone could have a piece. He would supply the necessary ingredients, and they would bake and bake and bake."

"How many children were at the orphanage when you were there?"

"Between ninety to one hundred. It varied slightly depending on when some arrived and when some left."

"That's a lot of cake!"

"It was a lot of cake. I'll never forget that first birthday. It was September 12—Sal's eighth. My father arrived with the Sterling full of boxes of cakes. It was a Monday, and everyone stood at the windows watching. It took Papa and

Uncle Samuel I don't know how many trips back and forth from the truck to the kitchen. They were both grinning ear to ear the whole time, and so were we. He overestimated how much to bring. We had enough cake for three days."

"I bet the kids loved it."

He nodded and smiled. "Oh, they did, we *all* did. And when the party was over and my father had to leave, there were no tears, just smiles and hugs. Papa became Uncle Georg at the orphanage after that first birthday party. All the children loved our Papa, their Uncle Georg. He wanted all the children to be happy. He was quite fond of the orphanage and the children. We were so proud of our Papa."

"I'd have been proud, too. So, every birthday, for five years, was celebrated there?" She ate another forkful of cabbage roll.

"Yes, every one of them."

"Five parties, five truckloads of cake. The neighbor ladies didn't mind?"

"No, they looked forward to it, actually. Some of them would come to help set up for the party. It did their souls good to see the joy that they helped bring to the children. Oh, and it was four parties—don't forget Mathilde and Diana share the same birthday."

"Oh, that's right."

"Now, you know my father had become quite attached to the children, and they to him. But he always wanted to do more for them. The following summer, my father had another idea. It was August 1933, just before school started. He wanted to have a picnic at the farm for the whole orphanage."

"That sounds like a lot more involved than a truck full of cakes."

"It was. But Papa made it happen. Uncle Samuel arranged to have all the children taken to our farm for the day. School buses from surrounding schools pitched in to transport us. Everyone got to see the animals. Peggy Marter brought her horses and gave horseback rides. It was a community effort. My father, he had a way with people, got all the neighbors and farmers to pitch in. They brought their tractors and wagons for the hayrides. Everyone brought their families and food. There was a weenie roast, and there were marshmallows to toast over the big bonfire. People from St. Paul and the Methodist Churches came. It was an all-day affair. I will never forget that day. I watched my father walking around like the mayor as he greeted everyone, making them all feel welcome. It wasn't until years later that I found out that my father had an ulterior motive."

Emily swallowed a half-chewed mouthful. "Ulterior motive?"

"Yes. He really did want to have the picnic so the children could have some fun away from the orphanage. And he wanted it to be a community effort. But Papa was a smart man. He knew that when the children were at the orphanage, they acted differently in front of strangers than when they were at the farm. They were at their very natural best, they had fun, and were themselves at the farm. No one knew, not even Uncle Samuel, that these summer picnics were really child adoption fairs in disguise."

"Adoption fairs?"

"Yes. Three children were adopted after meeting new families at the first picnic."

"Three adoptions. That's amazing. Wait, picnics—plural?" She held her beer glass in mid-flight from the table to her lips.

"Yes, picnics, plural. The first one was so much fun, not only for the children but for everyone who was involved, that it became a tradition. It gave all the farmers and neighbors and church parishioners something to feel good about during a time in history where there was not a lot to feel good about. And I think that it proved to my father that his idea worked. Every August, the summer fest at our farm is a highly anticipated event."

Emily took a sip of her beer. "Wait, *is highly anticipated?*"

"Yes, it continued after we left the orphanage and still does to this day; every August on the Saturday before school begins. It has become known as the Annual Beckenbauer Fest."

"Wait... your father... he's not still...?"

"Oh, no, my dear. If my father were still alive, he would be..." He did some quick math in his head. "...one hundred and three. He passed away in 1983; he was eighty-eight. We buried him next to our mother in the peach orchard."

"I assume that's where you're taking Sal." Her eyes softened as she looked into his.

"Yes, he's to be buried next to his parents."

"*His* parents... you mean *your* parents."

"His parents, as in the Cristoforos."

"The Cristoforos? I thought they were in a cemetery somewhere north of you, near where they lived?"

"They were buried in Hoboken when they died, that is correct." He waited for her enquiry. She just looked at him with an *and?* expression, waiting for him to explain. "My father told me years later, after the war, why Sal's parents were moved to our family cemetery. At my mother's funeral, he had observed Sal and Diana as they watched everything that was happening, and it dawned on him that he would be able to visit his wife's grave whenever he wanted. His children, his biological children, would be able to visit their mother's grave whenever they wanted. But Sal and Diana could not easily go to their parents' graves. They would never be able to pay their respects unless they drove to North

269

Jersey, quite a drive at that time. After my mother's funeral service, Papa had a talk with Father Kelly about having the Cristoforos exhumed and re-buried on our land. Father Kelly told Bishop Scully and Cardinal Bevilacqua the whole story. They arranged the exhumation and Father Kelly performed their burial service on the farm in the peach orchard."

"Your father... what a great guy. What did Sal and Diana think about their parents being moved?"

"At the time, they were happy to be closer to their mother and father. They hadn't forgotten about them, although visions of them and some memories had faded. Later in life, they understood what it had taken to accomplish something like that, and they were able to truly appreciate what my father and the church had done."

Emily forked another golumpki onto his plate, then one on hers.

"Thank you. You read my mind."

"I didn't read your mind. I read your face. I saw you eyeing them." Her smile was warm and sincere and without any sarcasm. "Go on with your story, don't let me interrupt you."

"My brother Karl took over the farm, and the responsibility of the annual picnic, when my father grew old and tired. And now one of his sons, Karl Jr., helps to run the farm, and consequently, the picnics."

"That is so lovely."

"Since the Annual Beckenbauer Fest began in 1933, one hundred and ninety-two children have met new parents."

"Oh my, that's wonderful." She dabbed at the tears in her eyes. "Did your father ever admit to his *ulterior motive*?"

"The closest I ever got to a confession was a smile once when I asked him about it. That's how I knew. It's not easy to lie to me. He knew that. He said yes with only his smile, technically keeping his secret to himself. He never wanted accolades for what he did, and I never gave his secret away—well, not when he was alive."

That did it. She couldn't hold back, and the tears flowed. "Oh, great, here I go again!"

He reached across the table and patted her hand. "Are you alright, my dear?"

With her other hand, she caught her tears with a paper towel. "Yeah, just peachy, thanks. Don't worry about me." She dried the tears. He waited a few moments and sipped some of his beer.

She composed herself, then went on with her questions. "And when you and your brothers and sisters came home from the orphanage, was there a big celebration?"

"No, it was a quiet reunion, just family. My father wanted us all to himself, and we felt the same way."

"I assume that you went back to your old school again, too."

"Yes, everything went back to the way it was before we left, except we were five years older and my mother wasn't there. We all missed her so very much, but we went on. After we settled back into our own home we helped on the farm. The old Sterling was retired from regular use and was used mainly for carrying crops from the fields and orchards. We all learned how to drive in that old truck. My father bought a second truck and a second tractor. Sal sure loved to ride the tractor." He paused, closed his eyes, and smiled for the memory.

She watched his face again as his mind traveled somewhere. No furrowed brow, no frown. Just a contented, easy smile, peaceful. She didn't interrupt this time. It was obviously a pleasant journey, and she waited for him to come back on his own.

When he opened his eyes, he stared off into the distance as if he was getting one last look. When he broke his stare at the fading memory, he turned his eyes to Emily, who was smiling as she watched him. "I did it again?"

"Yep, you went away. I let you go this time; you looked happy." She clasped her hands and rested her chin on her hammocked fingers, elbows on the table.

"I have so many memories. I relish them, all of them, the good and the not so good. They are all I have now. They make me who I am. When you are young, you don't realize that you are accumulating your *real* treasure, and that it is being stockpiled away in a big chest that you will open at the other end of your life, to keep you company when your company leaves. No matter how rich or poor you may become, you will always have your memories. So, my dear, make good ones now. Bad memories make for lonely futures."

"I think I am making some good ones right now."

"I believe we both are." His blue eyes twinkled like sapphires.

They both eyed the last two golumpkis and read each other's faces.

"I don't think I can eat another one," said Emily as she sat back into the banquette, rubbing her stomach.

"Saving room for dessert?" asked Hagen as he buttered two slices of rye bread. He put a piece on her plate, then started to sop up the remaining red sauce on his plate.

"Gee, thanks, dad." She looked at the piece of buttered bread then at him.

"Hmm?" He *hmm'd* through the piece of sopped bread he was chewing.

"I said, '*gee, thanks, dad.'* You buttered my bread." She picked up her bread. "Do you always butter other people's bread for them?"

He stopped chewing, then swallowed, realizing he'd done something that he used to do for Sal. He looked at the bread, then at her, and shrugged a little. "Force of habit, I guess, sorry." He put down his fork and sat upright. The golumpkis, the beer, the company; they conjured memories that triggered an unstoppable emotional response. His nostrils flared. His lips quivered. "I miss him terribly." He covered his mouth with his hand and sobbed deeply. His elbow landed on the table, causing his fork to fall off of his plate and the beer to ripple in their glasses.

Emily went around and scooched in next to him and put her right arm around him. She said nothing. Nothing seemed appropriate.

Just let this gentle soul release.

She held him with one arm as she wiped her own tears away with the other hand.

Hagen composed himself after a few minutes and sat upright. Taking a deep breath, "Whew. That was unexpected. Would you mind getting me a couple more paper towels?"

"Sure." She got up and pulled a couple of feet of paper towels from the dispenser on the counter and handed them to him.

"Thank you." He separated one of the towels, wiped his face, and then blew his nose. "I apologize if I dampened the dinner mood."

"Apologize? For having feelings? OK, Mister," she wagged her index finger at him. "You handed me some non-negotiable ground rules to work with if I was going to stay with you for this trip. Remember?"

"I remember. And so far, you've followed them remarkably well. There might even be a little extra something in your next pay check."

"Smart ass." She sat back down in her seat across from him. "My non-negotiable rule, and you must abide by this rule if you want me to hang around, is that you should never

273

hide your feelings in front of me and never, ever, apologize for having them. Can you handle that, Mister Smarty Pants?"

"My, you certainly do have a way with words. Yes, I can handle that." He dabbed his eyes again.

"Good. Like you said," her voice softened as she folded her arms on the table and leaned in, "we are going to be spending a lot of time together putting this family history of yours into book form. You must feel as uninhibited around me as I am becoming around you."

"Thank you, Emily."

"And Hagen?" She reached across the table and patted his arm.

"Yes?"

"You can butter my bread whenever you want."

He rolled his eyes and smiled. "Thank you," he said, and wiped a small rise of tears away again.

"OK," she sat upright. "When is the next train picking us up?"

He dabbed his eyes with the paper towel and looked at his watch. "At eight-thirty; we have about an hour."

"Alright, I'm going to put these leftovers back into the dish in the fridge and I'll do the dishes later."

"And we can have some dessert and coffee on the patio."

"Exactly. What's for dessert, anyway?"

"Well, there is a key lime pie and a cheesecake in the refrigerator. I can go either way. What sounds good to you?"

"They kind of go well with each other. My mom used to make a key lime cheesecake that was simply divine. I say a sliver of each. OK?"

"OK! Sounds *simply divine.* I'll make us a couple of nice, fat espressos. I don't want us to doze off again."

"Good idea." She retrieved the two desserts from the refrigerator and put slices of each side-by-side on two plates, while Hagen made the espresso.

She looked at the cups he was using. "You weren't kidding when you said *fat espressos*. I don't think I've ever had an espresso that big."

He looked at the slices of key lime pie and cheesecake she'd put on their plates. "Uh-huh, and that is your idea of a sliver? I can only imagine what your normal slice looks like."

"I'm just helping you make room in your fridge."

He patted his stomach. "And less room for my belt."

They laughed like old friends, their comfortableness not going unnoticed by each other. While Hagen finished making the oversized espressos, Emily gathered forks and clean napkins.

"Do you have a serving tray, or something that I could use to carry everything in one trip?"

"Under the cabinet next to the refrigerator you should find a tray, on its side next to some cutting boards."

She went to the cabinet and found a rectangular, silver tray and put it on the counter. She put the desserts, coffees, forks, and napkins on it, then picked it up. "OK, lead the way."

"Right this way, milady."

Emily followed him from the kitchen to the other end of the railcar. He opened his bedroom door and she followed him inside. He turned on more lights. She looked around at the furnishings and the artworks on the wall.

"More of your paintings?"

"Yes, the paintings are mine. The photographs are Sal's."

"Very nice work. He had a good eye. I really like these candid photos of the Native Americans."

"He had a passion for Native Americans and their causes. He did a lot of work with them."

Then she noticed that one of the larger black and white photographs looked very much like Hagen's painting on the wall over the dining room. She stared at it, cocking her head to one side.

"Yes, it is the painting in the dining room," said Hagen. "Sal took that photo from the west side, over near the volcanoes, in 1962, and I loved it so much that I painted it. I like his photograph better. His black and white is more dramatic."

"How come you didn't hang this in the dining room instead?"

He chuckled. "Because Sal liked my painting better and insisted that I hang it on the wall in the dining room. I always had a difficult time saying no to him." He sighed then looked from the photograph back to her. "Come, let's go sit down before we start moving again."

He opened the sliding door for her, and she went outside first and admired what she saw. It was like a small living room. To the right was a three-sided leather sectional, upholstered in the same leather as the sofas inside. It went along the wall that separated the patio from Hagen's bedroom, then along the left and end walls. Draped over the back of each section was a woven Navajo blanket. She put the tray down on the square mahogany coffee table in the nook made by the three sides of the sectional. There was a leather wingback recliner, like the ones in the living room, against the end wall, separated from the end of the sectional by a small table.

Hagen picked up the remote control from the little table and sat in the sectional with his back to his room. Emily handed him a plate of desserts, a fork and a napkin, then picked up her own and sat in the corner of the sectional to his right.

"Thank you. Let's have some fresh air, shall we?" He pushed a button on the remote, and all the windows descended into the walls. The February-cold Chicago air fell in on them as the windows opened. "That might be a bit much."

"Maybe a tad." She put her plate on the coffee table, pulled the blanket off the back of the sectional, and put it around her.

Using the remote, he raised the windows back up to about six inches from closed. "That's better."

"Much better. I really love this patio. The electric windows are very cool. Now all you need is a fireplace."

Hagen pressed another button on the remote, and against the right corner, from the floor, there arose a gas fireplace. After it ascended to its endpoint, thirty seconds passed, then it lit automatically.

"Ask and ye shall receive." He put the remote down and took a forkful of key lime pie and looked at her gawking face. "Earth to Emily."

"Uh-huh, more like Planet Hagen to Emily. You and your gadgets." She shook her head, forked a bit of each dessert into her mouth, and shook her head slowly.

"I do like my devices, this is true. Another of my patents, by the way." He reached out to pick up his espresso and took a big sip.

"I kind of figured. Any other patents on your train you want to tell me about?" She took a sip of her espresso. "Oh, this is good. I'll be awake for a while."

"I hope so. I'd like to get through everything tonight. And, nothing you can see. The newer diesel-electric engines utilize some electrical relays that I designed. They have also begun installing my transmissions in the newer models. I redesigned the mechanisms that connect the cars together. Oh, and the trucks, the things that the wheels are connected to that the car rides on, I designed a better suspension system for them which reduces the rocking and rolling. I have degrees in electrical and mechanical engineering, and I specialized in trains."

"Well, that explains it." She gave him a *that figures* look. "Does this car have that special suspension?"

"Yes, this one does. They are using my design when they build new railcars."

"I noticed the ride was so smooth."

"That's the beauty of my electromagnetic suspension. Anyway, enough about my inventions. Help me again, where did I leave off?"

"You were at the point where you and your brothers and sisters were going home."

"That's right. Let's pick up from there…"

Beverly, New Jersey
March 1937

As Karl's fifth birthday approached, Georg's children were counting down the days. Not because it was Karl's birthday, but because to them, March 9, 1937, marked the day when they would be going home; not just on Christmases and Sundays after church, but home for good. It marked the end of the five years that their father and Uncle Samuel said that they had to live at the orphanage. Georg wanted his children home with him as much as they wanted to be home. But Karl turned five in the middle of a school year. And their father did say, "until Karl is old enough to go to school." When Hagen had made the calculations, he didn't factor into his equation that there would be three months of school left when his baby brother turned five. Karl wouldn't be attending school until that fall. Logically, it would have been better for them to finish the school year at the orphanage, then go home and start a fresh new year, all five of them, at Shedaker School in September. Logic and children go together only when it means the outcome goes in their favor, and they didn't favor staying away from home any longer than they thought that they needed to. Now, don't get me wrong. Living at the orphanage wasn't all that awful for them. They never felt abandoned by their father. They made lots of friends. They had become well-admired by everyone, staff and fellow residents alike, as was Uncle Georg. And they knew there was an endpoint on the horizon, a finite time to their stay. It took some convincing, and of course Hagen had to calm his siblings, to talk them into staying until school ended. So, the date of departure was moved from Karl's birthday to the last day of school, and when that day came, they were packed and ready to go.

On June 8, 1937, the Beckenbauer children said goodbye to living at the orphanage, but not goodbye to their friends. They would of course visit often and would see them at the annual picnics on the farm. Many of them remained in touch for the rest of their lives.

When they got home, Heidi was there to greet them, along with Ethel Osterman. Ethel wanted to do something special for them, for their homecoming. She knew Georg wanted no fanfare, but she wanted it to still be special for them. So, she made a nice roasted turkey dinner, and when the family was all settled at the table, Ethel said her goodbyes and left Georg and his family to themselves to enjoy their June Thanksgiving.

The next few years saw the recession of 1937-38, then an economic turnaround in 1939, resulting in an end to the Great Depression. The economy slowly stabilized, and although it wasn't near its pre-depression greatness, everyone at the farm and around the nation breathed a little easier.

Europe, on the other hand, wasn't breathing well at all. Adolf Hitler and the Nazi party had come to power in 1933, and the letters that Georg received from Marta's sister, Mathilde, grew worrisome. She and her family did not like the path down which the Nazi dictator was taking Germany. The Schlessingers were in no way anti-Semitic, and feared reprisal for not supporting the new regime or becoming members of the Nazi Party. The devastation of the last war still haunted their memories. Mathilde would never stop loving Georg's brother Hagen or forget the image of the twins returning home in boxes. As the Depression in America ended, the war in Europe officially began with the Nazi invasion of Poland in 1939. After that, the letters from Germany became less frequent. The last one from Mathilde sounded stiff and matter of fact, very impersonal. She had signed it *Heil Hitler*. It was a complete turnaround from her previous letters. Georg sensed that she was fearing Nazi censorship of mail leaving Germany and understood that mail entering Germany might also be censored. By November 1939, all correspondence between Georg and his wife's family had ceased.

Georg had watched his children grow up into fine young adults. Diana and Mathilde were becoming young women. Boys were being noticed, and boys were noticing the girls in return. The girls were always best friends—unless they had their eyes on the same boy. Then civil unrest ensued, but it never lasted long enough to cause any permanent rifts. They were sisters first and foremost, and always would be.

Hagen and Sal were filling out in boy-ways themselves and stirred the local girls to swooning. Working on the farm had its physical advantages. Hagen grew tall, lean, muscular and as handsome as his father; almost the spitting image of Georg when he was Hagen's age. He ran track when he entered high school and took advantage of his family's farmland to practice running. His efforts at home helped his team become district champions his junior and senior years. Sal didn't grow as tall as Hagen, but he was no runt, either. At five-foot-nine, he was almost the same weight as six-foot-one Hagen. With broad shoulders and muscular arms and legs, he made a great addition to the Burlington High School football and wrestling teams. With Sal as their quarterback, the team won the state championship his senior year, and the wrestling team made it to the state finals with Sal as one of their best athletes.

Both boys were aware that they were the objects of many a young girl's attention. Hagen feigned interest but kept a gentlemanly distance. His soul belonged to Sal from the moment he saw him on the swing in the courtyard, and as he matured, his heart followed suit. Sal, feigning the same interest, let the girls get a little closer, but not too close. He harmlessly flirted, but never let anything get too serious. It drove Hagen crazy when he'd see a cheerleader fawning all over Sal after a football game. Sal knew this, and never let it go too far. Although he loved Hagen, his savior, his hero from day one, he wasn't as comfortable keeping too much of a distance from the girls. They both knew that it was something they needed to hide, but Sal felt that he needed to not play as hard to get as Hagen, in order to keep up appearances.

Karl was the free spirit of the bunch. His gentle demeanor and kind ways had some of the parishioners at St. Paul Church believing that he might one day become a priest. His compassion for mankind and animals alike was remarkable. When he was old enough, he did become an altar boy, but that was the extent of his tenure in the church. His love for animals and farming led him to follow in his father's footsteps and eventually take over the farm.

Besides growing into who they were becoming physically, the children were also realizing their abilities and aspirations.

Georg and Marta had known early on that Hagen had an innate talent for drawing. As he got older, he developed his skills and evolved from crayon to pencil to watercolor and oils. His artistic abilities earned him a scholarship to a prestigious art school in Philadelphia.

Hagen was tested at school and it was found that his IQ topped out at 177, although you would never have known it to talk to him. He seemed like your average, everyday high school kid. It was his genius intelligence that earned him the other scholarship; to MIT. He loved his art, but he was also passionate about knowing how and why things worked, and he let the art scholarship go to the next in line, Scotty Reed. Hagen enjoyed helping to fix the motor on the tractor with his father. And he was always trying to figure a way to make something work better. His passion for trains grew from watching them pass by on the tracks near the farm. He would later become an inventor, using his talents in electrical and mechanical engineering to design new technologies for trains, while at the same time making a small fortune.

Sal was drawn to photography from the very first time a photographer came to the school to take class photos. The shape of the camera, the film, the flash; they mesmerized him, and he asked the photographer a hundred and one questions the whole time he was shooting. The photographer didn't mind, and he answered Sal's questions with pleasure. For Sal's sixteenth birthday, Hagen bought him his first camera; a Rolleiflex TLR that he'd spied in the window of a pawn shop in Riverside; it was barely used fallout of the Depression. Sal took that camera and ran with it, taking pictures that would find their way into his yearbook, local newspapers, and National Geographic; yes, National Geographic. He entered a contest for amateur photographers and submitted a picture that he'd shot of one of their cows. A chicken was perched on the cow's back, looking down at Heidi, who was looking back up at the chicken. The cow was staring right at the camera. In the background, Georg was driving the old Fordson tractor with Karl standing on the hood, with his arms spread like wings. None of it was planned. It was entirely candid and impromptu. The prize was one hundred dollars, and his photograph featured in the September '41 issue.

Diana adored music. She loved it when Hagen dragged the family up to the balcony at church. She watched the organist with as much enthusiasm as Hagen had when he was younger. But it was the piano that really called to her. She loved to sit next to the music teacher at the orphanage and turn the pages for her. When Diana and her brothers and sister returned home to live, she asked her Papa if she could take piano lessons. They didn't have a piano, but she didn't care. She wanted to take lessons anyway. The orphanage's piano teacher gave her lessons at her home. Her pay was a dozen eggs, a quart of milk, and a hug per lesson. Diana did so well at learning to play without a piano at home, that Georg bought a piano—at the same pawn shop where Hagen had found Sal's camera. She studied education and music at Rutgers University, and eventually became the music teacher at Riverside High School and taught private piano lessons at home.

Mathilde was enamored by doctors and medicine. When she was old enough to know what she wanted to be when she grew up, she would tell everyone that she wanted to be a doctor. She became a volunteer at Zurbrugg Hospital, where she assisted with feeding patients, and performing light, non-medical duties. Dr. Small took her under his wing and mentored her. She studied hard and became the valedictorian of her high school graduating class of 1944. She attended Bryn Mawr College under a full scholarship, where she graduated with the highest distinction with a double major in philosophy and biology. She then went on to the University of Pennsylvania's Perelman School of Medicine, again under a full scholarship, and became the first female obstetric surgeon in the tri-state area.

And Karl, as we know, kept with the family tradition and became a farmer like his father, maintaining the farm and handing it down to his own children.

The Beckenbauers had survived the Great Depression, the death of Marta, a five-year separation, and had come through as a strong, loving family. Nothing in life is perfect. Of course, like any other family with five children, there would be squabbles and tiffs. But this family was a tight-knit unit held together by an unbreakable bond. Their love and faith kept them alive and sane in some of the darkest times of their lives.

Fate was about to put them to the test, again.

While the Nazis were infesting Europe, Japan was wreaking havoc on the other side of the world. It invaded China in 1937 and was working its way around the Pacific in an effort to dominate and rule all of Asia. In 1939, the United States renounced its trade treaty with Japan, and in 1940 imposed a ban on aviation fuel. These actions angered Japan and hurt its financial stability. It all came to a head in late 1941.

Beverly, New Jersey
December 7, 1941

Around the beginning of November, Hagen and Sal were scheming. They wanted to do something really special for their sisters' fifteenth birthdays. It was common knowledge that the girls were beginning to outgrow their room. They'd shared the same bedroom, as had Sal and Hagen, since Diana and Sal came to live at the farm in 1930. The boys didn't mind. They just didn't have as much *stuff* as the girls did. The girls didn't complain terribly, but the boys and Georg could sense that they needed to express their individuality. Hagen and Sal ran their plan by their father, and he thought it was a brilliant idea, so they put it into motion.

The third-floor attic was essentially one big room, with windows at each end and three windowed dormers on each side. There wasn't a lot of stuff stored up there—Christmas decorations, Sal and Diana's chest, and some odds and ends. The boys, with the help of their father, secretly built a wall at one end of the attic, with two doors, thus creating a storage room and a closet, then moved everything into the storage room. They scoured the local furniture and pawn shops for bedroom furniture—a dresser, chest of drawers and a couple side tables—and put them up in the attic. Then, they waited.

The Beckenbauers woke up to a sunny yet cold and breezy day that Sunday. It was not unlike any other December Sunday, except, it was December 7—Mathilde and Diana's fifteenth birthday. The girls were giddy. There was going to be a party, and they were so excited because this was the first birthday party that was going to include boys; not just any boys, but *boyfriends*.

Mathilde's beau was Chris Moyer. He was sixteen, from Delanco, and was his school's star wrestler. That's how they met. It was October, and the match was at Delanco. Sal had just shown Chris no mercy and had taken down Delanco's *number one*. On their way to their cars after the match, the Beckenbauers' and the Moyers' paths crossed in the parking lot. The two boys shook hands. Chris congratulated Sal. And then Mathilde spoke to him. She said, "good match."
WHAM!
Cupid shot an arrow into Chris with a thousand times more force than Sal used to take him down on the mat; you could have knocked him over with a feather. Cupid didn't need to shoot anything at Mathilde. He'd already taken care of that during the match. He had sat on her shoulder, directing her eyes to Chris before Sal had even begun to take him down. The only thing Cupid needed to do was ride on her shoulder until he could get a good shot at Chris. Cupid's buddy, Fate, helped with the *coincidental* crossing of paths in the parking lot.

Diana's beau was Kenny Storer. He was also sixteen, but from Burlington. They went to the same high school, but had never really noticed each other, or had the chance to. Kenny was a year ahead of her, and the grades stayed to themselves, mostly. One day, after school, Diana was playing piano for the auditions for the school musical. The choice that year was *I Married An Angel*. Kenny was up next, and he was going to sing *Stairway to the Stars*. He walked up onto the stage and handed his music to Diana without looking down at her. She barely looked up at him, just took the music from him and set it up on the tall, upright Ludwig & Co. piano, then commented to herself, *God, this again.*

This is the sixth guy to use this today. I think I could play this one with my eyes closed. The director and music teacher, Mr. Murray, gave her the cue to begin. She closed her eyes and started to play. *Yep, I can play this with my eyes closed.* Then Kenny began to sing. Diana's eyes popped wide open. It was as if she had heard the voice of an angel. Kenny's voice was velvety smooth, his phrasing perfect. She peeked around the piano to see who it was. It was as if she'd seen him for the very first time. *Kenny Storer?* She missed a note and he looked over and caught her peeking at him.

THWANG!

Cupid got two lovebirds with one arrow. Kenny smiled, then turned and walked over to the piano and finished singing the song, *to her.*

Oh, my, God. What is he doing?

She turned nine shades of red. Her hands got sweaty and her fingers started to slip on the keys. When the song was over, Kenny bowed to Mr. Murray, then turned to walk off stage. He stopped at the piano. "Thanks, Diana."

He knows my name?

He flashed a big smile, his green eyes twinkling in the stage lights.

"You're welcome." That's all she could muster. Then he walked off stage and disappeared through the auditorium doors. But not before he turned, looked over his left shoulder and gave her a wink. After that they were inseparable. She helped him rehearse for the part. Yes, he got the lead in the musical. After they had seen him perform, all the girls would say that he was *dreamy* like Sinatra and started calling him *Old Green Eyes.*

Anyway…

That Sunday, Hagen and Sal feigned having bad colds and played hooky from church. Their father was in on the ruse but made them promise to go to confession for skipping church. The girls were afraid that their brothers being sick would affect their party. The boys were supposed to help set up for it. Georg, Karl and the girls left for church, and the boys waited for the troops. Chris and Kenny were dropped off by their dads, and Lorraine Varsaci dropped off her son Luigi Jr. and his cousin Francis along with two enormous birthday cakes—one with lavender icing, Diana's favorite color, and the other with Mathilde's favorite, a light green icing.

Then the boys got to work. Hagen and Sal's beds were moved up to the attic, and Mathilde's bed moved to the boys' room. They painted each of the rooms one of the girls' favorite colors. Chris's dad owned a hardware store in Pennsauken and let them have the paint and brushes. After the painting was finished, they all went downstairs and decorated for the party, of course using the birthday girls' favorite colors.

After church, Diana and Mathilde were eager to get home and start getting ready for the party, which was to start at two o'clock. It was now close to eleven, and Georg wanted to delay getting home as long as he could, to give the boys enough time to finish their project. He stopped at the bakery to get some bread to go with Sal's meatballs, much to the dismay of the girls, who were having serious conniption fits. Then when he wanted to stop at Woodward's Feed Store, they went into hysterics. Georg gave in. The birthday girls were ranting about Hagen and Sal being sick and how they wouldn't be able to help and all the other kids who were coming and nothing was going to be ready... *deep breath*.

When Georg turned off Delanco Road on to Perkins Lane, the girls calmed down. As they got closer to their driveway, they saw their mailbox in the distance. The post was wrapped in green and purple streamers. The mailbox looked like a big present, their last name completely covered by the colored streamers, with two big bows on top. Georg turned onto the driveway. Nearing the house, the girls could tell that their brothers had been busy; obviously they had faked being sick. When they got out of the car they stared, mouths wide open, at the very decorated porch. Streamers wrapped around the porch railings, and balloons hung from the porch roof. The girls almost started to cry as they stood there marveling at the sight. Georg nudged them to go inside before they froze.

When they went inside, they were greeted with more decorations, and balloons. They giggled and jumped up and down. Stretched over the mantle was a long banner that Hagen had made, of course using their colors that said, "HAPPY BIRTHDAYS!"

Georg was smiling, proud of what his sons had done. He couldn't wait to see what the upstairs looked like.

When they went into the kitchen, the birthday girls saw the two cakes on *Tableosaurus*, a big bowl of punch, dishes of purple and green candies, and a big pot simmering on the stove. Sal had become quite the cook, by the way—another one of his passions—and he wanted the party to have more than just cake and punch. So, the night before, he had made an enormous pot of sauce, meatballs, and Italian sausage. The kitchen looked and smelled delicious.

Who the girls didn't see were their brothers. It was obvious that they were not sick. They went upstairs and knocked on the boys' door.

"*Come ii-iin,*" said Hagen and Sal from the other side of the door. Then, they c*ough, cough, coughed,* still continuing the ruse of being sick.

When they opened the door, the girls were greeted by the smell of fresh paint and the sound of six teenage boys shouting *SURPRIIIIISE!*

Everyone jumped, even Karl and Georg.

"What's going on here?" asked Mathilde. She looked at the walls, sniffed the air. "Hey, why is your room purple?"

"It's lavender," said Kenny. "It's Diana's favorite color. Go take a look at *your* room, Mathilde."

"*My* room?"

"Uh-huh," said Sal. "This is Diana's. You two have your own rooms now."

Mathilde ran to their old shared room and opened the door. Inside, she found the room painted light green. She started to cry. She couldn't believe what she was seeing.

"Aw, gee Mathilde, don't cry," said Chris. "Don'tcha like it?"

She looked at him, then at everyone else. "I love it. I absolutely love it."

Everyone had now gone into Mathilde's room. Diana joined her sister and they hugged. "What do you think, Di?" asked Mathilde.

"I don't know, Maddy, I kinda like this room better." She winked at Mathilde.

"Yeah, now that you mention it, I kinda like the boy's room better. Should we ask them to paint them over again?"

They looked at the six boys, who were now staring wide-eyed with their mouths agape. Georg was biting his lip to stifle a giggle.

"Just kidding, boys," said Mathilde.

"Yeah, you can close your mouths now," said Diana. "We love it, we really do. Thank you."

"Yes, thank you," said Mathilde. Then each boy got a kiss on the cheek from the girls. Even the Varsaci cousins, their cheeks already warm and blushed by the time the girls got to them.

"But where are you two going to sleep?" asked Mathilde.

"Oh," said Hagen. "We moved our stuff into Karl's room and moved him out to the barn with the cows."

Karl stared up at Hagen, then his father, then his sisters, then back to his father.

"Well, you are the youngest," said Georg, going along with the joke. "It was either that or the chicken coop."

Karl ran out of the room almost in tears. He threw his door open only to find that nothing had changed.

"Sal and I moved up to the attic," Hagen told the girls.

Karl stomped back to Mathilde's room with his arms crossed. "That was mean, you guys."

Everyone was giggling, except Karl. Diana leaned down and kissed him on the top of his head. "Yes, Karl, that was very mean. And just because of that, you get the biggest piece of cake."

Well, *that* changed his mood really fast. Karl's frown turned into a smile. He unfolded his arms, put his thumb to his nose and wiggled his fingers at the older boys, *thpthpthpthp'd*, then walked out of the room and went downstairs into the kitchen, sat down at the table and mapped out his piece of cake.

"Alright, girls," said Georg. He looked at his watch. "It is almost twelve-thirty. Your guests will be arriving in an hour and a half."

The girls were still dressed for church. The boys had already cleaned themselves up and dressed for the party. Chris, Kenny and the Varsaci boys had also changed, having brought their better clothes with them.

Hagen looked at his sisters. He looked them up and down. "You're not going to entertain your party guests dressed like that, are you?" he asked.

"What is that supposed to mean?" asked Diana, arms folded.

"Well," said Sal. "You don't really go with the theme."

The girls both put their hands on their hips.

"Excuse us?" said Mathilde.

"We can't be seen with girlfriends looking like *that* now, can we Kenny?" asked Chris.

"No way." Kenny folded his arms and shook his head.

"Well, I never!" said Diana, folding her arms back at him and stomping a foot.

Hagen took over before it could go too far. "What we are trying to say is, look in the closet."

The girls opened the closet door and hanging side-by-side were two new dresses, in their colors, and on the floor beneath them were matching shoes. Diana and Mathilde giggled with glee, jumped up and down and hugged each other, then the boys.

"Don't thank us," said Sal. "Thank Papa."

"Thank you, Papa," they said in unison as they gave him big squeezes.

"You are very welcome, my angels. Happy birthday."

The men left the ladies to get changed and went downstairs to await the arrival of the guests… and to keep Karl out of the cake. When the birthday girls came down the stairs all gussied up in their new dresses, they were greeted by whistles and applause. When the first car pulled up at twenty-till-two, Hagen and Sal retreated to the kitchen to put out the hot food and the bread, leaving the guests of honor and their beaus to greet their friends. By two-fifteen, all the guests had arrived. Uncle Samuel and his family showed up. Samuel and Ethel kept Georg company whilst the youngsters had fun. Sal's food was a hit. Steve Murphy brought his records and played disc-jockey on the old Victrola that Hagen had rescued from a junk pile and brought back to life.

At around two-thirty, everyone crowded into the kitchen around the big table. The birthday girls sat in front of their respective cakes and blew out the candles, after being serenaded by a quite harmonious rendition of "Happy Birthday." The cakes were cut. Karl got a nice piece of each and they all settled down somewhere, either standing or sitting in the living room. It was time to open the presents.

Diana and Mathilde could see that Chris and Kenny were just dying for them to open their presents first. The boys handed their girlfriends each a little box, wrapped too nicely to have been wrapped by a boy. *I bet their moms wrapped these,* thought Mathilde. When they removed the paper, they saw that they were each holding a little jewelry box with the same name on the tops: McElwie's Jewelers. The girls looked at each other, then the two boys looked at each other. When the girls opened the boxes, they found inside a little gold heart on a delicate gold chain.

"I thought I was going to get the necklace and you were going to get the bracelet," said Kenny.

"No, I was supposed to get the necklace and *you* were supposed to get the bracelet."

"Boys, boys," Diana cut them off. "We love them."

"We really do," said Mathilde. She handed her necklace to Chris then turned around so he could put it around her neck. Diana handed hers to Kenny and he did the same.

The girls spun around to show everyone their presents, then gave their boyfriends a big hug. The birthday girls had just sat down on one of the sofas to open more presents when there was a knock at the door.

Georg went to the door. When he opened it, he saw standing there with solemn expressions on their faces, Arthur McHugh and his wife, Sylvia. Their daughter Nancy was at the party.

"Hello Arthur, Sylvia. The party is not over yet. The girls just started opening their presents. Would you like to come in? Have some cake and coffee?"

"No, thank you, Georg," said Arthur. He peeked inside through the screen door and could see the girls on the couch smiling and laughing as they unwrapped gifts. *Sunrise Serenade* was playing on the old Victrola. "I assume you haven't heard yet."

"Heard what?"

Sylvia grabbed Arthur's hand. Her face was ashen. She looked absolutely terrified.

Hagen watched from the other side of the room. He couldn't hear them, but he could see through the screen door the postures and facial expressions of Mr. and Mrs. McHugh. They weren't smiling. Hagen looked over at Nancy, who was sitting cross-legged on the floor, holding a plate of cake, watching the birthday girls open gifts. Then his father went outside and closed the door behind him. Something wasn't right. Hagen walked over to the door and tried to hear what they were saying. He peeked around the curtains through the right sidelight. Mrs. McHugh was sobbing. Mr. McHugh was shaking his head, his arm around his wife. Hagen's father had his right palm planted on his forehead, his head was bowed and shaking slowly. Whatever was upsetting the McHughs, was also upsetting his father.

Hagen quickly moved away from the door when he saw his father turn. The door opened and the McHughs followed him inside. Hagen's heart was thumping in his chest. *Woah, something is really wrong.*

The teenagers turned to see who was coming in. Nancy stood up when she saw her parents standing near the door next to Mr. Beckenbauer. "Mom, Dad, you're early. The party isn't supposed to be over for another hour." Nancy saw her parents' expressions. "Mom, Dad, what's wrong?"

"Nancy, dear," said her mother. "You need to come home now. Mathilde, Diana, we're sorry to take Nancy home early."

"But Mom, why?" asked Nancy. She could see her mother had been crying and that her father did not look well; not at all like his normal happy-go-lucky self. He was always smiling, especially at parties.

"Georg," said Arthur. "You may as well tell them now. Some of the other parents are most likely on their way already to get their kids, too."

"Yes, I suppose you are right. Ladies, Gentlemen. I do not know how else to say this…" He cleared his throat. He was visibly shaken. Horrible memories of the last big war were taking the reins and causing his voice to waver. He looked around the room at the young men who were not old enough to go to war… not yet. He knew that if the United States entered into another military conflict, and it dragged on like The Great War, then some of these fine young men might grow into it, like his own brothers.

And may God help us all.

"…the Japanese have attacked Pearl Harbor, in Hawaii."

Gasps! Oh, no's! Oh, Gods! filled the room. Steve Murphy stopped the phonograph record. For many of these young people, *Sunrise Serenade* would forever invoke memories of that day.

Nancy's face immediately showed her panic as she ran into her parents' arms. All three were crying now, as were some of the teenagers, boys and girls alike. Not everyone knew, but many did, that Nancy's brother, the McHugh's only son, Artie, was in the Navy, and that he was stationed at Pearl Harbor. Artie McHugh was well-liked by everyone who knew him. He was smart, handsome, had his father's sense of humor. He had been a senior at Burlington High School when Sal and Hagen were freshmen. In the senior yearbook of 1938, was his picture, taken along with Mary-

Jo Halpern, and underneath their photo were their names and the title—*Funniest Boy and Girl.*

The phone rang. It was the first of the parents calling to relay, with fearful voices, the horrible news, and to say that they were coming early, *we are so very sorry,* to get their child. By three-thirty, all the guests had been picked up. Chris's and Kenny's parents stayed for a little longer, so their sons could console their girlfriends. Mathilde and Diana's day, their absolutely wonderful day that had started out to be the best birthday, ever, became the worst day, ever. It wouldn't be until several years after the Japanese surrendered, and the war was over, that their December 7th birthdays would be celebrated with any jubilance.

At the end of the driveway, Chris's father stopped the car so his son could get out and unwrap the mailbox. There would be no more celebrating that day. Samuel, Ethel, and their children stayed a little while longer. They helped take down the decorations that were supposed to remain up for at least a couple more days. Sal put the food and the rest of the cakes away in the refrigerator. When everything was cleaned up, they all sat around the living room and listened to the Zenith for news updates. At ten o'clock, the Ostermans went home. The Beckenbauers went to bed shortly after but didn't sleep well at all that night. Georg tossed and turned, worried for his family. He thought about Marta's family, stuck right in the middle of another world war, and he prayed for them, too.

The next morning, the children stayed home from school. Georg thought schools should have been closed, but they remained open. President Roosevelt was going to address Congress, and it was going to be broadcast on the radio. Georg felt it was important that they listen to him together. The nation stayed very close to their radios so they could hear Mr. Roosevelt address Congress. When war was officially declared on the Empire of Japan, Georg's heart sunk. His stomach started to do acrobatics he hadn't experienced since he drove his dying wife to the hospital. He looked at his two oldest sons and said a silent prayer. He prayed for a swift end to the war. He prayed that he wouldn't have to go through what his father had gone through—losing two sons. His eyes met Hagen's, and he forced a meagre smile. His son would be turning eighteen in less than three months, and Georg had an awful feeling that he would be watching Hagen go off to war all too soon.

Georg was glad that he kept his children home that day. There was an assembly in the auditorium at school so the students and faculty could hear Mr. Roosevelt speak. When the assembly was over, patriotism and duty to the country had half of the senior boys trekking down to the recruiting office to sign up. Many of them were not yet eighteen, but they lied about their age. December 7th would be forever known as Pearl Harbor Day, but December 8th would be remembered in their town as the day the Japanese stole the sons of Burlington County.

On December 12th, the day after Germany declared war on the United States, news spread quickly around town that an official military car had been seen pulling up to the McHugh's house around ten o'clock that morning. Sylvia McHugh's cries were heard a block away. Patricia Doerr, one of the neighbors, said that a doctor had to be called to sedate Sylvia.

Arthur "Artie" Matthew McHugh, Jr. was Burlington's first casualty of World War II, but not the last.

When the news of Artie's death reached the Beckenbauers, the mood in the household sank even lower. It was one thing to hear about the horrible attack and the devastation at Pearl Harbor, but to actually know someone who was there, someone you knew and highly admired—

well, it made it very personal. Hagen, usually the level-headed one in the family, was ready to go defend his country. If he hadn't had to wait until his eighteenth birthday, as his father requested, he would have enlisted that very day. Sal... well... Sal wanted to fight for his country right then and there, too, *to get those damned Japs back,* and it drove him crazy that he had to wait until September, and even crazier thinking that Hagen might be going off to fight without him.

Georg understood patriotism. He had fought for his country, albeit a country that went to war over politics and fidelity to another government. But when he had gone off to war, he didn't do it out of pride *for* his country. He did it because he was required to do it *by* his country. He resented then, and still did, the government that dragged on a senseless war that cost him his brothers and his parents. Listening to his sons sounding so eager to go fight the enemy was very upsetting. He understood what his helpless parents must have felt when they had watched their sons get dragged off to war. Hagen and Sal wouldn't have to be dragged. They would go freely.

God help them, and God help me!

As Hagen's eighteenth birthday loomed close, he and Sal chomped at the bit like horses at the gate, waiting to go off to war. Georg had managed, but barely, to convince Hagen to wait until he was legally old enough before he signed his life over to the military. He tried to convince Hagen to wait until he had graduated high school, but the best that he could do was keep him home, alive, safe, until February 19th. Sal would turn eighteen in September, and Georg felt a little relief knowing that Sal would at least graduate high school before leaving home for parts unknown.

Two days after Hagen turned eighteen, he went down to the recruiting office and joined the Army. Sal had tried to get his brother, his soulmate, to stay home until September so they could enlist together, and be together wherever they were going, to protect each other. Hagen could tell that Sal was desperate to keep him home, like his father. Hagen's logic was this: *If I don't join on my own, I'm just going to get drafted, and I'll look like a coward just waiting to be called up.*

That night was bittersweet for the Beckenbauers—their last night together as a family until the end of the war. Hagen was going to leave the next day for boot camp, and then off to fight the Japanese somewhere half a world away. After dinner, they tried to enjoy their time together. The Zenith did its best to keep everyone entertained with some upbeat swing, but the music was drowned out by thoughts of war, and of Hagen going off to be in the middle of it. The girls were becoming more and more emotional on the inside as the hands on the mantle clock counted down their time together. They wanted to keep stiff upper lips, stay strong for their brother. When their emotions began to leak through the cracks, they kissed their men goodnight, and went off to cry themselves to sleep. Karl was gung-ho for Hagen going off to beat the heck out of the enemy. He was proud of his brother. He was too young to understand what Hagen was about to do, what he was about to endure. He saluted Hagen and went up to bed. Georg turned off the radio when the news replaced the music, hugged his soon-to-be-soldier son, and bade him goodnight.

Sal and Hagen sat alone in silence for a few moments. Hagen turned to look at him, but Sal only stared straight ahead at the sleeping Zenith, then stood up. Without looking at Hagen, he put on his coat and left through the front door without saying a word. Hagen wanted to chase after him, but he knew that Sal needed some time alone. He turned off all the lights except for the porch light and lay down on the sofa.

His mind spun. He second-guessed his decision to enlist, instead of waiting for Sal. Then he justified it by reminding himself that some of the town's young men had been drafted so quickly. As his thoughts churned and roiled, he dozed off on the sofa. He was going to wait right there for Sal to come home. He wanted to hold him one more time before leaving him.

Hagen woke in the morning to the smell of coffee in the air and the sound of his father's voice calling his name. He rubbed his eyes.

"What time is it?"

"It is six-thirty, son."

"Six-thirty?" He realized he had slept the whole night on the sofa. He bolted upright. *Why didn't Sal wake me up when he came home?* "Where is everybody?"

"The girls went to collect some eggs for breakfast. Karl is around here somewhere."

"What about Sal?"

"I assume he is still asleep. I heard the front door last night. I thought you both went out but when I came downstairs this morning and saw you on the couch, I did not know what to think. Did you two have an argument?"

"No, not really. He was upset because I didn't wait until his birthday so we could enlist together. He walked out last night, and I figured he needed some time to cool down. I never heard him come home." Hagen got up and went to their room in the attic. He opened the door, hoping to find Sal sound asleep in bed. His heart sank when he found both beds still made. He looked in the closet, in the storage area, under the beds, hoping that Sal was playing a joke on him and he was going to pop out and hug him and hold him and try one more time to make him stay, even though signing on that dotted line was a done deal.

But no Sal.

He walked slowly down the two flights of stairs. When he got to the bottom of the steps, Karl, the girls, and Georg were in the living room.

But no Sal.

"Was he up there?" asked Georg.

"No." Hagen looked down at the floor.

"Didn't he come home last night?" asked Diana

"No. It doesn't look like it. His bed is still made." Hagen was verging on tears.

"Well, hey," said Mathilde. She could see the anxiety all over Hagen's face. "He probably went to the barn to think and fell asleep in the loft. You know how he does that sometimes when he's moody."

Karl took that as his cue, put on his coat and boots, still in his pajamas, and ran out to the barn to find Sal. Hagen's heart chinned up a bit at the hope that Mathilde was right. He had to be at the recruiting office at nine o'clock sharp and time wasn't slowing down.

Karl went into the barn and called out for Sal. No answer. He went up into the loft. No Sal. He walked back to the house feeling like he'd failed. He wanted to find Sal, to cheer up Hagen. Now he not only felt awful for Hagen, he worried about Sal.

Hagen looked out through the kitchen window and saw Karl coming back from the barn, alone. He looked at the clock on the mantle. It was almost seven. He had two hours left—well, an hour and a half—before he had to leave. The girls were making breakfast. The smell of sizzling bacon normally would have made his morning hunger even stronger. But no. His stomach was swarming with razor-winged butterflies. Hagen sat down to breakfast with his minus-two family (Marta's empty place was ever-present). The girls acted as cheery as they could while they served breakfast, then sat down. They all clasped hands to say grace, making Sal's absence even that much more upsetting.

After breakfast, they got ready to go to the recruiter. Hagen glanced at the clock every thirty seconds. He didn't want to leave without seeing Sal, and he couldn't believe that Sal didn't want the same thing. He was angry, sad, desperate, anxious. He wanted to cry. He wanted to scream. He wanted to punch a wall. He stood by the living room window like a statue, waiting until the very last minute.

Georg came up behind him and looked out the window. "Alright, son. It's time to go." Hagen turned his head towards his father. Georg's eyes showed signs of a recent cry.

Hagen grabbed him, put him in a bear hug that took Georg by surprise, and whispered into his ear, "I'm sorry, Papa." Neither one of them wanted to let go first. By the time they released each other, Karl and the girls were standing next to each other, watching them, their tears rain-dropping to the floor.

Karl insisted on carrying Hagen's suitcase to the car. He and the girls sat in the back. Georg drove as slowly as he could, hoping, praying that Sal would show up at the last minute. He knew that it was tearing Hagen apart that his brother wasn't there to say goodbye. Fury, worry, and love battled it out for control of Georg's heart.

The drive to Burlington reminded Georg of the drive to Mannheim when his parents took him to the German Military Office twenty-seven years before. He felt like throwing up. When they arrived, a crowd of families who were saying their goodbyes to their brothers, sons, husbands, and boyfriends had gathered in front of the recruiting office. Hagen and his family stood on the sidewalk across the street and watched as the other families tried to smile through their tears. Mothers clung to their sons. A grandmother stood arm in arm with her husband while she flicked through her rosary while she prayed for her grandson to come home alive. She had lived through the War to End All Wars, that did *not* end all wars, and she prayed for the best while fearing the worst.

Two military transport buses pulled up to the curb, right on time. A hush fell over the gathering of families. This was it—really *it*. Time to say goodbye—one more hug, one more kiss. It might be their last.

Oh God, don't even think that!

Hagen gave everyone one more squeeze, one more kiss. He told Karl to take care of his sisters and Papa. "Yes, Sir," said Karl with a salute. Hagen saluted him back, then walked across the street to join the rest of the recruits and waited to board the buses. Karl and his sisters never looked away from their brother the whole time he stood with the others. Georg scanned all the recruits. He recognized some of them and their families. He prayed for their safe returns although he knew that war did not pick and choose who was going to die, and who was to survive.

It was up to God—and the enemy.

The new recruits were checked in and assigned to a bus. Hagen disappeared into the group who was boarding the second bus and made it to a seat that faced the street. He slid the window open, leaned out and smiled one of those big, Hagen smiles that could light up the darkest moment. He did that for his family. They didn't need to know how terribly worried he was for them, for himself. At the same time, his soul wept for Sal. He didn't want to die with the last time that he saw Sal having been him walking out the door in a huff. He wanted, *needed* to hold him one more time before going to war, going to Hell, or Heaven. He wasn't going to see Sal today, and Hagen's heart mourned.

The bus engines started. Georg and his entire family, and the families across the street, all jumped at the sound.

The buses pulled away from the curb with their precious cargo squeezed out of every window, arms waving goodbye. As the sound of the engines faded, the sounds of women crying could be heard. No one moved until the buses turned left off of High Street onto Route 130, a quarter of a mile away. Hugs tightened. How many of them had just seen their child for the last time? Georg asked himself that question and shuddered at the thought as his soul slapped his inner voice for even saying it.

The ride back to the farm was quiet. So many thoughts on the tips of tongues, things almost said, so many sighs.

"He is going to be fine," said Mathilde, when she couldn't take the silence any longer. "I know it, I just do."

"You know, now that you mention it, I feel that way, too," said Diana. "I can see him now, coming home all handsome in his uniform, all smiles because we won."

Georg appreciated their optimism. It was at times like this that keeping positive and hopeful kept you from going insane and banging your head against a wall. "I think you are right, girls. He will be alright; I just know it." With the mood on an upswing, they made it home without any more tears. Their thoughts shifted to Sal, wondering where he was and if he was alright.

Their questions were answered when they pulled up in the front of the house. There was Sal, sitting on the porch swing, leaning over, elbows on his legs, his head bowed. He was wearing the same clothes he had on the night before. He looked up when he heard their footsteps on the walkway. His family stood at the bottom of the porch steps, staring at him. They didn't know whether to be happy to see him or throw a shoe at him for not being here to say goodbye to Hagen. They could see he'd been crying, and they waited for him to say something. Their silent expressions of concern and confusion were unsettling. He broke down and cried again, putting his face in his hands. He cried like someone mourning the death of a loved one. He was so mad at Hagen for leaving. He was so godawful angry at himself for not saying goodbye. He would never forgive himself, and he wouldn't blame his family if they didn't either.

The girls went up the steps and sat on the swing on either side of Sal. They put their arms around him, and he cried harder. Georg opened the front door.

"Come, Karl, let's go inside." They left Sal and his sisters alone for a while. Georg and Karl could hear Sal's crying through the window next to the porch swing. After about ten minutes, the three of them went inside and into the kitchen. Karl and Georg were sitting at the table sipping on glasses of milk. Sal sat down next to Karl and put his arm around him and squeezed him close. Georg smiled. "Are you alright, Sal?"

Sal was expecting the third degree and ice-cold shoulders from everyone, but he got none of that. They knew how much Sal loved his brother Hagen.

"I don't know, Papa. I messed up, I messed up really bad."

"I won't argue with you there, son. But I am not going to try to make you feel any worse than you already do. You are doing a fine job of that all by yourself."

Sal almost smiled—almost. "Was he mad?"

"No, son. I think he felt let down, though. Disappointed perhaps."

"Are *you* mad, Papa? Do you hate me?"

"No, son. I am not mad, and I don't hate you. I love you. We all love you."

He looked at his sisters who were nodding in agreement, their eyes glistening with fresh tears.

"I'm sorry, Papa."

"I know. We know. When you feel like talking about it, I will be here."

"Us too," said the girls.

"Me too," said Karl, as he did his best to wrap his arms around Sal's torso.

"I might as well tell it now." His face got very serious and the rest of them became concerned. "Last night," he took a deep breath. "Last night I needed to go for a walk. I needed to think." He stopped to think of what to say next. "Papa, I apologize, but I went to the barn and drank some of your beer. I guess I got a bit drunk. I started walking and I didn't turn around."

"Where did you go?" asked Diana.

"I was out on Delanco Road and a car stopped with some guys from school—Danny Snyder and Bobby Hesson. We drove around, we got some more beer, and the next thing I know, I'm waking up on Danny's couch."

"How did you get home?" asked his father.

"I woke up before Danny did. But his parents were up. His dad was getting ready to go to work at his store. Mrs. Snyder gave me a cup of coffee and Mr. Snyder gave me a ride to Perkins Lane. I walked the rest of the way. By the time I got here, you were all gone." Another deep sigh.

"I…"

Then the crying started all over again. Georg let him cry. The girls got up and went around to the other side of the table and stood behind him, rubbing his shoulders. Karl leaned into Sal and put his arm around him. When this wave of crying subsided, Sal rubbed his eyes. "Do you think there's any way to still say goodbye?"

"I do not think so, son," said his father. "He and the other recruits were taken to the training camp this morning. He is at Fort Dix by now."

Sal wanted to see Hagen so badly. What could he do? He needed to think, clear his head, find a way to see him. He got up from his chair. "I'm going to my room."

"Do you want something to eat?" asked Diana.

"No, thank you. I'm not hungry." Then he left the kitchen and went upstairs.

"Papa?" said Karl.

"Yes, Karl?"

"Can I go fight the Japanese?"

"No, son. You are not old enough."

Thank God.

"Is Sal going to go fight the Japanese?" asked Karl.

That question evoked a different feeling. Georg's heart jumped. "No, Karl. Not today." He looked up at the ceiling, in the direction of Sal and Heaven. *Dear God, please make this war end before September.*

"Papa," said Mathilde. "Diana and I are going to write letters to Hagen."

"Can I write one, too?" asked Karl.

"Of course," said Mathilde.

"That is a very good idea," said their father. "He is going to want to hear from you. Your letters will help keep up his morale." He remembered how good it felt to receive letters from his family during the first war. It wasn't only what the letters said, it was the feel of the paper in his hands. He was touching something that someone he loved, someone who loved him, had touched. Karl followed his sisters to Mathilde's room, and they began writing the first of many letters to their brother.

Sal was upstairs brooding and kicking himself. As he lay on his bed, he was scheming of a way to see Hagen and tell him that he was sorry. In the middle of scheming, he fell asleep.

When Sal woke up, it was after one o'clock. Karl and his father were out somewhere on the farm. The girls were downstairs listening to the radio. Whenever they would warm up the Zenith, they would say a prayer that they would hear news that the war was over. Sal came downstairs and Mathilde asked him if he was hungry. They had made tuna sandwiches and had saved him one in the refrigerator. He thanked them and went into the kitchen. They heard the refrigerator door open and close. The girls assumed that he was going to eat his sandwich. Then it got quiet. Eating a sandwich wasn't noisy business, so they went back to listening to the news. What they didn't know was that Sal wasn't hungry at all. He made noise to distract them, then quietly snuck out the back door. He walked out to Perkins Lane, then to Bridgeboro Road, and thumbed a ride to Burlington.

His ride dropped him right off in front of the recruiting office. He was glad to *help out a fellow patriot*. Sal thanked the man and got in the long line of other young men who were standing in front of the building. While he stood there, he struck up conversations with some of the others. He recognized a few from school, and he knew for a fact that they weren't eighteen yet, and they knew that he wasn't either. No one was going to rat out anyone. They were all there for the same reason—to fight for their country. But Sal also wanted to find Hagen.

He was there for about an hour before he made it inside to talk to the army recruiter. He lied about his age, said he was nineteen, which was not unbelievable given Sal's physique and that he'd been shaving since he was sixteen. Sal signed on the dotted line, said his oath of enlistment, and was instructed to return the next morning at 0900 sharp to be taken to boot camp for basic training. When he left the recruiting office, he ran into some of the guys outside whom he'd been chatting with earlier. One of them, named David Comeaux, *really* nineteen years old, from Cinnaminson, had a car, and gave Sal a ride back to the farm. He dropped Sal off on the side of the road near the orchards. David would pick him up in the morning at eight-thirty, at the same spot, and take him back to Burlington with him.

As Sal walked, his mind raced. *How am I going to tell my family that I just enlisted? What if Hagen gets so mad when he sees me that he tells the army I'm not eighteen? Why did I do what I did last night?*

As he walked past the cemetery, he turned his eyes away from the graves. He felt that if he looked at them, he would hear them whispering—*What did you do, Salvatore? What were you thinking?* He didn't need *that* guilt piled on top of the mound he had already made by himself.

When he walked into the house, the rest of the family were in the kitchen. The girls came running into the living room with Karl and their father behind.

"Where did you go?" asked Diana. "We were so worried about you."

"I went for a walk." He looked over at his father. "And no, Papa, no beer."

"Well, that is good to hear." He flashed his son a sympathetic smile. He was curious to know where he had been for the last five hours, but he wasn't going to press the issue so soon, even though his gut was in a knot with all the scenarios running through his mind.

"Are you hungry?" asked Mathilde. "You should be. You didn't eat your sandwich. I made lasagna for dinner."

"Sorry about that, I wasn't hungry earlier. But I am now." He wasn't really hungry, just kind of hungry, but he didn't want to let on how upset he really was. They went into the kitchen. Georg, Karl, and Sal sat at their seats and the girls served them plates of lasagna. When everyone was seated, they held hands, bowed their heads, and closed their eyes. Except for Sal. He watched them as Georg said the usual grace with the addition of a plea to God that he keeps Hagen and all the rest of the boys safe.

Amen.

Sal closed his eyes quickly on the *Amen,* then opened them with everyone else, picked up his fork, and slowly cut off a bite of his lasagna. Sal loved his family so very much it hurt and hurting them was the last thing he wanted to do. Georg could tell that there was something on Sal's mind, but he figured it was what had happened last night; he hoped it was about that, and not something stupid he might possibly have done while he was out.

Sal looked over at his father as he took a mouthful of lasagna. *I hope you can't read my mind, Papa.*

Georg saw the pain in Sal's eyes. He gave him an *it is going to be alright* look, reached over and squeezed his shoulder. Sal half-smiled a *thank you, Papa.*

After dinner, the family retired to the living room, as would be the case for nearly every night until the war ended, to sit glued to the Zenith as news reported the events of the war as they unfolded. When the news had nothing else new to relay, Georg changed the station and found some music. He sat back down and lit his pipe. Karl was sitting on the floor at the coffee table, drawing with crayons.

"What are you drawing?" asked Mathilde.

He held up the paper. "It's Hagen on a boat. He's going to Japan to win the war. I'm going to send it to him with my letter."

The sky was blue, the ship was grey, the sea was green. Hagen's hair was yellow, and the American flag was BIG.

"That's a very good picture," said Mathilde. "Hagen will love it."

Karl turned towards Sal, holding up the picture, smiling wide, looking for his brother's approval. "Look, Sal."

"That's very good, Karl." He tried to smile but it came out like a grimace. He got up and ran up the steps, two at a time, to his room.

Karl's smile turned to a confused frown. He looked at his father and his sisters. They understood why Sal got upset. Well, they thought they did. They only knew part of it. But Karl was too young to understand. "Papa, did I do something wrong?"

"No, Karl, he misses his brother. He is upset he did not say goodbye to him, not upset with you."

Karl sighed, then handed the picture to Diana. "Would you send this to Hagen with the letters, please?"

"I will put it in the envelope right now," said Diana as she went to Georg's rolltop desk.

Smiling proudly, Karl picked up a crayon and started a new picture.

Upstairs, Sal thought it was as good a time as any to write his goodbye letters. He wrote three of them—one to his sisters and Karl, one to his father, and one to Hagen. When each was finished, he folded them and put them in envelopes, then got ready for bed.

In the morning, Sal went downstairs dressed in his everyday clothes, carrying his Rolleiflex. His family was sitting at the breakfast table, dressed for church.

"Good morning, son," said Georg. His face looked confused. "You aren't dressed for church."

"I don't feel like going today. May I stay home?"

Georg could see that he was not behaving like his usual self. He attributed his demeanor to the events of the past couple of days. "If you don't feel like it, sure. I'd like you there with your family, but I am not going to force you." Any

312

other time, barring illness, he would insist that the whole family go to church together.

"I'm sorry, Papa. I'll go next Sunday."

"It would make me happy if you would at least sit and have some breakfast with us."

"OK, Papa." He gave him a kiss on the cheek. His guts felt like a python crushing its prey.

"Sit," said Mathilde. "Want some eggs and sausage?"

"Sure, thanks." He sat next to Karl and looked over at his drawing. "Whatcha got there?"

"Nothing." Karl curved his arm around it to hide it from Sal. "It's not finished, don't look."

Sal looked away, then down at the plate of fried eggs and sausage that Mathilde had put in front of him. The python squeezed harder. He knew he should eat. It was going to be a long day, and who knew when he'd be eating again? He grabbed the ketchup bottle and doused his sausage, then dug in, slowly at first. The python relaxed and allowed Sal to eat. It was gathering its strength for later.

"Karl, eat your breakfast," said his father, tapping on the table next to his plate. "You can finish that later."

Karl turned his head towards Georg, covering the drawing as much as possible with his folded arms. "It's almost finished, Papa." He looked pleadingly at his father then shifted his eyes in Sal's direction. Georg realized then that this was for Sal, maybe to cheer him up.

"Alright, you can finish it. But you will have to eat before we leave for church, deal?"

Karl smiled thankfully. "Deal!" He went to shake his father's hand but realized he'd be revealing the picture, then pulled his arm back.

"We will shake hands after you finish," said Georg. He resumed eating and Karl resumed his coloring.

When everyone had finished breakfast, except for Karl, the drawing was complete. "Close your eyes, Sal."

Sal had a feeling his little brother was fussing over him. He closed his eyes, so tightly he saw flashing lights on his retina.

"OK, you can open your eyes." Karl was holding up the picture, smiling even more than when he held up the one last night.

Sal opened his eyes and smiled but it quickly faded. He felt like crying. It was a picture, Karl's rendition, of Sal and Hagen. They were standing on a ship, on the ocean. Their arms were around each other. On the left side of the picture was supposed to be Japan. On the other side, was a crude United States. The ship was heading in the direction of home, not Japan.

"You hate it!" Karl pouted.

Sal grabbed his brother and pulled him off his chair and hugged him so tightly as tears fell onto Karl's shirt. Then he whispered in his ear, "I love it, it's perfect. Thank you, I needed this. You have no idea how much I needed this." He kissed both his cheeks, then put him back in his seat.

"If you love it, then why are you crying?"

"Sometimes people cry when they are happy, Karl," said Mathilde.

"I'm never gonna understand grown-ups. You cry when you're sad, you cry when you're happy." He shook his head and started to eat his cold breakfast. The *grown-ups* looked at each other and giggled. It felt good to Sal to laugh.

Pretty soon he won't be laughing. Pretty soon no one will be laughing.

Sal forced the last bite of his sausage and eggs down on top of the dozing python and got up from the table. He told everyone he was going to go out to the hayloft. It wasn't unusual. It wasn't unlike him to go there to think, and they

314

all knew he had been doing a lot of that over the last two days. Sal picked up the picture that Karl had drawn for him, and his camera, then gave Karl a kiss on the top of his head. "Thanks again." Karl smiled and *you're welcomed* him through his mouthful of eggs. "See ya later." Then he left out the back door and headed to the barn. As he walked, he folded Karl's drawing and put it in his coat pocket next to the one Hagen had given him twelve years ago. He cherished that picture. It was always pinned on the wall over his bed. Now it was going with him to war. Once inside the barn, he went up to the loft and waited.

Outside in the distance, about ten minutes later, he heard the Oldsmobile's engine fire up. He watched from the loft window as his family rode down the driveway and onto Perkins Lane. Then he came down from the loft, patted some of the cows in the pen outside the barn, said some goodbyes, then walked out to the path through the empty cornfield that led to the peach orchard. It was eight-fifteen by his watch. This time through the orchard, Sal stopped at the cemetery. He stood at Marta's grave.

"Thank you, Mama. Thank you for bringing me and Diana home. Thank you for being a great mother." Then he went to the Cristoforo's graves. "I know we didn't know each other very long. Thank you for bringing me and Diana into this world. I never forgot your faces; in case you were wondering. Thank you for doing your best to take care of us. And thank you for sending the Beckenbauers to us, especially Hagen to me." Then he addressed all three of them. "I love you. I miss you. If for some reason I don't make it home alive, or get to see Hagen again, save a place for me up there." He looked up through the barren February peach tree branches at the bright, blue morning sky. He squinted a tear from his eyes, said goodbye to his dead parents, and walked the rest of the way to the road.

When he emerged from the trees, David was just pulling up. As he got closer to the car, Sal could see that someone else was in the front seat with David. It was a girl, around the same age as David. Sal got in the back seat. "Good morning."

"Good morning, Sal. Ready to go win the war?" David was very excited. "This is my girlfriend, Angela. Angela, this is Sal."

"Nice to meet you, Angela."

"Same here." Angela didn't seem to share the same enthusiasm as David.

"Angela's coming with us so she can take my car back to my house."

"Does your family know you enlisted, Sal?" asked Angela.

"No." The python squirmed. "They don't."

"Neither does *his* family." She punched David in the arm. "Your mom is going to kill me, you know, when I show up to drop off your car."

"She won't kill you. She'll be madder'n hell at me for leaving. It's not like I didn't say goodbye."

"Yeah? Leaving a letter on your dresser isn't my idea of saying a proper goodbye." She shook her head then turned to look at Sal in the backseat. She saw the look on his face. "You left a letter too, didn't you?"

He sighed. "Yeah, three of them."

"What is it with you boys? You can't say goodbye to your mothers?" She looked back and forth at the two of them. David was crimson with embarrassment.

"My mama is dead," said Sal. He didn't want to go into the details of his two mothers, but that got Angela's attention. "I stopped at the grave this morning to say goodbye. Does that count?"

Angela lowered her head. "I'm sorry for getting so upset. I'm sorry about your mother." Then she looked at David. "I'm scared, that's all. You better come home to me, David, or so help me…" She stopped and put her face against his arm and put her right arm around him.

Sal watched David and the someone who loves him saying their long goodbye a piece at a time. He started to kick himself again for not giving Hagen the chance to say goodbye to him. The python twisted. "Stop the car."

"Huh?" said David

"Pull over, please!"

David pulled over onto the side of the road. As Sal was opening the door, David said, laughing, "You're not going AWOL already, are you?"

Sal got out, dropped to his knees on the dirt by the side of the road, and lost his breakfast. The python writhed, making sure Sal lost all of it. He wiped his mouth with the handkerchief from his jacket pocket. He got back in the car.

Angela was looking at him sympathetically. David looked at him through the rear-view mirror. "You OK, Sal?" he asked.

"I think so." He closed his eyes and took a deep breath.

"That's why I didn't eat anything this morning," said David.

"Sorry I had to make you stop."

"That's OK. I don't think Angela woulda liked driving home with your breakfast all over my back seat, anyway." She gave him another punch to the arm. "Heyyyy!" He rubbed his arm and faked pain.

"OK, tough guy," she kissed his arm, "you'd better get going before you're both AWOL."

David put the car in gear and pulled back onto the roadway. No one's thoughts made it to their lips. David had his mom on his mind. His father had died of a heart attack two years before, and he had had to go to work to help support his mom and sister. He never graduated high school. Joining the army would help his family. He would send his pay home to his mother. She would have one less mouth to feed, and when he returned, he would go back to school, get a decent job, and marry Angela.

Angela was worried about one thing—David coming back to her alive, and in one piece. She wanted to be his wife and the mother of his children one day. She loved him from the day they had met three years ago at a party. Inside she was screaming, telling him not to go. But she knew he had no choice. It's either go freely now or wait to be drafted. Either way, she had to say goodbye, and it was killing her.

Sal's mind was a whirlwind of thoughts. He missed Hagen. He already missed home, and he wasn't even gone twenty minutes. Going AWOL almost sounded like an option. But this was the only way for him to get to see Hagen. They would be at the same boot camp and then deploy together, fight together, and go home together.

David parked across the street from the recruiting office. Sal got out and stood on the sidewalk, watching the next batch of new recruits and their families across the street. Everyone had someone to say goodbye to them, except Sal. David and Angela got out and hugged one more time. She didn't want to let go. He put his hands on her shoulders and looked her right into her red-rimmed eyes.

"I will come home to you. I promise." They hugged one more time. When they let go of each other they looked over at Sal, standing there on the sidewalk like a lost puppy. Angela felt bad. She looked at David. He could tell what she was thinking, then he nodded. She walked over to Sal and put her arms around him. Sal stood there, dumbfounded, looking at David, his expression saying *what am I supposed to do?*

"It's OK, you can hug her. But don't get any stupid ideas."

Angela turned around and gave him a *really?* look and rolled her eyes. David shrugged.

Angela put her arms around him. It felt nice to be hugged, even if it was by a complete stranger. He squeezed back and whispered, "thank you."

When he felt her start to let go, he released her. She took a step back and looked right into his eyes. "You're a nice guy, I can tell. Take care of each other, for me, and when you come back, you can be the best man at our wedding, deal?" She held out her hand. He shook it and thought of Karl this morning at breakfast.

"Deal." After he shook her hand he reached inside his coat and felt the folded pictures in the pocket.

"Alright, Sal, let's get over there." He gave Angela one more hug, then a wink, then walked across the street with Sal and joined the crowd.

They didn't have to wait too long. A few minutes later, two military buses arrived. The recruits were loaded onboard. Sal and David stayed together and sat in a seat that faced the street. David opened the window and stuck his head outside. Angela was still in the same spot, arms folded, holding a handkerchief in one hand.

"I love you, Angie baby!"

"I love you, too, ya big lummox!"

The bus engines growled to life, spewing plumes of exhaust smoke into the crowd. People coughed and waved at their faces, taking back-steps to escape the cloud. As the buses pulled away, arms waved out of all the windows at their loved ones on the curb. The crowd reluctantly dispersed as the buses got further away. Angela waited until the buses turned right off of High Street onto Route 130, then got back

319

in the car and began the dreaded drive to David's house, and David's mother.

At Fort Dix, Hagen was on day two of boot camp. There were not going to be any days off for him, or any of the new recruits. Training was to be completed expeditiously in order to make room for the next batch of recruits.

On the bus, Sal and the rest of the recruits were informed that their destination had changed. Both Fort Dix and Fort Monmouth were at capacity. Their buses were heading to Philadelphia, where the recruits will board a west-bound train to California. Sal's heart almost stopped as the python twisted in his empty gut. He not only left his family without saying goodbye, but now he was being taken further from Hagen.

At church, the Beckenbauers prayed for Hagen's safe return. The pews were not as filled as they were before December 7th. Many sons and husbands had already enlisted, or had been drafted, and their absence was noticeable. After mass, people said their goodbyes to Father Kelly, and each other, and went home to their radios to listen for an answer to their prayers.

When they returned home and couldn't find Sal anywhere, Karl went to the third-floor bedroom to look for him. All he found were the three envelopes. He ran down the stairs as fast as he could. "Papa, Papa!" he yelled all the way to the living room.

The commotion had Georg and the girls on their feet looking at the staircase as Karl's voice got louder. When he got to the bottom of the stairs, Georg saw the envelopes. His knees weakened. He grabbed onto the bannister for balance.

"Papa, Sal isn't up there but I found these on his bed." He held out his hand with the envelopes to his father. Georg took them slowly and looked at each one. He handed the one addressed to Diana, Mathilde, and Karl to Diana. She stared down at it like she had never seen an envelope before.

Georg proceeded to open the one addressed to him. He read it out loud:

Dear Papa,

Please, don't be too mad at me. I had to enlist. I didn't want to wait until September. I have to find Hagen and fight alongside my brother. I owe it to him to be with him and fight with him. Hopefully, I will get to Fort Dix today and find him. I will write to you when I can.

Love,

Sal

Georg looked up from the letter at the children. Diana was still staring at the envelope in her hand. Mathilde slid the letter from her fingers and slowly opened it. She read it out loud:

Dear Diana, Mathilde, and Karl,

Please try not to be too upset with me. I hated lying to you and Papa, but I knew that you and he would have tried to stop me from leaving. I feel terrible that I wasn't here for our brother when he went away to fight the Japs. I went to find him so we can be together and protect each other until we come home. Take good care of Papa and Heidi.

Love, your brother
Sal

P.S. Please send the letter I wrote to Hagen with your letters just in case we don't find each other. Thank you.

"Now what are we going to do?" Asked Mathilde.

"I will drive to the recruiting office," said Georg, "to confirm if Sal really enlisted. If he did enlist, then I will drive to Fort Dix and bring him home. I need you girls to stay here with Karl until I return."

"Alright, Papa," said Diana. The children hugged their father, then he put his coat on and drove to Burlington. He walked into the recruiting office and spoke to the commanding officer and inquired about Sal. He found out that a Salvatore Cristoforo—age *nineteen*?—did enlist yesterday and that he was en route to California. The train from Philadelphia had left an hour ago. It was too late to bring him home. Georg went home and told the children the news about Sal and that they should probably send Sal's letter to Hagen with theirs. The only thing they could do now was wait to hear something from Sal and Hagen.

At dinner that evening, no one spoke except to say grace. After dinner, everyone said the same silent prayer as the Zenith warmed up: that the war was over and no one from their family was going to fight... or die. When they went to bed, the war hadn't ended, but neither had their hopes. They all cried themselves to sleep that night, including Sal, somewhere on a train in western Pennsylvania.

Hagen's Railcar
Chicago

Hagen stopped there when they heard a train horn and then felt the bump of the Amtrak train connecting to his car. The generator that had been powering his freestanding car shut off, and the lights flickered as power from the train took over. A few minutes later, the train began to move.

Hagen looked at his watch. "Well, that was a fast two hours." He picked up his coffee cup to take a sip and saw that it was empty. He didn't remember finishing his espresso.

"Time flies when you're captivated. I can't believe what happened! Did Sal ever find you?" She noticed that they were both out of coffee and water. "You want some more water, coffee?"

"Water, no coffee, thank you. I think I am awake enough. And no, he did not find me. I'll continue when you return."

Emily put the dessert dishes and coffee cups on the tray and carried it back to the kitchen and put them by the sink to clean later. She didn't want to waste any time. She grabbed two more bottles of water from the refrigerator and walked back to the patio. Hagen had dimmed the lights to a soft glow. She handed him a bottle of water and resumed her place on the love seat. She could see that he was thinking deeply. "Penny for your thoughts."

His expression softened. "I was thinking about the next chapter. I do not feel that it is necessary for me to go into the gory details about everything that happened during the war itself. Everyone knows war is hell. And you know that we both returned alive, but there are some things that I feel need to be told. My story isn't simply about what happened to me and my family, but about the connections you make along the way. The Universe can surprise you."

"Well, it sure had its way with your family, from what I've heard so far."

"Mmm, that it did." He sipped some water.

"I want to know when you and Sal finally got to see each other again." She saw Hagen's expression wax painful.

"The short answer is that we didn't see each other until after the war ended. A lot happened, though, between the last time he and I had seen each other at home and the end of the war. Those events will be the next phase of my story." He looked at his watch. It was after nine. "This might take us late into the evening."

"I don't mind. I had a nap and a bucket of espresso. I'm wide awake. How about you?" She settled deep into the corner of the sectional, wrapped in the Navajo blanket, and prepared for the next leg of the journey. "Are you OK to go on?"

"I'm fine."

Then he continued...

May 8, 1942

Hagen and Sal had never been farther apart than the distance from the pumpkin patch to the apple orchard, and never for more than half a day. Now, three thousand miles and seventy-seven days separated them. It may as well have been a three thousand light years and seventy-seven eons.

Hagen received the letter that Sal had written the night before he left for California. It was an apology/love letter. It upset Hagen to know that Sal hadn't waited until September to enlist. But he loved Sal and understood why he had done what he had done. Deep inside, there was a part of him that had wanted Sal to join the army with him. He couldn't admit it to anyone at the time. He knew that his father wanted Sal to graduate high school before enlisting. In his letter, Sal was sorry for not being there for him and the rest of the family. He told Hagen that he had enlisted in the army so he could find him, so they could be together. He did not want them to be apart, and he loved him more than the world. Along with Sal's letter were the ones from Karl and his sisters, and one from his father. Georg had written a letter after he had returned from looking for Sal. It explained that Sal had enlisted in the Army and was on his way to basic training in California. Hagen's heart sank when he read that. He knew Sal better than anyone else, and he was sure Sal was beside himself with anguish. Hindsight is twenty/twenty, and at that time Sal was not flush with foresight. It never, ever dawned on Sal that even if he and Hagen had wound up at Fort Dix at the same time, that it would not have guaranteed that they would be assigned to the same final destination.

Their basic training lasted ten weeks. In that time, letters were written to and from Sal, Hagen, and the family in Beverly. Georg and the children didn't stay mad at Sal for very long. They understood his motives, why he did what he did. They just wished that they had a proper goodbye, like they had with Hagen. Hagen was more worried than angry. He hoped that the Army would be able to tame Sal, help him contain his Italian fire, so if it came to a life or death situation, he would be capable of making decisions logically, not rashly.

All soldiers who successfully passed basic training received a three-day furlough before moving on to their assigned locations and special training. Fort Dix was not far from Beverly—about twenty miles—so Hagen was fortunate enough to be able to spend his three days with his family. Sal, on the other hand, was not that fortunate. It was bad enough to be where he was because of the circumstances surrounding his getting there in the first place, but the reality that going home to New Jersey was simply not logistically possible, just rubbed salt deep into the wound. Fuel was scarce and strictly rationed, and the national speed limit had been reduced to 35mph to help conserve fuel and rubber. Even if he could acquire enough gas for the drive, he would have to break land speed records to get home and back and chance being arrested for speeding. No one got to fly home for furlough, and a train would not make the six-thousand-mile journey in time for Sal to not go AWOL. He made the best of it. He went to the beach every day and did a lot of soul-searching. He wrote a letter to his father, a letter to his sisters and Karl, and six letters to Hagen; one each morning to tell him about his nightdreams and one each night to tell him about his daydreams.

After their furloughs, Hagen and Sal were assigned to special training. Hagen's high intellect and fluency in German made him an ideal candidate for the Army Counterintelligence Corps. After basic training he was sent to Washington, D.C., then Maryland for specialized training. He was subsequently transferred to England, where he worked alongside the British with their efforts to fight the Nazis.

Sal didn't have Hagen's IQ, but he was no slouch, either. During basic training, he tested highly in areas that would qualify him for flight training. Before Pearl Harbor, the military had had more stringent requirements as to who could become a flight officer, but when the United States entered the World War, the requirement that an officer candidate have at least two years of college experience had become unnecessary. Sal had lied about his age and attached to that lie was the assumption that he had graduated high school. After his three-day furlough, he was sent to Kirtland Army Airfield in Albuquerque, New Mexico for flight training. He excelled in air cadet school, especially in bombardier training, so much so that his fellow cadets nicknamed him "Bullseye." He was assigned to the 26th Bombardment Squadron and shipped off to Turtle Bay Airfield on the South Pacific island of Espiritu Santo and assigned to the crew of *Thor's Hammer*, a B-17F that had already seen some heavy fighting. She'd been beaten up so many times, yet always made it back to base. But sadly, on the last run, with fewer souls on board than when she had taken off.

Sal was sent to replace Second Lieutenant Hal Eckhardt, twenty-three years old, from Boise; a damned fine bombardier and officer. Hal had taken over the ball turret when the gunner, Sergeant Joey Howard, twenty, from Toledo, took rounds to the chest, neck, and face from a Zeke

(Zeke was a nickname for the Japanese Mitsubishi fighter, Zero Sen), who came up on them fast and furious. They had just finished the bombing run and made their turn back to Espiritu, when Joey got hit. Hal, who was a little guy too, pulled Joey from the turret, climbed down into the ball, and began firing the twin 50 calibre cannons at the fighters. Another Zeke came at them from out of the sun. Hal squeezed the trigger and the cannons spat their venom at the Zero and ripped off its starboard wing. The Japanese fighter rolled over and its port wingtip took out the ball turret, and Hal Eckhardt from Boise with it. When *Hammer* landed at Turtle Bay, she had lost four of her crew—the radio operator, Sergeant Gary Esposito, twenty-three, from Brooklyn; the tail gunner, Sergeant Freddy Shakney, nineteen, from Walhalla, South Carolina; Hal, and Joey.

Thor's Hammer was put back together by the ground crew in six days and was deemed ready for service. On the seventh day, Sal and the other replacements arrived. They were greeted with mixed emotions by *Hammer's* crew. The crew was a tight bunch, and the loss of their friends hit them hard. They had had seventeen successful runs, everyone returned alive, until that last one. But Sal and the other replacements were soon heartily welcomed and admired, and First Lieutenant Sal "Bullseye" Cristoforo, eighteen years… *ahem*, twenty years old, from Beverly, New Jersey, soon proved his worth.

The crew of *Thor's Hammer* resumed their bombing runs—eight, nine, ten runs without any loss of life aboard. Yes, there were the flack damage and the bullet holes, but the injuries were mostly bumps and bruises and a couple of cuts on sharp edges where the munitions damaged the aircraft. Downtime was never more than two days, and they'd be right back at it.

"Start by doing what's necessary;
then do what's possible;
and suddenly
you are doing the impossible."

—St. Francis of Assisi

Espiritu Santo
22 November 1942
0430 hours

The morning sun was still below the horizon, glowing faintly, its rays stretching up to the heavens through distant clouds as the squadron of B-17s took off into a clear, pre-dawn sky and steered northwest for a long bomb run over New Guinea. The flight was uneventful for the first eight hundred-or-so miles. As they descended from flight level two-five-zero, sporadic Japanese fighters would whiz by, strafing the planes, then get taken out by one of the B-17s' 50 calibres. As the squadron approached the target, the anti-aircraft barrage began. Not one B-17 was untouched, but they all managed to drop their payloads successfully and make the turn back for Espiritu and begin the slow climb to higher altitude. That's when all hell broke loose. An enormous squadron of Zekes swarmed upon them like angry hornets. *Momma Bomma* took a mean beating, losing engines one and three. Her tail gunner and ball turret had been wiped out by anti-aircraft flack, leaving her blind to the rear and dependent on the other ships in her formation to help defend her. Two Zekes came at her from underneath and took out engines two and four. That was it. There was nothing else to do. Over the radio, the other ships heard *Momma Bomma's* Captain's order to bail out. Six parachutes could be seen opening as the rest of the crew went with *Momma Bomma* to the bottom of the Coral Sea.

On *Thor's Hammer*, everyone was still breathing. There were holes everywhere, engine two was dead in the left wing, and the Zekes kept coming. Sal was up in the nose firing his 50 calibre at the moving targets. Another B-17, the *Gracie-Lou*, had just been shredded; her rudder almost completely blown off and she was down an engine, but still staying up. Just then a Japanese fighter strafed *Hammer's* underside. The ball turret was hit, but the gunner was OK; shaken up, but OK. The problem was that the track that it spun on was damaged, and the gunner, Sergeant Shilah Begaye, twenty, from Newcomb, New Mexico, was a sitting duck. The turret was jammed out of alignment and the tiny hatch was stuck closed. Shilah couldn't escape. The waist gunners were too busy fending off the attackers to help him. Shilah called on the com for help and Sal ran back there to rescue him. It took all of Sal's strength, using a crowbar, to realign the turret, open the hatch and pull Shilah out of the ball. Seconds later, the ball was obliterated by a speeding Zeke.

Sal and Shilah gave each other a quick smile. That was all the time they could afford for cordiality. They would celebrate when they returned to Espiritu. In the meantime, their squadron—what was left of it—was still dealing with the Japanese onslaught. The number of Zekes was diminishing, but the squadron wasn't out of the woods yet. The fighting went on for almost thirty more minutes. Most of the squadron continued to climb to higher altitude. Those with damaged engines straggled. The fewer working engines a B-17 had, the lower and slower it flew. Sal looked out of the right waist gunner's window to see who was still flying, then he looked out of the left window. Fifteen planes had taken off that morning. Eleven were heading home. Seven had all their engines intact and were pulling away. Sal looked back at the two waist gunners. They were leaning against the bulkhead, still riding the adrenaline high. Shilah was sitting next to the hole in the floor where the ball turret had been. He was cradling the crowbar like a baby. He looked up at Sal, who smiled at the sight.

"I told you that crowbar would come in handy," said Sal matter-of-factly.

"I'll never doubt you again." He stood up and walked over to Sal. "*Ahe` hee*. My family thanks you. My ancestors thank you."

"*Hágoshį́į.*"

"Very good, my friend, very good."

Just then, they heard the sputtering of one of the engines, some loud popping sounds, then they lost engine one. Now only engines three and four were keeping them aloft. The pilot feathered the dead props to reduce drag and pushed the throttle forward on the remaining two engines while he and the co-pilot mashed down on the pedal to keep a hard-right rudder. To make matters worse, a third of *Hammer's* rudder had been blown away by flack during the bomb run. It was a delicate balancing act of throttle, flaps, and rudder to maintain course. *Thor's Hammer* was not going to be able to keep up. They fell behind the other three ships that had still been with them. *Hammer* and her crew were going to be alone for the rest of the way home. It was going to be a long ride.

Everyone was back on high alert. The Solomon Islands were three hundred miles to the north of their route. They were still vulnerable to Japanese attacks as they passed near to the U.S.-Japanese battle zone.

Maintaining altitude was difficult. In the cockpit, there was talk of possibly having to ditch *Hammer*. It would be the last thing to do after all other attempts at staying aloft were made. The pilot talked to the men over the com.

"Gentlemen, I am sure you understand our situation, so I'll spare you the talk. We are closer to the Solomons than home. I think we should land there, get *Hammer* fixed up, and then head home."

The rest of the crew breathed a sigh of relief. They realized the seriousness of their situation. Heading to the Solomons was better than risking a water landing in the middle of the ocean, hoping to be rescued before the enemy—or the sharks—discovered you.

They were still within radio range of the other planes. The pilot radioed the squadron leader that they were changing their flight plan to land at Henderson Field on Guadalcanal. *Hammer's* radio operator tuned into Henderson's radar and they changed course. The crew was still on alert for any enemy ships or planes. If they were spotted, they were in no shape to fend off a squadron of Zekes and were vulnerable to anti-aircraft fire from any ships that might be lurking below them.

No one took their eyes off the sky, or the sea, or their hands off their guns. The sun had already crossed the sky and was screaming down into the cockpit. Off the port side, the left waist gunner spotted a lone Japanese fighter.

"Fuck a duck," the crew heard him say. "Ten o'clock low."

Everyone turned their attention to the Zeke, two thousand feet below them, heading west. No one spoke. They all prayed that they would go unseen as they watched in silence. The Japanese fighter remained on its course, getting farther away. Hearts pounded less against sterna. *Hammer* seemed to be at the Japanese pilot's back, in his blind spot.

Two hours later, Rennell Island came into view in the distance. It was the last bit of land they would see until Guadalcanal. *Hammer* lumbered along. The pilot and co-pilot's leg muscles were on fire from keeping her shattered rudder at hard to starboard. The flight engineer and Sal took turns giving the pilots a break, taking their seats at the yoke and pressing hard on the rudder pedals. Sal was in the left seat next to the co-pilot when flak exploded off the port side. Anti-aircraft fire erupted from below. A Japanese destroyer, four miles to the east, was taking shots at *Hammer*.

The already-out-of-commission engine number one got hit by flak, its oil tank leaking from the new hole. Engine two's prop took a hit to its hub and it flew up and over the wing, smacking the port horizontal stabilizer, damaging the elevator. To make matters worse, two Zekes were coming up at them fast from eleven o'clock low. Once the fighters were within range of *Hammer*, the destroyer ceased fire. The left waist gunner and top turret gunner began firing. The pilot resumed his place and Sal went back to the nose gun. One fighter went high while the other went low. When they got within striking distance, the Zekes let fly their bullets. The high fighter strafed across the port wing and into the cockpit. The pilot and top turret gunner were hit, leaving the co-pilot to struggle to maintain course. The co-pilot called Sal to help the pilot out of his seat and take over for him. Sal came up from the nose bubble to the cockpit, unbuckled the pilot, pulled his lifeless body out of the seat, then climbed in and pressed the right rudder pedal hard. The low fighter had come in from underneath and hit *Hammer's* belly and engine four. It was still working, but the oil leak, like a severed artery, gave away its impending death. Running on one engine was not impossible, but not with this much damage, and not while being taken apart piece by piece. The co-pilot told Sal he was going to try to make Rennell Island and ditch her as close to land as possible. He increased the throttle on the one remaining undamaged engine and steered towards

Rennell. Shilah helped the injured top gunner from the turret, put a tourniquet around his arm, and took his place.

The two Japanese fighters made hard turns and were heading back for the kill using the same one high, one low tactic. As they approached, their bullets hit *Hammer* on the top and bottom of the starboard wing. The right waist gunner hit the low fighter from prop to tail, taking out the engine and the pilot. Sal watched as it fell from the sky. How gracefully it drifted towards oblivion. For one millisecond, he wished he'd had his camera handy.

The higher fighter missed the engines, but on his pass over *Hammer*, he got two bullets into the cockpit. One went right passed Sal, right by his face and out through the window. The other one hit the co-pilot in the right shoulder, shattering his humerus. He was alive, but out of commission, and screaming in agony. Sal was on his own to maintain the aircraft in flight. His right thigh was burning with fatigue and his arms were shaking as he held the yoke.

The fighter was coming around again. Sal yelled into the com, "Shilah, you see him?"

"I got him. I got him." As the fighter was making his turn, Shilah aimed and squeezed the trigger. He was good at this. At home on the reservation, he hunted, and he was an excellent shot. He innately understood speed and trajectory. This time his instincts and his ability to understand the enemy's tactics had his 50 calibre cannons firing their ammo just before the fighter. The Zeke flew right into Shilah's stream of ordnance. The plane burst into flames and fell from the sky, following the other fighter to the sea below.

Sal got on the com. "Shilah, get in here!"

Shilah came down from the turret and into the cockpit.

"Shilah, take Jack to the back. Gerry and Mack can take care of him. Then get your ass back here." Shilah assessed the situation and helped the co-pilot from his seat and into the back with the waist gunners who were attending to Sergeant Bobby Shank, the injured top turret gunner, then rushed back to the cockpit.

"Take the co-pilot seat, I'm gonna need help keeping her straight."

Shilah sat down in the bloody seat and strapped in.

"Grab the yoke and hold on tight. Put your feet on the pedals and push the right one as hard as you can."

Hammer straightened out. Sal adjusted the trim and pushed both engines' throttles to help them maintain level flight. His plan was to follow through with Jack's plan to ditch near Rennell. He prayed that engine four wouldn't bleed out before they made it to the island.

Sal got on the com. "OK guys, we're ditching near Rennell. Gus, radio Guadalcanal."

"Aye, Captain." He messaged Guadalcanal, then sent out the SOS.

"Prepare for ditching. Follow procedures as best you can. Waist gunners, don't jettison your guns. I have a feeling they might come in handy."

Thor's Hammer was now six miles from Rennell. Sal could see the tiny island. It was completely forested, except for sparse bits of shoreline and a large lake. He knew there was a Japanese ship out there to the southwest. He wanted to make it to the north side and put the island between them. He looked over at Shilah, who looked so very calm as he scanned the sky and horizon for foe and friend. His right leg was locked straight, his hands white-knuckled on the yoke. Sal looked to his left and scanned the skies. So far, so good. Over the com, "OK guys, how you doin' back there?"

Gerry responded, "We're OK. Bobby seems OK. Jack not so good."

"Copy that. Hey, Stuey." Sergeant Stewart "Stuey" Werline, nineteen, from Scranton, Pennsylvania, was the tail gunner. And a mighty fine one, too.

"Yes, Sir."

"May as well crank the tail-wheel down now."

"Aye, Captain." Stuey admired Sal from the moment he joined *Hammer's* crew. He heard Gus call him Captain over the com even though he was Lieutenant Cristoforo. From all the commotion, Stuey presumed Sal was at the helm, keeping them all alive. Calling him Captain was a thank you for keeping them in the sky. He scanned the horizon all around from his viewpoint one last time and unbuckled himself to make his way forward.

"Scooter, before you leave the nose, I need you to dismantle the bombsight, toss it overboard and bring my camera up here to me."

"Aye Captain." Second Lieutenant Scott "Scooter" Magowan, twenty, from Philadelphia, was the navigator, whose station was in the nose next to Sal.

Shilah looked over at Sal, who was watching for any movement, his head slowly pivoting left and right. He looked up to Sal, respected him. Sal was a joker on the ground, but serious, dependable, and brave in the air. Shilah was the only one on the crew who Sal confided in about his real age. Age was just a number. It's a man's integrity that counts, and Shilah didn't know a better man than Sal for the situation they were in. Hagen wouldn't recognize him now, keeping a level head under such extreme conditions.

"Here ya go, Captain." Scooter handed Sal his Rolleiflex case.

"Thanks, Scooter. Tuck it under my seat, would ya?"

"Aye, Captain." Scooter pushed it under Sal's seat and resumed his duties preparing for ditching.

Sal turned *Hammer's* nose east, then turned her wide left, slowly, until she was aligned with Rennell's north shoreline. He began the final approach. He was only going to have one shot at landing her. There would be no go-around for another try.

Most of the island's shoreline butted right up against cliffs hundreds of feet high. There were very few places that had any beach, and those that did were tree covered almost to the water's edge. Sal spotted a patch of white sand about a third of the way up the island and steered towards it. He levelled the B-17 off at three hundred feet, trimming as much as he could to help maintain altitude. A thousand feet from the beach, he brought her down to one hundred and fifty feet. *Hammer* was flying parallel to the island and all that Sal and the crew could see were the cliffs to the left and water all around. He brought *Hammer* as close to the island as he could while bringing her slowly closer to the water; one hundred feet… seventy-five.

The water near the narrow beach was crystal clear, light blue and shallow. Sal prayed for shallow.

"Brace for ditching! Jettison the hatch cover!" Sal yelled over the com. As the plane eased below fifty feet, he reduced the throttle all the way, eased up on the rudder and pulled back on the yoke to keep her level with the water's surface. Ten feet from contact, Sal cut the engines and feathered the props. *Hammer* was now gliding to her final resting place. Just as she touched water, he would begin lowering the landing gear. Protocol dictated that the gear remained retracted in the event of emergency ditching. Sal's intention was to lower the gear after touching the water. They would extend while *Hammer* still floated and as she sank, the wheels would come to rest on the shallow reef, hopefully keeping some of her above water.

339

"Brace for impact," yelled Sal over the com. *Hammer*'s tail wheel sliced through the calm surface of the Solomon Sea just before her tail dug into the water. Sal pulled back on the yoke to keep the nose up as long as possible. The drag immediately reduced *Hammer*'s velocity, and her belly came down and skimmed across the clear, blue water. When the engines and wings hit the sea, the plane drastically slowed. The main landing gear continued to extend, eventually touching down on the reef six feet below. When the plane came to a complete stop, *Hammer* was resting slightly at an angle, her starboard wing tip just below the surface while two feet of her port wing tip extended over the sandy beach. The crew resumed their duties as her tail bobbed up and down, slowly sinking as it filled with the water coming in where the ball turret used to be.

Sal pulled the life raft handles and their hatches over each wing popped open as the rafts inflated. The crew exited the escape hatch one by one and got out onto the port wing. Sal and Shilah remained inside to hoist the injured men out of the hatch, then they gently lifted the pilot's body up into the other crewmen's hands.

From atop *Hammer*'s fuselage, Shilah could see that the life rafts were not going to be needed. The crew were walking down the port wing right onto the beach. "Nice parking job there, Cappy," said Shilah, patting Sal on the back. "Maybe when we get back to the states you can be my chauffeur."

"You're just full of jokes, huh chiefy?"

"I got a million of 'em."

"Well, that's just great. Maybe you can help Bob Hope entertain the troops."

"That's a good idea. I'll give him a call when we get back to base."

Sal shook his head. "Let's take the rafts on shore. We still might need them. Help me get the starboard one."

Together they lifted the raft and tossed it onto the port wing. Then they jumped down and each dragged a raft onto the beach where the rest of the crew had gathered.

"We should take shelter under those trees," said Sal. "We don't need the enemy shooting at us out here in plain sight."

Some of the men helped the wounded; some carried the dead pilot. The rest carried the emergency supplies and radio while Sal and Shilah dragged the rafts behind them. Under the cover of the trees, they put the wounded men in one raft and the supplies in the other and laid the dead pilot gently on the ground by a coconut tree. First Lieutenant Matthew "Matt" Morrison, twenty-two, from San Diego, would be sorely missed.

"Now what?" asked Stuey.

"We wait," said Sal. "Gus, did you get any response from your message to Guadal?"

"Aye, Cap'n, message was received."

"Good," said Sal. "And, you guys can stop calling me Captain. We're not on *Hammer* anymore. I appreciate it, though."

In unison, "Aye, Lieutenant."

The two wounded men were stable. First aid was applied, and the bleeding was stopped, but the co-pilot, First Lieutenant Walter "Wally" Porter, twenty-one, from Cheyenne, Wyoming, had lost a lot of blood and needed medical attention badly. They took stock of the emergency rations. They hoped they wouldn't have to worry about food and water and their rescue would be soon. Then they sat on the ground and waited.

Fifteen minutes passed, and Shilah stood up and walked out of the trees onto the beach. He was cocking his head, listening. "Do you hear that?"

Sal got up and joined him. "Uh-uh, no, what is it?"

"Engines, two of them, good size."

"I hear it. PBY?"

"Sounds like it." Shilah and Sal ran towards their stranded B-17 and hopped up on the wing, walked over to the fuselage and got up on top. In the distance, to the north, they spotted a plane. It was coming in low; a big, beautiful Catalina PBY, coming straight at them. Her outboard pontoons were lowered, and she was coming in for a landing. All of a sudden, the PBY raised her pontoons, pulled up and made a hard left. From over the cliff, coming from the south, two Zekes sped overhead in the direction of the American seaplane.

"Dammit," yelled Sal. "Shilah, follow me." He went over to the open hatch and climbed down and inside with Shilah right behind him. Sal got behind the right waist gunner's 50 calibre cannon and Shilah got up into the top turret. Sal squeezed off ten rounds. One of the bullets smacked one of the Zeros in the tail. It got the pilot's attention. That was Sal's intention. He wanted to distract them from the PBY. He went to the cockpit and got the flare gun, pointed it out the window and shot it into the air. That got the other pilot's attention. They turned around and came in low and fast. "Shilah, I got the one on the right."

"Copy that." They commenced firing at the Zekes, who returned fire. The Japanese bullets made trails in the water as they fast approached *Thor's Hammer*. Shilah and Sal both managed to hit their targets. Shilah's target began to smoke. Sal's target took a beating but kept on firing, hitting *Hammer*, but missing both of them. The Zekes went up and over the cliff, going high before turning around and coming down at the B-17. Shilah aimed and fired at the smoking Zero. It burst into flames and nosedived into the water fifty feet in front of *Hammer's* nose, rocking her with a wave of water from the impact. Shilah and Sal hung on tight as the other Zeke whizzed overhead, putting more holes in *Hammer's* fuselage. It throttled up and went high again before turning around and coming in fast, directly at them.

"Kamikaze!" yelled Shilah.

"GODDAMMIT!"

They aimed and fired. Sal squeezed off about thirty rounds, then ran out of ammo. "Shit! Shit! Shit!"

Shilah continued his barrage of cannon fire. Five hundred feet from *Hammer*, the Japanese pilot was on a course to destroy himself, his Zero, the American plane, and all who were in it. Then BLAMM! It exploded in mid-air. Its parts and pieces rained down into the sea about fifty yards from *Hammer's* starboard wing. The Kamikaze pilot had been so focused on destroying the American B-17 that he hadn't seen the PBY come back around. As the Zero sped towards *Hammer*, the PBY had flown to intercept. The nose gunner spat his 30 calibre rounds at the right spot, at the right time, and loaded the Mitsubishi from stem to stern, hitting all the right places. After the explosive mid-air victory, *Hammer's* crew came out from the trees, shouting and whistling.

The PBY made a hard right, then circled around, landed in the calm water and slowly made its way to shore. The pilot positioned her nose right up to the beach, right behind *Hammer's* tail.

At the PBY, *Hammer's* crew had brought their wounded and dead out from the trees to the shoreline and were putting them on board the seaplane with the assistance of the PBY's crew. Then one of the seaplane's crewmen shouted, "Jap sub surfacing, three-four-zero!"

343

Inside *Hammer*, Sal didn't hear the crewman shout about the sub, but he heard the others shouting at *Hammer's* crew to hurry up. He looked out through the window and back at the PBY and saw some of her crew looking northwest and pointing. He turned to look in that direction and saw what they were pointing at. A Kaidai class submarine had surfaced.

"Fuck a duck!" said Sal.

"What?"

"We got more company. Jap sub just showed up."

"A sub?"

"Yeah, and with a really big deck gun. We'd better get to the PBY before that sub starts shooting." He and Shilah went to the left gunner's window. "We better jump from here, keep *Hammer* between us and the sub. You can swim, can't you?"

"Very funny." He punched Sal in the shoulder. "You think because I am Navajo, I can't swim? We do have lakes and rivers in New Mexico. You ought to know that, you've been there."

"Yeah, I know, but I thought you people needed a canoe or something."

"You are a crazy white man, you know that?"

"Yeah, yeah, yeah, you keep telling me that. Tell the Army, why don'tcha, and maybe they'll give me that section eight I've been dreaming of."

"Ha, fat chance. They need crazies like you…"

"And you…"

"And me, to fly these buckets."

"Come on, let's get out of here," said Sal, gesturing to the window. "Ladies first." He laughed and braced himself for another punch in the shoulder.

"You are an asshole of the purest form, my friend." Shilah smiled when he said that. Inside he was saying *you saved my life, my friend, my brother. I will never forget you.*

"Why thank you, Chiefy. I take that as a compliment coming from you."

Shilah rolled his eyes, shook his head and listened to Sal's boyish laughter as he climbed out the window and jumped into the water.

Shilah swam alongside the B-17 towards the waiting PBY. He was alongside *Hammer's* sunken tail when he realized he hadn't heard Sal jump in. He turned around. "SAL! SAL!"

Sal poked his head out the window. "Keep swimming you dumb Injun. I'll be right behind you."

"I'm not leaving you." Shilah knew what was on Sal's mind and he was furious that he had been fooled into jumping overboard first. "I know what you're doing! You're not allowed to save my life twice in the same day."

"Swim dammit, swim." Then he went back inside *Hammer* and climbed up into the top turret. He saw the sub's crew coming up onto the deck and manning its 120mm deck cannon. They aimed it at the seaplane. The PBY's Captain saw it too and started the engines.

There was a flash from the muzzle of the 120mm, then the sound, then a big splash in the water just behind the seaplane's tail. *Hammer's* crew were now all on board. Shilah made it to the PBY while the sub's crew reloaded the deck gun. The PBY was a sitting duck.

Flash, boom, then an impact on the beach.

That shell went right over the seaplane's bow. The next one was sure to hit its target.

Sal knew what he was doing. He knew he couldn't take out that big 120mm, but he could slow them down, give the PBY time to take off. He aimed the twin 50 calibres just over the 120mm and fired. A direct hit. Two Japanese sailors fell overboard. The rest of them ducked behind the gun or hit the deck. Whenever Sal saw one of them attempt to man the gun, he fired again.

The Captain of the PBY knew what the man in the B-17 was doing. He knew he couldn't sit there just waiting to be blown out of the water. He also knew that the sub's captain had probably radioed the situation to other nearby enemy vessels. As the PBY maneuvered for take-off, Sal kept the Japanese sailors at bay. Then the seaplane went full throttle, blowing a salty mist onto *Thor's Hammer*, hazing Sal's view of the sub. The decision to take off and leave that brave man in the B-17 behind, would become the PBY pilot's most painful memory of the war.

Sal watched the seaplane leave the water and rise up into the safety of the sky. He stopped firing and ducked beneath the bubble. He thought that if he went silent, then the Japanese might assume that whoever was manning the top turret might have made it to the seaplane and escaped with the rest of the crew. He didn't need them aiming that big deck gun at him. He climbed down from the turret and went over to the left gunner's window, jumped into the water and swam to shore. Maintaining a low profile and keeping *Hammer* between himself and the sub, Sal went into the trees where the crew had been.

And he waited.

The sub didn't move; it just floated there with its deck gun now pointed at *Hammer*. The B-17 had now sunk all the way by the tail, her nose tilted up like she was sitting on the tarmac.

"What are they waiting for?"

He watched, heart pounding, breathing fast. Then the sub's gun pivoted back to its forward-facing position and the crew went back inside the conning tower. Slowly she sailed, turning north into deeper water, and sank beneath the surface.

Sal waited ten minutes after the sub disappeared completely, then walked out onto the beach. It was now very peaceful as the setting sun turned the sky crimson, splashing variants of gold and orange on the sparse clouds; a beautiful ending to an ugly day.

He was soaked, dripping wet, and contemplated stripping down to his skivvies and hanging his uniform somewhere to dry. He went back to the rafts and took one of their ropes and tied it tautly between two trees, then hung up his wet uniform and socks. He had taken off his bomber jacket when he and the crew had first gone ashore. It was still where he had left it, on the ground next to a tree with Shilah's jacket. It was the only dry article of clothing he had. He collected the food and water rations and put them in the clean raft and turned over the bloody one in which the wounded men had lain, and he lay on its bottom.

It was quiet lying there under the palm trees. Stars winked through the openings in the rustling fronds as the wind blew gently off the water. He thought about Hagen and the times they'd spent lying side by side in the corn field, looking up at the stars as the breeze rippled across the field. The last time was in the summer of '41, when they had talked about their futures after high school.

Sal sat up. He remembered that his camera was still in the cockpit. He got up and walked towards *Hammer* and stopped halfway. The full moon had risen an hour before and had taken over from the sun when it went to the other side of the Earth. It was big and brilliant, and it illuminated everything in a bluish-white light. He could see his plane sitting there in the water. It was a conflict of senses. Even though the air was balmy, *Hammer* looked cold in the moonlight.

347

He climbed onto her wing, then up on the fuselage and down through the hatch. The only light inside was the moonlight coming in through the right waist gunner's window. It was so quiet. He couldn't recall it ever being so silent inside *Hammer*. He went to the cockpit and felt around under the seat and found his camera case. He took the Rolleiflex out, put the strap around his neck and sat in the co-pilot's seat. His view was to the west with the water off to his right and the island's high cliffs to the left. The Solomon Sea was so very calm that night, so still, like it was mourning the death of *Thor's Hammer*, and those two dead Japanese pilots out there. He patted the instrument panel. "Well, old girl, there's no recovering from this. I'm really gonna miss you."

While he was communing with *Hammer*, something caught his eye; movement in the water, off to the right. The moonlight glinted off something floating out there. He fumbled in the dark for the binoculars. He found them and went to the top turret, put them up to his eyes and looked out. He strained to see what was out there. There it was again; another glint! The moonlight was reflecting off a wet conning tower. The sub was back! Sal's heart skipped two beats and then hurried to make up for it.

"Dammit, not again. What the hell are you doing?" He ran scenarios in his head and the one that seemed most logical was that they were looking for signs of life—firelight, flashlight, a cigarette's glow. He looked up to the moon and thanked it for being bright enough to keep him from needing his flashlight, possibly giving his presence away to the enemy. He climbed down from the turret and went to the right waist gunner's window, walking in knee-deep water.

The sub turned on its searchlight and scanned the beach and the plane. Sal moved out of sight. The bright light moved slowly over the plane, first lighting up the cockpit, then lighting up the inside when it came through the gunner's window. Ever the photographer, he removed his lens cover, and prepared for the return of the searchlight, hoping that the camera settings were correct. On its way back, he snapped a shot towards the tail as the light illuminated the interior and the water inside. Then he went up to the base of the top turret and snapped a shot into the cockpit when the light reached there. The sub turned off its spotlight and it went dark again.

He went back to the gunner's window, dialed in a slow shutter speed, stood in the window and held the camera on the frame to keep it steady. He looked down through the viewfinder and did his best to focus and snapped a couple shots of the sub in the moonlight. He wouldn't know how any of these photos would come out until he could get back to base and get them developed.

He looked up from the camera at the submarine as it slowly moved east. It then turned north to deeper water and went back out to sea. He put the lens cover back on and waited to make sure there weren't going to be any surprises, then climbed up through the hatch and back down the wing to the beach. He took two more shots of *Hammer* in the moonlight, then went back to the raft and lay down. He was tired but wired from his nocturnal experience with the Japanese submarine. He hoped that the PBY would be back to get him before the enemy decided to take an even closer look at *Hammer*.

Sal hadn't slept anywhere that wasn't filled with snoring, flatulent, belching men since before the war. He slept most of the night and awoke when the sun was just a faint glow beneath the eastern horizon. His uniform was dry for the most part, a few damp spots here and there, so he got dressed and ate something from the emergency rations and walked onto the beach with his camera around his neck.

It was peacefully quiet; just the sounds of seabirds, and the sea licking the beach. He sat on *Hammer's* wing, watching the sky get lighter in the east. As our nearest star broke the surface of the horizon, the landscape lit up with the glow of new morning light. He hopped off the wing onto the sand and aimed his lens at *Thor's Hammer*. He walked to the water's edge in front of *Hammer's* nose where the Japanese fighter had nosedived into the water. The Mitsubishi's tail and one wing protruded from the surface. Sal said a silent prayer for the Japanese pilot and his comrade a hundred yards away. Fearless men, although they were the enemy, now belonged to the sea, and Heaven.

Respect has no affiliations.

He took a few more photos and headed back to the trees. He was well aware that he could easily be seen by friend or foe. Friend knew he was there, foe did not.

Back under the trees, he looked around for places to hide, just in case. He found nothing. The only place to go was up the four-hundred-foot coral face. Not gonna happen! He went back to the rafts and waited.

One hundred fifty miles to the north, *Hammer's* crew watched the PBY take off and head back to Rennell. Fifteen miles from their destination they encountered the Japanese and their Kawanishi H8K; a bigger, faster and more heavily armed seaplane. The Japanese engaged the PBY, firing their 20mm cannons, quickly taking out engine one. The PBY returned fire, hitting the H8K along her bow but inflicting no significant damage. The PBY's Captain was now forced to turn around and try to maintain a heading back to Henderson field on only one engine. The Japanese were not going to let her go that easily and when the H8K came around again, she took out the PBY's other engine, and the right waist gunner. An SOS was sent to Guadalcanal as the American pilot glided her safely to a landing on the sea, doubly regretting having left that brave crewman, First Lieutenant Salvatore Cristoforo behind the night before.

Satisfied for now, the Japanese seaplane resumed its original course. Its crew was on a mission. If the American PBY and its crew were still floating on the sea when he returned, then they would finish them off.

On Rennell Island, Sal was hoping for the best and preparing for the worst. He couldn't take his mind off last night's visit by the Japanese submarine. Something was up, he could feel it. He put this camera back in its case and then wrapped it inside Shilah's bomber jacket, and then in his jacket, and found a place deep within the trees. He put the bundle at the base of one of the larger trunks and covered it with fallen palm fronds, then went back to the overturned raft and lay down. He thought of Hagen. He wondered where he was, what he was doing. Was he safe? He thought about the rest of his family, and the farm, and Heidi. He closed his eyes and pictured them sitting around *Tableosaurus Rex*, laughing. His thoughts, the island's calmness; they were hypnotizing.

His Zen-zone was interrupted. His mind came back to the present situation—airplane motors, more than two, big ones, unfamiliar. He sat up and looked out at the beach. He put the binoculars around his neck and went to the edge of the trees and listened. The sound wasn't coming from anywhere specific; it just *was*. He walked onto the sand and looked east, then west. He saw nothing. The engines got louder. He walked to the right, looking out to sea, and when he cleared *Hammer's* big rudder, the sound localized, its volume increased, and its source was revealed. There it was! The maker of the sound! Just as Sal had feared. The Japanese were back.

"SHITSHITSHIT!!" He ran back under the cover of the trees and cranked up the emergency radio hoping to contact someone, anyone.

Nothing! No one!

"Shit!"

He grabbed a canteen of water and the radio and ran west through the trees for about a hundred feet, stepping only on fallen palm fronds to conceal his tracks, then stopped and edged up to the beach and hid behind a tree. He watched the big four-engined seaplane turn west, then make a wide arc south then east and land in the smooth, blue water, parallel to the island. It coasted slowly as it turned inland. The pilot pulled her nose right up to the B-17's starboard wing and a crewman tied her up to *Hammer's* outboard prop. The crew exited their plane and boarded *Hammer*, walking on her wing then through the hatch on top of the fuselage.

Sal knew they were looking for any useful intelligence papers, the Norden bombsight, anything they could use against the Americans. They wouldn't find anything. Ditching protocol was followed, except with regards to the waist guns, and everything was jettisoned. He watched the Japanese, like ants on a dead grasshopper picking away at the carcass. The seaplane's pilot stood on top of *Hammer*, turning his head slowly, scanning the terrain, the trees. He looked like he was sniffing the air for the scent of prey. His gaze lowered to the left wing that extended to the beach, spying the trail of footsteps in the sand leading to the place where Sal and the others had been. He barked orders at his men. They jumped onto the wing and walked onto the beach. They unholstered their pistols and slowly followed the trail of footsteps, with the pilot leading the way. When he got to within ten feet of the trees, the pilot yelled something in English.

"Surrender, American pilot."

Sal froze, inside and out, forgetting for a moment to breathe. The pilot spoke perfect English and was acting as if he *knew* Sal was here. Sal's instinct was to run further, but he didn't want to chance that his movement would give away his position. He hoped he'd distanced himself enough from the rafts so that they'd search the local area, take their souvenirs, give up, and assume he'd made it to the PBY last night.

That damned sub Captain must have reported everything.

Sal let go of the palm tree, turned and slowly walked further west, away from the Japanese, walking slowly, silently on the sand between the dry, fallen palm fronds.

The Japanese pilot, Commander Hiromitsu Matsushita, and his crew, were inspecting the rafts, turning them over, rifling through the emergency provisions. The emergency radio was missing. They saw the blood. Commander Matsushita was a man of detail. He studied American ways, knew their ships, their planes, their language. He knew what to look for inside the B-17. When he saw the waist guns still in place, he had hoped to find other items: the bombsight, paperwork, maps. The Americans were thorough in sanitizing the plane, but the pilot had the foresight to keep the waist guns. The wreckage of the two Mitsubishis in the water was evidence of their usage, and the pilot's intuition. He was here somewhere; he could feel it. He told his crew to expand their search.

Sal stopped every thirty or so steps to turn around and peek out to the beach from behind a tree. He hoped each time that he would see them getting back on their plane. Each time, he saw no one, except the one crewman standing on *Hammer's* starboard wing.

Dammit. He's not giving up easily.

Sal resumed his stealthy retreat. He didn't need to keep checking on the status of his predators. He just kept walking. When he hears the H8K's engines, he'll know that the coast will be clear. He walked another hundred feet and the trees ended at a wall of ancient coral that went right up to the water's edge. There was nowhere to go but up, deeper into the trees, or into the water. He crouched down and waited, the sweat dripping into his eyes, his heart pounding in his ears. He kept his eyes on the trees, looking for movement.

He waited.

Minutes seemed like hours.

One by one, the seaplane's engines came alive. A wave of relief came over him. He crawled to the edge of the tree line and peered out. She was idling while the crew got back on board. The last man untied her from *Hammer's* prop, she reversed, turned and took off to the west. Sal waited until the engines' sounds became a very distant hum. He tried one more time to make contact on the radio. Static again.

As he walked back to the rafts, the H8K's exhaust wafted into the trees. The smell conjured images of *Thor's Hammer* and her crew, his friends, *all alive*, returning from a successful bombing run. He approached what was left of the rafts, still with his mind elsewhere. The sight of the deflated rafts made unusable by a Japanese bayonet, the tossed-about rations, brought him to reality, but not to his full senses.

Behind him, there was a click—a pistol being cocked—then, "Welcome back, American pilot," in a slightly Japanese-accented English.

SHIT! SHIT! SHIT! FUCKING!... SHIT!

Sal looked up and out through the trees at the beach. He was only ten feet from the edge of the tree line. He might be able to outrun the man, but not the bullet. He turned around to see his enemy.

"I did not think that you would have fallen for the ruse." Commander Matsushita grinned.

"I'm sorry if I disappointed you."

"I am not. Please, put down the radio and your sidearm."

Sal bent over...

"Slowly... please."

...and placed them on the sand at his feet.

"Thank you. Now, turn around, put your hands on your head, and walk towards your plane."

Sal obliged. His heart was back in his throat and the python was in his guts.

Near the waterline, just in front of *Hammer's* wingtip, they stopped. "Now, please, American pilot, get on your knees."

Sal dropped to his knees. In front of him, *Thor's Hammer* still drip-drip-dripped oil into the rainbow-slicked water from her dead engines, like a mother's tears of pain for her children—and for herself. She couldn't protect him anymore. Sal's thoughts went to Hagen. He wanted Hagen to be the last thing on his mind when the bullet went through his brain. He smiled. He sent out a thought transmission, hoping Hagen was sensitive enough to hear his goodbye. He always seemed to be able to read his mind at home. He looked up into the clear, blue Pacific sky. *I love you.*

"Are you praying to your god, American pilot?"

Silence.

Sal blocked out Commander Matsushita's words with thoughts of Hagen and his family. He thought about his real parents and Marta. He hoped they had saved a place for him. He thought of that first ride home in the back of the truck with Hagen. He thought of the hot chocolate Marta had made for them. A tear from each eye rolled down his cheeks. He sucked them into his mouth, so dry, the salty liquid loosening his lips from his teeth. Then he bowed his head and waited.

"If you are praying for it to end quickly, then your request will not be granted. If you are praying for your life to be spared, then you may consider the answer to be in your favor, but the conditions less than favorable."

Commander Matsushita said no more. Sal never made a sound. Forty or so minutes passed and from the west came the humming sound of the H8K's engines. Matsushita looked at his watch.

"If you had waited one hour, American pilot, I would never have had the pleasure of making your acquaintance. How do you say, 'Patience is a virtue'?"

The big Kawanishi made a smooth landing, then tied up to the B-17 one more time. Some of her crew remained on the seaplane while the rest walked on *Hammer* to the beach, and their waiting commander and his prize.

Sal was taken aboard the seaplane at gunpoint. Matsushita returned to his place in the cockpit, and the H8K took off into the western sky with Sal in its belly, swallowed whole by the flying whale.

Hagen's Railcar
Midnight

Hagen took a deep breath. "I would like to stop there for a bit, if you don't mind. I need to rest my brain, and my throat."

Emily sniffed, then blew her nose, then nodded in agreement. "I need a break, too." She got up to go to the rest room. "You need any more water?"

"Yes, please."

"Are you doing alright?" She laid a hand on his shoulder as she walked by him.

He put a hand on hers. "I am fine, my dear. How are you holding up?"

"Whew, I don't know. Emotionally drained, I guess?"

"If you weren't, you would not be human."

"I'll be right back." After the restroom, she went to the kitchen for some water. She was coming down from her caffeine high. She knew Hagen wanted to stay up longer, so she made a pot of pressed coffee and brought it back to the patio along with the water and the two rinsed out coffee cups from earlier.

"I'm back." She slid the door closed and put the tray on the coffee table.

"I smell coffee," he said with a smile.

"Well, I figured you aren't stopping there, at least I hope you're not. And the bucket of espresso is wearing off. Want a cup?"

"Yes, please, thank you. And, I will be continuing."

"Good." She poured for both of them, then resumed her spot in the corner of the sectional.

"I know what is on your mind," said Hagen. "You want to know what happened to Sal."

"I hoped you wouldn't leave me hanging."

"The short of it is, he became a prisoner of war."

"When did you find out? How did you find out?" She sipped her coffee.

"I was in England at the time, working with British Intelligence. I did not find out right away about Sal. My family was notified first, by telegram, that Sal was MIA. The Japanese did not release information about their prisoners as willingly as the Germans. When a search and rescue team finally made it to Rennell Island, they found evidence that the Japanese had been there before them. They searched everywhere; they did flyovers of the island. There was no sign of him. All they found were the deflated rafts, and the radio, and Sal's hidden camera wrapped in the bomber jackets. It was assumed he had been taken prisoner. They assumed correctly. I was notified by my commanding officer about Sal's situation. You may safely assume how I felt. I thanked my commanding officer and went to my quarters and cried, cried so very hard. Then I sent a telegram to my family telling them what I knew, that Sal was MIA. I knew he was alive. I could feel it. But it wasn't until three weeks later that we were informed by the Japanese that Sal was their prisoner."

"How long was he held captive?"

"Until the end of the war: nine hundred and ninety-seven days." Hagen stopped and swallowed. "I counted each day." He teared up and dabbed his eyes with his napkin. "I knew how the Japanese treated their prisoners. I never told my family. I knew they had enough on their minds and would find out when—if—he came home."

Emily scooted over and gave him a hug. Again, she had no words to say. Hagen cried at the memories.

"Thank you, my dear."

She kissed him on the cheek and went back to her corner.

He took a slow, deep breath, then let out a sigh. "Alright, I made it through that part without completely breaking down. I won't go into as much detail about what happened to me in Europe. As you know I was deeply involved with counter-intelligence. We had to stay ahead of the Nazis, figure out their ways, decipher their communications, and anticipate their moves."

He leaned forward, sipped his coffee and then sat back. "I would, though, like to tell you of a couple of profound experiences that I had."

"Please. I'm pretty sure your time was not uneventful."

"I don't believe anyone returns from war complaining about how bored they were."

"No, I wouldn't think so." She waited a few moments while he collected his thoughts.

"As the war neared its end in Europe, I was assigned to a group that was attached to the U.S. Seventh Army's 45th Infantry Division. It was the end of April 1945. We had received intelligence that a prisoner had escaped from a Nazi concentration camp and had made his way to the Americans, pleading for help. I was a witness to the liberation."

"Love and compassion
are necessities, not luxuries.
Without them, humanity
cannot survive."

—Dalai Lama

Dachau
April 29, 1945

As Hagen and his division approached KZ Dachau, a horrible smell permeated the air, getting stronger as they got closer. They entered the camp, yet despite the freezing cold, their senses were bombarded by the stench of death, decay, and despair. The sun shone brightly, contrasting the new snow which had fallen during the night against the bleakness of the surroundings. Prisoners were cheering for their liberators, becoming more jubilant with the realization that they were being rescued. Those with enough strength hoisted some of their heroes onto their collective shoulders like fans of the winning team. Others used their strength to impart justice upon the remaining SS and German soldiers who had remained behind to surrender Dachau to the Americans. There were many prisoners not so fortunate; weak and exhausted from malnutrition, disease, and mistreatment, they succumbed to their condition days, even weeks after being freed.

Hagen's sensitivities took a terrific beating. Being surrounded by the victims of the Nazi killing machine was overwhelming. Some of the souls he came into close contact with were battling hope against helplessness whilst struggling for life. Stronger friends helped weaker ones out of the barracks into the light, into view of the Americans. Some smiled, some cried, some did both. Some were too weak to emote at all. As the news spread throughout the camp that freedom had come, despair became excited confusion. Liberation meant freedom from captivity; but not a return to normalcy. Life would never be the same for the survivors. Some had no living relatives. Whole families had been erased; their homes were gone.

Hagen slowly walked deeper into the camp. Prisoners were making their way towards the front. A few hugged him in passing. They thanked him in so many languages—Czech, Polish, Hungarian, Romanian, French, German, Russian.

He walked against the stream of people, going deeper into the camp on the Lagerstrasse from the Appellplatz. People were coming from the barracks by the hundreds.

My God! How many are there?

From behind him, the cacophony of voices in their many languages echoed off the cold wooden barracks. Hagen saw women emerging from one of the buildings. Some walked easily, others not so well. Although the camp held mostly men, there were also women and children, some of whom had been transported just recently to Dachau from Auschwitz-Birkenau. They walked and shuffled towards the main gate, following the sounds of liberation. It was unlike anything anyone had heard during their incarceration at Dachau. It was neither threatening nor combatant nor evil. It attracted all who could walk, or shuffle, or crawl; like a lighthouse beacon to ships in distress.

A woman shuffled towards him. When she got close enough for him to see the features of her gaunt face, he was taken aback. She was probably no more than twenty-five. What was done to her, what she had endured, had made her look twice her age. His heart ached. She half-smiled through cracked lips at him as she passed. With each step, the cold April breeze washed the stench of death from her.

Hagen turned back to face the barracks the woman had emerged from and walked to the entrance. The shuffling woman had enough strength to ambulate. There could be survivors inside who might be too weak. He walked through the door. What he saw broke his heart. The living conditions were subhuman; the filth, the stench. *How could anyone survive living in this place?* But some of them had survived. The walking corpses he had seen outside proved that life is tough, it is brave, it is resilient and perseverant. As he walked down the aisle, he scanned the three-tiered bunks that had been the women's sleeping quarters. Most of the bunks were empty. A few were still occupied, but Hagen could tell that only their shell remained. They had already passed on, out of this hell on to a better place. Their eyes stared blankly at something not in the room—a death gaze. He made the sign of the cross at each of their remains, then continued down the aisle. Off to the right, on a bottom bunk, were two young women, side by side. They were holding hands. Their heads were turned to face each other. Hagen cried at the sight. He could no longer contain his emotions. He got down on his knees at their side, leaned on the cold wood of the bunk, closed his eyes, put his clasped hands up to his face and prayed.

He prayed aloud through his tears. He prayed to God for their peace, for their souls, and for their loved ones. Then something brushed his hands. He moved them down and opened his eyes only to find that the woman closest to him had turned her head away from the other woman and was staring at him. She was watching him pray. Even in her weakened physical condition, a peaceful look came upon her face. She reached out to touch him again. Their eyes met; souls met. He held out his hand to take hers, so cold and frail, and he took it into both hands to give her some of his warmth. Her sleeve moved and he could see the last three numbers of the tattoo on her left forearm—463

Then she said something in Polish. "*Błękitny Anioł.*"

"I'm sorry, I do not understand."

She turned her head and gave the dead woman next to her a kiss on the forehead, then her hand. *"Dopóki nie spotkamy się ponownie, droga siostro."* She turned back to Hagen. She smiled and nodded and held out her hand. He understood the meaning and took her hand in his.

He gently helped her out of the bunk. She could barely stand up without assistance. Her clothes were threadbare. Her shoes, what was left of them, were bound with rags to hold them together. She was shivering, either from the cold or fear or exhaustion or all three. Hagen took off his long military coat and put it on her. He walked with her for a few steps and caught her in mid-collapse, then put his right arm under her legs with his left behind her shoulders and picked her up.

My God, there is nothing to her!

She put her right arm around him as they walked out of the barracks and into the cold air. Her eyes were fixed on Hagen's face. She was in the company of a pure, kind soul. She saw only him, and nothing else. The rest of the world was out of focus. The sound of his boots crunching the cold, hard ground sounded so very distant, like he was holding her fifty feet up into the sky. With each step he took, her spirit came to life, infused by the essence of goodness, sloughing off the residue that evil had slathered on her; tarred and feathered with hot pitch and the devil's plumage. Tears coursed down his cheeks like salty springs. He wasn't sobbing, just flowing. He was furious, sad, confused— humbled.

The woman reached up with her hand and wiped away his tears. She whispered, *"Nie płacz, mój Błękitny Anioł."* She could not remember when she had last cried or had anyone cry for her. He looked down into her eyes. Her visage spoke volumes. He smiled down at her, then kissed her on her forehead. She wrapped her arm around him as tightly as she could and rested her head against his chest. His thumping heart hearkened her soul back to before her body entered the world, hearing the beating of her mother's heart from inside her womb. Her soul was safe now. She was being reborn.

Hagen had now reached the fringe of the mêlée of people. The sight of his approach, his tears, the woman in his arms, gave people pause. Some of the other women came to their side. They were talking to Hagen and the woman in Polish. One of them said something that made the woman in his arms take her eyes from Hagen. More words were exchanged. Then one of the women left the group and ran into the crowd yelling someone's name. Hagen couldn't make it out. The woman in his arms turned back to him and said something. He responded in English. "I do not understand." Then he tried German. *"Ich kann Sie nicht verstehen."*

Her eyes widened! She understood him. *"Helen ging, meinen Ehemann zu finden."*

"Husband? *Ehemann?"*

"Ja, meinen Ehemann."

From out of the crowd came Helen, with a young man in tow. He was short in stature, dressed in tattered, striped clothes, and was as undernourished as the woman in Hagen's arms. When he saw his wife in the arms of the American soldier, his knees buckled and he fell to the ground, clasping his hands together, looking up to the heavens. Helen and another woman helped him stand back up and he hobbled to his wife, crying tears of joy. He kissed the woman's face, her hands. She looked up at Hagen. *"Ich denke, dass ich gut jetzt sein werde. Siekönnen mich setzen niederzuwerfen."*

Hagen put her gently down onto her feet. The couple embraced, then the man put his wife's face in his hands. She said something to her husband in Polish and he turned to Hagen. He stood up straight, composed himself as if he was about to address royalty, then said something in Polish. His wife tapped him on the shoulder and told him that this man speaks German.

"Danke, dass du meine Frau vom Abgrund zurückgebracht hast."

Then he grabbed Hagen and squeezed him as tightly as he had the strength to do. Hagen put his arms around him and felt his bones. The man was trembling. He had no shoes. The man's wife put her arms around both of them. Hagen let go of the man, pulled open his coat that the woman was wearing, and tucked her husband inside with her.

"Gott segne dich," said the woman.

"Nein, gnädige Frau, Gott segne dich. Gott segne euch alle."

She put her hand up to his face one more time, closing her eyes, breathing deeply the cold air between them, as if smelling springtime and new life.

Helen came over and walked them back to their little group. Hagen stood motionless, numb, watching all of the survivors rejoicing in their freedom. The woman turned around once more to look at her savior. Hagen did not move until they melted into the crowd, then he rejoined his outfit as they continued to give aid and comfort to other survivors of Dachau.

Germany surrendered unconditionally on May 7, 1945. The war in Europe was over. But the damage inflicted upon the countries, the cities and the people, would take years to overcome.

The American public wanted their family members home as soon as possible. Demobilization of the Allied military forces in Europe after the surrender was not a fast process. Not everyone returned home right away. Some servicemen remained until the following year. The war in the

Pacific had not yet ended, and although it was apparent that an Allied victory was almost certain, some personnel were transferred to the Pacific theatre.

Hagen needed to be home again. He needed to be with his family, and they needed him. With Sal still in Japanese captivity, his mind was now focused on finding him and bringing him home. He asked his superiors to keep up with their attempts to find Salvatore Cristoforo. He made it known that even though they had different last names, Sal was his brother.

Six months after Sal was officially declared a POW of the Empire of Japan, Georg and the family received word from Washington, D.C. that Sal was to be awarded the Congressional Medal of Honor. Everyone prayed that it wasn't going to be awarded posthumously. The Army assured Hagen that every effort was being made to locate his brother and bring him home alive.

Back home in New Jersey, the Beckenbauer family was so relieved that Hagen had made it through the war and would be coming home—maybe not right away, but he would be walking through the door, alive, on his own two feet. Georg's memories of Hagen's namesake lying in a box next to his twin brother Karl in the family chapel haunted his soul. Every day he had prayed that he would not have to go through that with his sons. One was safe. One was missing. By now, Georg was aware of how the Japanese treated their prisoners. Again, and again, he prayed that Sal was safe, unharmed, alive.

Hagen spent the next three months in Germany, assisting with the translation of Nazi papers and the interrogation of captured German soldiers and officers. When it was time to go home, he requested that he make a detour to visit his family's home in Lampertheim. Permission was granted and, on his way west from

Nuremberg, he got off the train at Mannheim. The city was in shambles, having been bombed over and over again throughout the war. The railway lines had only recently been repaired.

Once off the train, he began to walk in the direction of Lampertheim. He had walked about half a mile when a worse-for-wear Opel Olympia pulled up next to him. The driver was an older man in his sixties, who seemed as tired as the car. He offered the American soldier a lift. Hagen gratefully accepted, and on the way a conversation was struck.

"Thank you for the ride."

"My pleasure, young man. You are an American, yes?" He gazed at Hagen's uniform.

"Yes, sir, why do you ask?"

"Your German is quite good. Your American accent is almost non-existent. Are you from Germany?"

"No, sir, but my parents are from here. Lampertheim, actually. We had a farm here. That is where I am going."

The man looked over at Hagen. The boy's features bore a resemblance to someone he knew years ago. "What is your family's name?"

"Beckenbauer, sir. My father is Georg Beckenbauer."

The man's eyes widened. "I knew it, I just knew it." He smacked the steering wheel with his right palm. "I thought you had a familiarity about you. I knew your parents and your grandparents. You look just like your father. When you got in the car, I thought I was seeing things, but I thought no, it can't be. It has been over twenty years since I last saw Georg, and you do not look any older than your father was when he left for America."

Hagen's interest was piqued. "How did you know my family?"

"Their farm, of course. My wife and I frequented your grandmother's little market for eggs, cheese and milk. Your grandmother spun wool, as well. I still have a sweater that my dear departed wife knitted for me from wool spun by your grandmother. Your grandfather, he smoked the best Rauchschinken and brewed his own beer."

"It sure is a small world," said Hagen. "I cannot wait to tell my father I met someone who knew him. What did you say your name was?

"Krüger, Josef Krüger. My wife was Maria." He put out a hand for Hagen to shake.

"Hagen Beckenbauer, pleased to meet you, Herr Krüger."

"Josef. Please call me Josef."

"Pleasure to meet you, Josef."

"Tell me, how is your family, besides this damned war?"

"My father is well. My mother passed away in 1932."

"Oh, I am so sorry to hear that. Your poor father. And you. Do you have any siblings?"

"Yes, sir, two sisters and two brothers."

Josef pursed his lips and shook his head. "Five children without their mother. How did your father manage?"

Not wanting to go into details about the orphanage, "Our family managed with the help of close friends."

"Good, good. We all need each other to help us through tragic times. It binds us together and helps us appreciate the better times. What does your father do in America?"

"We have a farm in New Jersey, much like we had here, crops and dairy."

"Very nice." They arrived at the entrance to the little road leading into the farm. "Here we are, the entrance to your old farm. Shall I drive you in?"

"No thank you, Josef. I can walk." They shook hands once again.

"Very good then. Take care, and don't forget to remember me to your father."

"I will not forget, and thank you again, Josef."

"My pleasure, young man. Take care."

Hagen got out of the car and waved as the Opel drove off, then turned to look at the long dirt drive that led into the farm. It looked like it hadn't been traveled upon in some time. He began walking towards the house in the distance. As he approached, he could see that the buildings appeared to be uncared for, unused for some time. There were missing boards on the barns. Shutters were askew on the main house; some of its shingles strewn about on the ground along with the flotsam and jetsam of the war and many seasons.

He went up onto the porch, rubbed the grime from a window with his sleeve and peeked inside. No furniture was visible, but he could see the layout of the living room, the stairs that led to the second floor, the stone fireplace. He looked off into the distance and could see the chapel in the stand of trees on the other side of the unkempt barley field. He remembered the stories his father told of the cemetery, the ancestors buried there—his parents, his brothers.

He went down the porch steps, stepping over a missing board and walked to the field and into the waist-high barley. He closed his eyes as he walked, holding out his hands to his sides, feeling the tops of the barley with his open palms. He breathed in deeply the smells of the dirt and grasses. Images of him and Sal running through the fields of grain their father grew for the cows to graze in flashed through his memories. He smiled as he pictured the good times, the good memories, but those images were shattering as made-up ones of Sal somewhere in a Japanese prison camp slammed through his mind. Hagen stopped walking, and closed his eyes so tightly, as if squeezing the negative thoughts from his mind. One more deep breath, and he opened his eyes and continued the walk.

As he got close enough to make out the chapel's features—the stained-glass windows, the shapes of the headstones, the fence that surrounded the little cemetery—memories of the cemetery in the peach orchard back home came into his head. His mother's face was still clear—her voice, her laughter. He smiled again, and whispered, "I love you, Mama," onto the breeze and let it carry his words up to Heaven.

The chapel appeared to be in good condition. All the windows were intact, and there were no holes in the roof. It seemed the grounds had been kept up as well. The area was clear of debris and there was evidence of someone having recently placed flowers at one of the graves. Hagen opened the gate, walked in and browsed, reading the names of his ancestors with dates from centuries ago. The most recent ones—his grandparents, and uncles—were now before him. He read their names, their dates of birth and death. It was an odd feeling to see his and Karl's names on the headstones at the side-by-side graves. It was his Uncle Hagen's grave that was the recipient of the recent floral arrangement. He closed his eyes again and visualized the story his father had told him of the day that he returned from the war with his two brothers in boxes. It was a surreal feeling to think about that, to put it into a vision whilst standing right over their graves. He prayed he would not be returning home with Sal in a box and shuddered at the very thought of it.

As his shudder faded, a sound came from behind him. He turned around to see a woman standing at the open gate with her hands holding onto a bicycle. She gasped and let go of the handlebars. The bicycle fell to the ground, her hands to her face, mouth agape. Her face twisted with curiosity and disbelief.

She spoke German. "Georg? Is that you?"

Hagen sucked in a breath. This woman knew his father. She looked and sounded like his mother. He was shocked into speechlessness.

"It is not possible; you have not aged a bit!"

"I am not Georg," his voice wavered. "My name is Hagen."

Now it was her turn to lose her tongue to emotional paralysis. Her eyes looked from him to the flowers on the grave back to him. "Hagen. Hagen?" Her head cleared a bit when she saw the American uniform; connections were made as assumptions were constructed. Hagen could see her thoughts on her face. Her feelings were not difficult to read. Then he looked down at the flowers that were in the bicycle's basket on the ground. He also put two and two together.

"Aunt Mathilde? My mother's sister?"

"Mother? You are the son of my sister and Georg? This is too incredible! You... you look just like your father. My God, I thought I was seeing a specter." She went to him and grabbed hold of him, hugged him, pulled back and looked into eyes that were hauntingly familiar. "Oh my, so like Georg. I have not heard anything from your father since Hitler took over. I thought I would never hear from him again. How is he? I miss him. I miss your mother." Tears were parading down her cheeks as she spoke. "We could not believe what happened." She sniffled. "We were so sad that we could not go to the funeral." Memories of the past came torrenting through her mind, engulfing her present emotions as she tried to comprehend what was happening. "I had hoped that he would forgive my parents, me, us, for not coming." Sobbing took over her speech momentarily. She composed herself, shook her head and wiped the tears from her eyes with a handkerchief from her dress pocket. "My father, your grandfather, went into a deep depression after that. You would have thought it would have been my mother, but it was my father. She was the strong one, she kept us going until he recovered, came back to his senses. Then that bastard Hitler took over. It gave us little time to grieve for my sister. Then the goddamned war." She looked at the chapel and made the sign of the cross. "Now, it is just me."

Hagen was taking it all in, but not as quickly as she spoke it; rapid firing so much emotionally-charged information at him that there was about a five-second delay in his head. When his brain got to *Now, it is just me,* the emotional roller coaster halted. "Just you?"

"Yes, just me." Her tears were replaced by anger. "Mannheim was constantly being attacked by the Americans or the British. We always worried about living so close to the bombings. One night—I was not home; I was working at the tavern—we heard airplanes in the distance. We listened as they got closer, then went over us; then came the whistling of the falling bombs and explosions all around us. The ground shook under our feet; windows shattered; the lights went out. I ran out of the tavern and ran all the way home." She swallowed hard. "There was nothing left. A bomb had landed right on our home. It was completely destroyed— with my parents inside." She took a big breath and let out a long sigh. "And now, I am alone."

Hagen put his arms around her and said softly, "Aunt Mathilde, it is not just you anymore. You are not alone." She hugged him so very tightly as she cried onto his shoulder. Hagen's tears dripped into her hair. He looked up into the sky through the trees.

Dear God, hasn't this family endured enough?

Their crying subsided and they let go of each other. She went over to her bicycle, picked it up, and leaned it against

373

the gate post. She picked up the flowers that had fallen on the ground and a little blanket that was in the basket. She laid the blanket on the ground over Hagen's grave and replaced the old flowers with the fresh ones, then sat down on the blanket. She saw Hagen watching her. "Come, sit with me. I have come here to visit this cemetery, and Hagen, at least once a week since he died." She put a hand on his headstone. "I don't know if your parents ever told you that he and I loved each other very much. We were intended to be married."

He sat cross-legged across from her on the blanket. "Yes, Papa told me." He looked into her eyes, so blue like his mother's, twin oceans. He felt her sadness and the weight on her shoulders. It was benthic.

"I never loved anyone else. I never stopped loving him." She ran her hand down the side of the granite stone, caressing it tenderly.

"Then it is you who cares for the cemetery?" He looked around again at the headstones.

"Yes, and the chapel. When your parents sold the farm before moving to America, the cemetery and the chapel and the land it sits on was not part of the sale. It was to remain in the family. My parents and I took it upon ourselves to be the caretakers. I hoped your father would not mind that I buried my parents here as well. They are on the side of the chapel facing the river."

"You are family, Aunt Mathilde. I know my father would want it that way." He reached over and squeezed her hand.

"Your father, he is a good man. My sister married a good man. I can see they made a good son." She smiled as his face faded from today's Hagen to yesteryear's Hagen to Georg and back to the present. "Do you have time to sit with me a while longer?"

374

"Of course, of course. You don't think that I could meet my mother's sister, under the circumstances of our coming together, and simply walk away casually after a quick how-do-you-do, do you? *'Papa, guess who I met. Aunt Mathilde. She says hello.'*"

They both laughed. She asked him to catch her up on what happened after Marta died. Hagen told her about Reverend Samuel and the orphanage and the circumstances surrounding Sal and Diana becoming part of the family. He told her about living at the orphanage, his father's diligence in keeping the family together, the annual picnics at the farm for the children. He told her about his sisters having the same birthday, and what happened when Pearl Harbor was attacked. He told her about Sal enlisting after he did; and where Sal was now. He told her everything about everything. Well, almost everything. He didn't go into detail about *how* he and Sal loved each other, just that there was a strong bond between them.

She could see that her nephew had a way about him. His maturity and sensitivity made her feel like she was talking with a man twice his age. *You made a good man, Marta. Mama and Papa would be so proud of their grandson, and you.* She could also see something in his eyes when he spoke about Sal. His words said *brother*, but his eyes gave away something else. She knew. She could see it in those eyes that his heart was breaking. Sal was his everything and it was eating at his soul that his whereabouts and condition were unknown. She could also feel that it was a secret that was draining Hagen to keep hidden.

"Hagen, my dear nephew, would you like to go into the chapel and pray? It belongs to you and your family. It seems only fitting that we pray for Sal together in your family chapel." She stood up and offered her hand. He took it and stood up.

She knows.

His heart skipped a beat and a half. He followed her to the door. She pulled a large and very old iron key from her pocket and unlocked the chapel door. The squealing of the hinges echoed off the stone floors and walls as she pulled it open. Inside he saw the pews and the stained-glass windows. He closed his eyes and for a moment thought he could hear the centuries of whispered prayers echoing from the marble and wood.

He followed her down the short center aisle and she stopped and looked down. They were standing over the graves of the first Beckenbauers to live and die here.

Adolphus Beckenbauer

1616⸱1688

Brunhilde Beckenbauer

1620⸱1691

There was a moment of reverent silence before she genuflected and then sat in a pew. Hagen followed and they knelt and prayed. Hagen prayed for all the departed who were buried around him. He prayed for his living family. He prayed for Aunt Mathilde. He reserved the lion's share of his prayers for Sal. He bowed his head into his folded hands.

Mathilde prayed for the living, the departed, and for God's forgiveness for praying for herself. She gave thanks to Him for the serendipitous meeting of her nephew. She prayed for his peace and for Sal's safe return.

Hagen began to cry. At first motionlessly, just a flow of salty rivulets down his cheeks and around his hands, down his wrists. Something came over him; it was uncontrollable. It took command of his very being. Maybe it was the awareness of where he was, or who was with him, or the culmination of his life's experiences up until that very moment. Maybe it was all of it, *plus* that he could feel his aunt was praying for him. He didn't know how or why, but he heard, *felt,* his name. Then he *felt* Sal's name. She said *Amen,* and he felt her hand gently rubbing his back. It felt just like when his mother would rub his back when he was a child. He leaned over, into her. She counterbalanced and leaned back.

"There, there. Let it out. You have kept it inside for far too long."

The flood-gates opened. Hagen cry-moaned, very much like Ingrid had for her sons Hagen and Karl, so much so that it hurt Mathilde's heart. *This boy cares too much about others to grieve for himself.* He unloaded all the pent-up feelings of helplessness, hopelessness, despair, anger, and anxiety that he had accumulated and kept inside. Duty and the honor of wearing the uniform kept those acerbic emotions bottled up and fermenting, the pressure ever mounting. To keep the cork in the bottle, he'd kept twisting and tightening the cage that held it in place. He couldn't show weakness. He'd had to be strong for the men he served with. But the war, for him, was over. His duties now lay elsewhere; at home in New Jersey, and somewhere, God knows where, in a prison camp on the other side of the world. Aunt Mathilde had loosened the cage with her prayers and gentle affection, and the cork blew off. The relief was overwhelming. His mind cleared as the bottle drained. After he had turned it upside down to let the last drop fall, he sat up, wiped his face and sighed. He looked up at Christ on the cross over the little altar, then into his aunt's eyes.

"I love him, Aunt Mathilde."

"I know, dear, I know." She caressed his hair, ran her fingers through it to put it in place. "There is nothing to be ashamed of. Love is nothing to be ashamed of."

She was the first person to whom he had admitted his true feelings for Sal. Her non-judgmental compassion and understanding were what his heart and soul needed. "Thank you, Aunt Mathilde. You have no idea what that means to me."

"Maybe one day I will get to meet your Sal." She held the side of his face with her hand.

He smiled and leaned his face into her palm.

Then he sat up straight. "Aunt Mathilde, you said you are all alone now. And I said that you are no longer alone, and I meant it. I am here for you. There is a reason we met today. I believe God put us here so that we may save each other."

Tears welled in her eyes. She knew exactly what he meant. He needed the acceptance. She needed to know that she still had a family who loved her.

"Aunt Mathilde, I want you to come home with me to New Jersey." He got excited at the thought.

"What? Hagen, I cannot simply leave. It takes time to do such things. I could not think of imposing on your family. I will make do here, but we will always remain in touch."

"Impose? Are you insane? Sorry, I mean no disrespect. But you are my mother's sister. You are the only remaining connection that we—that I—have to her. My father speaks of you so often. When this damned war began, even before that, when your letters ceased, he was so concerned for your safety, and my grandparents. We may not have been in contact for some time, but that does not mean that you were forgotten. Impose? Never!" He held her chin in his hand and made her look right into his eyes. "You are coming home with me. Unless you do not wish to; then that would be kidnapping."

She laughed through fresh tears, then hugged him and spoke into his ear. "Your mother is smiling down on us now.

I can feel it." She sat back. "I had a dream last night, about her. She was walking through fields of grain. She was smiling, the sun was shining, a breeze was blowing. As she walked, she was joined by our parents. They walked side by side, your mother in between them. When they stopped, they were standing at the gate to this cemetery. Marta opened the gate and the dream ended. When I awoke, I remembered the dream, and I thought that it might be an omen portending my death. Now I know that it was not, that it was foreseeing my continued life, with family. Oh, Hagen, how God works, I will never understand, but I thank Him for bringing you here today. Oh, my, I feel alive again."

"You see, we did save each other." He wrapped his arms around her and said, "Let us say our goodbyes to the dead. Then I will take you home to live." He stood up and took her hand. When they got to the door they turned around and took in the sight of the little family chapel. They said their silent goodbyes and she locked the door behind them.

They went over to her parents' graves and said a prayer and goodbye. Then to the graves of Hagen, Karl, Ingrid, and Horst. After some more silent prayer, Mathilde spoke aloud, first to all of them. "Look, your grandson, your nephew, has come to take me home." Then to Hagen's grave, "Goodbye, my love. Until we meet again in Heaven."

She turned to her nephew, and they left the cemetery and closed the gate behind them. He rode the bicycle into the village with his aunt on the handlebars. When they got to the friend's house where she had been staying, she introduced Hagen to everyone, and then packed the few belongings she had remaining. A friend drove them to the train station in Mannheim. From there the train went to Calais, then they took a ship to England. Hagen brought his aunt with him to the Army base and spoke to his superiors. He explained to them who she was, her situation, and that he intended to take her home with him. He was given permission to bring Mathilde aboard the transport ship so they would be together. He then sent a telegram to his father:

```
TO GEORG BECKENBAUER
   RR 1
   BEVERLY NJ
   USA

DEAR PAPA

STOPPED IN LAMPERTHEIM STOP VISITED THE
FARM STOP AM BRINGING HOME AUNT MATHILDE
STOP SEE YOU IN A WEEK STOP KEEP THE PARTY
SIMPLE STOP

LOVE HAGEN
```

Georg read the telegram out loud to his family. They all jumped up and down and hugged each other. Everyone, even Karl, cried happy tears. To hear that Hagen was at last returning home, well, it goes without saying that that was one of the most wonderful things that the family could have heard. Oh no, Sal didn't get lost in the celebration. They understood exactly what Hagen meant in his telegram. Keep the party simple meant that the homecoming will be official, and enormous, when *everyone* was home. Georg telephoned Samuel and Ethel to tell them the news. When they heard that Hagen was not only returning safely but that he had found Marta's sister, Mathilde, *AND* she was coming with him...??

God working in His mysterious ways again.

Georg was ecstatic. He adored his wife's sister. He had looked forward to watching his brother and her get married, raise a family. The first war changed that. This war separated him from his wife's family, and that hurt terribly. The war separated him from his two oldest sons, and that was killing him. *Thank you, God, for bringing Hagen home. Thank you for reconnecting us with Mathilde. Now please, dear Lord, send Sal home to us. Amen.*

He thought about it for a moment. Mathilde is coming to America. Hagen didn't mention anyone else. Now he worried about Oskar and Louisa. He would have to wait to hear everything when Mathilde arrived.

Back in England, Hagen and Mathilde were preparing for their journey. They were still on base, waiting for their departure in two days. It was August 10, and the news of the Hiroshima and Nagasaki nuclear bombings was spreading around the world quickly. Everyone knew that the war in the Pacific just had to be over.

But Hagen could not take his mind off Sal. If the war was over, then where the hell was he? Panic percolated from his gut to his mind. What was he going to do if Sal was dead, or worse, never found? His aunt was watching the emotions transform his face, like an artist's hands molding clay, as he pondered the worst scenario. She sat beside him on his bunk.

"Dear heart, have faith. You love him very much, yes?"

He pursed his quivering lips and nodded.

"Can you still feel him, his presence?"

He nodded, sniffed, his lips quivered harder.

"Then he is still with us. I never told this to anyone, but when your Uncle Hagen died..." She closed her eyes in recollection and took a deep breath. "...I knew it. When he and Karl went off to fight, I always *knew* he was alive. I felt his presence around me, day and night. He came to me in a dream the night he was killed. It was so real, he touched my face, I thought he was already home. He told me how much he loved me and that he was sorry for not coming home.

When I woke up, I was frantic. I was afraid to say anything, to anyone, not even to Marta. Everyone believed that your father, Karl and Hagen were on their way home. I didn't want to upset anyone. What if my dream was simply a nightmare?

"When the day came, the day I saw the two military vehicles rumbling down the street in the direction of the farm, my heart sank. I rode my bicycle as fast as I could the whole way, almost catching up with them. I saw the men in the back. I saw the boxes and the look on one of the soldier's faces when he saw me following them. I didn't want to believe the worst. Up until I saw the boxes being pulled from the backs of those trucks, I still had hope that all three of them were alive and were simply being dropped off, praying that the boxes, God forgive me, were meant for someone else's family to suffer the loss. After the dream, I could not feel his presence. That's how my soul knew the truth. Sal is still alive. I know it and you feel it."

"Yes, I do feel it. It is killing me not knowing anything and I know there is nothing I can do but wait." He sighed and stood up. "I cannot sit still. I am going to go for a walk. Would you like to join me?"

"Of course. The air will do us good." They took a stroll outside the camp into the nearby countryside. It was so beautiful, green, and peaceful. One would never know from the serenity that chaos had reigned over the world for the past six years. They talked more about their lives, before the wars, after the wars. They talked about their hopes for the future. Mathilde hadn't had much of that until Hagen appeared out of the blue and changed everything. Now, her hopes were to be happy and content on the farm with her family.

They got back to the base as the sun was touching the horizon. They had worked up an appetite and Hagen escorted

382

her to the mess hall. They went through the line and carried their trays to a table and sat across from each other.

"Wait until you see the gigantic kitchen table my father made. It is so heavy. Mama told me that it took seven men to carry it inside. He made all the chairs, too. All twelve of them." Hagen's pride for his father was very evident.

"My goodness, seven men! Twelve chairs!" She took a forkful of stew from her tray.

"Yes, he wanted a big family." He swallowed his food and stopped moving. His gaze went off into the distance. His mind went back to the farm before his mama died. Her laughter echoed in his heart. He smiled.

Mathilde could see that his mind had wandered somewhere else. It wasn't bad; she could see from his expression that he was recalling something good. She didn't interrupt. She waited until he returned.

When his mind came back to the mess hall, he looked at his aunt. She was smiling. "Something good, dear?"

"Yes, I was thinking about Mama. I wish she were alive to see you again."

"So do I. But I believe that we see our loved ones again, in time. That is what comforts me and gets me through the difficult times."

"Beggin' your pardon, Sergeant Beckenbauer." A PFC was standing at attention at the head of the table.

"At ease, Private," said Hagen.

He stood at ease and continued. "Colonel Jameson wishes to see you right away in his office, Sir."

Hagen looked down at his barely-eaten dinner then back at across the table. "Sorry, Aunt Mathilde." He shrugged. "Save my seat?"

"Absolutely. I will be right here waiting for you." She reached across the table and patted his hand.

"Alright, Private, let's go." Hagen got up and left the mess hall and followed the private to the colonel's office. Hagen stood at the colonel's door with the private standing off to the side. He was looking at Hagen, staring at him, into him. "Is there anything else, Private?"

"No, Sir, Sergeant," his focus coming back to the foreground.

"That will be all, Private." The PFC turned and walked back in the direction from whence they had come. As he rounded the corner to another hallway, he glanced back at Hagen. Their eyes met again. He saw something in the private's eyes but couldn't quite figure it out. Was he flirting? He didn't smile. Did he know Hagen was different? He didn't seem to be judging. Did the private butter his bread on the same side as Hagen? He gave no signs that he did or did not.

When the PFC disappeared, Hagen turned back to face the colonel's door. His mind scanned all the reasons why he would be asked to see the colonel.

Sal!

His heart and stomach bare-fist boxed each other. The wood grain on the door blurred. He leaned against the doorframe and took a few deep breaths, stood up straight, removed his hat, ran his fingers through his hair and knocked.

He heard the colonel's muffled voice from the other side. "Come in."

Hagen went inside and closed the door. Colonel Jameson was standing on the other side of his desk. Hagen approached and saluted his superior officer. "Sergeant Beckenbauer reporting, Sir."

The colonel returned the salute. "At ease, Sergeant. Please, sit down." He waved a hand to the two chairs on the other side of his desk.

Hagen was trying to read the colonel's face, his mood, the tone in his voice. He was very poker-faced, difficult to read. "Thank you, Sir."

The colonel went around to the other side of his desk, turned the other chair to face Hagen and sat down. He leaned forward and looked Hagen right in the eye. "I don't know how else to say what I have to say other than just saying it plain."

WHAM!! went Hagen's heart. The pulse shock-waved to the very tips of his fingers.

"Salvatore Cristoforo, your brother, has been found." His expression showed no signs of relief, no signs that it was good news, no signs that Sal was even alive. His tone was suggestive of bad news to come. Hagen's innards froze and the feeling spread outwards to his extremities. His knuckles whitened as he squeezed the arms of the chair. His mouth dried up. His jaw clenched; the muscles visibly flexed. He said nothing. He didn't blink, didn't encourage the colonel to continue. He just waited for him to go on at his own pace.

Colonel Jameson watched Hagen turn into a marble statue, the blood running from his face despite his heart doing double-time in his chest. When it was apparent that Hagen was slowly slipping into a mild state of shock, he continued. "Captain Cristoforo is alive. He is in a military hospital in Manila."

Hagen's demeanor changed slightly; his petrified muscles relaxed a little. He knew there was more, and it wasn't good. He peeled his tongue from the roof of his mouth. "Go on, Sir." He still hadn't blinked.

"As you are aware, the Japanese didn't treat their POWs very kindly…"

"Please… Sir… with all due respect… spare me the prologue." Hagen blinked once, never moving his eyes from the colonel's.

385

"He is in critical condition. I've been told that he is suffering from malaria, malnutrition and extreme physical abuse."

Hagen regripped the arm of the chair; the wood creaked. His breath came out in short bursts. His nostrils flared. In his mind he saw Sal the way he remembered him; so strong, so handsome. Hagen's soul contorted in pain. In his head, he screamed in German. He began to mumble. *"Was zum Teufel hast du meinem Sal angetan? Diese verdammten Bastarde!"*

"Sergeant, he is in good hands." He stood up and put a hand on Hagen's shoulder.

Hagen closed his eyes and a tear came down each cheek. "My apologies, Colonel. I meant no disrespect."

"No apology required." He patted his shoulder before walking back to his side of the desk. "Sergeant…" He picked up a piece of paper and held it up in front of him.

Hagen was staring somewhere far, far beyond the wall.

"Hagen? Son?"

Hagen turned his head and eyes toward the colonel. "Yes, Sir?"

"Not that it will lessen the pain that I know you are feeling, but I can sympathize with you. My son, First Lieutenant Walter Jameson, is MIA somewhere in the Pacific." His eyes looked briefly down at his desk then back to Hagen.

"I am sorry to hear that, Sir." Hagen's demeanor softened. The blood filled the capillaries in his knuckles as he released his grip from the chair. Empathy knocked on Hagen's door and he answered.

"His B-24 was shot down over the South China Sea in 1943. The plane was never found, nor were any of the crew." He stopped and looked down at the picture of his son, in his military dress uniform, facing him on his desk. He had not told anyone about his Wally since being transferred to that base. He sat down, laid the paper on the desk, opened a drawer, and retrieved two shot glasses and a bottle, and put them gently on the desk. Hagen's eyes moved from the colonel to the bottle. His head cocked a little to one side with curiosity when he read its label—*Jameson's Irish Whiskey.*

The Colonel looked at Hagen, then the bottle. "Oh, no relation. I wish. It was introduced to me by my CO when he sat me down to inform me that Wally's plane was shot down." He poured a full shot into each glass, held up one for Hagen to take and then picked up his. Hagen slowly stood up and took the glass. "To Captain Salvatore Cristoforo," said Colonel Jameson.

"To First Lieutenant Walter Jameson," said Hagen. The whiskey went down fast, its warmth immediately fanning out and replacing the arctic chill that had taken over Hagen's core. He put his glass down on the desk and sat back in the chair.

"Sergeant, your brother is able to communicate. He has asked that you escort him home stateside." He picked up the piece of paper again.

Hagen's face illuminated. When the colonel had said Sal was alive, he wanted to run out of his office and find the fastest way to Manila. How would he have done that? He had no idea. Now, it seemed Sal might be granting Hagen his wish.

"This is a special order from President Truman. It is an order to extend your tour. You are to be flown from here to Manila to escort your brother home to receive the Congressional Medal of honor."

A state of mild shock prevailed over Hagen again, but this time not horrific shock. It was proud shock. Proud to have been recognized by his President. So very proud of Sal.

Colonel Jameson stood up straight and serious. "Sergeant Beckenbauer. I hope that you will fulfill the duties of the mission that you have been assigned by the President of the United States."

Hagen stood up straight and saluted. "Yes, Sir!"

The colonel returned the salute. "Dismissed! Now, go get your brother and bring him home." He handed Hagen the orders and sat back down behind his desk.

"Yes, Sir, thank you, Sir." He turned to leave. Halfway to the door he stopped and spun around. "Beg your pardon, Sir."

"Yes, Sergeant?" He was pouring another shot of whiskey.

"I was supposed to be going home by ship, in two days, Sir. My Aunt Mathilde—you met her when we arrived here from Germany—doesn't speak English, and she will be taking the trip alone now."

"I have already taken care of that, Sergeant. I didn't think you'd refuse the orders from President Truman, or the opportunity to bring your brother home." He raised an eyebrow as he confidently smiled.

"If you don't mind my asking, Sir, how did you take care of it?"

"One of my staff was scheduled to ship home this week. I have arranged for him to take your place. He speaks fluent German. You met him a few minutes ago—PFC Pfeiffer. While you and I were talking, he walked back to the mess hall to explain everything to your aunt. He is waiting there for you to return."

Hagen remembered the private's face as he turned to look at him. *That was the look in the private's eyes.*

"Thank you, Sir, for everything."

"My pleasure, son. Take care, and God's speed."

Hagen turned and left the office. His heart was punching his sternum like a prize-fighter. His palms were sweaty; he felt feverish. He would finally see Sal again. But under what circumstances? His soul didn't know whether to be happy, frightened, or angry.

When he entered the mess hall, Private Pfeiffer was sitting in Hagen's seat across from Aunt Mathilde, who was crying into her napkin. As he approached them, Private Pfeiffer started to stand to attention.

Hagen spoke in German. "As you were, Private Pfeiffer." He waved a hand in a sitting motion.

Mathilde stood up. "Oh, Hagen, I am so happy to hear the good news that Sal has been found." She wrapped her arms around him, teary-eyed and sniffly.

Hagen's emotions were all so mixed that his response came out flatly. "Yes, Aunt Mathilde, good news."

Good news? He is alive, but barely. Good news?

"You are aware that you will be traveling to America without me."

"Yes, dear, I am. I will not be alone, though. Robert and I will be keeping each other good company. Right, Robert?" She looked down at Private Pfeiffer, who was watching them and was as *at-attention* as he could be while sitting; his back as straight as the imaginary pole bolted to his spine.

The private smiled and nodded. "Yes, Mathilde, we will."

Sergeant Beckenbauer looked down at… *Robert?* The look on his face said, *did you just say, Mathilde… Robert?* The smile melted from the private's face when he saw the sergeant's expression, then he looked down into his lap like a scolded child.

Mathilde saw their silent interaction and intervened. "Now, Nephew, do not be mad. I insisted that Robert call me by my first name. After all, we are going to be traveling thousands of miles together. I don't want to hear *Miss Schlessinger,* or *ma'am*, five thousand times all the way to America."

Hagen sighed, relaxed his stance. "Alright, Aunt Mathilde. Please, let's sit." Mathilde resumed her place at the table. Hagen sat to her right and looked over at Private Pfeiffer, still sitting at-attention, looking as awkward as he probably had looked on his first day of basic training. Hagen knew he was being a little too stern. And he knew his own emotions were bleeding into the mood at the table, and it wasn't fair.

"Private?"

"Yes, Sir, Sergeant?" He sat even straighter.

"You will take good care of my aunt, yes?"

"Oh, yes, Sir, absolutely, Sir."

"Good, very good. I can tell you are a man of your word." And he really could tell that Private Robert Pfeiffer, from Burwell, Nebraska, was a man of his word. He was shy, obedient to a fault, and trustworthy. But something else lingered in his dark, black-brown eyes. When he looked at Hagen, there was an underlying sense of respect emanating from those eyes, mixed with sadness. The look that he had given Hagen in the hallway earlier was not just because he knew why the colonel wanted to see Hagen in his office.

"How old are you, Private?"

"I am nineteen, Sir." He wondered why the Sergeant wanted to know but was not about to ask.

"When did you enlist?"

"I enlisted when I turned eighteen, Sir."

"You got discharged rather early." Hagen was fishing. Something else was going on with Private Pfeiffer.

"Yes, Sir." A sadness surfaced in his eyes. He tried to look respectfully at the sergeant. He averted his eyes briefly and looked at Mathilde. She saw the sadness too. Then he looked down at Hagen's tray of cold stew.

"Private, who are you mourning?" Hagen hit the nail right on the head. Private Pfeiffer's nostrils flared. He was trying to keep his emotions in check.

Mathilde turned her head to look at Hagen, then back to Robert.

"My brother, Sir." His voice cracked as he spoke down at the stew.

"I am sorry to hear that. When did it happen?" Hagen couldn't help becoming emotionally involved. This was hitting a little close to home.

"Last week, Sir." He lifted his gaze up from the food to look at Hagen and could see that the sergeant's face had softened. The discerning glare was gone.

"Last week? Private, the fighting ended three months ago. What happened?" Hagen could see the pain in his eyes.

"It was a landmine, Sir. Jimmy's regiment was marching through a field that was supposed to have been cleared." He averted his eyes to stare at the clock on the wall. "I am taking him home."

Mathilde reached across the table and touched his arm. He took his eyes off the clock and looked into her sympathetic eyes. He clenched his jaws as he forced himself not to cry, *again*.

"With your permission, Sergeant, may I be dismissed?" His voice wavered.

"Of course, Private." It was not protocol for a junior rank to request permission for dismissal from a senior rank. Hagen wasn't going to be a stickler for rules and regulations now. The boy was in pain.

Private Pfeiffer stood up, nodded to Hagen, then to Mathilde. "Good night, Mathilde, Sergeant."

"Good night, Robert. See you in the morning," said Mathilde.

He turned and left the mess hall. Hagen folded his hands in front of him, elbows on the table, chin on his thumbs and turned to look at his aunt. She was still looking at the door through which Robert had left. "What a shame, Hagen. To go the whole war and then get killed when it is over."

He closed his eyes and tried not to imagine Sal dying in a hospital bed, six thousand miles away.

Six thousand miles! It may as well be six million!

He had no idea of his exact condition; malaria, malnutrition, severe physical abuse!

Oh my God!

Hagen knew how horribly the Japanese treated their prisoners. Since Sal was captured, he had worried about what they might have been doing to him. Oh, the many nights he had cried himself to sleep. He knew that Sal wasn't a POW. He was a victim. When he opened his eyes, his aunt was watching him.

She knew what was going through his mind. "He will be fine, Hagen." She put an arm around him. "When do you leave?"

"My orders are for me to leave tomorrow at 0900." He looked at his watch. "It is getting late. I need to send a telegram to my father."

"You did not eat your dinner. Aren't you hungry?" She pulled his tray to their side of the table and slid it in front of him.

"I am not hungry, Aunt Mathilde. If I ate anything, I do not think that I could keep it down. Are you finished eating?"

"Yes, dear, I am finished." She rubbed his back and put her head on his shoulder. He tilted his head and rested it on hers. They sat there for a little while, both caught up in their thoughts. She patted his back as if to say, *ok, let's go.* They lifted their heads and she said, "come, walk me to my room, then you can go send the telegram to your father."

They got up and put their trays on the pile with the others on the table under the clock and left the mess hall arm in arm. When they got to Mathilde's room—it was really just an empty office with a folding bed—they said good night. Hagen walked to the communications room and sent another telegram home:

```
TO GEORG BECKENBAUER
   RR 1
   BEVERLY NJ
   USA

DEAR EVERYONE

CHANGE OF PLANS STOP AUNT MATHILDE ARRIVING
WITHOUT ME STOP SAL IS ALIVE  STOP GOING TO
MANILA TO BRING HIM HOME STOP WILL LET YOU
KNOW WHEN I ARRIVE THERE STOP PRAY FOR US
STOP

ALL MY LOVE

HAGEN
```

Hagen went to his quarters to pack for the trip. Before retiring for the night, he wrote a letter to his father.

Dearest Papa,

I leave tomorrow to bring Sal home. My commanding officer has informed me that Sal's condition may not be good. Apparently, he was not treated well while in captivity. I did not want to say that in the telegram and upset the whole family. Keep it to yourself until you hear from me again when I know more. Aunt Mathilde does not know, either. I do not want her to cry all the way home. Please, Papa, light a candle for Sal and say a prayer for him. Do not worry about me.

Love, your son,

Hagen

He put it in an envelope, sealed it and then went to bed.

In the morning he picked up his duffel bag and met Mathilde for breakfast. As they were eating, Private Pfeiffer walked in and got into the chow line. He sat down by himself four tables away, unaware of their presence. He closed his eyes and bowed his head to say grace. Mathilde saw him and nudged Hagen.

"Look, there's Robert. Would you be too upset if I invited him to join us? I don't want him to eat alone." She reminded him so much of her sister. His mother cared for everyone, every living creature she met. Compassion apparently was a prominent trait in the Schlessinger family.

"Of course. You are right, he should not be alone. Please, ask him to join us."

She kissed him on the cheek. "Just like your father, you are." She got up and walked over to Robert. Hagen watched Aunt Mathilde lean over and speak softly to him, her hand on his shoulder. Hagen could not hear her, but he could read her lips as she asked him to have breakfast with them. His reaction melted Hagen's heart. He looked over at Hagen, his expression asking if it was alright. Hagen nodded and waved him over. Robert picked up his tray and glass of milk and followed Mathilde back to their table.

Private Pfeiffer put his tray and glass down across from Hagen and started to stand at attention.

Before he could fully straighten, Hagen interrupted. "As you were. Please, sit, eat." He sat opposite Hagen. Mathilde sat next to Robert and pulled her tray over from across the table where she had been sitting.

"Thank you, and good morning, Sergeant."

"Good morning, Private."

"I wish to apologize to you, and your aunt, for my behavior last night. I was out of line with my request for dismissal. I meant no disrespect." He sat up straight, at attention, looking first at Mathilde, then into the Sergeant's eyes.

This boy's parents ought to be proud of their son. Even in pain over his dead brother, he apologizes for an error in protocol. "There is no need to apologize, Private."

"Thank you, Sir." He half smiled, looked down at his tray, and moved his eggs around with a fork.

Hagen didn't know what to say next. *How did you sleep? Ready for your trip home?* He could not think of anything positive or upbeat to say, knowing that the private's brother was in a box somewhere waiting to be loaded into the cargo hold of a steamship. Small talk seemed inappropriate when that funereal elephant in the room was parading around the table. Nothing he could think of sounded right he wanted to avoid an awkward silence. "I have a favor to ask."

The private was in mid-sip. "Yes Sir?" Then wiped the *milkstache* from his upper lip. It made Hagen think of Karl. He always mustached his upper lip when he drank milk.

"I would like you to drive me to the airstrip this morning. My plane takes off at 0900." He looked at his watch. It was only 0810, plenty of time.

"Absolutely, my pleasure Sir." He cheered up a bit up at the thought that the Sergeant asked *him* to drive him to his airplane.

"Good, good." Hagen fiddled with his eggs. The awkward silence was closing in around them again. Hagen didn't want any more formality between them. The war was over. He was tired, and he wanted to be himself again. "I will be so glad to eat real eggs again." He held up a forkful of the powdered eggs in front of him.

"Me too, Sir, and sleep in my own bed." He smiled, blushed and looked sheepishly down at his food. He was getting too familiar with the Sergeant.

"I look forward to that as well. The Army didn't build those bunks with comfort in mind." He smiled at the private who seemed relieved to have a normal conversation with someone, and a sergeant to boot.

"No Sir, they sure did not." Another bite of eggs, another smile.

"Where is home, Private?"

"Burwell, Nebraska, Sir."

"Where did you learn to speak German?"

"My parents are German. They moved to America with my grandparents after the first war. We speak mostly German at home."

Memories of the day Marta and Georg left for America bubbled up through Mathilde's thoughts. Her mind drifted back to 1922 and the last time she saw her sister and Georg. Melancholy came over her like a slowly rising tide, as her attention drifted away from the two men's conversation.

"My parents left Germany after the war as well," said Hagen. "That is also how I learned the language. We have something in common."

The private was feeling more comfortable with the conversation. "What does your father do?"

No more formalities for Hagen. No more barriers or walls. "We are farmers in New Jersey. What does your father do?"

"My father has a grocery store in Burwell. It is our family business. My brother was going to take it over one day and I was going to go to college to learn business. That has all changed now." How quickly a mood can go from light and chatty and then nosedive into the abyss. "I am sorry, Sergeant. I did not want that to be a topic of conversation this morning."

"Please do not apologize, Robert." He reached across the table and patted Robert's arm.

Robert? Did he call me Robert? Did he just touch me? Oh, God help me, what am I doing?

"You may talk about anything you wish. And please, no more Sergeant; call me Hagen." He lifted his hand from Robert's arm and offered it to shake. Robert took it and held it firmly. Their hands clasped for slightly longer than a normal handshake, not queerly long, just long enough for their eyes to meet and exchange a million words.

"Thank you, Hagen. You can call me Bobby; all my family and friends do." They released each other's hands; Bobby's having gotten immediately sweaty; not going unnoticed by Hagen. Bobby did not know what he was feeling. He had felt it before with other boys, but never told anyone about it. He didn't even have a name for it other than it was sinful, probably.

"Is there a girl waiting for you at home, Bobby?" Hagen was fishing a little; just harmless fishing caused by curiosity with a smidgen of attraction. He loved Sal, always had, always would, but every once in a blue moon someone like Robert, of his *persuasion,* would swing into his orbit; maybe ever so briefly, just enough to spark an interest and trying to ignore it was impossible because it was like finding a five-leafed clover.

"No girlfriends, Sir—uh sorry… Hagen—just my mother." He smiled with a whisper of coquettishness. For a nineteen-year-old, he certainly knew how to say what he really wanted to say without really saying it. "Do you have anyone special waiting for you?"

By this time, Mathilde had returned to the present from her mind's journey to her childhood. She quickly deciphered the conversation and was waiting as well to hear Hagen's answer.

The simple, yet loaded, question—*do you have anyone special waiting for you?* —was not answerable in simple code. There was only one answer.

Hagen answered solemnly, looking deeply into Bobby's eyes. "Yes, someone is waiting for me." It was the way he said it. Bobby knew that any further questions might evoke dangerous answers for the time and place they were in.

"I see. Well, hopefully someday someone will be waiting for me, too, besides my mother." All signs of interest other than professional blew away on the breath of that sentence. He went back to fiddling with his breakfast. The conversation was over. He was no longer interested in finishing his cold eggs.

Mathilde knew what Hagen's answer meant. He was leaving in less than an hour to go to that someone who waits for him. Bobby assumed Hagen had someone back home.

Bobby looked at the clock on the wall. It read 0821. He got up from the table, "I think I should go find a jeep."

"OK, Bobby, we will meet you outside." Hagen watched him deposit his tray on the table under the clock and leave by the side entrance that went directly outside. He had lost his appetite as well and pushed his tray away. He looked over at his aunt's breakfast. She hadn't been doing most of the talking and had finished hers before it had gotten coagulated and cold. "Are you ready, Aunt Mathilde?"

"Yes, dear, I am. I am not going to ask you if you are. Your face is a portrait of angst."

"Is it that bad?" He felt like crying.

"Not bad, just obvious. There is nothing bad about having feelings and emotions. What I think is bad is that society dictates when and where we may express them."

"You know, Aunt Mathilde, I don't think I need to worry about Bobby taking good care of you. I think you are quite capable of taking care of yourself." He kissed her on the cheek. "I think *you* might be taking care of *him*." He picked up his duffel and they headed for the door.

When they got outside, it was warm; the sun was shining. There were birds singing in nearby trees. Men and women in uniform were walking to their destinations. In the distance, the sounds of airplane engines purred. Mathilde put her arm through his and leaned against him.

"Hagen, I do not believe I thanked you." She hugged his arm with both of hers.

"Thanked me for what?" He turned his head and looked down into her face. She was beaming; her eyes, her face, her smile so much like his mother's. It caught his breath.

"For everything; for being there in the cemetery that day; for being my sister's son. I thanked God for you, but I never thanked *you* for you. You are a wonderful man, and your mother would be so very proud of you. I cannot wait until I see your father so I can brag about you."

He was smiling down at her, trying to think of something to say, trying not to cry in uniform, when Bobby pulled up in a Jeep. He sat behind the wheel, motionless, waiting for his passengers to get in.

Hagen put his duffel in the back and helped his aunt into the passenger seat. He took the seat behind her so he could see the side of Bobby's face. Bobby never turned around to look at Hagen, just to Mathilde to make sure that she was settled in.

The ten-minute ride to the airstrip seemed much longer to both young men. The closer they got to Hagen's departure, the more anxious each felt. The feelings they could not control were bullied by the fact that who they were, and how they felt, had to be kept hidden. Hagen was not falling in love on first sight—just attracted to Bobby at first sight. There were many times he wished he could have been comforted by, or had comforted, another man. Other

400

servicemen had wives or girlfriends back home, or they found solace in the arms of local women. Men like Hagen and Bobby would simmer alone in their frustrations.

Bobby… well, he was different. His heart beat double-time as he first approached Hagen in the mess hall the day before. His attraction was physical at first. It was love at second sight when Hagen returned to the mess hall and they spoke. This morning at breakfast, Bobby's heart made a place for him. He knew nothing of Hagen, yet he romanticized that they would continue to know each other after the war was over. As far as he had known, this Sal he was flying off to see was his brother, but when Hagen said that there was someone waiting for him, his breaking heart closed the door on the place it had made. The realization of the difficulty of ever being truly happy brought his mood down to a very low point. He was so angry that he had let himself get caught up in the momentary joy that came with being so close to another one of his kind. He was also mad at Hagen, who seemed to know what he was doing. To him, the touch on the arm at breakfast was a signal that they were in synch. Nothing could have been further from the truth. He wanted to scream, cry, stop the Jeep and run away.

When they arrived at the airstrip, Bobby pulled the Jeep right up to the plane. There were other GIs already on board the C-47 transport who were leaving the European theatre and bound for the Pacific. The flight crew were preparing their flight plan for the 6,500-mile trek as a tanker was topping off the plane's fuel tanks. Hagen hopped out of the back and grabbed his duffel, then helped his aunt out of the Jeep. Bobby got out and came around to the passenger side and leaned against the rear fender, arms crossed, and watched Hagen and his aunt say goodbye.

"Goodbye, Aunt Mathilde. Will you do me a favor?" He pulled the letter he had written to his father out of his coat pocket and handed it to her. "And give this to Papa for me?"

"Absolutely, first thing. Now, you take care of yourself on this long, long trip and do not fret. Everything will be fine; I just know it."

"Thank you." He dropped his duffel and gave her a big hug that reminded her of Georg's hugs.

She held his face in her hands and kissed him on each cheek. Just then, one at a time, the C-47's engines came to life, their propellers blowing exhaust and dust at them.

"I had better get on board." His eyes went to Bobby, who looked lost and awkward standing there against the Jeep. "Bobby."

He had to talk loudly to be heard over the plane's engines. "Yes, Sir?" Back to formalities again; a way to re-distance himself.

Hagen walked over to the Jeep and put out his hand. Bobby slowly reached out and took it. As they shook, Hagen spoke in English. "I hope your trip goes well, under the circumstances. I am sorry for your loss. Please take good care of my aunt."

"Yes, Sir, thank you, and I will, Sir."

Hagen feigned not being able to hear him over the engine noise, and he pulled Bobby closer to him, and whispered into his ear. The sound of Hagen's voice, his breath right in his ear, standing so close they could smell each other's scent, made Bobby a little lightheaded.

"I'm sorry, Bobby. I know you're upset, and I know how you're feeling. One day, it won't be so difficult. Please, take care of yourself." Hagen pulled away and they stared at each other, again saying a million silent words.

Bobby nodded and half-smiled. His face had flushed, and his mouth went dry as their sweaty hands let go of each other. Hagen walked back to his aunt for one more hug, then up the steps into the plane.

Mathilde walked over to Bobby, who was still in a slight fog. "Come, Bobby, before we get blown away by the propellers." She nudged him with her elbow and got into the Jeep. Bobby stood there and waited until Hagen disappeared inside the plane, the stairs pulled away, and the door closed. He went around the Jeep, got behind the wheel and drove off the tarmac to a grassy area and parked so they could watch the plane take off.

The plane taxied to the runway and held short as a B-17 came in for a landing. Mathilde could see that Bobby had been smitten with her nephew. She didn't know whether she would be comforting him on this trip for a grieving heart— or a broken one.

A few minutes later, the tower cleared the C-47 for take-off. It turned onto the runway, straightened out and then went full throttle. It gained speed. The tail rose, and a few seconds later it left the ground, rising gracefully up into the sky.

As the plane took off, so did Hagen's mind. He closed his eyes and sent his thoughts out to Sal. *I am on my way. Hold on. I'm coming.* He felt the hairs on his whole body rise with goosebumps. He laughed out loud. He opened his eyes, relieved that none of the other men noticed him. Most of them had their eyes closed, some were already sleeping, some were praying, rigor stiff with fear.

The plane banked to the right and the airstrip came into view from his window. Hagen saw the Jeep sitting in the grassy area near the field. He hoped Bobby would be able to find peace one day, find someone like he had in Sal. The plane finished its turn. It was a turbulent ride on the way up to cruising altitude. Hagen's already churned insides were tossed about. He never liked flying, never felt safe off the ground. He closed his eyes again, breathed deeply, slowly, and tried to daydream peacefully about good times past.

It wasn't until the plane was a mere dot in the sky, disappearing into a distant cloud, its engines no longer audible, that Bobby started the Jeep and drove back to the barracks. His heart was still thumping hard and fast, and his face was still flushed. He dropped Mathilde off at the building where she was staying and went back to his quarters to keep his mind busy preparing for his—and his brother's—journey home.

Hagen's Railcar
Ohio-Pennsylvania Border

Emily and Hagen sat there, silently and still, the only noise coming from the wheels on the tracks and the occasional sound of the horn blowing from the engines at the other end. Hagen was still gazing out into the darkness where he had stared during most of his time talking. Emily watched him. She didn't know if he was continuing or not. He seemed so far away.

Hagen wanted to stop there, for now. He relished the reverent silence, like the fading echoes of the orchestra in the concert hall before the next movement began. He was almost at the end of the story, his family's saga. He looked at his watch—3:38 AM. He made some calculations and figured that if they called it a night, just a few hours' rest, he could finish the story by the time they reached Philadelphia. He turned his gaze to Emily. He looked de-energized. It was the lateness of the evening mixed with the emotional journey that had him wanting to take a break.

Emily sat bundled in the Navajo blanket; only her face was visible. She cocked her head quizzically to one side. "Hagen? You OK?"

"Yes, dear, I'm fine. I think I may have bitten off more than I can chew for one night." He crossed his arms, hugging himself.

"I had a feeling. I wasn't going to interrupt you, though. We can stop for the night and pick it up in the morning if you want to."

"I think maybe a few hours rest will suffice. Pittsburgh is coming up soon, and another disconnect. The layover will be about an hour. From there it is only about seven hours to Philadelphia. I feel I might be running out of time."

"You won't run out of time." She smiled. "And you know I am not going anywhere."

"I know, but when we reach New Jersey, things will become busier and interruptive. Anyway, let's take a break." He slowly rose, leaning on his cane. Emily unbundled herself and got up to help him. He pressed a button on the remote and the fireplace extinguished then descended into the floor. She followed him through the sliding door into his room and walked with him to his bed. He sat down and looked up at her. "Go get some rest, dear. I'll be fine." He lay down on the bed, on his side, facing her, still clothed. She pulled the Navajo blanket over him, rubbed his back and gave him a little kiss on the cheek.

"Get up when you're ready. Sleep well, dream swell." She turned and left the room. In the living area, it was dark except for the lights illuminating the painting of Sandia Crest and the random lights shining in the windows as the train passed through civilization. Instead of heading downstairs to sleep, she curled up on one of the sofas. Her body was tired, but her mind spun wildly, keeping her awake. She knew she needed to sleep. Hagen said that things would become hectic once they arrived in New Jersey, which meant no rest for the weary.

She recounted in her mind what Hagen had told her so far. It was all too fantastic to believe. She had to believe it, though. It had all happened; the lives he and his family had lived. Suddenly, a wave of realization came over her and chased away any semblance of dozing. Her life was changing forever with each click-clack of the wheels on the tracks beneath her. She and Hagen were now bound together

406

by common knowledge. He let her in, and she was now privy to his private, personal life. There was no going back and un-knowing it.

So many questions flew around in her head. *What happens next in the story? Who are the Morawskis? Who was the Native American at the train station in New Mexico? How did Sal die?*

Just then, a sound like a Native American flute, a few notes only, high and fluttering like a red-tailed hawk, broke into her thoughts. She focused her attention on the room, listening for it to repeat. She waited. Nothing—just the train sounds and her heartbeat. She waited a few more minutes, then returned to her original thoughts. Her tired body eventually overcame her spinning mind, and she dozed off.

The *thump-bump* of Hagen's railcar connecting with the next train jostled her.

Pittsburgh.

Her busy mind rose out of the depths of the dream she was in, a dream she would not remember.

When she opened her eyes, the sun was just a faint glow beneath the horizon. She sat up, rubbed at the sleep, and looked at her watch. It said 6:37 AM. The train was moving, gaining speed. There were no signs of Hagen. He wasn't sitting in a recliner, sipping an espresso, waiting for her to wake up. She got up, stretched and went down the elevator to freshen up and change into some clean clothes and take advantage of the shower in the guest bathroom.

I might as well be clean when I meet the rest of his family. Rest of his family! What am I getting myself into?

Her traveling wardrobe was simple—casual slacks, blue jeans, a few tops, a sweater. She kept no skirts or dresses with her as she never needed to dress up for anything.

What am I going to wear to a funeral? Am I going to the funeral? Why wouldn't I, after all he's told me? I am his assistant now, right?

As she and Benny Goodman rode up the elevator together, her mind was going a mile a minute; so many thoughts, so many questions. She ascended through the floor and could see that the living area was still Hagen-less. She went to the kitchen first to see if he was starting coffee. Nope, no Hagen in the kitchen. Then that mind of hers took a sharp left. *He is always an early riser, so he says. Is he alright? Shitshitshit! What if he's not alright? He isn't young. What if he's sick, or worse? Stop it! I'll go check on him. Not doing it would look uncaring, right?*

She dilly-dallied no longer and quickly walked from one end of the railcar to the other. At Hagen's door she stopped, put an ear to it, listened for signs of movement. Nothing. *Now what?* She knocked three times then hesitantly, slowly opened his door and peeked inside. The room was lit from the rising sunlight coming through the open drapes. The Navajo blanket was neatly folded on his bed and he was not in the room. She peeked through the glass doors to the patio; not there either. She went to his bathroom and put her ear to the door. No sounds, no water running. She knocked. Nothing. A wave of moisture and the scent of fresh soap wafted out into the room when she opened the door. "Hagen?" Nothing.

OK, this place is not that big. She walked back to the living room and there he was, on a sofa, showered, dressed, bright-eyed and raring to go.

"Good morning, Emily. I trust you slept well." Her *where-the-Hell-have-you-been* look on her face was just too funny not to play along with.

"Uh, good morning. I've been looking all over for you."

"Well, you found me." He smiled and opened his arms as if to say *ta-dah*. He was wide awake and in good spirits. "I looked for you, as well. I guess we missed each other in our searches and, as they say, if you are ever lost, stay in one place and you will be found. So, I stayed put."

"I've heard that. I've never had to search for anyone before today. I guess it works."

"It looks like it does. I've never had the pleasure of being rescued before today. Thank you."

"My pleasure, Boss." She smiled warmly. "Want some coffee?"

"Oh yes, please. There's a pot already steeping in the kitchen." He stood up rather spryly, still using his cane though.

She followed him to the kitchen. "My, weren't we the busy bee? And, awfully chipper for someone who went to bed three hours ago."

"I think it might be the wee bit of extra adrenaline flowing through me this morning. It's a big day, as you well know." He didn't tell her that he hadn't slept at all. After she had left him to go get some rest, he went back to the patio with the Navajo blanket from his bed. He didn't want to sleep; too much on his mind; so much to still tell her. Oversleeping would have been too easy to do, and timing was crucial.

He sat at the banquette and she pressed the coffee and poured for both of them. "Shall I raid the fridge for something?" She opened the refrigerator and scanned the contents, hoping something might look breakfasty. "I don't know how you feel about golumpkis and eggs for breakfast."

He scrunched his face. "It is a little too early in the day for my stomach to take on cabbage. Let's splurge and order out."

409

"Alright, what are you in the mood for? I'll go to the dining car and bring something back for us."

"Have a seat." He patted the banquette seat. "We'll have something delivered."

She cocked her head. "Delivered?"

"Why not?"

They sat at the banquette and sipped coffee while they perused the menu. Hagen put his menu down, his face telling her he had made up his mind. "I don't need the menu. I already know what I'm having."

She looked over her menu at him. "What are ya' having?"

"Eggs Benedict. I've been craving hollandaise sauce. I don't know why."

"Ooh, I love Eggs Benedict... and home fries. But they never give you enough hollandaise."

"Well, that's settled; Eggs Benedict and home fries for two."

"Absolutely. But, are you sure they'll deliver it? Shouldn't I just go get it?"

He gave her the look that said *watch me* and picked up the phone that was on the wall near the banquette. He pressed a couple numbers and waited.

"...."

"Good morning."

"...."

"This is Hagen Beckenbauer. How are you today?"

"...."

"I am well, thank you. I would like to order some breakfast to be delivered to my car."

"...."

"Thank you, yes, I would like two orders of Eggs Benedict with home fries, please."

"...."

410

"Juice? Hold on please…" He cupped the phone. "What kind of juice would you like, Emily?"

He caught her staring out the window at the passing scenery, her mind had wandered for a moment and she came back to the present when she heard her name. "I'm sorry, what did you ask?"

"What kind of juice would you like?"

"Anything, you pick."

"…Hello? Sorry about that. Two large carafes of juice; one orange, and one grapefruit. If you will freshly squeeze them, I will be most appreciative. I will pay extra for the service."

"…."

"No, I think that will be all, thank you. Oh, wait, I apologize, I did forget something. Please add an extra pint of hollandaise sauce on the side, in addition to what comes with the Benedicts. I know there will be an extra charge incurred."

"…."

"Who am I speaking with?"

"…."

"You have been most kind, Marjorie, thank you."

"…."

Hagen hung up the phone and sipped his coffee. He smiled and gave her another *ta dah* look.

She leaned on the table with both elbows. "I keep forgetting that I left the real world behind in New Mexico." She leaned back, picked up her cup and squinted her eyes a bit, then sipped.

"You are still in a real world, my dear, just a different one. How you handle it is up to you. Now, while we wait for breakfast, let us discuss the rest of the day."

"Good idea. How much time do we have left before we reach Philly?"

He looked at his watch. "Hmm, about seven hours, ish." He looked back at her. "Plenty of time."

"Will you be able to finish before we get to New Jersey?"

"Oh, yes. I have to. The funeral is today. The train will pull right into our farm, then we go straight to the cemetery. I need to get this all out before we are no longer alone."

"Oh, wow, that fast. I didn't realize that it was today. Do you want to talk while we eat?"

"Not this morning. I want to continue where I left off and I would rather not do it over breakfast. I want to get through it without distraction in one final chunk."

"I understand. Well, hmm. Wait, am I going to the funeral?"

"I assumed you would be going. You are my assistant and I would like you there."

"Uh, Hagen, I have nothing appropriate to wear to a funeral. The fanciest thing I have with me is what I have on now."

"You look just fine. No one there will fault you for not bringing your funeral attire with you to work."

"If that was supposed to be funny, it wasn't." She folded her arms.

"I wasn't trying to make light of it. I appreciate you wanting to look nice for my family. They will understand the situation. When we get there, I will see if Mathilde or Diana have something for you to wear. OK?"

"Thank you. Sorry for acting so pissy."

"That is quite alright, dear. It was for a good reason."

Ten minutes later, there was a knock on the door. Through the glass, they could see a young man standing there on the gangway, wearing the familiar Amtrak uniform. Hagen and Emily both got up and went to the door.

Hagen opened it. "Good morning…" he peeked at his name tag, "…Eóin. Please, come in."

Eóin was a handsome, mid-twenties young man with jet-black hair and eyes blue as lapis. His fair skin contrasted against his dark hair. Hagen's assumption that he was Irish was confirmed when Eóin responded in a lilting Irish accent.

"Good morning, Mr. Beckenbauer." He pulled a rolling cart through the doorway into the kitchen. "Where would you like me to set up your breakfast?"

Hagen turned and nodded in the direction of the banquette. "On the table over there, please."

Hagen and Emily followed Eóin to the table. "If you and your guest would like to sit down, I will be pleased to serve you."

"Thank you, Eóin, that would be lovely." Hagen waited for Emily to take her seat, then sat down.

"My pleasure, sir." Eóin surely did come prepared. He brought glasses for the juice and silverware, which he placed in front of them. He then uncovered the plates of Benedicts and potatoes and placed them on the table, first in front of the lady, then the gentleman. "Would you like grapefruit or orange juice, ma'am?"

"Grapefruit, please. Thank you." She stifled a giggle. She'd never been served breakfast on a train, only served it to passengers.

"My pleasure." He filled her glass. "And for you sir?"

"I will have orange juice, please, Eóin, thank you."

"My pleasure, sir." He poured for Hagen, then left the carafe on the table next to the grapefruit juice. He placed a white, covered ceramic bowl on the table in between them. "Your additional hollandaise sauce." Next to it, he placed a ladle that matched the same pattern as the silverware. "Will there be anything else, ma'am, sir?"

Emily's turn to speak. She was afraid to ask and began to stumble over her words. "Well, yes," she winced a bit, "there is, but I'll get up and get it, it's silly."

"I will retrieve it for you, ma'am. What is it you would like, and where will I find it?"

Hagen knew what it was. "In the refrigerator door, Eóin, you will find the ketchup." Hagen smiled over at Emily, who was now blushing multiple shades of red like a cuttlefish.

"You must think I am just a cheesy American, Eóin." She looked up at him with hopes of redemption for the sin of ketchup at breakfast.

"No ma'am, I do not. I believe everyone is entitled to their preferences." He went to the refrigerator and retrieved the ketchup, placing the bottle in front of Emily. "I personally enjoy it on my shepherd's pie. My mother does not know." He gave her a smile and a nod, and then looked at Hagen, who was thoroughly enjoying the interaction between the two young people. "Will there be anything else, sir?"

"No, thank you, you have been most attentive."

"Thank you, sir." He handed Hagen a waiter's book and a pen. Hagen signed the check, slipped a crisp one-hundred-dollar bill inside, then handed it back to Eóin. "Thank *you*, sir! Enjoy your breakfast."

"Thank you, Eóin. I am sure that we will."

Eóin bowed slightly, then turned and walked to the door, slid it open and went out into the gangway. They watched him disappear into the next car before beginning to eat.

"He was a very nice young man. Have you ever worked with him?"

"No, I've never seen him before. Are you always such a good tipper?"

"In general, I am a very good tipper, where the tip is due. His service was exemplary, and I tipped him accordingly."

"That was very nice of you. I think you made his day." She cut off a chunk of the benedict and took a mouthful. "Good choice for breakfast." She opened the ketchup and squeezed a small, red pond next to the potatoes, then put the bottle in front of Hagen. "Ketchup?"

He picked it up and jiggled it to see how much was left while looking at her plate.

"Alright, alright, we've already had the ketchup discussion. I… like… ketchup." She forked some potatoes and dragged them through the red puddle, then put them in her mouth and over exaggeratedly chewed, swallowed, and then smiled.

"You are a gem, Emily, a real gem."

"Thank you, Hagen, so are you." She forked another ketchup-swabbed chunk of potato into her mouth.

She was so comfortable with him now, and he with her. It was like they'd known each other before; maybe in another time, another life. He opened the ketchup and squeezed some onto his plate next to his potatoes. The bottle *burped* as air mixed with the last of its contents. A memory took over his thoughts and he paused for a moment with the bottle in mid-air.

Emily swallowed and saw him freeze. "Hagen, are you alright? I'm sorry if I used the last of the ketchup."

He came back to the present moment. "No, it's not that. I have more ketchup in a cupboard. I just had a senior moment there for a second."

"OK, just making sure you're alright." She watched him put the bottle down, then take a bite of his Benedict.

415

"This isn't bad hollandaise, not bad at all." He lifted the cover off the bowl of extra sauce, then dipped the ladle in it. "Care for a splash more?"

"Yes please, a double splash if you wouldn't mind."

He doused each of her eggs with a healthy ladle of sauce, then did the same for himself.

"Thank you. So, tell me," she asked, "how long do you think it will take for you to put this book together?"

"Well, I am not really sure. Six months, maybe? We already know the content; well, I know it all and, in a few hours, so will you. It will have to be edited, and that takes time."

"Six months. Where will we be working? New Jersey? New Mexico?"

"We may be going back and forth; I haven't thought that far ahead. I will purchase a computer for the train so we can work while we travel."

"Somewhere along the line, I will need to get some things from my apartment. I have houseplants I'll need to give away, or maybe bring with me, and I will have to talk to my landlord about mailing the rent to him."

"You will be able to tidy your affairs back home. The simplest solution would be for my accountant to take care of your rent while you are away. It will be one less thing for you to worry about."

"Accountant? Accountant." She said it like it tasted strange. "That feels so weird to say. I'm so used to doing everything for myself. I agree though, if it is taken care of it would make things easier. You can deduct it from my pay."

"Is your rent due soon? If so, we will need to get that taken care of quickly."

"No, it's not due until the first. What is today's date? I've lost all track of time."

"It is the nineteenth. We have time."

"Yes, there's time." Then something flashed in her brain. "Wait a minute. Today is the nineteenth? It's your birthday, right?"

"You listened well. Yes, it is."

"Aw, why didn't you remind me? I feel so stupid."

"Please don't feel bad. What is there to say? I don't go around on my birthday announcing it to the world so everyone feels obligated to make a fuss. The people in my life who are close know what today is. Technically, you did remember."

She frowned. "For what it's worth, happy birthday. I know we all wish the circumstances were better."

"Thank you, my dear. Next year we will celebrate the big *seven-five*. This year I am going let it slide by."

"Call me, and I will try to arrange my time off around your birthday. Or, you could call *Warren* and do it for me." She gave him a sly smile.

"If it would make it easier for you, then I will make the call."

"While you're at it, see if I can get a raise, too."

"If that is what you want. You may feel differently about your career after I publish. Why don't we see what the future holds for both of us?"

They had been eating during their chat, and when they finished the last bite, Emily put their plates and silverware back onto the cart. "Shall I take this back over to the dining car now?"

"No, not now. It can wait. Let's adjourn to the patio."

"Do you want more coffee?"

"No, I'm fine with just water and juice. Press another pot if you want more."

"That's OK, I'm fine with water and juice, too."

She put the carafes and glasses on a tray and followed Hagen to the patio. They took their places in their seats.

417

Emily wrapped herself in a blanket. Hagen relit the fireplace and resumed his story from where he had left off.

"If you are not too long,
I will wait here for you all my life."

—Oscar Wilde

Manila
September 1945

The C-47 landed in Manila three days later. There were stops in Italy, Egypt, Iran, India, and China; too many ups and downs as far as Hagen was concerned. Nothing was comfortable about this trip. Each long leg was cold, and at times turbulent. The food was either military rations or something strange and local from vendors near the airstrips. Whether they ate or not, some of the men had difficulties with airsickness. One group who had no digestive issues took bets on who would puke the most before they reached Manila. A tally was kept in chalk on the bulkhead. There were eight "contestants," and Hagen was in the top three. At one point he was neck and neck with Private Kurt Merriweather, twenty-two, from Cincinnati. When the C-47 touched down on the Manila airstrip, Kurt lost his lunch one more time. A very happy Corporal Sven Thorsen, twenty-six, from Iron Junction, Minnesota, won the betting contest and walked away with $22.50.

Hagen was now tickled pink, instead of airsick green. Just the thought that he was going to remain on terra firma for a while put his insides at ease, and he vowed he would never fly again.

From the airstrip, he was driven by Jeep to a boat that took him to the island of Corregidor, near the entrance to Manila Bay. From there, it was another Jeep ride to the hospital. That last, short leg of his trek half-way around the world was the most nerve-tingling for Hagen. He was now in the same part of the world, on the same small island, within a few miles of Sal. His heart galloped in his chest. His palms were sweaty. His eyes burned.

The hospital came into view and he almost started to cry. He knew Sal was in a bad way. Was he supposed to hope for the best and prepare for the worst? Would he be able to contain his emotions in front of Sal; and everyone else? There was nothing he could really do at this point. He had thought long and hard during that 6,500-mile journey about how he would handle himself when he finally saw Sal. Best case and worst-case scenarios had played out in his mind in between vomiting sessions. The men onboard the plane with him had assumed he was just airsick. That was part of it. A major influence on Hagen's digestive condition was his mental state as he thought about Sal being beaten like an animal by the Japanese.

The Jeep pulled up to the hospital's entrance. The driver, Private Joey Magowan, nineteen years old, from Bala Cynwyd, Pennsylvania, looked over at Hagen, who was sitting motionlessly staring up at the building. "Sergeant, Sir, we're here. Are you alright?" Hagen didn't move. "Sergeant Beckenbauer?"

Hagen snapped out of his daze when he heard his name. "Yes, Private, I am fine. Sorry about that."

"That's quite alright, Sergeant. I know why you're here. I can imagine that you have a lot on your mind."

"Thank you, Private. I appreciate that." He looked at the private's face. He was young but seemed so old.

So many of the young have lost their innocence; so many of the old have lost their young.

"You don't have to wait for me, Private. I don't know how long I will be here."

"Yes, Sir, just call the base when you want me to come get you. There is a bunk in the barracks waiting for you when you want to get some rest. You look like you need it, beggin' your pardon for saying so, Sir."

"Thank you, Private." He looked back up at the building. He took a deep breath and let out a long sigh. "I guess I had better get inside." He got out of the Jeep and retrieved his duffel from the back seat.

"I'll be waiting for your call, Sergeant." The Jeep pulled away, leaving Hagen standing there staring at the door.

Medical personnel were coming and going. One nurse came through the door and saw Hagen standing there, looking like a lost child. "Good afternoon, Sergeant. May I help you?"

"Yes, ma'am. I am here to see my brother. I guess I am a bit nervous."

She could see from the look on his face that he was more than nervous. He was terrified. "Come inside Sergeant, and we will find him together. My name is Sylvia Barrow. What's yours?"

"Hagen Beckenbauer." She put her arm through his and walked him to the door.

"It's nice to meet you, Sergeant Beckenbauer."

"It is nice to meet you as well, Miss Barrow."

Once inside, they walked to the front desk where a nurse named Maggie sat writing notes in a chart. "Hi, Mags."

"Oh, hi Syl." She saw the handsome young Sergeant standing with Sylvia and perked right up. "What's up?"

"The Sergeant here is looking for his brother. Last name, Beckenbauer."

Hagen spoke up. "His name isn't Beckenbauer. It's Cristoforo, Salvatore Cristoforo."

Maggie and Sylvia's eyes locked on each other's. They were very aware of who Salvatore Cristoforo was. He had come to the hospital a week ago; bad shape; Medal of Honor. Everyone talked about him; wondered how he was still alive.

Sylvia took her eyes off Maggie and looked at Hagen. She tried to smile, but it was worse than if she had just cried. He looked back and forth between the nurses. He was very aware of their reaction to hearing Sal's name, and his heart thumped painfully. Their new demeanor and facial expressions made him weak at the knees. Maggie ran around to the other side of the desk and grabbed his right arm while Sylvia got his left. They walked him over to a bank of chairs against a wall and sat him and themselves down.

"Sergeant Beckenbauer..." said Sylvia.

"Please, just call me Hagen."

"Alright, Hagen, I'm sorry I reacted that way. When your brother came to us, he was in a very bad way. I think that I should warn you before you see him, that you might need to prepare yourself. He probably looks nothing like how you remember him."

"I was told he was starved, beaten, had malaria. I hoped it wasn't that awful. The looks on your faces said all I needed to know."

"We're sorry if we scared you, honey," said Maggie, rubbing him on his back. "Let me get someone to watch the desk and we'll take you to see him." She got up and picked up the phone at the desk. A few moments later another nurse arrived. Maggie quietly told her who Hagen was going to see and asked her to page Dr. Cutter and have him meet them in Ward 3C. She had the same reaction that Sylvia and Maggie had when they heard Sal's name, but Hagen wasn't paying attention to them. He was listening to Sylvia whilst he stared at the floor. Maggie came back around from the desk and over to Sylvia and Hagen. They stood up and he followed the nurses to the elevator. The ride up was vacuously silent; even time seemed to disappear. Hagen was afraid to speak for fear of hearing something else terrible.

Oh, and Captain Cristoforo has no eyes. Oh, and Captain Cristoforo has no legs.

Maggie and Sylvia watched Hagen, just as afraid to say anything.

The door opened and they stepped out of the elevator onto the third floor, in front of the nurse's station. Maggie led the way as Sylvia and Hagen followed arm in arm.

The hallway was long. It had six doors on each side, thirty feet apart, with the nurses' station dividing it in half. Wards 3A through 3L contained thirty beds each, fifteen on each side. At the end of each room, there was a large window that looked out over the island. The hospital sat high on a hill and from some of the wards, the view was quite breathtaking, the ocean so blue and serene in contrast to the black agony that some of the patients were enduring.

Dr. Cutter was standing by the door to Ward 3C, waiting for them. He was dressed in military uniform and his insignia denoted that he was also Captain Cutter. When within proper distance, Hagen came to attention and saluted the doctor.

"As you were, Sergeant."

Hagen relaxed his stance. "Thank you, Sir."

"Before you go inside, I want you to know that we are doing everything in our power to help Captain Cristoforo. I am sure you were apprised of his condition. I do not see any reason for him not to make a full recovery. It will take some time, though."

Hagen nodded. He couldn't pry his tongue from the roof of his mouth to say anything, so nodding was the best he could do. The doctor couldn't think of anything else to say. He opened the door and walked into the ward. Hagen followed at a three-pace distance with Sylvia and Maggie on each arm.

Each bed was occupied by a man who was suffering some degree of malnutrition, physical abuse, disease, or a combination of all three. Most suffered all three. Skeletons with ashen skin stretched over their bones lay there, some with wide gazing eyes, some with eyes closed. Flashbacks of Dachau flickered along the back wall of Hagen's mind. He scanned each face, looking for some familiarity, thanking God that *that last one wasn't Sal.* Down the aisle they walked until they approached the last bed on the left. The man under the sheets barely made two lumps with his shoulder and hip as he lay on his side in a fetal position, his back to the door and Hagen.

Dr. Cutter stopped and turned around to face Hagen. He could see that Hagen was shell-shocked. The doctor stepped back so Hagen could go around to the side of the bed that faced the windows. There, with just his head poking out from under the sheets, was Sal. His eyes were wide open, sunken deep in their sockets, staring blankly out the window at the blue sky. His face was gaunt, his cheekbone prominent; his ear looked too large. From his vantage point, all Sal could see were the blue sky, the angelic, high-flying Frigate birds, and clouds. His eyes were unmoving, his breathing almost imperceptible beneath the sheet that resembled a cockeyed circus tent that stretched from his shoulder to his hip. Tears flooded Hagen's eyes as he walked to the side of the bed, casting a shadow over Sal's face, blocking his view of Heaven.

"Sal…"

Sal blinked, then continued to stare through Hagen at the same distant place in the sky.

"Sal…" He knelt down, putting his face directly in front of Sal's. Hagen touched his head, caressing his hair, felt the shape of his skull. "Oh, God, Sal." Holding it in was impossible now. His head fell forward against the bed and the floodgates opened, his chest heaved, but he never lost touch of Sal.

Dr. Cutter, after all he'd witnessed in this war, never would get used to the pitiful sights of once virile, strong, young men lying in hospital beds with their lives sucked out of them like a spider's prey. He looked at the two nurses, who shared his feelings. They were dripping tears onto their uniforms. The doctor nodded in Hagen's direction. Understanding his meaning, Sylvia and Maggie went to Hagen's side and knelt beside him, each putting an arm around him. Maggie covered Hagen's hand on Sal's head. Hagen's life with Sal up until that moment played over and over again in his mind. Milliseconds long was each re-run, but not a precious moment forgotten. Over and over it played. Deep inside his soul, the projector kept running. The replaying of all that was good before the war was an incantation, a prayer to the Almighty to *please, please help us. Save him.*

For the second time in his life, Hagen prayed beside the bed of a victim of evil, and for the second time he felt God's answer. Something touched his head. It wasn't Sylvia, nor was it Maggie. Sal had lifted his right hand to console his savior; the man who once as a boy first saved his soul, was here now to save his body. "Hagen." His voice was raspy, weak. "I knew you would come for me and take me home."

Hagen laughed through tears. "Yes, yes, yes, I'm here and we are going home." He pressed his head to Sal's; his tears fell on Sal's face.

Sal put his hand on the back of Hagen's neck and pulled him weakly into a hug. He kissed his cheek three times and whispered in his ear. "You are my angel coming to take me home." When he let go, Hagen sat back so he could see his face. It seemed his countenance had rejuvenated slightly. His color was less grey; his eyes showed more life in them.

Sylvia and Maggie stood up and went to the doctor's side. "If ever there was a reason to believe in God, this is it," said Sylvia.

"I doubted throughout this whole damned war," said Dr. Cutter, "that there was a God. So much pain, so much death and devastation. I honestly didn't have high hopes for Captain Cristoforo, but I do now. Look…" he nodded at Sal and Hagen. "Look how the presence, the simple touch of a loved one, can do what medical science cannot. You're right, Sylvia. God exists. The power of love proves it." He went to Hagen and leaned down, put a hand on his shoulder and spoked softly. "We're going to step out now, leave you two alone. I don't recommend you keep him up too long, though. He needs his rest and by the looks of it, so do you."

"Yes, Sir, thank you."

"Alright then, come see me before you leave. I'll be at the nurse's station."

The doctor rejoined the nurses and led them down the aisle and out into the hallway. It was now Sal and Hagen, just the two of them—well, except for the twenty-nine other men lamenting in their agony of abuse. Hagen and Sal didn't have to verbalize how they felt. They spoke to each other with their eyes; their souls were dancing again and oh what a feeling.

"Hagen, how bad do I look? Be honest. I haven't seen my own reflection since before…" He stopped in mid-sentence. It hurt to cry but he couldn't help himself. He hadn't cried in so long. He had always been too numb to cry; or under threat of a sound thrashing by one of the guards if he showed any sort of emotion. If you smiled, they'd beat you until you cried. If you cried, they'd beat you until you screamed, and if you screamed, they'd beat you into unconsciousness. He jumped when Hagen touched his shoulder. Pavlov's dog drooled at the sound of a bell. A tortured man recoils from even the kindest touch. It would take months before Sal would not jump when someone touched him.

Hagen put his arm around him. "Shh, shhhh. You're safe now. I will not let anything hurt you, ever again." He could feel Sal's bones through the sheets. Hagen's soul screamed. It was awful, and again the flashbacks of Dachau howled like ghouls in his head—emaciated, dysenteric, starved, tortured shadows of humans walking aimlessly around in dazed torment. Thank God that Sal wasn't that far gone. He still had his mental senses. That was a good sign. His soul wasn't dead.

Hagen held Sal until his crying subsided. He sat back in the chair by the side of the bed, still keeping one hand on him.

"You had better get some rest. The doctor said you're going to be fine, but I need to let you sleep."

"Oh, Hagen, please don't go, stay until I fall asleep. I promise I'll rest if you just stay." Oh, that look that he always gave Hagen when he wanted to get his way. It always worked.

"I'll stay. Now, get some rest, please. The trip home is going to be long, and you will need your strength. If I'm not here when you wake up, don't worry. I won't be far. I will have to pee eventually, and I hear there's a shortage of bedpans in this hospital. I don't fancy you'll want to share yours."

That had Sal laughing—it was weak and raspy but laughing, nevertheless. It hurt good to laugh. Laughter had not been in his vocabulary for nearly three years.

It didn't take long for Sal's eyes to close. He fell deeply asleep, twitching occasionally. Maybe it was bad dreams, maybe it was his battered body trying to heal. Ever since his rescue, his spirit had been cocooned in a shell. Nothing could

428

get through. It wasn't until Hagen arrived that the shell fractured and let someone in. Torment still reigned inside his mind, and it was leaking through the cracks.

Hagen caressed Sal's hair and stood up. Before walking away, he noticed a prayer card on the bedside table. He picked it up. On one side was a picture of an angel. He had enormous, widespread wings of blue and white, and a shining halo over his head. In one hand he held a staff, and in the other, a glowing orb. Hagen turned the card over and there he saw the prayer to Saint Raphael the Archangel. He wondered who had left that there. He put the card back and walked down the aisle, looking at the other bedside tables for prayer cards. It seemed Sal was the only one who had one.

He left Ward 3C, and went to the nurse's station, where Sylvia was sitting behind the desk going through charts with Dr. Cutter. They heard his boots on the tile floor as he approached the desk. The doctor looked up and Hagen stopped to stand at attention.

"As you were, Sergeant. Let's just keep you as you were until I say otherwise. You're going to be here a while and we're going to be seeing a lot of each other while your brother recuperates sufficiently enough to handle the journey home."

"Thank you, Sir. How long do you think he will have to stay here?"

"Honestly, I had no idea up until now. He was almost catatonic at times, difficult to feed him anything. I was fearful that his malnourished state would get worse. I've kept him on IV fluids to keep him hydrated. Today, Sergeant, I saw a very different Captain Cristoforo. His reaction to your presence has me very hopeful that in a month's time you will be able to take him home."

"A month?" Hagen's face gave away his thoughts.

"A month is just a guess. If you can get him to eat and get up, move around, gain some strength, then I will assess his condition on a weekly basis, and keep you apprised."

"Thank you, Captain." Hagen was just then emboldened with a mission to rehabilitate Sal faster than anyone would have expected. "Captain?"

"Yes, Sergeant?"

"Would it be possible to have a cot put next to Sal's bed? Maybe if I stayed with him, he'd improve faster."

"I don't see why that would be a problem. It shouldn't get in the way. He is in an end bed. I'll see what I can do."

"Gee, thanks Captain, I really appreciate it." Hagen's heart lightened a little more. He didn't want to leave Sal every night and go back to the base to sleep. He knew that Sal needed him, and it did not go unnoticed by Hagen how Sal had perked up when he realized Hagen was there.

"I think you being here is going to make a big difference in Sal's recovery. But you, Sergeant, you need rest yourself. You look dead on your feet. I order you to go get some chow and a hot shower. In the meantime, I'll procure a cot, and have it brought up."

"Thank you, Sir. And thank you, Sylvia." He nodded at her behind the desk.

"Oh, my pleasure, Hagen. Now, go get something to eat, and I'll see you when you get back."

"Yes, ma'am. Thank you, both of you, for everything." He walked to the elevator and pressed the button. Six seconds later the doors opened. Downstairs, Maggie was back at the main desk. She called to have the private bring the Jeep back and take Hagen to the base.

He thanked Maggie for all she had done to help Sal, then went outside to wait for his ride. Ten minutes later Private Magowan pulled up in the Jeep. The private could see that Hagen had been crying. He was on the fence on whether to

430

inquire about Sal or not. About half-way back to base, he fell off the fence. "Sergeant?"

"Yes, Private?" He knew what the private was going to ask.

"Are you…"

"I'm fine, thank you. I'm just very tired from the trip here."

"And Captain Cristoforo? Is he OK?"

Hagen could see that he was genuinely concerned.

"I think he will be." *Dear God, I hope he will be.* He looked over at Private Magowan, who was staring ahead at the winding road. There was an expression on his face. He wanted to say something else, Hagen was sure of it. "What's on your mind, Private?"

"Permission to speak freely, Sir?" He was still paying attention to the road ahead.

"Absolutely, please do."

The private pulled the Jeep over to the side of the road and stopped. He turned in his seat and faced Hagen. "I want to thank Captain Cristoforo, either personally, or through you."

"May I ask for what?"

"My last name is Magowan. My brother, Scott Magowan, was the navigator on your brother's B-17. He saved Scotty's life, and the rest of the crew."

When you save someone's life, whether it be theirs, or the life of their loved one, a bond is formed. It might be only a gossamer filament that keeps you attached spiritually over thousands of miles, or it may become a lifelong friendship with bonds as thick as the cables on the Golden Gate Bridge. If Hagen could have put a special filter over his eyes and looked at Sal, he would have seen hundreds of gossamer strands of love entering Sal's soul, coming at him from every

431

direction; from their own family, from the men he saved, and from their families.

Some of us believe in prayer. Some don't. Even if you have no faith at all in any higher power, the simple act of thinking good thoughts for someone is a prayer in itself. No matter what the religion, or lack of religion, we are all connected by an energy that binds us to it, and to each other. If you have the capacity to love and be compassionate, then you have a faith.

For the rest of Hagen's life, he would never cease to be amazed by the connections people make and the consequences of those connections. He turned in his seat and stared wide-eyed at Private Magowan. His mouth was slightly open in disbelief, although he did believe.

"What is your first name, Private Magowan?"

"It's Joseph, sir. But everyone calls me Joey."

"It is a pleasure to know you, Joey. Please, call me Hagen."

"Thank you, Hagen. Your brother is a brave man. Scotty wrote to us about what he did on his B-17. I hadn't enlisted yet and was still at home. My family has prayed for Captain Cristoforo—"

(gossamer strands of love)

"—and still do. They couldn't believe it when I told them that he was here on the same island where I'm stationed."

"How is your brother, if I may ask?"

"He's fine. His crew got a new pilot, co-pilot and another B-17 and continued their missions. He's going home soon."

"I'm glad to hear he's safe. Sal will be glad, too. Have you seen my brother since he arrived?"

"Yes, once. When I heard he was here, I went to see him. He wasn't awake. I didn't have a chance to talk with him, but I talked to him anyway."

"*You* left the prayer card."

"Yes. When I told my family that Captain Cristoforo was here, they told me to find a Catholic Church and get the Saint Raphael card."

"Thank you, Joey. Thank your family for me, too. Sal is going to need all the prayers anyone can pray right now."

Joey pursed his lips a bit and lowered his gaze, as if he was looking at something in his mind. Then he looked back to Hagen. "I'd better get you back to base. You look beat." He sat straight in his seat, put the Jeep in gear and continued the drive.

"Joey, I'm going to need a ride back again tonight. I'm going to be staying at the hospital with Sal while he recovers. Would you be able to take me back after I clean up and eat something?"

"Absolutely, Sir."

"Thanks, Joey, and skip the *Sir* when we are alone, OK?"

"OK."

Joey dropped him off at the barracks. Hagen went off to shower and get some food. Joey was going to meet him in an hour to take him back to the hospital. On the ride back, Hagen got to know Joey a little better. He and his family were Catholic, like the Beckenbauers. His father, though, was not a farmer. He was the District Attorney of Philadelphia and Joey wanted to follow in his father's footsteps. Law was his passion. He believed in everything that was right and true. When they arrived back at the hospital, Hagen said, "Joey, park the Jeep. I want you to come in with me."

"Are you sure?"

"Yes, I am. I know Sal will want to meet you."

He parked the Jeep and they walked to the entrance. Hagen hoped Sal was awake. Meeting a fellow crewman's brother might really perk up his spirits, knowing his crew was alive and well.

When they walked through the door, Hagen could see that Maggie was still behind the desk. She quickly stood and came around to greet them.

"Well, hello again, Sergeant." She almost reached out to give him a hug but stopped herself. That's not proper protocol. She didn't know him that well, but something about him made her feel so darned at ease.

"Maggie, I told you; it's Hagen, remember?" He opened his arms. He felt she needed a hug. He surely needed one. Now he gave her permission.

She opened her arms and they hugged quickly, yet sincerely. When they let go, she looked up into his eyes. "Thanks, Hagen, I really needed that."

"So did I."

Maggie kept her composure well, but not completely. Being in an environment surrounded by the fallout of the war—the physically, emotionally and spiritually mangled men—took its toll on the medical staff. This wasn't your local hospital where little Suzie was having her tonsils removed and she could have all the strawberry ice cream she wanted. Or, where little Johnny had to have his appendix taken out; *whew, good thing he's ok, God bless him*. Or, Mrs. Appleby just gave birth to her third little Appleby and Mr. Appleby and the other Appleby children were on the other side of the big window, cooing at the new addition. For the men upstairs in their beds in all manners of pain, the nurses were their source of compassion, and the doctors their source of hope, hopefully.

Hagen followed her eyes to the private, who was watching the exchange between them. "Hey Joey, nice to see you again," said Maggie. "Are you going to play for us?" Still in hug-mode, she went over to him and gave him one too.

He hadn't had a hug in a long time. It sure felt nice. He gave her a good squeeze. He missed his mom's hugs, and this just felt so good.

"Good to see you again, too. I might. Are you OK?"

"Oh, I'm fine, I'm fine." Big sigh, then she let go of him. "Sorry gentlemen, I don't know what came over me. Sometimes I think that all the world's problems could be fixed if everybody just got together and gave each other a hug once in a while."

Hagen always had known the power of a hug. *God, I wish it were that easy, then none of us would be here now. Sal wouldn't be up there now.* "You two know each other."

"Of course. Joey comes here once in a while, sits with some of the men. He plays piano beautifully. There's a piano in the rec room and he plays for the men, and for us too, sometimes."

"Aw, go on, Maggie," said Joey.

"It's true, Hagen, he's brilliant. The men love it when he plays, and so do we."

Joey blushed; the heat emanated from his cheeks.

"OK, Maggie, I'll try to get down there."

"Joey's brother was on Sal's B-17." That's all that Hagen needed to say. Maggie looked at Joey.

"And your brother?" She looked at him with cautionary, hopeful eyes.

"He's fine, he's on his way home, thanks to Captain Cristoforo."

Thanks to Captain Cristoforo.

Pride swelled in Hagen, and Maggie could see him beaming with it.

"You two go see him. I'm sure he's waiting for Hagen to come back, and I think meeting you, Joey, will be real nice."

Hagen and Joey took the elevator up to Sal's floor. When they exited the elevator, Sylvia got up from the desk and came around to see them.

"He's been asking for you. He woke up about half an hour after you left. He was crying and trying to scream. For a moment he didn't know where he was. He thought he'd dreamed you were here earlier. I held him a while. When the orderlies brought in your cot and I told him he wasn't dreaming, that you just went to eat and clean up, he calmed down a bit. I told him the extra bed was for you because you were going to stay with him. Then he settled down."

"Thank you, Sylvia. Do you know Private Magowan?"

"I sure do. Hey there, Joey. What brings you to the third floor? The piano is downstairs."

"I asked him to come with me. His brother, Scott, was on Sal's B-17. I figured it might do Sal good to meet him."

"And I wanted to thank him in person, for me and my family, for saving my brother and the rest of the crew. He sacrificed himself so they could be rescued."

"That is the news going around the hospital," said Sylvia. "Some of his fellow POWs have been telling stories of some of the things he'd done while in captivity. One of them told me Captain Cristoforo took a beating that was meant for another man because he knew the other man would not have survived it."

Joey winced. Hagen's breath hitched; he cleared his throat and swallowed hard as he tried to not envision the love of his life having the shit beaten out of him. He closed his eyes. A tear squeezed out and ran down to the corner of his

436

mouth. Joey shivered at the thought of being beaten helplessly.

"I'm sorry I blurted that out like that." She handed them each a tissue from one of her pockets. She had spilled more tears in that hospital than she would for the rest of her life after the war, and she always kept a pocket full. "You boys have good hearts. Try not to let them break too much in here."

Hagen gave her one of those Beckenbauer, take-your-breath-away fantastic hugs. "Thanks, Sylvia."

She hugged him back as hard as she could. When she went to pull away, he held her even tighter. This woman had a beautiful soul; he felt its pain. When he let her go, she pulled a fresh tissue from her pocket and dabbed at her eyes. "Oh God, you have no idea how I needed that."

Oh, but yes, he did.

"May I walk with you to see Sal?" She wanted to see him perk up when Hagen returned with Joey. Sal's change when Hagen was around him was remarkable. And she knew why, too. There was something about Hagen that just made you feel good. And now, she felt like she had the strength to handle the sadness after that energizing Hagen hug.

"Of course. You're family now." He put his arm through hers and they walked down the hallway to Ward 3C, with Joey close behind.

As they neared the door, Joey's heart beat a little faster. He was finally going to meet the hero who saved the life of his big brother. The Magowan family would be forever grateful to Sal. The Beckenbauers would eventually become very close to the families of the men Sal saved on *Thor's Hammer*, and with men who suffered with him in the Japanese POW camp.

Sal wasn't facing the window when the three of them walked into the ward. He was on his right side, facing in the direction of the door, his hawk-eyes waiting to catch a glimpse of Hagen. When he caught sight of Hagen's blond hair from over the mound of the soldier in the next bed, his heart quickened just a bit and he tingled with joy; a feeling he'd not had in quite some time. As the three of them approached, he tried to sit upright but fell back onto the bed. Sylvia quickly went to his aid and sat him up, propping him up against the wall with his pillow.

Even in his weakened condition, Sal beamed. His smile seemed unusually broader; his face so gaunt. His big brown eyes were like saucers in their sockets. His voice was still not its usual bright tenor, but he could be understood. And he was gaining strength spiritually from Hagen's presence. As awful as his life had been for the past almost three years, and as crappy as he felt at that moment, he knew everything was going to be just fine. He had Hagen. His savior. Again.

"That feel better, honey? Are you OK sitting up for a bit?" Sylvia was finishing the final tucking of the pillow.

He nodded. "Mmhmm. Thank you, ma'am." He looked back at Hagen with those adoring brown eyes that never lost their effect on him. Hagen smiled and gave him a wink, his heart a vortex of emotions.

Sal looked past Hagen at the young private standing just behind him to the left. He closed his eyes, and his mind skipped back to *Thor's Hammer*, sifting through the images of the crew. This young man looked familiar; he was trying to remember from where. He opened his eyes "Private, you look like someone I know, but I can't place it."

"Captain Cristoforo, Sir, my name is Joey Magowan. I'm Scotty Magowan's younger brother. We do look a lot alike. Sometimes people mistake us for twins even though he's three years older than me."

Sal closed his eyes again and he saw the faces of his crew as vividly as if he'd just closed his eyes on the lot of them. He relived that day on Rennell Island when they were last together. He smiled as he watched in his mind the PBY rising off the water, climbing high into the sky with his crew tucked safely inside.

He opened his eyes. Joey had come closer to the bed; a tear was drawing a wet line down his cheek as he tried not to react to Sal's condition. He looked worse awake than when he first had seen him sleeping the day that he left the prayer card on his bedside table.

Sal looked up at Joey's familiar Magowan face. "Did Scotty make it?"

"Yes, Sir, the rest of the crew all made it, thanks to you."

"Good, good." He let out a long, raspy sigh. That was one big load off Sal's mind. He had worried about his fellow crewmen, wondered if they made it to Guadalcanal safely. Now he knew. "Tell Scotty I said hello."

"Yes, Sir." Joey laughed a little, sniffled a little. "I sure will, Sir. May I shake your hand, Sir?"

Sal slowly raised his right arm. Joey came to the side of the bed and took it in both his hands and squeezed gently, feeling the bones so close to the surface, afraid he was going to break them. As they shook hands, a flash of light filled the room, startling some of the conscious patients, stirring a few of the dozing ones.

Off to Hagen's left, stood two uniformed men. One was holding a camera, changing out the flash bulb. The other man held a notepad and pencil. A private man as much then as now, Hagen's anger rose. "Excuse me, Privates. Don't you think that saluting a superior officer should be the first order of business before invading his privacy and taking unapproved and unsolicited photographs?"

The two privates from *Stars and Stripes* came to attention and saluted. They stood there waiting for a return salute. It wasn't coming from Hagen. They were waiting for Sal.

"Captain Cristoforo," said Hagen. "They are waiting for you."

"Captain?" Sal barely whispered the word. He looked from Hagen to the two red-faced privates as they maintained their salutes, unmoving.

"Yes, Sir," said Hagen with a grin. "While you were away, your rank rose to Captain."

Sal raised his hand and saluted the two embarrassed men. "At ease, Privates."

The two reporters went at ease. "We apologize, Sir," said the one with the pad and pen.

"I didn't mean to offend, Sir. It was a good shot, so I took it."

"Next time announce yourselves properly," said Hagen.

"Yes sir, Sergeant," they said in unison.

Sal put a hand up as if to quiet a commotion, clicking his tongue against the roof of his mouth. He knew how the photographer felt. If the shot is good, take it, and deal with the improprieties later. "It's OK, Sergeant. Apologies accepted."

"Thank you, Sir. I'm Private Holkom," said the one with the pad and pencil. "And this is Private Wicznowski. We're from *Stars and Stripes*. We were sent here to hopefully get an interview with you and get some photos for the paper. You're a hero, ya know."

"So I heard." He flushed a little with embarrassed modesty. He looked at Hagen, who knew exactly what Sal was feeling, then back at the reporters. "I didn't do anything that anyone else wouldn't have done."

"That might be true, Sir," said Private Holkom. "But, not everyone did what you did, and that makes it a story—

and you a hero. A Congressional Medal of Honor is waiting for you back home stateside."

"I heard that, too." He shook his head and closed his eyes. He didn't believe in medals or trophies. When he wrestled and played football in high school, it wasn't the trophy or the accolades that made him want to be the best. He did it for the good of the team and the school. When he did what he did on *Thor's Hammer*, on Rennell Island, he didn't have his eye on any prize. He had his crewmen—his team—and his country in his heart. Knowing that his crew, his friends, were all safe, that was his reward.

Hagen could see that Sal had had enough excitement for today. "Private Holkom, Private Wicznowski, as much as we all know the importance of telling the country about what Captain Cristoforo has done, he needs to get better so he can get home to his family as soon as possible." He looked over at Sal. His eyes were closed, but he wasn't asleep. He was listening to Hagen's voice, like music, soul-soothing, a whisper of a smile on his lips.

"Yes, Sir, I understand," said Private Holkom. Private Wicznowski nodded in agreement.

"Captain Cristoforo?" Those words coming from Hagen sounded so funny. Sal opened his eyes to see Hagen and the rest watching him.

Trying to remain serious. "Yes, Sergeant Beckenbauer?"

They gave each other such a look that only they could understand; they were laughing hysterically on the inside.

"Will you permit these two reporters to interview you and take photographs?"

"I will." It sounded like a wedding vow. Then to the two reporters, "But if they wouldn't mind coming back tomorrow. I'm beat." Maybe a poor choice of words, but

441

apropos for the time. The others made side glances at each other as the unintended pun was not lost on them.

"No Sir, we understand you need to rest," said Private Holkom." We'll come back tomorrow. We won't just pop in."

"Thank you," said Hagen. Then to Sal, "Ten o'clock sound alright to you?"

Sal nodded. "That's fine."

"OK," said Private Holkom. "See you tomorrow morning. Oh—" He addressed Hagen and Joey. "How do you two know the Captain?"

Hagen and Joey looked at each other. "You first, Joey."

"Captain Cristoforo saved my brother's life and the rest of the crew on his B-17. I'm here to thank him." He looked over to Hagen, giving him the floor.

"I am Captain Cristoforo's brother, Sergeant Hagen Beckenbauer."

The slightly confused looks on the reporters' faces were understood by Hagen. "We grew up together. We are as close as blood brothers, maybe even closer." No truer words were ever uttered.

Sal's story just got more interesting. *The Stars and Stripes readers are going to love this.*

The reporters said their goodbyes and left the ward, with Sylvia, Joey, and Hagen watching as they disappeared through the doors. Sal never took his eyes off Hagen. He hadn't felt so safe since the last time Hagen had come to his rescue on that cold January morning in 1930. He never forgot, never would forget, the ride to the farm in the back of the Sterling, all bundled up next his hero.

Hagen turned to Sal. "Are you OK with all this publicity?" He sat down on his cot next to Sal's.

"If I don't do it now, I'll have to do it later. May as well get it out of the way."

"Well, if you ever want it to stop, if you're ever too tired to deal with it, let me know and I'll make them go away."

"Thanks." He looked over at Sylvia and Joey. "Joey, you go tell your family for me that I'm OK, I'm going to be OK. And, please come visit whenever you want to. I have some stories about Scooter that he might be too modest to tell. He's a good man."

"Thank you, Captain, I'd like that very much."

"Sal, it's Sal. OK?"

"Sure thing, Sal." They shook hands. He shook Hagen's hand then gave Sylvia a hug before he left the ward.

"He's a good kid," said Sylvia. "Kind of like a mascot around here."

"What do you mean?" asked Hagen as he turned around on the bed to look at her.

"Every chance he gets he's up here, making the rounds like a priest, consoling the men, sometimes individually, sometimes a whole group, playing the piano downstairs. He sings and plays beautifully, but I wouldn't be surprised if he got into politics someday."

Hagen could tell he was a good guy. He had that energy that made you want to know him, and he looked forward to Joey's next visit with Sal.

"Well, boys, I gotta scoot. Gotta make *my* rounds, too. See you boys later."

"See you later, Sylvia." Hagen smiled as he watched her leave. When she was out of sight, he turned his attention to some of the men in the other beds. None of them looked older than twenty-five. Some were alert, chatting to other men in other nearby beds. Some were in terrible shape, more gauze and plaster cast than flesh. There were no enforced visiting hours, but then, there were no visitors other than the medical staff and the occasional off-duty private or corporal, guys like Joey who extended their duties to help their injured

443

fellow servicemen pass the time. Hagen was the only visitor who was family.

Sal lay down all the way, put his head on the pillow and closed his eyes. He was tired. All the commotion took it out of him. He dozed off and the bad dreams abused his subconscious like a marauding band of demons; the screams of tortured men, the sounds of canings, beatings, beheadings; the lightning-bolt-searing pain as the butt of a rifle impacts your skull right behind the ear; the taste of bile and blood in your mouth as you're kicked in the gut when you hit the ground.

Sal whimpered. His arms and legs moved under the covers, like a puppy running in his sleep, and it brought Hagen's attention back to him. He put a hand on Sal's forehead, and he calmed down a bit. He didn't want to wake him; he needed his restorative sleep. But what kind of sleep helps the body to heal whilst demons are attacking the mind? *Oh God, how could you allow humans to treat each other so horribly?*

Sal sank deeper into sleep, his sunken eyes darting about under their thin lids. The whimpering quieted; the jumping extremities settled. Hagen sat back against the wall and closed his eyes and listened to Sal's breathing, one hand touching his arm through the sheets, then extended his awareness to the other men, their chatter, their breathing. He fell asleep sitting up, without any dreams.

The days passed, turning into one week, then two. Sal regained his strength and weight slowly. Two weeks to the day that Hagen arrived, Sal took his first steps unassisted, shedding the wheelchair that had been his only mode of transportation. It wasn't simply the ability to walk on his own that was his goal. It was also to no longer require the use of the bedpan. Such an embarrassing way to do personal business—a necessity of course, but an embarrassment, nonetheless. Hagen helped him when he was there, which was most of the time, and assisted without complaint as love does conquer all. Later in their lives, they would joke about the *bedpan times*, finding the humor of it.

Three weeks after Hagen arrived in Manila, the doctors cleared Sal for travel. He was going home. The reporters from *Stars and Stripes* interviewed Sal, took photographs of him, and had written a very good story, the whole time being very respectful of his privacy and when he needed his rest. The article in the paper was a hit with service personnel and civilians: "POW Congressional Medal of Honor Recipient Goes Home."

Although some of the photos of Sal were disturbing, they were published anyway. It showed humanity that it had ways of lowering itself to becoming less than human. Sal insisted that they be shown to the world in hopes of preventing such atrocities from ever occurring again.

The night before Sal and Hagen were to leave Manila, Joey came to visit. Some of the staff and servicemen gathered downstairs around the piano. Sal had a request that Joey play *I Don't Want To Walk Without You.* Sal wanted to dance with Hagen, but well, you know that couldn't happen, not in those days. He danced with Sylvia while Hagen danced with Maggie. When they looked at each other over the nurses' shoulders, their eyes met, and they danced with their hearts. Halfway through the song, they changed partners. When the song ended, they all hugged. Sal tired easily; his road to recovery was still miles long. He said goodnight to everyone, gave Maggie and Sylvia kisses on their cheeks, and walked with Hagen back to Ward 3C.

Sal climbed into his hospital bed for the last time. He turned onto his left side, facing Hagen, who had climbed into his cot, and whispered, "Goodnight, Hagen," then mouthed the words, *I love you.*

"Goodnight, Sal," and mouthed back, *I love you, too.*

Sal was out cold thirty-seven seconds after his head hit the pillow. Hagen, on the other hand, was wide awake, his mind spinning, full of thoughts about the past, the present, and the future. Sal was a fly-by-the-seat-of-his-pants kinda guy. Hagen wanted—needed—everything planned out, choreographed, under his control.

The war was a lesson in *not* being in control; taking orders from others when he knew a better way but could say nothing due to his rank. He was taking control now of Sal's situation. He was going to be there for every step of his recovery.

He left the horrible thoughts of the war in a locked closet, far in the back of his mind, and concentrated on the here and now. Sal's breathing was slow and deep, with an occasional sound leaking from a dream. He had bad dreams. Some nights were better than others. Tonight was a fairly quiet night in Sal's dreamscape. Hagen focused on his own breathing and matched his with Sal's, thought about the next leg of their journey together, and fell asleep facing Sal.

They were up early the next morning. Hospital attire was no longer required for Sal. A new uniform was provided, replete with Captain's insignia. Hagen stood back and admired how Sal looked in his new uniform. "Very nice, Captain Cristoforo. Very nice indeed. Papa is going to be so proud when he sees you."

"Thank you, Sergeant." He stood motionless, staring at Hagen.

"What?" His face showed his puzzlement.

"Did you forget something, *Sergeant?*"

Hagen thought a moment, then realized his faux pas, and stood at attention and saluted his superior officer. "My apologies, Sir."

Sal looked around for any eavesdroppers—there were none within earshot—then he whispered, "I was only joking. Relax, will you? If you ever salute me again, I'll punch you."

"Yes, Sir." He finished the salute to Captain Cristoforo, then winked.

Sal shook his head then looked around again to make sure their conversation was still private. "You better be careful, or you'll get us both court marshalled."

Hagen walked over to him and leaned in close, whispering in Sal's ear. "Yes, dear."

Sal punched him in the arm. Hagen laughed heartily, stirring some of the men in their beds. "C'mon, Captain, time to go home." Hagen picked up both of their duffels and followed Sal down the aisle. They said goodbye to some of the men in their beds as they walked to the door, then hugs and goodbyes at the nurses' desk. When they got out of the elevator downstairs, Maggie and Sylvia were waiting for them, ready for their hugs. Sylvia had already prepped Maggie with tissues. They were so happy to see Sal go home, but at the same time, it was a melancholy feeling. They were going to miss him and Hagen more than they would the others. They didn't quite understand why. It was just a feeling they had.

Joey was outside by the Jeep waiting for them. He put their duffel bags in the back while Hagen helped Sal get into the passenger seat. Hagen hopped in the back, and Joey got behind the wheel, started the engine, and off they went to the dock. Waiting for them dockside was the hospital ship, *USS Benevolence*; bright white with a wide, green stripe from her bow to her stern that was interrupted in three places by her big Red Cross crosses. It was an interesting contrast to the

447

other ships docked nearby; all a dull grey, some still bearing their battle scars.

When they pulled up to the dock, other men were being carried, wheeled, or were crutching themselves onboard for their trip stateside. Hagen helped Sal out of the Jeep and started a slow walk to the gangway with Joey following them with their duffel bags. When onboard, a nurse took them to where Sal and Hagen were going to sleep. Their beds were against the starboard wall, with a porthole in between them. Although the nursing staff thought it quite irregular for Hagen, who was not a patient, to be sleeping in a bed alongside the other patients, the condition of Sal (*they should have seen him three weeks ago*), and the obvious emotional requirement for Hagen to be with him, overrode any irregularities. Plus, Hagen had Presidential Orders in his pocket.

Sal sat on his bed, looking absolutely drained. Hagen turned to Joey. "Thank you so much for all you've done, Joey."

"It was my pleasure, the least I could do."

"Joey, you're from Philadelphia, right?" said Hagen.

"Well, it's actually Bala Cynwyd, right outside Philly. No one has ever heard of it, so I just say Philly."

"I've heard of it, and you're pretty close to our farm in Beverly, just a little north of Philadelphia, in New Jersey. Don't be a stranger. You and your family are always welcome."

"Thank you, Hagen. I know my family would like to meet yours. We have already talked about taking the ride to Jersey." They shook hands.

Then Joey looked down at Sal. "Thank you again, Captain. I know you hate it, but—" and Joey took two steps back and gave Captain Cristoforo a perfect salute. It was the sincerest, most respectful salute Hagen had ever seen. It was heartfelt and emotional, as far as salutes go. Sal tried to stand, a little wobbly, not wanting to deny Private Magowan the returned respect. Hagen grabbed hold of his left elbow. When he was upright, Captain Cristoforo returned the salute and held it, looking deep into Private Magowan's eyes. He had a feeling that Joey and his family were going to be part of his family's life, that this wasn't the last he'd see of Joey, or Scooter. He finished the salute. "Thank you, Private." He smiled and sat back down on the bed.

Joey finished the salute and smiled at the two of them. "Safe trip home. See you in the funny papers." On those words, he turned and left.

The beds around them were receiving their occupants, the room filling with clatter and chatter. Hagen looked out the porthole at the gangway leading down to the dock. The flow of patients had thinned. Most of the military transport vehicles had left. He saw Joey walking down the gangway. There was something about him, he couldn't put his finger on it, but something about him made Hagen feel pretty confident that Private Joey Magowan of Bala Cynwyd, Pennsylvania (just outside Philadelphia), was going to make something of his life.

An hour later, the gangway was lifted away, the ropes untied and pulled in, and the ship slowly left the dock and made its way west out into the South China Sea, turning north to go around Luzon. From there it made its way east. Three days later, the ship docked in Hagåtña, Guam, to pick up more injured servicemen. Patients from the temporary military hospitals in Agat and Anigua were shuttled to the ship over the course of the evening. The *Benevolence* shoved off with first light, on the way to Oahu, six days away, where injured servicemen from the 147th General Hospital waited for their ride home. The hospital ship docked in Pearl Harbor in the middle of the sixth night, near the entrance to Southeast Loch.

Hagen, always an early riser, was up before the sun. Sal used to be that way. His battered mind and body kept him asleep more than awake as they both healed. Hagen sat up in his bed and listened to the sounds around him. Some men snored. Some were dreaming things that made them cry out from the hellscape that entered their minds and took over when they were vulnerable. He watched Sal sleep. It was another bad night with nightmares of beatings and torture. Sometimes he cried out in English, sometimes in Japanese.

"Shinaide kudasai! Watashi o yurushitekudasai! Watashi wa yoku narimasu! Watashi wa yoku narimasu!"

(Please don't! Please forgive me! I will be good! I will be good!)

Hagen clenched his teeth so hard that his ears rang, and his temples pulsed. He knew that after those words came the beatings. He got up several times in the night to put a hand on Sal's head and whisper in his ear, *"You're safe, Sal, I'm here."* The whimpering and the muttering would stop, only to return a couple hours later.

Through the porthole, Hagen saw the sky getting lighter with the rising sun. He stood up and looked out. Navy personnel were preparing the ship for departure. He could hear movement as nurses walked amongst the patients, helping them with their morning routines, checking vitals, administering medications and compassion. Sal's nurse came by to take his blood pressure. She was a little thing, Filipino, no more than five feet tall, with skin the color of cappuccino foam, her hair tied up in a bun that was hidden by her nurse's cap.

"Good morning, Gabriella." Hagen's bright eyes and smile had been a pleasure to see each morning since they left Manila.

"Good morning, Sergeant Hagen. How did he sleep?"

"It was a rough night. Three times I got up to quiet him."

"Poor thing." She clicked her tongue.

Sal stirred as the cuff tightened around his left arm with each squeeze of the bulb. His eyes opened as Gabriella watched the gauge and listened with her stethoscope. He turned his head on his pillow and smiled at Hagen, sitting on his bed, quietly watching. Hagen winked at him. Sal blinked back.

"Good morning, Captain." Gabriella's voice was sweet music in the morning.

"I told you, Gabriella, it's Sal."

"Good morning, Captain Sal." She stuck a thermometer under his tongue, shutting him up for the moment.

He sighed. Every morning was the same banter between them. She never gave in, a stickler for using the rank. She couldn't salute men of rank. Insisting on addressing them by their rank was her salute. She was a softy in all other ways but stood her ground when it came to military ranks. Hagen gave up trying halfway to Guam to get her to stop calling him Sergeant.

"Nice try, *Captain*." Hagen giggled at Sal's daily attempt to convert Gabriella.

Sal moaned. He was outnumbered, and he had to pee. He held up his arm for Hagen to pull him up.

"Ah, ah. One minute, Captain Sal. I'm not finished with you." She looked at her wrist and watched the second-hand ticking.

Sal stood there, jiggling with the need to pee.

"I told you before, if you stay put while I finish, you would not have to pee-pee so bad. Standing up makes it worse." She pulled the thermometer from his mouth and looked down at it. "OK, you will live. Go pee-pee." She giggled as he shuffled as fast as he could, with Hagen's help, to the bathroom.

On their way back to the beds, Sal had an idea. He wanted to see Pearl Harbor. So, the two of them climbed the stairs up to the highest promenade deck. From the starboard side of the ship, they could see where Battleship Row had been. It had been repaired, reconstructed better than before the Japanese had destroyed most of it almost four years before. All but three of the heavily-damaged warships were repaired better than new. The *USS Oklahoma* was raised but sank in a storm as she was towed to San Francisco. The *USS Utah* remained on her side, out of sight on the west side of Ford Island, sunk in the muck of the bottom of the Harbor. The resting place of the *USS Arizona* was visible as she poked out of the water where she and 1,102 of her crew eternally rested at the bottom of the Harbor, an oil slick on the surface rising from her hull like the blood of a wounded beast. Other patients and service personnel gathered along *Benevolence*'s starboard side. No one spoke. There were salutes, shaking heads, rising prayers, and falling tears. It wasn't until they were clear of the harbor that people spoke and walked about, told stories and returned to their places.

When the ship shoved off it was at full capacity, with 797 injured servicemen and 558 crew and medical personnel. Four days later, in Los Angeles, medical transport vehicles were waiting to take the injured to the train station, where hospital trains bound for different parts of the country waited to be filled with patients and staff. It didn't take long to empty the ship, and in a few hours, Sal and Hagen were on board their train. Bunks for the men were lined up on both sides of the train car where seats had been when it was a passenger train. At eleven-thirty that night, the train left the station and made its way into the American Southwest.

Of all the different modes of transportation that Hagen had experienced during the war, it was the train that he fell in love with; the sounds, the smells, the feel of the wheels on the tracks beneath him. You can get up and move about, have dinner in a different car, a cocktail in the lounge, and meet people and have conversations. Steamship travel was as nice, with the same abilities to eat one place and then take a stroll on deck before retiring to your cabin. But just as the flying made him airsick, the movement beneath his feet, not being on terra firma, just hovering above nothing, had his stomach on edge the whole way from Manila to Los Angeles. He had never thrown up, yet the feeling that it might happen would occasionally juggle his guts with its fingers, keeping him aware that anything was possible. If the time ever came to travel to another continent, Hagen would go by steamship by default because, as we know fair well, flying was his least favorite. He didn't dislike airplanes. He could appreciate their design, their splendor, the ability to leave the ground and return safely, as long as he wasn't inside one of them when they did it.

As their train snaked through the California darkness, Sal was tucked in and dozing into semi-consciousness. Hagen was wide awake, his mind was all over the map with thoughts of the future: of himself, Sal, of Sal and him, of his family and the farm. There would be school to attend. They both needed to graduate high school and get their diplomas. The last letter he had received from his father was a happy letter. Aunt Mathilde had settled in nicely. She was staying in Karl's room, while Karl took the attic bedroom. They'd figure something out later when he and Sal returned home.

As the train picked up speed somewhere between Anaheim and Riverside, Hagen's mind slowed down, and he drifted off to sleep in the bunk above Sal. His hopeful dreams of the future came back to occupy his mind while Sal's nightmares of the recent past tormented his sleep.

The morning sky lightened in the east as the train was passing through Williams, Arizona. Hagen was already up, dressed and waiting for Sal. Some of the other patients were awake. Those able to walk got up to use the restroom, while those unable to get up waited for their nurse. Hagen sat on the edge of Sal's bunk near his feet and watched his face. His change in breathing signaled his rising from slumber. A deep breath, then a deeper one, then a long, deep one and a stretch. His eyes opened with a smile at the sight of Hagen's bright blue eyes gazing down at him.

"Good morning, sunshine," said Hagen. "How'd you sleep?" He knew Sal slept fitfully. He had heard his sleep talking and tossing about; no begging for mercy in Japanese this time. *Thank God.* Sal never remembered his dreams the next day, just felt the draining effects they had on his mind and body.

Sal moved his tongue around the inside of his mouth and moistened his dry lips. "Good morning." His voice was dry. He managed a smile. "I don't know how I slept. You tell me."

"Smart ass." Hagen scrunched his face up in fake disgust, then pretend-pinched Sal's leg; not much there to pinch; more than when Hagen first got to Manila, but not enough, not like before the war.

Sal pulled off his covers, his bony extremities still painful for Hagen to look at, and sat up, turned, and put his feet on the floor. "I have to pee. Where's the head?"

Hagen pointed towards the front of the train. "That way, at the end of the car. You need help?"

"No, I think I can manage, thanks." He stood up and held onto the top bunks for balance against the occasional rocking of the train as he walked down the aisle towards the bathroom. When he returned about ten minutes later, he was smiling.

"What are you smiling about?" asked Hagen.

"I just saw one of the guys who was in the same POW camp I was in. He looks good; so much better than the last time I saw him. I didn't think he was going to make it."

I don't think anyone thought that you were going to make it.

"That's great, Sal."

Sal leaned over to look out of the window. "I wonder where we are."

"I heard one of the nurses say we just passed a town called Flagstaff, Arizona."

"I thought Arizona was all desert. The mountains out there have lots of trees."

"That's what I thought. Are you hungry, Sal?"

"A little bit. You?" He sat back on his bunk.

"Yeah, I'm hungry. I'll go find out what we do for chow around here."

Hagen patted him on the shoulder and went off in search of breakfast. Sal lay back down and turned towards the window. The mountains of Arizona slid by in the distance; a vast, moving panorama. The gentle rocking and rhythmic sounds of the train soothed Sal back into a snooze. The touch of a nurse's hand on his shoulder startled him awake. He jumped so much that the nurse was as startled by him as he was by her.

"Oh honey," her Tennessee drawl as thick as cold molasses. "I'm so sorry." She rubbed his shoulder, he jumped again, and she took a step back. "I thought you heard me coming up behind you."

He rolled over to look at her. He needed to see her face. He needed to separate her from the bad dream that was forming when she touched him and became part of the nightmare. Her kind face, her gentle southern dialect, calmed him. Hagen returned at that moment and could see Sal's face. "Sal, are you alright?"

"I'm OK, I guess I fell back asleep."

"And I scared the dickens out of him," she said to Hagen, then looked back at Sal. "I'm really very sorry. I'd seen you two talking a few minutes before and I thought you were awake."

"It's OK, nurse, I have been a bit, uh, jumpy lately."

Hagen looked from Sal to the nurse. *That is an understatement.*

She took a deep breath. "My name is Charlene, and I'm your nurse for your trip home."

"I'm Hagen, Sal's brother." They shook hands. He liked this nurse. She was older, his father's age, with a kind face, a twinkle in her eye and her greying hair up in a bun.

"It is a pleasure to make your acquaintance, Hagen. And you are," she looked at her clipboard, "Salvatore Cristoforo, Captain Salvatore Cristoforo."

"Yes, that's me, but, call me Sal, please."

Unlike Gabriella, who was a stickler for using their ranks, Charlene was happy to oblige Hagen and Sal. She had the utmost respect for them, for the servicemen they were, but to her, if an officer insisted on a first name basis, then she wouldn't argue. It was about their request, and a return to normalcy, not protocol.

"Alright, Sal. How are ya feeling today?"

"I'm OK. I wake up tired."

"He has bad dreams," said Hagen.

She put her hand on Sal's head. "You're not the only one, honey. They'll fade. I've been doing this since the first war, trust me, they'll fade away. It takes time" —she looked at Hagen— "and the love of family." Her smiling eyes twinkled like Mrs. Claus. "You two should get some breakfast. Can ya walk, honey?"

"Yes, ma'am."

"Good, the exercise is good for ya. But, if ya'ever need me to bring your meal, I'd be glad to fetch it for ya. And, y'all call me Charlene, ya' hear?"

"I will, thank you, Charlene," said Sal.

"I'll see you boys later." She winked and moved on down to the next man, spreading her kindness and good spirit, sharing her infectious smile.

After breakfast, there wasn't much to do; not a lot of room to go exploring like there was on the *Benevolence*. Sal napped a lot, and, in between naps, he and Hagen talked. They reminisced about the farm and the orphanage. They talked about what was going to happen when they got home; school and careers. Hagen even got Sal to talk a little about what had happened on the B-17 and afterwards on the island. He didn't pry into Sal's experience as a POW. That would have to happen when Sal was ready—if ever he would be ready—to talk about it.

Later that day, in the late afternoon just before sunset, the train pulled into Albuquerque station. Sal was asleep, his belly full. Dinner was beef stew and was surprisingly tasty, and Sal, much to Hagen's delight and surprise, ate quite a healthy serving. He had gained a little weight since Hagen had first seen him; his body was slowly regaining strength despite the nightmares running amok in his mind at night. When the train stopped, Hagen looked out the window. What he saw made his heart skip a beat and his soul do a double-take. Sal jumped a bit in his sleep. Something was going on in his dreams again. He put a hand on Sal's head. He settled down, and Hagen headed for the exit.

When he stepped out onto the platform, the scenery laid out before him gave him pause, and momentarily took away his breath. In the east, Sandia Peak was aglow in the light of the setting sun that silhouetted the extinct volcanoes in the west. An enormous full moon had just cleared the mountain's crest. It seemed so close that Hagen reached his hand up to the sky as if to caress it. It was a scene similar to this that Sal would catch on film in 1962.

Then there were the smells. All along the platform, locals offered their culinary creations to weary and hungry travelers. Hagen closed his eyes and breathed in the symphony of aromas: green chile stew, fresh tamales, Indian Fry Bread. The smells stirred his appetite in spite of the fact that he'd just eaten a hefty bowl of stew himself. He opened his eyes. The moon rose slowly higher. As the smells of New Mexico took their turns tickling his olfactory system, the sounds of the train and the people milling about the platform faded into silence. The smells were still there, but the sounds were gone. He screwed a finger into one ear, then the other, trying to unclog them. Still, no sounds could be heard. He watched the people around him like he was in the middle of a silent movie.

From off to his left came the sound of a Native American flute. It was haunting, yet beautiful, calming, and sounded as if it were right in the room with him, if he was in a room. But he was not in a room. He was out in the open air that had all the surrounding sounds removed and replaced by that one flute. Hagen looked in the direction from where it came. Off to the left, with the other purveyors of local fare, about fifty feet down the platform, was an old Navajo woman. She sat cross-legged on a beautifully woven Navajo blanket. Displayed on the blanket around her were her wares: pottery, blankets, silver and turquoise jewelry. She stared directly at Hagen with a slight smile on her face and a twinkle in her eye. Her lips moved, and he heard her as if she were right in front of him.

"Wóshdéé'."

He turned around to see if perhaps she was looking at someone behind him. She was speaking Navajo to *him*. Why would she be addressing *him*? And, how could he hear her so clearly and nothing else?

"Wóshdéé'." She nodded directly at him.

He put his hand on his chest. "Me?"

"Yes."

That was English for sure. And she heard him as plainly as he heard her.

With a wrinkled, sun-leathered hand she waved him over. As he approached, she never removed him from her gaze, and with each step closer, the sounds on the platform gradually returned, so that by the time he was standing in front of her, everything was back to normal.

Sitting on the blanket, a little behind and to her right, was a young Navajo boy, about ten years old. He was watching Hagen with the same smile as the old woman. A neatly folded woven blanket rested in his lap. She began to speak to Hagen again in her native tongue as the young boy stood up, holding the blanket out in front of him.

"Gah-than."

"Take this," the boy said as he offered up the blanket with both hands.

Hagen reached out and took it from him. "Thank you. Uh, here…" He reached into his back pocket and pulled out his wallet.

She spoke, then the boy. "No money. Take it and cover him."

Hagen's confused look needed no words to say what he was thinking. He still had to ask, "Cover him. Cover who?"

The old woman and the boy turned their heads and looked directly at the railcar where Sal was sleeping. A light emanated from Sal's window, glowing red, pulsing like a heartbeat.

Hagen rubbed his eyes and shook his head. *That couldn't be. Must be the sunset reflecting somehow.* He turned back to look down at the two Navajos, who now smiled broadly up at him. Without looking down, still with her gaze affixed to Hagen's, the old woman reached off to her left and picked up a dreamcatcher. It was about six inches in diameter, its spider web-like mesh adorned with stones, fetishes, and feathers. She held it up to Hagen with two hands. Touching it made his hand tingle, and he reflexively pulled back.

The woman spoke again, and the boy translated. "You feel it. That is good. Take it. Hang it over him."

"What does it do?"

"It will keep away the bad dreams," said the boy.

Hagen looked back at Sal's window to see if the glow had returned. It hadn't, but he was sure now that he was in the presence of something spiritual and more powerful than himself. When he looked back down at the two Native Americans, they bowed their heads.

The train whistle blew.

"Thank you," said Hagen.

They both looked up at him again and nodded. He walked away, holding their gifts close to his heart. When he got to the entrance to the train, he turned back. Their eyes were still on him, and for one brief moment all the sound around him faded again and he heard the old woman's voice once more,

"Nááí'ahideeltsééh."

"Until we meet again," said the young boy.

Hagen stepped up and held on to the handle with one hand, while clutching the blanket and dreamcatcher in the other. The sounds returned, and the train whistled and started to move forward. He remained there for as long as he could, wanting to see as much of Sandia's majestic beauty glowing in the setting New Mexican sun.

When Hagen returned to their bunks, Sal was still asleep. He was twitching again. The demons had returned. Hagen unfolded the blanket. The detail in the weaving was remarkable. The design depicted five Navajo figures standing between stalks of corn. The two ends and the top were framed by a stretched sixth figure; his feet in the bottom left and his head in the bottom right. He laid the blanket over Sal's body. Then he tied the dreamcatcher to one of the slats in the top bunk over Sal's head, using the twine that was attached. When he touched it, he felt an energy. It was scary. It was captivating. It was enlightening. When he let go of it and it hung freely, the webbing vibrated ever so slightly, like violin strings, jiggling the fetishes and semi-precious stones that were strung onto it. In his sleep, Sal took a deep, long breath, then sighed, and then returned to normal breathing.

That night, Sal slept his first night's sleep without his soul being tormented by horrific visions of the past three years. When he woke up the next morning, he was noticeably rested, more so than any other morning. When Charlene came by to see him on her morning rounds and asked him how he was feeling, he actually said, "I didn't wake up tired today."

"Well, that's good, honey. Didn't I tell you it would get better?" She smiled, patted his arm, then moved on to her next patient.

Hagen didn't tell Sal about his encounter at the station in Albuquerque. His explanation about the sudden appearance of the blanket and the dreamcatcher was quasi-true. He went out to get some air when the train stopped in Albuquerque. He got the blanket and dreamcatcher from a little old Navajo woman; the plain and simple, sanitized truth. It wasn't until years later, when Sal and Hagen had moved to New Mexico, that Hagen told Sal about what really happened that late afternoon at the train station in Albuquerque.

Three days later, the train pulled into Philadelphia. Waiting for them were the whole Beckenbauer family, Uncle Samuel, Aunt Ethel and their Muriel and Joey (Sam Jr. had not yet returned from his tour in the Pacific). Hagen spied them standing on the platform and waved out the window at them. Mathilde and Diana were jumping up and down, running to the window to touch Hagen's hands. Karl ran after them, shouting his brothers' names. Sal stood up and leaned out with Hagen. His appearance caught them by surprise. The last telegram that Hagen had sent to his family, from Manila the night before he and Sal had embarked on their journey home, advised his father to prepare the rest of the family for their first sight of Sal. Nothing anyone said could have prepared them enough. It was a good thing they hadn't seen him as he was when Hagen had first seen him.

Georg's breath hitched. He bit his lower lip, hard. Aunt Mathilde put her arm around him and whispered, "It is OK, Georg, it will be OK. He has Hagen. He has you, the family."

The girls did their best to keep smiling, keep up the enthusiasm. Their brothers were finally home, alive. Karl stopped running for a moment when he saw Sal's condition. When the train stopped, he caught up to his sisters, who were now waiting by the door for their brothers.

Hagen immediately felt their mood. It was not difficult to see it on their faces. Uncle Samuel and Aunt Ethel stood just behind Georg and Mathilde. The shock on their faces was very apparent. Hagen hoped they all could contain their emotions, for Sal's sake. Sal already felt bad about himself as it was. He needed smiles, hugs, laughter; not frowns and tears of pity.

Hagen exited first, holding their duffels. He dropped them as the girls tackled him with hugs and tear-wetted kisses on the cheeks. Karl was next. He was thirteen now, and Hagen almost didn't recognize him. He grabbed Hagen, squeezing so hard, surprising him with his strength.

From behind Hagen came Sal's voice. "Hey, guys, you're blocking the pipes here. I'd like to get off this train sometime today."

Karl grabbed the duffels and moved them out of the way. Hagen reached up to grab hold of Sal. A step at a time he emerged from the train, leaning the whole while on Hagen. He stepped onto the platform and was immediately surrounded by his other siblings. They didn't tackle him like they did Hagen, but he was smothered in love just the same.

Hagen turned to look at his father, with his Aunt Mathilde and the Ostermans. They were standing a few paces away, patiently awaiting their turn to hold Hagen and Sal again. Hagen walked towards them. Sal followed, with the others surrounding him like bodyguards.

"Hello, Papa." There were tears streaming down Hagen's cheeks, magnifying the blue in his eyes.

Georg was so proud to see what a fine young man Hagen had become. He opened his arms. Hagen went to him, slowly, like a ship gently docking at home port. No tackle. No grizzly bear squeezes. Just a comforting, welcoming embrace. They let go of each other and Hagen hugged his aunt.

"Welcome home, Hagen. It is good to see you again," she said in German.

"It is good to see you again, Aunt Mathilde. How do you like New Jersey?"

She couldn't help but laugh through the tears. "I liked it very much. I love it even more now." She hugged him as hard as she could. When she let go, "Now, I must meet Sal."

While Hagen and the Ostermans hugged and talked, Aunt Mathilde and Georg went to Sal. As they approached, he stood up straight. He steeled himself. During his years in captivity, he'd dreamed of coming home. During the trip home he'd wondered how this day was going to feel. He wanted to remain strong. He knew his condition would be upsetting to his family. He refused to become too emotional, for their sakes.

Hagen had told Sal about Aunt Mathilde, about how they found each other and how much she looked like their mother. As she and his father got closer, Sal could see the resemblance.

Georg opened his arms and took Sal into them, gently engulfing him, feeling Sal's frailness. "Welcome home, son. We are so very proud of you."

"Thank you, Papa. It's good to be home."

Aunt Mathilde put a hand on Georg's shoulder. He looked at her and slowly let go of Sal. "Sal, I want you to meet someone."

Hagen had now joined them and was standing beside his aunt. She asked him to translate for her. "Welcome home, Sal. I am your Aunt Mathilde. I am so happy to finally meet you. I have heard so much about you."

"Hello, Aunt Mathilde. It's a pleasure to meet you as well." The resemblance to her sister was remarkable. Memories of Marta came into his thoughts. She could see it on his face and took him in her arms just as the floodgates opened. The others gathered around them, all placing a hand on Sal, feeling his bones as his body shook with the sobs.

"There, there, Sal," said Aunt Mathilde. Hagen stopped translating. The meaning of the words came through loud and clear with the sentiment. "You are safe now. Shh, shh." She gently rubbed his back.

Hagen observed his aunt and Sal. Memories ignited.

So much like Mama.

Strangers around them, who were waiting for their own loved ones to emerge from the train, briefly stopped what they were doing. The Beckenbauer reunion was a touching and heart-breaking sight to see. When *their* son, brother, husband, got off the train, it was their turn to shout, cry, and jump up and down.

Georg put his arms around his two oldest boys. "Let's go home."

They walked in a tight formation, arm in arm, to the exit. The girls were so excited. They had cooked for days. There was a pot of meatballs and sausage in red sauce on the stove; Sal's favorites. Hagen had many favorites. One of them was pot roast. His mama's was the best. Sometimes, on special occasions, there would be sauerbraten; tangy and tender. Georg still kept the handwritten recipe. It was Marta's mother's recipe, handed down from her great-great-grandmother. Georg had asked the girls if it would be alright if Aunt Mathilde made the sauerbraten. She was moved to tears when Georg and the girls showed her the recipe in her mother's handwriting. She'd lost all of her parents' things in the bombing and this was a wonderful reunion with something of her mother's. Naturally, Aunt Mathilde made the sauerbraten.

Georg was always thinking about other people's feelings. When the time came to go to Philadelphia to pick up his sons, it wasn't a simple picking up of a relative from the station, who was returning from a pleasure trip. The bringing home of his two sons, who had been to Hell and back, matched significance with the fateful journey to Zurbrugg with his dying wife. Completely different

465

circumstances, indeed, but of the same importance, the same emotional magnitude. He told his children and Samuel what he wanted to do. They all agreed that his idea was perfect.

Sitting at the curb in front of the station, waiting to take Hagen and Sal home, was the old Sterling. It had been retired from regular use many years before, only used around the farm occasionally during harvest and for hayrides at the annual picnics. Georg and Karl kept it very well maintained. It held a significant place in their lives, like an old loved uncle. It was their first purchase when he and Marta arrived in America. Karl was born in it. Marta went to Heaven in it. It was sheltered in the barn most of the time and was in remarkably fine condition for its twenty-three years.

Hagen and Sal stared at the old Sterling like a long-lost friend. The significance of its presence did not go unnoticed by them. They looked at their father. Georg was watching their reactions. When they saw the look on his face, they knew it was he who was behind the gesture.

Georg and Hagen helped Sal climb up into the back, and then Hagen hopped in with him. There were two blankets on the floor near the hay bales—the same two blankets that covered them when the Sterling carried Sal and Diana home fifteen years before. It was October. No snow dunes on the ground yet, but it was still chilly enough to need the blankets.

After they settled into the hay, Hagen pulled the blankets over them. Georg and Aunt Mathilde got into the cab of the Sterling with the girls squeezed in between. Following behind were the Ostermans in their car with Karl, Muriel and Joey in the back. Samuel saw Hagen and Sal sitting next to each other in the back of the Sterling, in the same places they'd been that cold January in 1930. The vision of the two as little boys, riding away from the orphanage, played in his heart. Hagen waved under his blanket at them, jiggling the fabric, just like he had fifteen years before, and Samuel started to cry.

It was a perfect ride home; the chilly air whipped around their faces in the back. Under the blankets, Hagen put his arm around Sal, holding him close, keeping him warm. They stayed like that for the entire ride. Not a word was spoken. None were needed.

Their homecoming was low-key; quiet, family only, no press, just the Beckenbauers and the Ostermans. Everyone enjoyed the feast, and after coffee and the best chocolate cake, ever (made especially for the occasion by Lorraine Varsaci), the Ostermans went home, bellies and souls full.

As the days passed, the house was visited by neighbors and friends, clergy and parishioners from the church, to pay their respects to Hagen and Sal. When the news first spread that Sal had earned the Congressional Medal of Honor, his notoriety for his heroism was the talk of the town. The hubbub started up again when word got around that he was coming home. There were a couple of visits from local newspapers as well.

"It is amazing what you can accomplish if you do not care who gets the credit."

—Harry S. Truman

November 1, 1945

One day, after the buzzing quieted down and life was returning to almost normal, there was a knock on the door. When Georg opened it, standing there was a young man, a Second Lieutenant, in military dress. He was holding an envelope.

"Good afternoon, sir."

"Good afternoon, Lieutenant."

"My apologies for the intrusion. I have a letter here for Captain Salvatore Cristoforo."

"He lives here. I can give it to him, he is my son."

"I beg your pardon, sir, but my orders are to hand this to Captain Cristoforo personally."

"Well then, do come in. Have a seat and I will go get him." He showed the Lieutenant to the living room and offered him a seat.

The Lieutenant took off his hat and stood perfectly straight. "Thank you, sir, I will stand."

"Alright, Lieutenant. I will be right back." He went upstairs to get Sal. Hagen and Sal came down the stairs behind their father.

The Lieutenant stood at attention. "Captain Cristoforo?"

"Yes, Lieutenant, I'm Captain Cristoforo."

"I have a letter here for you, Sir, from the White House." He handed the envelope to Sal, then walked to the door. "It is an honor to meet you, Sir." He put his hat back on and left the three men standing there in wonderment.

Georg shook his head. "Well, that was quick."

Sal was turning the letter over in his hand. He saw his name and the official White House seal. You would have thought that ripping it open would have been the first thing on his mind. But no. He stood there, silently turning the envelope over like a blind man examining a holy relic, feeling the texture, the seam along the seal where a White House staffer had licked and sealed it shut.

Georg and Hagen patiently waited for Sal to do something other than fondle the envelope. After a couple of minutes, Hagen had to say something. "Well, are ya going to open it or ask it out on a date?"

Sal smirked and cocked his head a little to the left. "Smart ass." Georg handed him a letter opener from the desk. Slowly he inserted the tip and gently slit it open like a surgeon. Inside was a single tri-folded page. He pulled it out, unfolded it and read it to himself. His face turned white, he needed to sit and slowly sat down on the couch, holding the letter in both hands, staring up at Hagen and his father.

"Well? Sal?" Hagen was a little scared. He couldn't make out Sal's emotions. He looked terrified. Why? What could a letter from the White House say that would make the blood run from Sal's face? He took the letter from Sal and read it aloud so his father could hear it:

To: Captain Salvatore Cristoforo
       RR 1
       Beverly, New Jersey
From: Harry S. Truman
       The White House
       Washington, D.C.

Captain Cristoforo,

It has been brought to my attention that you have spent almost three years as a prisoner of war of the Japanese Imperial Army and have only recently returned home to your family. I have read all the documents concerning your account. I have also received numerous letters from your fellow crewmen and their families praising your heroic efforts aboard your B-17. I am sure you have been made aware that your heroic deeds have garnered you the Congressional Medal of Honor. Captain, I have presented many a serviceman with the Medal of Honor. Normally, you would come to Washington, D.C. to receive your medal. I would like to step out of the norm and come to you, to your home in New Jersey, to personally award you the Medal of Honor. I have set the date, Saturday, 10 November, to arrive at your farm.

I look forward to meeting you and your family.

Sincerely,

Harry S. Truman

Harry S. Truman
President of the United States

Hagen and his father slowly sat down on either side of Sal. They turned their heads to look at him with dramatic slowness.

"Son." Georg put his arm around Sal. "I think we should get your uniform pressed."

Sal closed his open mouth. "He is coming… here. The President of the United States is coming… here?"

Hagen laughed and patted Sal on his back, stood up at attention and saluted. "Yes, Sir, Captain, Sir. He is coming *here*…" He leaned over and looked right into Sal's deer-in-the-headlight eyes and poked his shoulder. "…for *you*."

Sal punched him in the arm. Notoriety was not Sal's cup of tea. The constant flow of congratulators, hand shakers, well-wishers, bringers of casseroles and cakes could not have died down fast enough for him. He wanted things to go back to normal. He wanted his old life back. But his old life ended the moment he took control of *Thor's Hammer* and landed her and her crew on the shore of Rennell Island.

Hagen punched him back. "We talked about this on our way home." Hagen looked over at his father. "He knew he was getting the medal." Then back to Sal. "What did you think, Sal, that they were just going to mail it to you?"

"I had kinda hoped, yeah." He shrugged his shoulders.

"Well, Sal, it doesn't work that way."

"I'm aware of that now."

Georg put his arm around his son the hero. "We know you are a modest man, son. What you have done was extraordinary. It made a difference to so many lives. With brave acts come the gratitude of those whose lives you have touched. Allowing them to thank you is a continuance of the duties you performed in the war. You have received letters of thanks from your crew members' families. Scott Magowan and his family visited you from Philadelphia.

472

Now you must graciously accept the gratitude of your country, and your president."

"Don't worry about Mr. Truman," said Hagen, sitting down and putting an arm around Sal from the other side. "We'll get through it and then go back to our normal lives, OK?"

Sigh. "OK." Sal knew deep inside, in that place where common sense and logic grew as the boy became the man, that his life would never be the same. He would always remember the day his childhood ended; the day he sneaked off to enlist.

Georg informed the rest of the children of the president's visit when they arrived home from school. The excitement in the Beckenbauer home reached a level approaching that which engulfed them when they heard their boys were coming home. *Approaching* is the key word in that last sentence. There would never be another moment in their lives with such a positive impact upon their hearts and souls as the day Hagen and Sal came home, not even a presidential visit.

It was decided by the family, with Sal's insistence *and* a threat of running away to South America, that the news of President Truman's impending visit was to be kept hush-hush.

"Loose lips sink ships and lose me," he told them, making them all cross their hearts and hope to die.

The only person outside the family whom they trusted to let in on the secret was Uncle Samuel, and *only* Uncle Samuel. He was not permitted to tell Ethel or their children. The Ostermans would come over that day under the pretense that it was a friendly lunch visit. Aunt Mathilde was making pot roast. *Yum, yum.* While they visited in the living room, talking about this and that, Mr. Truman would knock on the door like a door-to-door salesman. *"Good afternoon, my name is Harry, Harry Truman. May I interest you in a set of encyclopedias, a Congressional Medal of Honor, or Liberty and Justice for All?"*

After the letter from the president arrived, the only thing present on everyone's mind was, well, the president. The letter didn't give a time, just the day. Two days before *the day*, the phone rang. Sal answered it.

"Hello, Beckenbauer residence," said Sal.

A woman's voice spoke, plainly, courteously but to the point.

"Good afternoon, Mr. Beckenbauer. This is Rose Conway, President Truman's secretary."

Christ, now what? Sal lost his tongue and the spit in his mouth dried up. His blood pounded in his ears.

"Hello, Mr. Beckenbauer? Are you there? I am calling from Washington, D.C. Can you hear me?"

"Yes ma'am, I can. This is Sal Cristoforo."

"Well, Captain Cristoforo, how fortuitous that I get to speak with you personally. The President and Mrs. Truman are looking forward to meeting you and your family, as am I. You're quite the American hero."

All Sal heard was "*…and Mrs. Truman.*"

Aunt Mathilde came out of the kitchen and saw the look on Sal's face. Her English wasn't the greatest yet, but she didn't need a translator to understand the shock on Sal's face. She put a hand on his shoulder and gave him a concerned look.

He ignored her. "Thank you," he mustered back to Rose Conway.

"Mr. and Mrs. Truman will be leaving Washington this Saturday morning and will be to your house at noon. They will be accompanied by his press secretary, some members of the press, and me of course."

Members of the press.

He was in auto-pilot mode now. "Thank you, ma'am, we look forward to your visit. Good-bye." He hung the phone up slowly and put it back on the desk.

In Aunt Mathilde's new, thickly German-accented English, "What is the matter? Who was that?"

"Mrs. Truman is coming, too."

"You just spoke to Mrs. Truman?"

"No," he shook his head solemnly. "That was Rose Conway, his secretary. They will *all* be here at noon on Saturday. The President, and his wife, and his press secretary, and the press, and Miss Conway."

"Good thing Georg made such a big table." She giggled. "I must get busy preparing for Saturday's lunch."

Sal could not believe she was so calm. It wasn't the Varsacis or the Hennings or the Kronenbergers or the Blohms who were coming for a visit. This was the man who sat with, ate with, drank with President Roosevelt, who ended the war, who leads our country. Sal could not wait until Sunday, when it would all be over.

November 10, 1945

The sun rose three hours after Sal opened his eyes for good, two hours after Aunt Mathilde got up to start things in the kitchen, and an hour before everyone else went down to join her. Sal didn't get up right away. He lay in bed, his heart beating like a Tahitian drum, and listened to the silence of the house, and Hagen's slow, quiet breathing. He wondered, as he looked at Hagen's shape in the bed next to him, highlighted by the moonlight from the window, *how can anyone sleep? Am I the only one in this house who can't sleep?*

The answer was yes.

Naturally, as Saturday drew nigh, the excitement level rose. Aunt Mathilde had planned lunch—enough for an army, should Mr. Truman decide to bring it with him. Mathilde and Diana cleaned the house, spotless, top to bottom, three times—and made that many peach pies, times two, from their canned orchard peaches.

Karl tidied the barn and mended anything that needed mending. *"Mr. Truman grew up on a farm; he'd notice things."* Karl had become quite the farmer, by the way. He cleaned *and* polished the tractors, even the old Fordson, rust spots n'all.

Hagen went through the orchards the day before to collect wood for the fireplace. It planned on being a chilly day and a fire would be nice. He dragged Sal with him out into the orchards, thinking the clean air and exercise would do him good. And it did. He needed to move his body—and his mind—out of the house, even if only for a few hours.

Georg sat back and watched the buzz of activity around him. The smells of a clean house and peach pies were soothing. Was he nervous about the presidential visit? Not in the least. He and his family had recently returned from an emotional trip (physically and mentally for Sal) to the deepest, shittiest part of Hell. This was going to be a piece of cake (or in this case, a slice of pie, peach, to be exact). He had his family. The farm was thriving. His two oldest boys were alive. Oh, and the president was stopping by. A slice of pie indeed!

When Hagen woke up, he stopped at the foot of Sal's bed and pulled on one of his toes through the covers. "Get up, Captain Hero. Gotta get spiffy for the photographers." He laughed at his own words. Sal threw a pillow at him in mid-guffaw and hit him right in the face. Hagen tackled him and tickled him. Sal grunted; he hated being tickled. He finally gave in to Hagen. Which was unusual as Sal, although shorter, had been a wrestler and stronger than Hagen. He lay there under Hagen's weight, his arms pinned over his head, looking up into Hagen's eyes.

He frowned. "I hate being this weak, Hagen. I hate it. I look like shit. I feel like shit. Everybody looks at me like I'm a disease."

Hagen got up off of him and sat on the edge of the bed. "Is that why you're so edgy about this, about the publicity and people coming to see you?

"What do *you* think? I'm half the man I was, literally. I used to be able to bench press you and, just now, I couldn't even push you off me. I want to go to sleep and wake up when it's all over."

"Sal, I love you, but you are an idiot."

"Excuse me?"

"Yeah, you don't look like the old you, but you will again, and you know it. This new you went way, way, *way* above and beyond what anyone would have ever expected from a normal human being. You... are extraordinary. You are... amazing. And I am so very, very proud of you."

Sal looked back up at the ceiling. A tear leaked backward into each of his ears. "I'm sorry I've been such an asshole. I guess I should apologize to everyone, huh?"

"You don't have to apologize to anyone. They know who you are, and they all understand what you are feeling. They want this for you, not for them. That's why everyone is making sure everything is going to be perfect today. Not for them, or for the president—for you."

He turned his head back to Hagen. "Thanks, Hagi."

"Sure thing, Sali. Can you do me a favor, though?"

"Sure, what?"

"Next time you're feeling this stupid will you just talk to me?" He poked Sal's ribs. "OK, Captain, my Captain?"

He didn't giggle or wriggle, just smiled up at him, "OK, Sarge my Sarge, I will. Can I lay here for just a little bit longer?"

"Sure." He gave him a peck on the cheek. "I smell coffee, I'm going down for some. I'm sure Aunt Mathilde is going to need help in the kitchen." He held his nose high and sniffed the air. "I smell bacon, too. Better not dilly-dally too long. You know how Karl likes his bacon, and everyone else's." He went downstairs to the kitchen in his pajamas, where the rest of the family had already gathered around *Tableosaurus* with coffee and breakfast.

The aromas of bacon, toast, and coffee tugged hard at Sal's nose until he couldn't lie there any longer. Once up, he showered, put on some regular clothes and pulled his military dress uniform out of the closet. He held it up and looked in the mirror. He wasn't going to fill it out today the way he did when he first put it on over three years before. There was nothing he could do about it now. Everything was in motion and it was out of his control.

Downstairs looked like any other day, when he finally joined the rest of his family. Apple and peach logs were crackling on the hearth. The Zenith in the living room was playing an upbeat tune from the Philadelphia station. Aunt Mathilde and the girls were cleaning up from breakfast. Georg was at the table—*The Philadelphia Inquirer* in hand—sitting where Sal usually sat, sipping coffee in between puffs on his pipe. Hagen was sitting next to his father, peeling potatoes. Karl had already had his fill of bacon and eggs and was outside tending to the chickens and cows.

Aunt Mathilde saw Sal first. "Good morning, Sal. Come, sit, eat."

Then the girls, almost in unison, "Good morning, Sal."

"Good morning," Sal responded. He paused and took in the normality of the scene.

Aunt Mathilde pulled out the chair at the head of the table, the seat his father usually sat in. "I hid some bacon from Karl. I will make eggs." She poured coffee into the cup in front of him.

Georg looked up from the paper. "Good morning, son. Beautiful day out today. Not too cold or windy." It was indeed a beautiful day. The sun was rising brightly in a cloudless sky.

Sal turned his head and looked out the window over the sink. "Yes, sir, it is a beautiful day."

Aunt Mathilde cracked four eggs into the cast iron skillet that still had some bacon grease in it. The kitchen air became re-baconized and the smell, mixed with the coffee under his nose and his Papa's pipe smoke, was a panacea for his soul. The smell from the toaster joined the aromatic symphony and just at that moment, all was right with the world. A few minutes later, Aunt Mathilde placed a plate with the eggs, bacon, and buttered toast in front of him.

"Thank you, Aunt Mathilde."

She placed a hand on each shoulder, leaned over and kissed him on the top of his head. "You are welcome, *Liebchen. Guten Appetit*."

The girls, who were standing at the counter, turned their heads to look at Sal, then smiled at each other and went back to helping with the lunch prep. Hagen smiled as he peeled potatoes, never looking up, not wanting Sal to get the feeling that everyone was watching him, because, well, everyone *was* watching him. When Hagen went downstairs that morning, he told everyone how Sal was feeling. It felt like a betrayal of confidence, but he also felt that they should know. So, they all decided that not making a big deal out of what was going to happen would be best for Sal. They were going to act like it was any other day. It seemed to work. Sal ate his breakfast. He had a second cup of coffee. Georg offered him the funny papers, which he gladly took. He even laughed a couple of times out loud.

Sal knew what the rest of them were doing; he was watching *them* as well. He played along. He appreciated their efforts to keep calm when, in less than—he looked over at the clock on the wall—three hours and nineteen minutes, the leader of the free world was coming for lunch. Inside he was nervous, but not panicky nervous, not anymore. His talk with Hagen upstairs earlier, and the kitchen filled with the love of his family, made it all bearable.

Sal finished his breakfast, put his dishes in the sink and turned around to face the room. He looked from Hagen to his father to his sisters, who were now dredging chicken pieces in flour, to Aunt Mathilde, who was sifting flour for biscuits. One by one they realized that it was Sal who was now watching them and they, one by one, looked back at him, stopping in mid-sip, mid-dredge, mid-sift, mid-peel.

"I don't know how you are doing it," Sal said to the room, "keeping it in, but, thank you. I'm fine, I really am. Hagen, if you keep biting your lip, you're gonna chew it right off, and Diana, Mathilde, I can just about hear your seams busting. Papa, you have been reading the same article for the last fifteen minutes. Aunt Mathilde, you are good, you are *rrreally* good. I can't tell if you're acting or if nothing ruffles your feathers. So, please, as they say in the Army, at ease."

The room filled with sighs and *Oh thank Gods.*

As Sal left the kitchen he said, "Besides, it's only the President of the United States who's coming for lunch…"

Their mouths opened, not believing what they were hearing.

From the living room, they heard him still talking, *"…to eat your fried chicken, Aunt Mathilde. I hope he likes peach pie, girls, you sure made enough of them."* He could still hear Hagen's and Papa's boisterous laughter as he grabbed his coat and went out to find Karl and help him with some of the chores.

Uncle Samuel and his family arrived thirty minutes before T-time. Samuel kept his promise, as a man of the cloth, or a best friend should, and never let on to Ethel or their children about who was coming to lunch. Ethel, thinking it was just going to be the twelve of them, made two coconut cream pies for dessert. Under his breath, Sal whispered to Hagen, *"Oh look, more pie. Good thing they don't have a peach orchard, too."*

Hagen almost choked on his own spit and elbowed Sal in the ribs. "Don't you think it's about time you got dressed instead of dilly-dallying?"

Sal looked at the clock on the mantle, and realizing he was cutting it close, ran upstairs to get dressed.

When Ethel and Muriel took the pies into the kitchen, they saw *Tableosaurus Rex*, set for twelve. At one end of the kitchen, they also saw another table, one of the wooden ones with folding legs that lived in the barn, that was pulled out once a year for the annual Beckenbauer Picnics. It was set for eight, with eight folding chairs. On the counter at the far end of the kitchen sat the six peach pies. Ethel looked around at the two tables with their settings for twenty, then she and Muriel put the pies next to the others. Before going back into the living room, she lifted the lid off the pot of mashed potatoes. Her eyes widened. It was enormous. A pot almost as large sat next to it, filled with gravy. Another pot was full of green beans. She opened one oven to see the mountain of a dozen cut-up fried chickens, and the other oven with a tray mounded with six dozen biscuits.

When Ethel walked back into the living room, Sal was coming down the staircase all decked out in his military dress uniform and all eyes, and hearts, were on him. After the applause ended, Ethel had to ask. "What is going on? How many people do you plan on feeding today?"

Georg spoke. "We are not sure how many exactly."

"You could feed half of Burlington County, by the looks of things in the kitchen."

"We didn't want to run out of food, so we made extra, just in case," said Diana.

"Who is coming? Samuel, what's going on?"

"I'm sorry, dear. I couldn't tell you because I was sworn to secrecy. Sal is being awarded the Congressional Medal of Honor today."

"That's why he is wearing his uniform," said Hagen proudly, grinning ear to ear.

"Here, at your house?" Ethel was trying to understand. "Aren't those usually awarded at the White House, by the president?"

"Yes, usually," said Samuel. "For some reason—well, not for some reason. We all know the reason. Sal did an amazing thing, saving those men, then being captured and..." He choked up. He looked at Sal, whose eyes glistened as he listened to his proud Uncle Samuel.

Samuel cleared his throat, as did some of the others. "...President Truman is going to present Sal with the medal, today, here at the house."

Ethel and the Osterman children had about thirty seconds to absorb Samuel's last sentence. Diana spotted movement out of a window, across the empty field, way out on Perkins Lane. "I think they're here."

483

Anyone sitting stood up and anyone standing stood straighter. Sal's demeanor changed. His nerves calmed. All sophomoric expressions of distaste for the pomp of the upcoming ceremony were replaced with pride for his country, for himself, for his family, and the utmost respect for his Commander in Chief. He said not one word as he walked out onto the porch, stood at the top of the steps, and looked out towards Perkins Lane as the third of three enormous limousines made its turn onto the driveway.

The others gathered around Sal and watched as history pulled up in front of the house and parked like yachts at a dock. "They drove all the way from Washington!" said Georg.

The first to exit the vehicles were the Secret Service detail from the first and third cars, affectionately nicknamed the Queens by President Roosevelt for the ocean liners Queen Elizabeth and Queen Mary. Eight men in overcoats and hats quickly got out of each Queen and took positions near the house at all corners, on the porch, and around the president's car.

The president's car, nicknamed the Sunshine Special by the man for whom it was customized after the start of the war, was the longest car anyone on that porch had ever seen in person. One of the agents opened the back door, and out stepped President Truman in a grey topcoat and hat. He helped his wife, Bess, out of the car, then his daughter, Margaret. Next was Rose Conway, then White House Press Secretary Charlie Ross, and Abbie Rowe, the White House photographer. Sal took a deep breath and backed up three steps as Mr. Truman led the small group, flanked by Secret Service agents, to the steps of the porch.

Who was supposed to speak first? No one on the porch knew that, or what to say. There was no manual attached to the Constitution or the Declaration of Independence or the

Bill of Rights instructing the average American on what to do when the President of the United States is standing at the bottom of your porch steps with the First Lady and their daughter.

Sal stepped up to the plate, stood at attention and saluted. "Good afternoon, Mr. President. I am Captain Salvatore Cristoforo. Welcome to our farm, Sir."

Mr. Truman returned the salute. "As you were, Captain Cristoforo," and marched right up the steps, Bess at his side, and extended his hand for Sal to shake. "It is so good to meet you, Captain," taking Sal's hand with both of his.

"Thank you, Mr. President. It is an honor to meet you, Sir."

"No, young man," he turned his head to look at the others who came with him. "I assure you the honor is ours." Everyone in his entourage nodded, even the Secret Service agents who were within earshot. "I would like you to meet my wife, Bess."

"Pleasure, ma'am." They shook hands.

"The pleasure is mine, Captain."

Everything stopped for a moment, frozen in time as everyone on the porch watched the hero of the house talking to the President of the United States and the First Lady.

Hagen felt a pregnant pause forming. "Captain Cristoforo, why don't we go inside where it is warm, and we can continue with the introductions?"

"Of course, of course, I'm sorry, Mr. President." Captain Cristoforo turned and opened the door. The Trumans, the secretaries, and the photographer walked in, led by two Secret Service agents, followed by the Beckenbauers, the Ostermans, then Sal.

Once inside, Aunt Mathilde took everyone's coats and hats and hung them on the hall tree. Everyone was introduced. There was a lot of handshaking—lots and lots of handshaking—and flashbulb flashes.

In the living room, the Trumans settled next to each other on one of the couches. They seemed like neighbors paying a friendly visit. They commented on the Beckenbauer's lovely home, the beautiful farm, and the wonderful smells coming from the kitchen, and seemed quite pleased to know that lunch would follow the presentation of the medal. Sal told them that the ladies of the house had been cooking for days. Diana and Mathilde blushed. Aunt Mathilde beamed.

Hagen felt very comfortable around the Trumans. They were everyday people in extremely un-everyday positions. He sensed that they needed this getaway from Washington. He noticed there were no press, no police escort, no throngs of public massing on the lawn. It was revealed later in conversation over Aunt Mathilde's fried chicken that when Rose Conway spoke to Sal on the phone two days before, she heard his panic. She and her boss discussed the option of a low-key ceremony; no press, just a photographer. A story would be given later to the Washington Post to publish along with photographs of the president and the war hero.

The presentation took place at twelve-thirty in front of the mantle with the fire glowing on the hearth below. Mrs. Truman and Margaret stood behind the president. Georg and Hagen stood behind the hero. The president spoke of Sal's bravery under extreme conditions, the lives he saved, and the sacrifice he had made that resulted in his becoming a prisoner of the Empire of Japan. He spoke of men like Captain Cristoforo, who did what they had to do, not for the accolades, but for the good of the country, for Liberty, for Democracy.

Sal bowed as the president put the necklet and medal around his neck. They held their pose in mid-handshake, the families clapped, and the photographer snapped away.

After the ceremony, they adjourned to the kitchen for lunch. The Osterman children, and Mathilde, Diana, and Karl sat at the folding table. Everyone else sat at *Tableosaurus Rex*. The president allowed for a group picture of everyone at the table but didn't think it necessary for the rest of America to see him eating fried chicken with his fingers. He insisted that Mr. Rowe join them and sit in the remaining chair at the big table because the president knew that greasy fingers and a Graflex Speed Graphic camera do not go together.

Aunt Mathilde's fried chicken was a hit, as were the mashed potatoes, gravy, biscuits, and beans. The first Mrs. Truman, the president's mother, had made her son's favorite fried chicken. Mathilde's came close, but the president didn't say that. As far as Aunt Mathilde knew, it was the best he'd had yet. He had a second helping to prove it. Yes, politics crept into kitchens as well. The second Mrs. Truman was thoroughly impressed and asked if she could have the recipe for herself. She had no intention of insulting Vietta, the cook at the White House, by showing her any recipe. Vietta never used a recipe, and her fried chicken, gravy and biscuits were indeed delicious. As far as Bess Truman was concerned, Aunt Mathilde's came in second behind the first Mrs. Truman's. She knew that one day, she and her husband would be returning to Independence, Missouri, and she would be cooking again, gladly, for her Harry.

The table was cleared. Everyone was stuffed. Dessert would have to wait. Mr. Truman, having grown up on his family's farm, had the notion to take a walk and let lunch settle. He wanted to see the Beckenbauers' farm, get some air and rejuvenate.

So, out they went; all of them: the Trumans, the Beckenbauers, the Ostermans, both secretaries, and the photographer, for a stroll around the property. They talked as they walked, about farm stuff, trading farm stories. Mr. Truman was genuinely interested in how the Beckenbauers came to be farmers in New Jersey. Georg still had, would always have, a German accent, and it was purely simple and sincere interest in the history of one American family that compelled the president to enquire. Georg told of how he and his wife had moved to New Jersey after the first war, the subsequent children, the orphanage, the Ostermans, Marta's death and the orphanage again. Their stroll led them into the peach orchard and to the little family cemetery. Mr. Truman and his wife said a silent prayer over their graves. Even Rose Conway, usually stoic and by-the-book, dropped a few tears as she listened to the story of Marta.

They returned to the house refreshed physically from the walk and the brisk air, and emotionally touched and inspired by what Georg had told them. Coffee and pie (peach *and* Ethel's coconut cream) were served, much to the delight of all the guests.

When it was time for them to leave, the Trumans admitted that they would have loved to have stayed longer. It was a delightful day away from the hustle and bustle of Washington, and they thanked the Beckenbauers for the delicious getaway. They rode home to Washington with their hearts and stomachs full, and a whole peach pie.

On Monday, the Washington Post printed Sal's story and several photos (a copy was sent special delivery from Charlie Ross, along with prints of photographs taken that day, and the pie plate with a handwritten thank you note from the First Lady), and a resurgence of interest in Sal by the local press ensued. Sal handled it with grace and humility, and within a couple of weeks, everything was back to *almost* normal at the farm.

Sal and Hagen took their equivalency tests and earned their high school diplomas. The following year, Hagen used his scholarship and attended MIT as an undergraduate, earning degrees in both mechanical and electrical engineering, graduating top in his class.

Sal never lost the shutterbug itch. A new school, the Hussian School of Art, opened in Philadelphia that year. Using the GI bill, he attended the four-year program, earning his Bachelor of Fine Arts degree. His photographic talents were admired by many prominent people in the art community. Upon graduating, several positions were offered to him by prospective employers in various parts of the country. He took his time as he contemplated each offer. There was one factor—a very important factor—that played a large role in his decision making.

Hagen.

They had been apart for four years. They both wanted to be near each other full-time, not just on summer breaks and holidays. Hagen wanted to pursue his master's degree. Sal didn't care where he did it. He would find work wherever Hagen decided to continue his education.

Then one day, The Universe put in its two cents.

Hagen was offered a position, right out of MIT, with GE Transportation. His achievements in school, and affinity for trains, gained him recognition by their research team. They were aware of his desire to continue his education and were very supportive.

One of the offers made to Sal came from the New Mexico Bureau of Land Management. They needed a photographer to take pictures to catalogue the state's various natural resources.

It just so happened that the University of New Mexico had a wonderful engineering department. It also just so happened that General Electric had a research and development office in Socorro, about an hour south of Albuquerque.

Ever since that day at the train station in Albuquerque, Hagen knew he would be returning to New Mexico. It called to him in his dreams, but he never forced the Universe's hand, instead, he let everything unfold as it should. It was all now unfolding.

In the Spring of 1951, Sal and Hagen moved to Albuquerque. They rented a little adobe house near Old Town. Hagen worked diligently at his career and studies. He proved himself to be a great asset to the company and rose higher in the ranks in the research and development department.

Sal dived lens first into his position with the Bureau of Land Management. His travels across the state enabled him to see the wonders and beauty of New Mexico. Occasionally, Hagen would join him if time permitted. Whether it was a wide-open mesa, or desert, or mountain, or lake, New Mexico sang to their souls. Hagen would bring his easel and paint the grand scenery. In addition to shooting the photos required by his employer, Sal always had his old Rolleiflex with him, and shot photos for his own personal pleasure. Together, Sal and Hagen created a collection of stunning photographic and painted works, and by 1954, they had begun to be recognized by the art community.

One of the men from *Thor's Hammer* who Sal never lost touch with was Shilah Begaye. After Sal returned home from Manila, he received a letter from Shilah. The Newcomb, New Mexico return address and postal stamp excited both Sal and Hagen. Shilah thanked him again for saving his life, twice, and hoped that the friendship they made would

490

continue, now that the war was over. He hoped Sal was doing well and extended an open invitation to come to New Mexico and visit anytime. "*My teepee is your teepee.*"

Sal and Shilah maintained a pen-pal relationship until the move to New Mexico. After the move, Shilah and Sal's relationship turned into an *I-would-take-a-bullet-for-you-* best-friendship. Shilah and Hagen got along famously. Hagen wasn't the jealous type and was happy that Sal had a good friend, especially one who could relate to what Sal had been through during the war.

One thing that had always bothered Sal was the plight of the Native Americans, and it became a cause he fought for most of his life after moving to New Mexico. Many Native Americans fought, and died, for their country. Many of them returned to their homes only to be forgotten, falling back into the cracks of bureaucracy, suffering from poor educational standards, poor medical care, and poverty. On his journeys around the state, Sal saw first-hand much of the suffering of the Native Americans and documented it with his photography. After several years working for a government agency that seemed to not care about the indigenous peoples, he began to suffer from a moral dilemma. After discussing it with Hagen, Sal resigned from his position with the Bureau of Land Management, putting his efforts and energy into rallying for the Native American cause. Hagen's position with GE paid well, so Sal was free to fight for what he believed in.

In 1961, Hagen created and patented design improvements to the diesel-electric locomotive— *revolutionary* design improvements. By replacing DC generators with alternators that utilized silicon diodes, the reliability, safety, and productivity of the locomotives were greatly increased, and Hagen and Sal's bank account balance increased as well. This was the beginning of their financial freedom. Hagen had purchased stock in GE earlier in his career, and in the years since, his stock increased in shares and value many, many times over.

In time, other patented inventions continued to increase his net worth, and by 1968, he and Sal no longer needed to work for anyone except themselves. Sal's photography and Hagen's paintings were selling in fine galleries in Santa Fe, Taos, Albuquerque, and Sedona, and with the income from Hagen's patents, they were able to create a non-profit organization—The Cristoforo Native American College Fund. Sal and Hagen believed that the way to improve one's position was to have a quality education.

Back in New Jersey, the farm was thriving, as were the rest of the Beckenbauers. All three siblings were eventually married and had their own children. Karl married a girl from Burlington, Dottie Jackson. They had two children, Karl Jr. and Debbie. They were the next generation of Beckenbauer farmers. Diana married Kenny Storer. After the war, he was hired by RCA Victor in Camden and remained there until he retired in 1991. They had four children—Kenny Jr., Kathy, John, and Jim. Mathilde married Scotty Magowan, who became a lawyer like his father, and had two children, both girls, who they named Marta and Jennifer.

"Life shrinks or expands
in proportion to one's courage."

—Anaïs Nin

December 21, 1979

Sal and Hagen were enjoying a fruitful life together in New Mexico. They moved to Santa Fe in 1970 and purchased a lovely adobe house in the foothills of Atalaya Mountain. They soon became well-liked and admired members of the Santa Fe art community.

Hagen and Sal hadn't splurged yet on their own railcar, but the train was still their preferred means of transportation for traveling across the country. Sal did not despise flying like Hagen, but he knew there was no way of ever getting Hagen on a plane unless it was in a museum, and Sal enjoyed the comfort of riding on a train; seeing the country from the windows, and meeting people.

They were on a train going home to New Jersey for Christmas. They'd left on the 20th and were enjoying the ride, as usual. The train pulled into Kansas City Station at nine in the morning on the 21st. They had an hour to kill, so Hagen talked Sal into getting off the train for a bit, to stretch their legs and breath some fresh air. Out they went into the cold December Kansas City air. The station was decorated for Christmas. Wreaths hung from light poles outside, and lights and ornaments on a very tall tree in the lobby glowed a multi-colored welcome to travelers while Christmas music played in between train announcements from hidden speakers.

They went out the main exit, onto the sidewalk. Up and down the street, lamp posts were decked with lights and garland in the shapes of bells and wreaths. Most of the stores were also decorated for the holidays. There was a bookstore, a highly-decorated candy store featuring homemade fudge and holiday treats, a tobacco shop, and a little café. A bakery sign caught Sal's eye. He was in the mood for something baked and sweet. A quaint little antique shop across the street caught Hagen's attention. He walked over to browse the antiques while leaving Sal to pick out some baked goodies for the ride.

The bakery sat on the corner of West 22nd and Central at the end of a row of businesses. Sal stood in front of it and looked up at the three-storey fieldstone structure. The two upper floors appeared to be a residential dwelling—most likely the baker's home. Curtains hung in the windows, and here and there an air conditioner poked through a wall. The bakery on the bottom floor was simple on the outside. There were two large windows with neatly handwritten signs in them advertising bagels, danishes, breads, rolls, cakes, and cookies. A sign hanging from a chain in the window of the door had been turned to OPEN long after the bakers rubbed the sleep from their eyes and had gone downstairs to start their day. Above the door a sign read "MORAWSKI," and at the bottom of the left set of windows was a menorah with seven lit bulbs.

Sal grabbed a railing and climbed the three steps up to the door—taking note of the mezuzah—and went inside. When he walked in, his senses were pleasantly met by the smells of baked goods, both sweet and savory, and the display of those gastronomic delights in glass cases along the right and far walls. To the left was a rectangular wooden table with eight chairs for those customers (the regular ones, no doubt) who wanted to nibble, sip coffee and schmooze with the bakers. This was a very warm and inviting atmosphere, and Sal thought Hagen should have been with him. *Hagen loves these kinds of places.*

495

Behind the high counter, at the far end, was a swinging door that led into the kitchen. On the walls on either side of the door, there were tilted shelves with wicker baskets loaded with various rolls (croissants, kaiser, challah) and loaves of bread (seeded, plain, round, and long). Behind the counter in the left corner was a coffee maker with a full pot of fresh coffee and a pot of water at the ready for the next batch. Nothing fancy, just coffee, and the undernote of the coffee smell mingling with the other aromas, like the bay leaf in a pot of chicken soup, turned a business into a home away from home. The jingle of the bell on the inside of the door announced Sal's presence. A few seconds later, the door to the kitchen swung open and a young woman in her twenties, twenty-five-six-seven-ish, walked through. She was wearing a sleeveless top underneath a white apron, and her hair was held neatly back by a blue and white tie-died kerchief.

She spoke with a thick, Polish accent. "Good morning, sir. How may I help you?"

"Good morning ma'am. I—I really don't know yet, it all looks so good."

"Thank you, thank you. Take your time." A male voice came from the kitchen through the crack around the door.

"Krystyna, kto to jest? Czy to jest Jakub? Powiedz mu, że potrzebuję więcej jajek, dwanaście tuzinów."

She poked her head into the back, *"Nie, Piotrze, mamy klienta."*

"OK, powiedz mu, czego potrzebujemy, gdy przyjdzie. Muszę skończyć to ciasto dla Plotniks."

"OK." She turned back around. "My apologies—my husband," and pointed to the door behind her.

"That's OK. I'm ready when you are." As Sal pointed, she plucked the goodies from the case. By the time he finished picking and choosing, there were two of almost everything in a big box. She tied the box closed with a string. Then Sal chose a few croissants (some with chocolate inside) a variety of mini challah rolls with various seed toppings, and a variety of bagels. If Hagen had been there, he would have governed the amount that Sal was ordering, but he wasn't there and, as always, Sal was like a kid in a candy store.

When all was packed and ready to go, the lady walked to the other counter, with Sal's box of sweets and bag of breadstuffs, where the cash register sat on the counter against the wall. As she walked from the back counter around to the side counter holding Sal's purchase, she passed the break at the corner of the room. That's when Sal could see that the young woman was with child—*very* with child. She put the box and bag on the counter and tallied up everything on the register. She told him the total and he handed her cash.

As she was counting the money he asked, "Do you have a restroom?" His two cups of coffee earlier that morning before the train stopped had just kicked in.

"Yes sir." She pointed to a little hallway on the other side of the room that led back to a public restroom. "Down there, at end of hallway."

"Thank you, ma'am. I'll be back for the change." He left her to count his money and went to use the bathroom. Down the little hallway, on the wall, were some photos. He recognized the young woman behind the counter; she was a bit younger in the pictures, but it was her. In one photo she stood next to a man—*the disembodied voice from the kitchen probably.* Both were smiling, arms around each other, standing in front of the bakery at the top of the steps. A sign on an easel (GRAND OPENING!) stood on the sidewalk next to the steps.

Other older photos hung nearby. In one there were four people: the young lady and the man, and an older man and

497

woman. They were standing in front of a house somewhere in a rural area. The license plate on the car that was parked in the driveway told Sal that they were not in America. A dog, a little schnauzer, was in the arms of the older woman. In another photo, six people—the four in the last photo plus another older couple—sat at a table, with big smiles. A few had turned to look at the camera, holding up glasses of champagne. As a photographer, he appreciated all manners of photography. These photos told a brief segment of the lives of a happy family who had lived in another country and had come to America to start a new life; not unlike the Cristoforos and the Beckenbauers had done so many years before.

Two minutes after he locked the bathroom door, he heard a loud voice, a male voice, coming from the bakery. The voice sounded agitated and had no Polish accent.

Not the husband.

Sal couldn't hear it all clearly, but what he did hear alarmed him. The profanity interspersed between the muffled words was louder, more distinct. Ever so slowly, quietly, he unlocked the door and opened it just enough to better hear what was going on. The male voice sounded young, nervous. He was instructing the young woman to empty the cash register.

"Put the money in a bag and don't do nothin' stupid."

Sal heard the husband's voice telling the robber to *"please not to shoot. I give to you the money. Please not to hurt wife, she is pregnant."*

He has a gun. SHITSHITSHIT.

"Just do as you're told, and no one gets hurt, OK mister?"

Sal opened the door enough to slip out of the bathroom, slowly, praying the hinges wouldn't squeak. He couldn't remember if they squeaked when he had opened it the first time.

No squeak.

Thank Christ.

Stepping only on the balls of his feet, he crept to the end of the wall of photos and peeked around into the room. With his back to Sal was a white male wearing jeans, very worn tennis shoes, a dark blue sweat jacket, and a black knitted hat. He held his right arm out in front of himself, towards the couple behind the counter with his left hand tightly clenched into a fist at his side. Sal couldn't see the weapon, but the stance of this man was all he needed to know that he wasn't poking his finger at them from inside a pocket, pretending to have a gun. The gun was real and visible to the baker and his wife.

Sal revealed a little more of himself. He didn't take his eyes off the frightened couple. He made eye contact with the woman. He slowly shook his head and put a finger to his lips; a silent *shhh*. Her husband's back was to him and the robber, as he put all the cash into a bag, like the one Sal's rolls were in. She spoke to her husband without taking her eyes off of the man with the gun.

"*Piotr, po odwrócić nie patrzeć na klienta za człowiek z pistoletu. Go zignorować, OK?*"

Piotr understood exactly what she meant. In his mind, he saw a faceless man creeping up behind the agitated asshole with the gun pointed at his pregnant wife.

He nodded, as he fumbled with the money with shaking hands, that he understood his wife, and said to himself, *'Och, B-g nam pomaga!'*

"What did you just say?" shouted the robber.

"I tell my husband to make hurry with the money."

"Oh, OK, good."

When the baker turned, he purposely stared right into the assailant's eyes and held out the bag of cash. "Here is money. Take and go, please."

The thief stepped forward; that is when Sal made his move. He figured that if the man with the gun was perfectly still, then his sense of awareness would be heightened. He waited for the thief's mind to be distracted by his victim's voice and the bag of money dangling in front of him like a carrot.

Hoping the ruse would work, Sal shouted, "Freeze! Police!"

In a blurry half-second, the startled gunman spun on his heels and squeezed off two rounds. The baker and his wife dropped to the floor behind the counter as Sal lunged forward in an attempt to tackle the man. One of the bullets whizzed past Sal's left ear, hitting the wall by the table. The other one went into his chest, grazing his left collarbone and coming to a halt right behind his left shoulder blade, stopping Sal in his tracks. The robber, shocked by his own gunfire, ran for the door. Sal was hit, but not down for the count—not yet. He grabbed one of the chairs from the table with his right hand and hurled it at the robber as he mad dashed for the door. It made contact with his legs, tripping him, and at full speed he fell face first onto the floor. He dropped the gun and slid headfirst into the wall underneath the window, knocking himself out cold.

Sal wobbled over to the gun and kicked it back towards the far counter, then fell to his knees and sat down next to the gunman, leaning against the wall under the menorah. The baker stood up from behind the counter. Sal looked up at him. "Your wife is OK?"

The baker looked down at his shocked, frozen wife. "Yes sir, she is not hurt."

"You... you are alright?"

"Yes, sir."

Sal smiled, and half closed his eyes. "Good, good. I think you might want to call the police now." He sighed, then passed out as he was thinking about how mad Hagen was going to be.

The baker picked up the phone and dialed 911. He told the operator in his excited, Polish-accented English to *send police, send ambulance*. His wife, still sitting on the floor, leaning against the back of the display case, winced, then began to scream as she held her abdomen. Her husband looked down at his wife as amniotic fluid spread out from under her.

"Oh, G-d, no. Please, please to send two ambulance. My wife is having baby."

While the events inside the bakery were unfolding, Hagen was finishing making a purchase. He'd found, in remarkably pristine condition, an old cast iron toy model of a Fordson Tractor, much like the one his father had purchased in 1922. He thought his father and Karl might get a kick out of it. He left the antique store and scanned the sidewalks on both sides of the street for Sal. He had expected Sal to be standing out in front of the bakery with two armfuls of baked goodies with a huge grin on his face.

God help us. He's buying everything again.

He waited for a break in traffic to cross over to the other side. As he stepped off the curb the two gunshots rang out from inside the bakery. At first, he didn't know exactly where they had come from, just that they emanated from somewhere on the other side of the street. He fast-walked towards the bakery as he scanned the windows. He heard the thud of the gunman's head slamming into the wall as the windows rattled in their frames. As he reached the other side, he saw Sal wobbling in front of the window, looking down, then collapse and disappear. Hagen sprinted up the steps and threw open the door. He took in the scene: the gunpowder smell overpowering the resident aromas, a man on the phone behind the counter, an unseen woman screaming, another man lying face down on the floor, and Sal unconscious against the wall.

He ran to Sal. "Sal, Sal. What happened?" He saw the hole in Sal's jacket and the blood on the floor. "OhGodOhGodOhGod." Hagen pulled open Sal's coat and saw his blood, a lot of blood, seeping into the fabric of his shirt. He held Sal's face in both hands, held it straight. "Sal… SAL! Goddammit, SAL!"

No response.

He jammed his fingers into Sal's neck, feeling for a pulse.

Bum, bum… Bum, bum… Bum, bum.

"Oh, thank Christ." He turned around to look for the man who was on the phone when he walked in. He was not in sight, but he could hear him talking loudly in Polish to the screaming woman. She was in pain. *Was she shot, too?*

He shouted, "Hey, you behind the counter!"

Nothing.

He didn't want to get up and leave Sal, but he needed to assess what was happening. He quickly went over to the counter and behind the display case. The husband was kneeling on the floor holding his wife. Hagen saw she was pregnant and in labor.

"Hello," he shouted. The man looked up, tears in his eyes. He was praying in Hebrew. "Is your wife injured?"

"No, but baby is coming."

"Did you call 911?"

"Yes, police and ambulance come now."

"Good, good." Hagen looked over at Sal. He had fallen over onto his side. "Noooo, God help me!" He ran back to Sal, knelt beside him and put him back into a sitting position.

Hagen then sat next to him on the floor between him and the gunman and waited.

Sirens in the distance got louder. Three minutes after the baker got off the phone, three police cars and two ambulances stopped in front of the bakery, blocking traffic in both directions. The gunman began to stir and moan and started to lift his head. In his blind fury, Hagen balled his hand into a fist and backhanded the man on the base of his skull, slamming his head onto the tile floor. "Stay down, asshole."

The baker came from around the counter as the police cars screeched to a stop outside. He smiled when he saw Hagen knock the gunman out again.

"*Dziękuję.*" He kicked the unconscious man in the ribs. "*Kurwa dupek.*" He opened the door; the police pulled their weapons and aimed at the baker.

"Freeze, put your hands in the air."

He did as they told him, then spoke. "There is man inside, hurt very bad. My wife is having baby. Man with gun is inside on floor."

The police quickly deduced from the man's panicky voice, tears in his eyes and his baker's apron that he was not the bad guy. Once they were inside and deemed it safe, they allowed the paramedics inside to attend to Sal and the baker's wife.

The woman was quickly assessed, put on a gurney and wheeled out to a waiting ambulance, with her husband following right behind her. The siren blared, the lights flashed, and off they went to Truman Medical Center.

Sal's condition was not as straightforward as the baker's wife. He was losing a lot of blood; his pulse was weak, and his blood pressure was dropping. The paramedics started an IV, stabilized him for transport, then lifted him onto the gurney and rolled him out to the other ambulance. As the ambulance pulled away, with its sirens howling and lights flashing, the train sounded its horn and left Kansas City without them.

Sal arrived at the same emergency room ten minutes after the baker's wife. By the time Sal was lifted from the gurney to the ER table, the mother-to-be was on her way upstairs to Labor and Delivery. Sal was prepped for emergency surgery. A mobile X-ray machine took a picture so the surgeons, who were scrubbing up in OR-5, knew where to find the slug.

Although by 1979 it was not uncommon for expectant fathers to accompany their laboring wives into the delivery room, the baker did not. He was not a man with a strong stomach when it came to such things; the blood, the sight of his wife being stretched open by something far too large to be emerging from, well… from down there… would have proven to have been too much for him to handle. He and his wife agreed from the beginning that he'd wait in the waiting room, like their own fathers had done, and pace the floor until it was over.

The nervous baker had just called his parents and had taken a seat in the waiting room. He didn't feel the need to pace. His mind raced enough on its own with thoughts of what had happened less than an hour ago. It was a relief to know his wife and baby were going to be alright. His thoughts wandered to the stranger who had saved them. That is what he believed. That the stranger saved them. Some would later say that if Sal had just kept quiet, had maybe remained hidden in the bathroom until the gunman left with his bag of money, then no one would have gotten hurt. And they may have been right about that. Hindsight is 20/20. Those people didn't know Sal.

The baker would never believe that. He saw the crazed look in the eyes of the robber, who was mentally unstable. It would be discovered later that he was a junkie looking for money to pay for his next fix. So, as far as the baker was concerned, Sal took a bullet for him, his wife, and their baby.

He was deep in thought when Hagen walked in, carrying his coat, stained with Sal's blood. He had just called his family in New Jersey. The baker stood up when he saw him.

"Sir, how is your friend?" He could see Hagen had been crying.

"I do not know. He is in surgery now. The bullet hit an artery; he lost a lot of blood." Hagen felt faint; he needed to sit down. He went to the closest chair and sat. The baker sat down beside him.

Hagen hung his head and stared down at the intersecting lines in the tiled floor. *I almost lost him once. Dear God, wasn't that enough?* The crying began again. Tears plopped onto the floor. The baker put his arm around the crying stranger.

"Sir, have faith. It was good thing he did. G-d will protect him."

Hagen raised his head and looked at the man's face; a kind, gentle face of a good man. "Thank you, sir."

The baker stood and extended his hand. "My name Morawski, Piotr Morawski. No more *sir.* You call me Piotr, yes?"

Hagen stood and took the man's hand. "Yes, Piotr. My name is Beckenbauer, Hagen Beckenbauer. You call me Hagen."

They sat back down. "Hagen, your friend, what is his name?"

"His name is Salvatore. We call him Sal."

"Salvatore. Is a good name. Means, 'Savior.'" He smiled; his eyes twinkled.

Oh, don't I know it.

"He is a good man—always thinking of others." Hagen plucked a tissue from a box on a little table nearby and wiped his eyes. He observed that there were quite a few tissue boxes around the room. *A room for crying.* "And your wife, what is her name?"

"My wife," he smiled when he said *my wife,* "her name, it is Krystyna."

"Krystyna, pretty name. She is a beautiful young lady."

"Yes, beautiful, very beautiful. I am lucky man."

So am I.

"Yes, Piotr, you are."

The conversation paused. Their minds returned to their loved ones with intermittent distractions from the "Laverne and Shirley" sitcom rerun playing on the television mounted on the wall. "Family Feud" followed "Laverne and Shirley", and Hagen restarted the chat.

"Piotr, you are from Poland, am I right?"

"Yes, yes, from Poland. Five years ago we come to United States."

"May I ask, why Kansas City?"

"My parents, they have friends in Kansas City, so, we move to Kansas City. You and Salvatore, you are from Kansas City?"

"No, we are from Santa Fe, New Mexico. We were on a train, going to visit family in New Jersey for Christmas. We got off the train to get some air and look around. While Sal was in your bakery I was across the street in the antique shop."

Piotr understood most of that. "Your baggage, your clothes…"

"On their way to New Jersey without us." He had to laugh at that. "I could use some coffee. Would you like some coffee, Piotr?"

"I would, thank you."

506

Hagen went over to the vending machine on the far side of the room and slipped a dollar bill in. "Piotr, how do you take your coffee?"

"Black, please."

He pressed the "black" button and watched the cup drop and fill, then put in another dollar. While he was waiting for the second cup to drop and fill, the waiting room door opened as a very anxious and upset older couple burst into the room and ran to Piotr with open arms.

"Mama, Papa."

Mama spoke first, *"Piotr, Piotr, co się stało? Co z Krystyna? Jak dziecko? Tyle krwi w piekarni!"*

("Piotr, Piotr, what happened? How is Krystyna? How is the baby? So much blood in the bakery!")

"Krystyna i dziecko są w porządku."

("Krystyna and the baby are fine.")

Both parents, in Polish, thanked G-d.

"Człowiek próbował okraść piekarnię, klient interweniował i został ranny."

("A man tried to rob the bakery and a customer intervened and was hurt.")

Hagen stood by the coffee machine with a cup of coffee in each hand watching them talk. Piotr turned to him and pointed. *"To jest Hagen. To jego przyjaciel, który został zastrzelony i jest w chirurgii teraz."*

("This is Hagen. It is his friend who was shot and is in surgery now.")

Hagen recognized his name and nodded to the couple. "Hello."

"Hagen, these are my parents, Ryfka and Zelik Morawski."

Zelik nodded back to Hagen. Ryfka stood motionless, wide-eyed, and whispered, *"Błękitny Anioł."*

Zelik looked at his wife, then back to Hagen, then back to his wife. *"Błękitny Anioł?"*

"Tak, Błękitny Anioł."

Piotr had heard stories about his mother's *Błękitny Anioł. "Mamo, co mówisz? Czy on jest Błękitny Anioł?"*

Hagen saw the look on Ryfka's face. He felt an enormous mood change in all three of them. "Piotr, is everything alright?"

"Hagen, Mama says you are her Blue Angel."

Confused, "her—her what?"

"Blue Angel." As Piotr spoke, his mother slowly walked towards Hagen, her arms outstretched. "In the war, you were in Germany?"

"Yes, I was." As Ryfka got closer, he recalled a memory. *It could not be. It cannot be.*

Ryfka was now standing right in front of Hagen. She looked up into his blue eyes. Such blue eyes—she never forgot those blue eyes, like the sky, like Heaven. She held his face gently in her two hands. *"Hallo, mein Freund. Es ist gut, Sie wieder zu sehen."*

("Hello, my friend. It is good to see you again.")

It hit him all at once. It was her—the woman from Dachau. His whole body, his entire being tingled, and everything in the room opaqued as if he was looking through gauze. Piotr and Zelik realized what was happening and quickly went to them. Each took one of the cups from Hagen's hands before he lost his grip on them.

Looking down into the eyes of the woman who had the same expression on her face which he had seen thirty-four years ago, he knew it was her. He could *feel* it was her. He put his arms around her, pulled her close, not feeling every bone like when he first held her. She was healthy, a little plump. He kissed her on the top of her head, and she laughed through tears. Hagen saw the two men, father and son, standing there watching the miracle reunion.

It was Zelik's turn. He stood next to his wife and told Hagen how they thought often about the man, the Blue Angel. How they had told the story to friends and family about the day Ryfka was pulled from a deathbed by an American soldier and carried to him.

Hagen asked her why she called him her Blue Angel. She asked her son to tell him. She didn't like to talk about herself.

"Hagen, my mama is modest woman. She keep to herself what she can do, what she can see."

Hagen looked back down into Ryfka's eyes. She was not looking at his face now, but over his head—around his face, not at it.

"You see, Hagen, my mama, she sees your light."

"My light?"

"Yes, your light. Mama say is very blue, deep blue. In Dachau, you prayed for Mama. She thought you were angel coming to take her and sister to Heaven. Your light, very bright, very big. Is far around you. I know well this. Mama, she tell story to all family, all friend. I cannot see your light, Hagen, but can feel it. I felt when saw you in bakery, looking down at us. You are Earth Angel."

Ryfka understood enough of what Piotr had said. She continued in German as Zelik translated for his son. "Hagen, I did not recognize your face, not right away. I can see it is you now. It was your light I saw from across the room. That is how I knew who you were. I believe G-d does things for a reason. He brought us together again. The circumstances are not the best; I am sorry about your friend."

"I remember your eyes," said Hagen, "how you looked up at me, like now."

"It was you, dear, who helped restore my faith in humanity. I have seen others like you, walking amongst us, and it is good to know that G-d has put men and women, like you, on the Earth to help us. But your blue is so pure, the purest royal blue. You have a way with people, do you not? You calm people with just your presence, am I right?"

He did not know how to answer her. It is not like he interviewed everyone he met and asked, *"So tell me, how do you feel now that you have met me?"* He did know that he had always felt the pull, the need, to help someone in emotional distress.

"I can see you are searching for something to say. No words are necessary. Angels do not boast." She pulled his face to hers and kissed each cheek. "Now, come, sit. We will catch each other up on our lives."

They sat in a row of chairs. Ryfka patted him on the leg. "You first."

Hagen told them the basics—college after returning home after the war, his career, his family in New Jersey. He wasn't ready to explain exactly who Sal *really* was to him, just that he and his sister had become family during the Depression, and they grew up as siblings. He did, of course, brag about Sal's Medal of Honor and his heroism on his B-17. When the Morawskis heard that, they all nodded. "*Salvatore, Zbawiciel*," said Piotr to his parents.

Ryfka translated in German for Hagen, "My son said, 'Salvatore, Savior.' It is quite apparent that Sal is a natural protector."

"I sometimes call him 'The Underdog's Hero,' a bully's bully—always sticking up for the neglected and abused."

"I am sorry Salvatore's good deed in bakery cause him harm," said Piotr.

"Do not be sorry. He is unstoppable when he sees an injustice" Hagen paused as memories flew in through the

510

windows of his mind. "Enough about us." Then, in German, to the elder Morawskis, "Tell me about you, about what you did after the war."

Ryfka began to tell him about the struggles of rebuilding their lives after Dachau. The difficulties in making their way home to their village of Olszyny, almost nine hundred kilometers to the east. They found their home intact, but their belongings all gone. They had lived above their bakery like they do now. It took over a year and a half to begin a somewhat normal life. The village would never be the same; whole families were gone. In some instances, only one member of a family would return, a parent or a child, who would wish they had never survived the war. You know the saying "It takes a village to raise a child?" It took the village of Olszyny, what was left of it, to raise each other, to come together and become a family. As Ryfka continued, the door opened. A doctor, wearing scrubs, came into the waiting room asking for the family of Salvatore Cristoforo.

Hagen's heart paused in his chest. The Morawskis held their breath.

Hagen stood up and tried to read the doctor's face. Nothing to read. Like the day Colonel Jameson sat him down to tell him about Sal's rescue. "I am Salvatore Cristoforo's family." Ryfka held one hand, Zelik grabbed the other and squeezed.

The scrubbed man walked over to the waiting Hagen. "Hello, I'm Dr. Fenlin, I'm one of the surgeons who just operated on Salvatore. He's going to be fine."

Hagen clapped his hands together and looked up. "Oh, God, thank you."

"We had to repair damage to his subclavian artery but there was no other major damage. We removed the bullet and he's in recovery now."

"When can I see him, doctor?"

"We are going to keep him in recovery for about an hour. You may see him briefly, in a few minutes. He'll be transported to ICU and you'll be able to spend more time with him there."

"Thank you, thank you so much." They shook hands.

"I heard what Salvatore did," said Dr. Fenlin. "He's a brave man. A nurse will come and take you to recovery after we have him settled in."

The doctor left the room. Piotr had been translating in Polish for his parents (as best he could), what was being said between Hagen and the doctor. They were relieved to know that Salvatore was going to survive. Hagen turned to look at the smiling Morawskis. He sat back down with them, and they waited together for the nurse.

A few minutes later, the obstetrician came into the waiting room to announce the arrival of the new Morawski. Krystyna was doing fine, as was their baby.

"Is boy or girl?" Piotr's face was aglow with anticipation. He did not care one way or the other. He and Krystyna had been double thinking, not knowing if they were having a boy or a girl, and he just needed to be able to start thinking in blue or in pink instead of lavender.

"Congratulations, Mr. Morawski, you have a beautiful, healthy baby girl—seven pounds, eight and a half ounces.

"Oh, thank you, thank you, thank you," as he grabbed the doctor's hands with both of his and shook him like he was trying to shake fruit from a tree.

Speaking through jiggled laughter, "You are very welcome, Mr. Morawski." Piotr let the doctor's hand go. "Your wife and your daughter are being taken to their room. Someone will come to get you in a bit and take you to them."

"Thank you very, very much."

"It was my pleasure, sir. Best of luck to you and your family." He nodded to the others in the room and took his leave.

Piotr grabbed hold of his parents. They were jubilant, talking a mile a minute in Polish, while Hagen absorbed much of their goodness. He needed a recharge, and the Morawskis were a perfect source as they celebrated their new addition. Piotr turned to Hagen and looked up into his eyes. "You. And Sal." Tears. A smile. He put his arms around his Mama's angel and held him tightly. *Błękitny Anioł* saved his mother, and in turn she made a son, who now has a daughter. "Because of you I have Mama. Because of Salvatore I have wife and baby. Thank you."

Hagen found no words and resigned himself to silently accepting the man's gratitude graciously. He understood now why Sal didn't want, or need, recognition, preferring to be his fellow humans' silent partner in life.

They all sat back down in their seats and waited for their escorts. Hagen's entered the waiting room about fifteen minutes later. He hugged the Morawskis before being led to the recovery area. There, in a bed, hooked up to IVs and monitors, lay Sal. He was still heavily sedated, and his left shoulder was wrapped up like a mummy. At the side of the bed, Hagen looked down at the hero, watching his chest rise and fall, the jugular pulse in his neck. He held Sal's left hand in his, while caressing the top of his head. A flicker of a smile, just a minute twitch, caught Hagen's attention. "You son of a bitch. You're laughing at all this, aren't you? When are you going to stop being the goddammed hero?" He stayed only ten-or-so minutes, kissed him on the cheek, then went back to the waiting room.

He wasn't sitting with the Morawskis for more than three minutes when a nurse came in to show them the way to Krystyna's room.

Ryfka grabbed Hagen's hand as she followed her husband and son. "Come, dear, you are family. I want you to meet my daughter-in-law and new granddaughter."

How could he refuse? He and Sal now had five new additions to their galaxy of loved ones.

"I would love to meet them," replied Hagen. Arm in arm, he and Ryfka followed the proud men and the nurse. In the elevator, Piotr's excitement was palpable. Hagen and Ryfka rejoiced quietly, occasionally looking into each other's eyes in silent conversation.

They entered Krystyna's room and found her beaming with love for her new child sleeping peacefully in her arms. She couldn't wait for her husband to meet their new daughter, and giggled when he walked in.

She spoke in Polish. "Piotr, come, meet our daughter." She was glowing with joy as she lifted the pink blanket so he could see his daughter's face for the very first time. He leaned in and kissed his daughter on the head, then his wife, tenderly on the lips.

Ryfka, Zelik, and Hagen were standing at a respectful distance near the door when Krystyna noticed them there. "Piotr, who is that man standing next to Mama?"

He waved his parents and Hagen over to the bedside. He went back to speaking English for Hagen's sake. "Krystyna, this is Hagen. His friend was brave man in bakery."

Hagen nodded. "Mazel Tov."

"Thank you. Where is friend? I want to thank him." She looked around the room to see if Sal was behind them somewhere. She did not know Sal was shot. Her world had closed in on her when her water broke, and the pain started. Not wanting to upset her, no one had told her yet about Sal.

Hagen pursed his lips and looked at Piotr, whose look said, *shall I tell her, or shall you?*

Ryfka stepped in and said, in Polish, "Krystyna, Salvatore, Hagen's friend, was shot."

"Oh, G-d, no. Is he… is he…?"

"No, dear, he is going to be alright. He was in surgery while you were in labor."

"I am sorry. Such nice man, brave man," said Krystyna to Hagen in English.

"Thank you, Krystyna. Yes, he is a brave man." *Brave and stupid.*

"Krystyna, I would like to—" said Piotr in English.

"Name baby after Hagen's friend," Krystyna finished his sentence for him.

"Yes, yes. If you agree."

"That is a nice gesture," interrupted Hagen, "but not necessary. Krystyna, I do not want you to say yes because I am in the room. And you will not hurt anyone's feelings if you say no."

Ryfka was looking confused so Hagen repeated to her in German what he had just said to Krystyna. Then she looked at her son and his wife, and in Polish, "It is up to you. I know that you had your heart set on a different name."

"I know," said Piotr, still in Polish. "Krystyna, it is up to you."

"No, Piotr, it is up to us. And I agree, he saved us, and our baby. But a girl named Salvatore?"

The Morawskis laughed at the thought of a girl named Salvatore?

Hagen caught the gist of the subject. "Like I said, not necessary," in English and German.

Krystyna had an *ah-ha moment* come over her face, and in Polish, "Sally. Sally? Sally, we will call her Sally."

Eyebrows raised as they thought about it. "I like it," said Piotr. "Mama, what do you think?"

"I like it, too." Then to Hagen, in German. "Krystyna suggested, 'Sally.' What do you think?"

"It is a pretty name. Sali is what his parents used to call Sal when he was a little boy."

Ryfka translated into Polish what Hagen had said. Piotr, in Polish, responded, "We will call her Sally, but we will ask Salvatore for his permission before we make it official."

Krystyna and Sally needed to rest. They'd both had an exciting morning. The others were drained in all ways that they could be drained. Hagen was overwhelmed by so many emotions coming from so many people. But his mind was only on one thing.

Sal.

He said his goodbye first, then stepped out of the room so the family could have a little privacy.

In the hallway, nurses and doctors passed by, entering and leaving rooms. A new-born wrapped tightly in a chrysalis of blue, with just his pink scrunched-up little face visible, rolled by in a bassinet, pushed by a nurse and into the room next to Krystyna's. Another nurse approached, and Hagen asked her for directions to the ICU.

"Go to the elevators at the end of this hall," she pointed in that direction. "Go to the fourth floor and you can't miss it."

"Thank you, nurse." He smiled cordially, covering up his anxiety about Sal as best he could.

"My pleasure." She returned the smile and continued on her way down the hall.

A few minutes later the Morawskis came out, smiling and talking. Ryfka saw that Hagen's light was reaching for something, pointing in one direction, like a compass needle pointing north—in the direction of the ICU. "Hagen, you need to see Salvatore. Come, we will go together. We all need to see our hero." She put her arm through his as he led

516

them to the elevators. On the fourth floor, they followed the signs to the ICU.

Inside they were met by a nurse who informed them that patients in the ICU were only allowed to have one brief visitor at a time. Hagen introduced himself, then asked her if she knew why Salvatore was in the hospital.

"Yes, I do. Mr. Cristoforo was admitted with a gunshot wound and only just arrived from surgical recovery."

"That is all correct, but, Nurse…" He looked at her nametag. "Nurse Alonzo, do you know the circumstances surrounding the shooting incident?"

"I'm sorry, but I do not."

"Miss Alonzo." He shifted into bragging gear. "The man in that bed," he pointed to Sal's glass-walled room, "is a Congressional Medal of Honor recipient. He saved the entire crew of his B-17 in World War II. He suffered and survived almost three years in captivity as a POW of the Japanese. Today, he took a bullet as he intervened in a robbery attempt." He put his hand on Piotr's shoulder. "This is Piotr Morawski. His wife Krystyna gave birth to their daughter while Sal was in surgery. It was their lives he saved." He waved his hands to Piotr's parents. "These two people are Piotr's parents. I met them thirty-four years ago in a Nazi concentration camp and only reconnected with them today, *today,* because Sal cannot stop trying to save people. I do not know if you see the cosmic implications in today's serendipitous crossing of paths, but I do. And so do they. They need to see him as much as I do, and together. I promise we will be brief, and I promise we will return. Sal has cheated death in far worse circumstances without any loved ones nearby. That is not going to happen again. He needs us as much as we need him."

"Mr. Beckenbauer…"

"Hagen, please."

"Hagen, you had me at Congressional Medal of Honor. Please, go see him. Pull the curtains so no one sees all of you in there with him. And please, be as quiet as possible. I don't need another write-up because I broke the stupid rules again."

As they walked into Sal's little room, Ryfka whispered, "I understood only a few of your words to that nurse, but you sure do have a way with them."

"If you present your case in a logical, respectful and thoughtful way, most people will see your point clearly."

Hagen quietly closed the sliding glass door and pulled the curtains around them. Sal was breathing slowly and steadily. His IV dripped as the monitor displayed a strong and steady heartbeat.

Ryfka went to the other side of the bed, opposite Hagen, and held Sal's hand. "Hagen, Salvatore is your soulmate, isn't he?"

He looked up from Sal into the all-knowing eyes of a woman who was, in her ways, as sensitive as him. "Is it that obvious?"

"To me it is. Salvatore's light is multi-colored, but with a very large amount of pink. He is a true defender. When we walked in, his light was reaching for yours, as yours was for his. In fact, I could have followed yours right to him. It led the way."

Hagen always knew there was the attraction between Sal and him. *Soulmates* was the best way to describe their relationship, as it transcended the physical. Ryfka's description put it in a whole new light. No pun intended.

"How long have you known each other?"

"We met fifty years ago."

"Your souls knew each other long before that. You are lucky to have found each other again. The world is a big place."

518

Sal was beginning to wake up. He gave no sign that he was, keeping his eyes closed, listening to Hagen and an unknown female voice conversing in German. It did not matter what language Hagen spoke. His voice was like a cool compress on a feverish forehead. He set his eyes to look in the direction of Hagen's voice, to his right, before he slowly opened them. The first thing he saw was Hagen, just as a tear fell from his chin onto Sal's hand. Ryfka's words moved Hagen in a way he'd not been moved before. Sal followed Hagen's gaze to Ryfka and listened to their conversation. He did not understand German. A few words here and there that Hagen tried to teach him—I love you, kiss me, I'm hungry, goodnight. That was about it. But the way the words were being spoken told Sal that Hagen and this woman had a connection, and it was becoming stronger by the moment. Another tear fell on Sal's hand.

Always the jokester, always looking for some humor in the dark, "Is that your idea of a sponge bath?"

Hagen tightened his grip on Sal's hand and wiped his eyes with the other hand. "Hey, you."

"Hey, you." Their eyes locked. Ryfka watched in wonderment as the two souls spoke without uttering one word.

"If you wanted to stay longer in Kansas City you should have said so."

"You could have found a nicer hotel. These double-digit thread count sheets are chafing my delicate skin."

Hagen laughed and cried. "Such a smart-ass. Yeah, you'll be fine." He saw the Morawskis watching, looking confused as they listened to them laugh. Hagen translated into German for Zelik and Ryfka, who then told Piotr. The laughter made its way from Germany to Poland as Sal looked from Hagen to the three Morawskis.

"Hagen. Are you going to introduce me to the United Nations?"

"Oh, yes, sorry. This is Piotr Morawski, from the bakery."

"Oh, yes the man behind the counter with the…" He stopped and remembered the nice lady, the nice, very pregnant lady. "Where is his wife? Is she OK? The baby?"

"They are both fine. While you were being shot, she went into labor."

"You never miss a chance, do you?"

"Nope. Piotr and his wife have a new baby girl. Because of you they are all fine."

"Not because of me. And no medals please. I'm done with medals. Can we just go home now?"

"I wish it were that simple. You are probably going to be enjoying these lovely accommodations, and the exfoliating sheets, for a while."

"Damn. I'm sorry to put you through this again, Hagi. I really am."

"It's not your fault, my little hero. It's who you are. But I have to thank you as well."

"Thank me. For what?"

Zelik was now standing next to Ryfka. "This is Ryfka and Zelik Morawski. They are Piotr's parents." They nodded to Sal. He nodded back. Zelik was smiling. Ryfka was grinning from ear to ear. "Do you remember the story I told you about when I was there for the liberation of Dachau?"

"Uh-huh, of course, I do." Then he stopped. He saw the look on Hagen's face. That look that said, *you are SO not going to believe this.* Sal turned his head on his pillow and looked up into Ryfka's eyes. She squeezed his hand in hers. When he looked down at her hand, he saw the tattoo on her left forearm and the last three numbers, *463.* "You have got to be fu…"

"Ah, ah aaah. Language, mister."

"...kidding me."

"If it weren't for your stupidity, she and I may never have met again. So, thank you for getting shot today."

"My pleasure. If you think of anyone else from your past who you need help getting in touch with, let me know."

"Jeez. You should do stand-up, you know?"

"Thank you, ladies and gentlemen. I'm here all week. Hey, I know what I want for Christmas."

"What's that?"

"A Kevlar jacket."

"Ba dum-dum-tss"

The door slid open, and Nurse Alonzo entered from behind the curtains. "Ah, you're awake. I thought you might be by now. How are you feeling?"

"Like a million bucks. You should see the other guy."

"Ah, a comedian. Humor is good." She checked his IV, then his monitor. "Are you in any pain?"

"No, not really."

"You might be when the morphine wears off." She handed him a cord with a button on the end. "If you start to feel the beginnings of pain, press this button once. It's governed to prevent overdosing, so pressing it ten times won't make a difference. Once pressed, you have to wait fifteen minutes for another dose. Got it?"

"Got it."

"Now, you folks really should let him rest. He is only spending the night here for observation and will go upstairs to a regular room tomorrow. You'll have all the time you want with him then."

Sal pressed the button at the end of the cord. The *ding* sound got their attention. A fresh dose of pain medicine entered Sal's veins and his eyes fluttered.

The nurse pointed to her patient. "My point."

Hagen shrugged in agreement and looked down into Sal's fuzzy eyes. "They're kicking us out now." Sal didn't say anything, just smiled drunkenly. "Let's go," he said to Ryfka. "We will come back tomorrow."

Ryfka gave Sal a kiss on the forehead, and they quietly left the ICU. Knowing that Sal would be fine gave Hagen the opportunity to think. Since all of his and Sal's clothes were going to Philadelphia without them, he was going to need something to wear besides the bloodstained clothes he was wearing. He also needed a hotel and a vehicle.

Ryfka wouldn't hear any of it. "Hagen, we have plenty of room. We live above the bakery and it is much larger than it looks from the outside. Please, stay with us."

Piotr and Zelik wholeheartedly agreed. They wouldn't think of him staying in a hotel all alone, especially at this time in their lives.

"Hagen, my Angel, it will give us time to know each other even better."

Hagen accepted the Morawski's offer to stay with them while Sal was in the hospital. But he still needed clothes. Once at the Morawskis, he cleaned up. His shirt had to be thrown away, and his coat was saturated with Sal's blood. It was December. It was cold outside. He'd have to go shopping without a coat, without a shirt.

Piotr wasn't Hagen's size, but he did have a sweater his mother had knitted for him. It was oversized; it might fit. He tried it on. It did fit. Hagen would chance the cold weather, coatless.

While he was trying on Piotr's sweater, Ryfka came down the stairs holding something long, in a bag, on a hanger. She was carrying it in her arms like Hagen had held her in his arms thirty-four years before. She handed it to him.

Hagen took it from her and held it up by the hanger. Ryfka unzipped the bag. "My coat. You still have it?"

"Of course. It belonged to you, my Angel. Keeping it safe was like taking care of you. I would take it out of the closet to look at it, to touch it. It kept my body warm with your heat when you gave it to me. It kept my soul warm all these years just touching it. It belonged to you. It still belongs to you. Put it on."

He took the coat out of the bag and off the hanger, then handed it to her and turned around. She held it up and he slipped his arms into the sleeves and turned to face her. "It still fits you. I had wanted to find you sooner, to return it to you somehow, to thank you. There was no identification inside, so I left it to fate. And, here you are."

"And here we are. I still cannot believe it."

She nodded her head in the direction of the kitchen, where Zelik and Piotr were talking over a cup of tea. She held his face in her hands. "Neither can we." She kissed each cheek. "OK, Zelik is going to drive you to the mall while I make dinner. Piotr is going back to visit Krystyna and the baby for a little while. We will eat when everyone returns."

Off to the mall Zelik and Hagen went. To the other shoppers and store clerks, they looked like two middle-aged men, one in an antique military long coat—*is that the style now? A new fashion trend?* They were just friends perusing the men's section. Hagen's coat was the only thing about his appearance that might have given away a tiny bit of his history; his rank, army intelligence in the European theatre.

When we go out into the world, amongst our fellow humans, we see only the at-that-moment exterior. We don't hear the thoughts of the woman behind the checkout counter. We see her smile, hear her cordial words, when inside her head a whole other storyline is playing out. Her child may have just gone off to college and she misses him. Or, her husband may have just been deployed and she's worried sick. Or, what will she be making for dinner tonight after a double shift selling shoes to rich women with bad feet?

To see Hagen and Zelik walking through Macy's men's department, chatting in German, smiling, checking tags for sizes, no one would have guessed what was going through their minds. Their outward demeanor would never have given away their very distant past and very recent histories; that one of those men had, hidden under his coat sleeve, numbers tattooed on his left arm; a reminder of a time when some men were at their evil worst and others were at their compassionate best.

And that the man in the antique military long-coat was some woman's *Błękitny Anioł*.

And that *that* woman was married to the man with the tattoo.

And that they would have a son who is right at that moment holding his new daughter.

How about this? The man with a tattooed souvenir of one of the most horrific times in humanity's existence was helping a man (a man who had given him and his wife a coat when they had no coat) look for a new coat because the one he was wearing that morning was now saturated with the blood of his friend—a man who saved three people: the tattooed man's son, his son's wife, and their new-born daughter.

When Hagen and Zelik returned to the house above the bakery, Piotr had already returned from the hospital. He was helping his mother set the table. It was Chanukah, and that night the eighth candle was to be lit. It brought back memories for Hagen of St. Paul church and the vestibule at the bottom of the balcony steps, where the rows and rows of red candles sat under the statue of an open-armed Jesus; a Jewish man sacrificed for humanity.

That night above the bakery, prayers were said. Many thanks were given up to G-d for so many things. Then they stuffed themselves with brisket, noodle kugel, and potato latkes. They stayed up late with hot tea and sweets from the bakery and talked deep into the night. Their friendship, forged by compassion in the darkest of times, was now an unbreakable steel bond.

In the morning, Hagen called the hospital for an update. Sal was fine, there had been no issues during the night, and he was to be moved to a private room on the eighth floor that morning, around nine. Then he called his family in New Jersey again with the latest news. He could feel the relief in their voices from twelve hundred miles away. Christmas would be postponed until he and Sal made it home. Karl was going to go to the station in Philadelphia and retrieve their belongings. Amtrak had been notified of the situation and an attendant had already gathered their possessions together and kept them safe.

Hagen and the Morawskis left early for the hospital. Piotr couldn't wait to see his wife and baby, nor Hagen to see Sal. More for Sal's sake than his own. Sal was a tough man. He could take a beating and keep on going, but what kept him going was knowing Hagen would always be there for him. Hagen let the Morawskis off on the second floor, then went to the fourth floor to see if Sal had been moved yet. The elevator door opened and waiting on the other side was Sal, in his rolling bed, surrounded by four nurses and two dangling IV bottles. He was wide awake. The nurses were laughing. *Always making someone happy, aren't you?* Sal saw Hagen standing there in the elevator with a look that said what he was feeling.

"Hey there, elevator man."

"Hey there, mister. Going my way?"

The nurses rolled the bed into the elevator as Hagen and Sal continued their banter.

"Yep, if you're going to Jersey, I sure am."

"Sorry, sir, this isn't the Wonkavator."

"Damn."

"Sorry, Charlie."

The nurses laughed at the little show the men were putting on for them. The elevator door opened on the eighth floor and they rolled the bed out and down the corridor to Sal's private room. Hagen stood by the window while the nurses plugged in Sal's machines and bed. In the distance, Hagen could see the train station. When all the gadgets were beeping and flashing and dripping properly, the nurses left. Sal and Hagen were alone now, finally.

"I assume you called the family."

"I did, several times."

"How mad are they?"

"Not mad. Worried. Happy you're alive. A little upset when I told them not to come. It wasn't easy to convince them to stay home. You know how obstinate Diana can be."

"I do. I sense a couple of punches in my good arm when we get home."

"I wouldn't be surprised." Hagen chuckled and smiled. "How do you feel?"

"Eh, it hurts. The morphine helps—keeps me from talking like a sailor."

"Keep that button handy. You're probably going to have lady visitors again today."

"You would think my chest would hurt the most. Most of the pain is in my back, under my shoulder blade. I saw the surgeon after you left yesterday. He said the bullet punched a dent on the inside of my scapula. Oh, here…" he reached under the sheet and pulled out a plastic container and shook it. Something rattled inside. "…an early Christmas present."

Hagen took the container and looked at the contents through the opaque plastic, then unscrewed the cap and looked inside. Rattling around was the deformed slug that the surgeon had removed from Sal's chest. "Gee thanks. Is this what I think it is?"

"Yep. 38 calibre. Sorry I couldn't afford a bigger one. Fixed income, you understand."

"It's the thought that counts. I love it."

Hagen was about to lean over and steal a kiss when there was a knock at the door. The door cracked open and Ryfka peeked her head in, smiling. Hagen waved her in. She opened the door and there were all the Morawskis; Ryfka, Zelik, and Piotr pushing Krystyna in a wheelchair holding Sally.

Hagen turned. "Here they are. How are the mother and baby?"

Piotr wheeled Krystyna to the side of Sal's bed. "We are fine, thanks to you, Salvatore."

Zelik and Ryfka joined Hagen on the other side of the bed. Hagen put a hand gently on Sal's bandaged left shoulder. "Sal, this is Krystyna, and their new baby girl."

"I remember you from yesterday in the bakery. I hadn't met your baby yet. She's beautiful."

"Thank you. Thank you for what you did. How we can ever repay you?"

"How about half a dozen danishes and a gallon of milk?"

Piotr started to leave, and Sal put up his right hand. "Stop, I was kidding. I don't need repayment. I would have done nothing differently."

Hagen interjected, "Believe him when he says that. If there is an injustice within fifty miles Sal is there to stand up to it."

Krystyna lifted her sleeping baby. "Salvatore, you want to hold baby?"

He looked up at Hagen, then at each Morawski, one by one. Piotr picked her up and gently laid her on Sal's chest. He cradled her in his good right arm.

"Oh, my. This makes getting shot worth it." He leaned down and sniffed the new baby smell, kissed her on the top of her little pink hat. "What's her name?" They all smiled; even Ryfka and Zelik understood the question.

Hagen cleared his throat. "Piotr, you tell him. It was your idea in the first place." Sal scrunched his face in confusion and looked at each of their grinning faces.

"Salvatore," Piotr began. "We are naming daughter 'Sally,' with permission and blessing, of course."

Sal's eyes widened. His heart monitor beeped a little faster. His mind was a little numb from the morphine, but he still put two and two together rather quickly. It wasn't hard to distil 'Sally' from Salvatore or Sal. He looked up at Hagen, who nodded, eyebrows raised, lips a long thin smile.

"How's that for a medal of honor, Captain Sal?" asked Hagen.

Piotr continued. "Krystyna and I thought would last longer than danish and milk."

Sal looked back down at the sleeping child. "And so much better for the heart."

Ryfka was watching the interplay of lights. Sal's light was surrounding Sally, like a translucent protective shield, while Hagen's deep blue had extended outward, and was engulfing everyone in the room. She held her husband's hand and squeezed tightly. Zelik squeezed back and looked at his wife. She was aglow with peace. He knew she was witnessing something no one else in the room could see. He gave her hand a quick double squeeze to get her attention, and she looked at his face. "It is wonderful, Zelik. I wish I could take a photograph and show you."

"The look on your beautiful face is all I need." Then he kissed her gently on the cheek.

Sal started to feel a tinge of pain returning. He kissed his namesake on one of her little pink cheeks, then looked up at Hagen. He half-lifted her up.

"Here, Uncle Hagen, it's your turn to hold Junior."

"Junior?" Hagen smiled, knowing where this was going. He leaned over and took her, cradling her in his left arm.

"Yes, Sally Junior." He smiled and winced a little, with the pain rumbling like thunder in the distance. He could feel his own pulse, like someone tapping on the inside of his left shoulder blade with a lead finger. He refrained from pressing the *Zen Button,* not wanting to make his guests feel like they needed to leave because their host needed rest. That little baby was better than all the morphine in the bag that hung from the *Zen Dispenser.*

Hagen caressed Sally's cheek, admiring her newness. "Well, I think that's adorable. What do you think, Junior?"

Zelik asked Hagen in German, "What is this '*Junior*' you say?"

"Sal called her Junior, Sal Junior."

"Ah, I see. Junior."

Ryfka laughed, translating in Polish to Krystyna and Piotr. They all laughed and agreed it was an endearing nickname. From then on Sal would call her Junior. She was Sally Cristina Morawski to everyone else, but always Sal's little Junior, which eventually became shortened to SJ.

So, now you know.

Three days later, on Christmas Day, Sal was released from the hospital. Krystyna and Sally had been released the day before and were settled nicely at home above the bakery. Hagen had procured train tickets for the Sal and himself for the following day, and the two of them spent their last night in Kansas City in the company of their new friends.

The next morning, Sal and Hagen said their farewells to the Morawskis. Piotr and Krystyna stayed home with Junior. Ryfka and Zelik walked with them to the train station. Hagen carried the two new suitcases containing new clothes. Zelik carried a box of sweets, Ryfka a bag of breads, rolls, and bagels. As they waited for the train to arrive, they talked about the future. Nothing would separate them again.

The train pulled in and the tears began. Ryfka knew she would see her Blue Angel again, but she wanted more of his company. She wanted to make up for thirty-four years of lost time. Hagen promised that they would see each other often; she might even get tired of seeing his face.

"Never, never, never will I tire of your face." She hugged him; then said to Sal, "Or yours. You two are family." One more round of hugs and tears, then Hagen handed their suitcases to a train attendant and took the baked goods from the Morawskis. Sal climbed aboard the train, then Hagen, and they made their way to their cabin.

Zelik and Ryfka sat on a bench and waited for the train to leave. She never wanted to be the one who left first. Only when the train disappeared from sight did she kiss Zelik on the cheek. "Alright, my dear husband. We may go now."

Hagen's Railcar
Approaching Harrisburg

Hagen stopped there. Emily was amazed into silence. A zillion feelings, words that could not be formed, unlabeled emotions whirlpooled around in her mind. Her expression said it all.

"Are you alright, Emily? I know that was a lot to take in. Believe me, it was a lot to get out."

"I can't believe what I just heard. I mean, I believe you. It is all just so... incredible. I do have questions."

"I'm sure you do. Ask away."

"Before we get to the Blue Angel subject, there's one thing that's been on my mind—your dog."

He smiled reminiscently. "Heidi."

"Yes, Heidi. You haven't mentioned her since..."

"Since 1942, when Sal and I went off to war."

"Right. Whatever happened to her? I mean, I know dogs don't live as long as humans. Was she there when you and Sal got home?"

"No. I wished she had lived until we returned. We grew up with her. She grew up with us. She was as much a member of our family as any of us." He smiled as he was remembering Heidi and the last time he'd seen her.

"When did she pass away?"

"I had received a letter from home. I'll never forget where I was, either. It was April 12, 1944. I was in London at the Intelligence Office. Since I moved around a lot, my mail was sent there. When I opened it, it seemed like the usual letter, replete with *we miss yous* and *we love yous* and news of the family, the farm, neighbors, friends. It finished with news of Heidi. Two days before Papa wrote the letter, we lost her."

She leaned her elbows on her crossed legs, chin in her palms. "What happened?"

"They woke up one morning. It seemed like any other day. They let Heidi out to roam the farm like she usually did. She didn't return for breakfast. She always came back to eat breakfast with us. After they ate, my father and Karl walked around the farm looking for her, calling her name. They checked the barns, the fields, the orchards." He stopped for a moment. Hagen always got emotional when he thought of this story. He cleared his throat. "They walked into the peach orchard and eventually came upon the cemetery. When they got close enough, they could see Heidi. She was lying on the ground. It looked like she was sleeping. They called to her. She didn't move. She did what most dogs do when it is their time; she went off somewhere alone to die. She lay down on my mother's grave, curled up against her headstone, and went to sleep forever. It was her time. She was fourteen, a good age for a German Shepherd."

Emily sniffled, wiped the tears away with her sleeve. "She loved your mother."

"Oh, my, did she ever. I told you how heartbroken Heidi was after my mother died. She loved all of us, but Mama… Mama was her best friend. Papa and Karl buried Heidi deep in the ground at Mama's feet."

"I *knew* you were going to tell me that." She grabbed a tissue from the box on the table and dabbed at her eyes again. She sat up straight and took a quick deep breath. "OK, now, this double encounter with you and the Morawskis. That blows my mind. And, Blue Angel? I mean, you're not an

angel, are you? You're not going to suddenly sprout wings."
She fake-smiled Cheshirely "Are you?"

"No, my dear, I am not an angel."

"I mean, if you were, that would be OK. I just want to
be ready for whatever you're going to spring on me." She
spread her arms out like wings. "Just in case."

He shook his head. "You are something else."

"Thanks. You say the sweetest things." She glanced at
her watch. "How long until Philadelphia?"

He looked at his watch. "Three hours, or so. Then
another hour-ish to the farm."

She curled back up under the blanket. "Are you
nervous?"

"Nervous?" His face went pensive. "*Thoughtful* aptly
describes my feelings. If I had taken this trip alone, or with
my regular, ahem…" He sarcastically smiled. "…*help*…"

Emily rolled her eyes, shook her head.

"…I would have reminisced to myself, pieces and parts.
Instead, I brought it all up and out… and all the emotions
with it."

"And mine along with them. But that's OK. I'm in for
the long haul. I am emotionally invested and there's no
turning back now."

"I am so happy to know that." He turned his head in the
direction of the bedroom. He was thinking, and Emily felt
the shift in mood.

"What's up? Are you OK?"

He turned back to her. "Hmm? Oh, yes, I'm fine. Just
thinking, always thinking." He paused a moment, putting a
hand to his chin in thought. "There is something else I would
like to go over with you."

"Oh? Do tell." Her interest was piqued.

"I was going to wait until after Philadelphia, on the last leg to the farm. But we seem to have a little extra time and I think we should do it first."

"Do what?"

"Emily, why don't you take the breakfast cart back to the dining car, and it will give me time to get ready."

"OK, you're killing me. I know you *must* have a reason for teasing me this way."

"I have a reason. Trust me."

She sighed a big sigh of resignation. "OK. You win, again."

"I usu…"

"I know. *You usually do.*" She stood, hands on her hips. "How much time do you need to get ready? Should I sit at the bar and toss back a few?"

"It's only ten-thirty, dear. It's kind of you to sacrifice your liver on my account." Another sarcastic smile. "I will be ready when you return."

She squeezed his shoulder before opening the sliding door. An endearing squeeze. A touch that said *I care.* She had almost closed the door behind her when she opened it again and poked her head out. "Hey—oops, sorry, *hay* is for horses."

He dropped his head and smiled at the floor, giggling. "Yes, Miss Manners?"

"Would you like anything from the dining room? Something for lunch later?"

"I don't think so. My stomach is still coated with hollandaise. If we hungry later, we can raid the fridge, if that is alright with you."

"That's fine with me. See you in a bit."

Looking over his shoulder, "I will be right here waiting for you."

Once the sliding door closed, he counted to thirty, then went into his bedroom.

When Emily returned twenty minutes later, she found Hagen right where she had left him, almost. He was on the patio, only now he was sitting, arms folded, on a big, rectangular box that was covered by a beautiful crocheted blanket. It was on the floor next to the coffee table.

"Where did that come from?"

He was a little nervous and covered it with a little humor. "I pressed a button and it popped up from the floor."

"Ha-ha. Seriously."

"It was at the foot of my bed. Hiding in plain sight."

"I never noticed it. You dragged it out here by yourself?"

"I did, yes."

"With that hip? You could have hurt yourself. Why didn't you wait for me to come back?"

"The effect would have been different. I wanted to surprise you. Besides, it isn't that heavy."

"Well, I'm surprised. Happy?"

"Eh, it's the wrong kind of surprised, but I will take it." He stood up. "Emily, have a seat, please," he said, waving his hand to the coffee table. He was now quite serious.

"Why so solemn? Should I be concerned?"

"No, I want you to sit and face the box."

"OK." She sat on the coffee table, hands in her lap. "Now what?"

He pulled the blanket off the box and she understood the reason for his solemnity. In front of her on the floor was the Cristoforos' steamer trunk.

"Oh, my. Is this…?"

"Yes, it is. Open it."

Her reaction was very much like that of Marta and Georg on that day, sixty-eight years before, when they sat in

535

front of it. Her face said *really?* He smiled and nodded. She put both hands on it and closed her eyes. Visions she had made up in her mind when Hagen told the story of the trunk, its contents, and the Cristoforos, played in her mind; an old silent movie. She leaned in and smelled it; its scent sweet, old, like an antique saxophone case filled with clean linen and dried roses. Hagen sat on the love seat and watched her intently. She opened her eyes and turned the key. Slowly, gently, she opened the trunk.

It was still half full. There were items inside that weren't there when Marta and Georg first looked inside. The first thing she saw made her hold her breath. One hand went to her mouth, the other gently felt the old leather of Sal's bomber jacket. It lay there flat, arms folded inward as if in a casket, lying in state. Her eyes welled and met Hagen's.

His eyes went to the trunk. "You should have seen him, wearing that jacket. Heads turned when he walked into a room."

Emily lifted it, just a bit, hesitated, then asked, "I'm sorry, may I?"

"Of course, please." He watched her lift it, like a baby from a cradle, hold it close and smell the leather and the fleece lining.

Under the jacket was the Navajo healing blanket that Hagen had been given at the train station in Albuquerque. He had taken it off his bed and put it back in the trunk. On top of the blanket lay the dreamcatcher. Emily laid the jacket on her lap and picked up the dreamcatcher, hoping it would vibrate for her, like for Sal.

"You must have bad dreams for it to work," he said.

"Reading my mind again?"

"Just your face."

She picked up the blanket, held it up, then put it over her lap. "It's beautiful. Isn't this the one I saw on your bed?"

"Yes, we kept it in the trunk for safekeeping, but I took it out after Sal... after Sal became ill."

She held her left hand out to him and he squeezed it. She smiled, although her heart ached for him, empathy for the empath.

"You are so sweet, Emily. I really am so glad we met."

"You too, and me too." She looked down at the next treasure, then reached in with two hands and picked up an old camera case. She opened it. Inside was Sal's old Rolleiflex. "This is it? The one you gave him? The one he left on the island?"

He nodded. "Yes, that's the one."

"It's in really good shape."

"Sal took such great care of his cameras. That one especially. It was his first. He had other cameras, but this was his baby. He shot that photo of the moon rising over the mountain with that camera."

"I love it. It still works, I assume."

"Of course. I'll get some film for it in a few days and you can play with it if you want."

"Really? Are you sure? I'd love to."

"Absolutely. The best way to keep something in good condition is to use it."

She placed the camera gently in its case on the coffee table and looked in the trunk. There were three items remaining: Giuseppe's hat box, the small box with Sal's bronzed baby shoes, and the photo album.

She picked up the album and opened it. "These photos are amazing. And in really good shape for their age."

"That is not the original album. And you may have noticed that a few items were not in the trunk. Diana has the wedding dress, the Bible, the silver candlesticks, the original photo album, and her baby shoes. She wore her mother's dress when she married Kenny."

"That is so sweet."

"Naturally, Sal and Diana both wanted the photo album. We had it professionally duplicated, right down to the scalloped edges on the photographs. Even the *Homeric*'s postcard and tickets were reproduced. That album is an exact replica of the original. Side by side you would not be able to tell the difference."

"Sounds like an expensive project."

"It wasn't cheap, but it was well worth it."

As she turned the pages, she observed the same progression in the timeline of the Cristoforos' lives, as Marta and Georg had all those years before. She examined each photo like an artist in a gallery. The faces, the places, the period apparel—all had an impact on her. After turning all the pages, she pulled out the hat, put it on (a little big for her, going over her ears), then put it back in its box inside the trunk. Then she examined the bronzed baby shoes, feeling the creases and the laces frozen in bronzed time.

"So small, so detailed. I always wondered how they did that." She put them back into their aging cardboard box and back into the trunk. "Is that everything?"

"There should be one other item in there. Maybe under the hat box."

She looked again into the trunk and slid the hatbox to the left, revealing a manila folder that was held closed by a string. She retrieved it and held it in both hands. "What's this?"

"Open it and see."

She untied the string and peeked inside. "More photos?"

"Yes, and these are originals, and old. They are not decrepit, just old. But, be careful anyway. I trust you."

She slid the stack of eight-by-ten black-and-white photos from the envelope. When Emily realized what she was holding—

"Are these…?"

"Yes, the ones from Sal's camera." He nodded to the Rolleiflex. "These are from the roll of film that was in it when they found it on the island. I think you will be impressed. I sure was, as was the Smithsonian."

"The Smithsonian?" She looked back down, reverently, like she was holding the Dead Sea Scrolls. The first photo was a group shot of Sal's crew in front of *Thor's Hammer*, with her painted nose art depicting a huge hammer being swung by a very muscled arm, smashing a Japanese rising sun flag. They were gathered near her nose, in their bomber jackets, all smiles, best buddies. Her hand reached under the blanket to feel Sal's jacket. She spotted him right away in the photo. He was the only one who looked Italian, and he was standing next to the shortest guy in the bunch. *Shilah.* There were a few more of the crew, some with *Hammer*, a few of them at the beach, another in their quarters. Sal had also managed to get some of the most poignant shots on a B-17 during the war. Some were candid; some were not. He shot each crewman, with their cannons at their posts or killing time with a deck of cards on a long run. A photo of Shilah crammed into the ball turret smiling up at the camera through the tiny hatch. One of the cockpit, the pilots turned towards Sal, grinning, with thumbs up. Another looking up into the top turret as the flight engineer stared down between his arms as he gripped his twin fifties; photos of men, frozen in time, on dangerous bomb runs, smiling for the camera, not knowing if it was going to be the last image of them alive. He took photos of his squadron in flight over the expanse of ocean below, contrails streaming behind them like long white cat-scratches against the sky.

A picture speaks a thousand words, so they say, and if that is true, then the last five each spoke a thousand and one. They left Emily speechless. They were the ones that Sal shot

539

on Rennell Island. The first one, very dark, was of the outline of the Japanese submarine, glinting in the full moonlight just offshore. The next was of the interior of *Thor's Hammer* illuminated by the Japanese sub's spotlight; eerie, the water so strange and out of place on the inside as the tail angled down into the sea. In the next photo, *Hammer* sat ghostly, seeming to float above the water, glowing in the moonlight. The last two shots were of *Hammer* the next morning, dead in the water, the oil slick spreading out around her, and the wreckage of the Japanese Zero poking through the surface.

"I can see why the Smithsonian would have been interested. These are amazing photos." She slid them gently into the folder and tied the string.

"They were on display for a time in an exhibit at the Air and Space Museum. Copies are now in the National Archives. He was such a good photographer; a very passionate artist."

Emily put all the items back in the trunk just as she had found them, then closed the lid, turned the key and patted the chest of treasures, gently.

Neither spoke. Hagen was sifting through old memories while Emily created new ones.

She took a deep breath and let it out slowly. "Thank you, Hagen, for sharing this, these priceless things with me. That's all I can say, really. I cannot put proper words together to convey to you how I really feel right now."

"You do not have to, Emily. It was my pleasure to show you."

"May I ask a question? If it's too difficult to talk about then I will understand."

"Ask away."

"How did Sal die?"

Hagen smiled, then it faded. "Sal was always healthy. Hardly ever sick, rarely a cold. His body had been run through a meat grinder, but once he was healed, he was as strong as an ox." Memories of a young, vibrant Sal had him closing his eyes for a moment to recollect. *Take time to smell the roses even if the blooms are old.* He opened his eyes and resumed. "Then, last December, right after Christmas, Sal started to tire easily. His skin color changed, and he began to lose weight. After the new year, I took him to the doctor. By that time, he was jaundiced, orange as a pumpkin and itching like crazy. They gave him a prescription for an anti-itch pill. They ran tests to rule out Hepatitis and discovered the cancer in his pancreas. When I heard that I just about lost my mind. I knew, we all knew about pancreatic cancer from Michael Landon. Once you have symptoms, it is really too late to do anything. We had very few options."

"I'm so sorry. God, I hate cancer."

"I don't know anyone who doesn't." He sighed. "A procedure was scheduled for a shunt to be put in to reroute the bile from his liver. It would not have been a cure, but it could have made him more comfortable, maybe given him a few more months. It was scheduled for February 14. A few days before the procedure, Sal took a downward turn. His health declined very fast and we had to take him to Presbyterian Hospital in Albuquerque on the tenth. He slipped into a coma in the middle of the night and passed away at 12:30 the next afternoon."

Emily found no words. When her mom died, the best things people said to her were nothing at all.

"He was surrounded by family and friends. Everyone had flown in from New Jersey. Shilah was there. He chanted a Navajo prayer to help him on his way to the next life."

"Shilah sounds like a nice man." She grabbed a tissue from the box.

"Indeed, he is. He was Sal's—is our—best friend."

541

"Was he the man speaking to you at the station in Lamy?"

"That was Shilah. You will be meeting him today."

"Oh?"

"I am flying him and his family in for the funeral. Here's a story I haven't told you yet. Do you remember the old Navajo woman I told you about?"

"The one at the station in Albuquerque, who gave you the blanket and dreamcatcher."

"Yes, her. It was a while before I told Sal that story. But then, one day, I told it again, to Shilah. He listened, very seriously, arms folded. When I finished, he smiled at us, chuckled, and said, 'I wondered when you were going to tell me.' Sal and I looked at each other, very confused; neither one of us had ever told anyone else that story. Shilah was the first. Then he said, 'That old woman was my grandmother. That young boy was my brother. Spirit brought you together that day, to help the man who saved my life. Twice.' You could have knocked us over with a feather."

Emily held up her arm. "Same here. Look at these huge goosebumps."

"I get them every time I think about it. Shilah has a wife, three children, six grandchildren and eleven great-grandchildren. His is just one family that was able to continue because of the bravery of one man."

"Incredible."

"And now, Shilah Begaye is the President of the Navajo Nation."

"President?"

"Yes. Shilah comes from a long line of Navajo chiefs. He was a chief for a time. Now, the Navajo Nation is structured like a democracy." He looked at his watch. "Emily, we have about two hours until Philadelphia. I have something to confess to you."

"Oh, what is it?"

"I never went to sleep last night."

"Hagen, no."

"I couldn't take my mind off today."

"Why didn't you tell me earlier? You could have laid down after breakfast."

"I felt fine at breakfast, and I wanted to make good use of the time we had remaining."

"Why don't you go and lie down for a while, and I'll wake you when we reach Philly."

"You wouldn't mind?"

"Of course not, silly. Come on," she stood and offered her hand. "Let's go inside."

He took her hand and they went into his room, where he lay down on the bed. She pulled off his shoes. Realizing that the Navajo blanket was in the trunk, she went back to the patio and got the crocheted blanket and put it over him.

"This is a nice blanket."

"Aunt Mathilde made this for us for Christmas, 1988. She was very crafty. She could knit, crochet, tat, sew, quilt."

"My mom tried to teach me to knit, once. It was a frustrating experience for both of us. Anyway, get some rest and I'll see you in Philly."

"Thank you, Emily."

She kissed him on the forehead, then left the room. The thought of lying on one of the sofas, taking a cat nap herself, entered her mind. It sounded good, but, oversleeping again did not.

Downstairs in the guest room was her alarm clock, one of those traditional types that you wind up, with the two bells on top, noisier than all get-out, impossible to sleep through unless you were sedated for surgery. Figuring that it was a way to get in a catnap of her own, she brought it upstairs, set

543

the alarm, put the clock on the coffee table in between the sofas, lay down and dozed off.

At one o'clock the alarm rang, startling her out of her nap. Bolting upright, shaking her head to throw off the confusion, she stopped the alarm, squeezed her eyes closed, opened them, then looked outside. They were still moving. Hagen wasn't visible anywhere. *Probably still sleeping.*

She went to his room. The smell of men's cologne was in the air, faint, woodsy, pleasant, but different from what she smelled before in his room, and on him. She gently opened his door. His form was visible under the blanket. She hated to wake him; he needed the rest, but the train would be arriving in Philadelphia soon.

Putting a hand gently on his shoulder, she whispered, "Hagen, time to get up."

He stirred; his eyes flickered open. "Sal?"

"Hi there."

Realizing where he was, "Hi there."

"It must have been a nice dream. You woke up smiling."

He sat up. "Oh, it was." He put his face in his hands and rubbed up and down, clearing the remaining fog.

"You said, 'Sal.' He was in your dream?"

"Mm, I was home, walking through the peach orchard. It was spring, and the trees were in full blossom. Funny thing was, they didn't smell like peach blossoms. There was a faint smell of English Leather in the air."

"English Leather?"

"That was Sal's fragrance. He loved it. Anyway, as I walked through the orchard I came to the cemetery, and there he was, standing near the tree. He was wearing his uniform and bomber jacket. He held out his hand and I walked towards him. He was smiling. And those brown eyes… He could get me to say yes to anything with just a look." He sighed, looked up at Emily's face and smiled. "The scent became stronger as I approached him. Our fingers touched. I was about to grab hold of his hand when I woke up."

She frowned. "I ruined your dream. I'm so sorry."

"My dear, don't be sorry. I am sure it won't be my last dream." He turned to look outside. The train was slowing down. William Penn could be seen in the distant skyline out of the window, perched high atop city hall. "We are pulling into the station soon. I'd like to freshen up."

"Me too, see if I can make myself look presentable to your family."

"You worry too much."

"I have nothing appropriate to wear. I'm going to feel so out of place."

"You look fine just as you are."

"Says you."

"Says me. Besides, you're with me and anyone with me looks fabulous by association."

"Well, that sure makes me feel good."

He grinned, stood up slowly and headed to the bathroom. Before he closed the door, he said, "Meet me on the patio when you're ready."

Frustrated with not having anything to wear, she huffed under her breath and went downstairs. She washed up, put on some makeup, and put her hair up into a neat twist. In her small traveling wardrobe, she found a dark blue blouse that Hagen hadn't yet seen her wear. It went with the khaki pants she had on. Standing in front of the mirror over the dresser she said to herself, "Well, Emily, this is as good as it gets. I feel like Cinderella without a fairy godmother." A breath in, and a sigh out, then she went up to meet Hagen on the patio.

In the meantime, the train had stopped at the station just long enough to drop off and take on passengers. Then it traveled a mile and a half to an area where numerous tracks veered off from the main ones. Hagen's car was

545

disconnected from the main train. It sat alone on the tracks, under its own power, until Hagen's waiting switch engine connected to it and then began the last leg of Sal's final journey home.

Walking into his room, the usual smells were back. Scents from Hagen's soaps wafting from his bathroom were melding with his cologne. It was pleasant, soothing, just like Hagen. She peeked through the glass door. He was sitting in the recliner, wearing his black suit, and was fidgeting with something in both hands. He stopped fidgeting when he heard the door slide open.

"Hey there, boss." She slid the door closed and sat on the sofa close to his recliner. He was holding an envelope. "Are you doing OK?"

"I think so. Part of me wants this train to never stop. Just keep going around and around like a toy train under a Christmas tree."

Emily put a hand on his arm.

He smiled; his blue eyes twinkled. "Emily." He turned the envelope over and over, slowly. "I forgot to tell you part of the story." He paused, then sighed. "No, that's a lie. I left out part of the story."

"OK. Is it something bad?"

"I don't think it is. But…" Sweat beads glistened on his forehead. He dabbed his face with a handkerchief from inside his coat. "…did it ever cross your mind—did you ever count the years that Sal and I had known each other?"

"As a matter of fact, I have. Sixty-eight years. That's a long time. Not many people can say that."

"Did you ever wonder if Sal and I ever had problems, or strayed from each other?"

"Honestly? No. Nothing of what you've told me would have led me to believe that you and Sal were anything but each other's soulmates."

"I believe—we believed—that we were. But, sometimes in a person's life, they have moments of weakness—physical weakness. It's not unhuman to be in a situation where the physical comforts of another human lead to intimacy."

"Are you trying to tell me you cheated on Sal?"

"No, dear. I never cheated on Sal. The closest I ever came to that was in England. I admit there was an attraction between me and Bobby Pfeiffer. It never manifested into anything more than words and sweaty handshakes."

"If the situation had been different, if you were alone with him, do you think something might have happened?"

"I honestly don't know. We were young. Maybe, maybe not. But since then I have had other opportunities, and never once did I do anything. I had matured. I didn't need anyone else. After the war, Sal and I were totally committed to each other, in all ways."

"After the war? Did something happen before the war?" The envelope turned again in his hands.

"Yes."

"Who? You? Sal?"

"It was Sal."

"Really? When did you find out?"

"Sal told me about it after we moved to New Mexico. It was a one-time thing. The circumstances surrounding the occasion catalyzed the connection."

"Did you know the other guy?"

"I knew the other party, yes. Not very well. It was someone we went to school with. It happened the night before I went off to basic training."

"The night that Sal went off alone and didn't come home? Was it one of the guys in the car that picked him up?"

Hagen shook his head. "No. The story Sal told everyone the next day was that he drank some homemade beer from our Papa's supply, then wandered off and got picked up by

Danny Snyder and Bobby Hesson. That was true. It was also true that they continued drinking and had become sufficiently inebriated. Sal did wake up on Danny Snyder's couch the next morning and Mr. Snyder did give him a ride. It was what happened in between Sal getting picked up by Danny and Bobby and waking up on the Snyder's couch in the morning that Sal intentionally left out. After Sal got picked up, the three of them wound up at a party at Doug Minette's house. There were some girls there. Sal was feeling awful about me leaving in the morning. One of the girls at the party was also down in the dumps about her boyfriend enlisting a few weeks earlier. She missed him. She was lonely and miserable. And as you know, misery loves company. One thing led to another and Sal and this girl consoled each other… biblically, shall we say?"

"Oh, my. A girl? How did that make you feel?"

"I was a bit shocked, but not like I might have been if he had told me when we were younger. By the time he told me I was old enough to understand what had happened."

"So, how does this fit into your book? Is this something you want everyone to know about?"

"No. I do not think it is necessary to tell the world about it. Just the people who I think it would matter to."

She got quiet. She thought for a moment. "Why the need to tell me?"

"Because, my dear, I think it will matter to you." He handed her the letter. She took it, slowly. The postmark was dated February 7, 1943. It was addressed to Salvatore Cristoforo at the Beverly address. The return address said the letter was from an Irene Wells in San Diego. "Go ahead," he said. "Read it."

She pulled the one-page letter from the envelope and unfolded it. Hagen's heart beat fast and hard as she began to read.

Dear Sal,

The last time we saw each other my fiancé had just gone off to fight and your brother was leaving the next day to do the same thing without you. We were both very upset. We had a few too many drinks and cried in each other's arms and, well, I am sure you remember the rest. You enlisted the next day just like you said you were going to do and that was the last we saw of each other.

A month after you enlisted, my father died suddenly of a heart attack and my mother and I moved to California to live with her sister. Two months after you and I had last seen each other, I discovered that I was pregnant. Please, Sal, I am not telling you this because I want anything from you or that I am blaming you for what happened. No one is to blame. I let everyone believe that the baby was Stanley's. I didn't know how long I could keep up with that story because Stanley and I had never been physically intimate. I had never been physically intimate with anyone before you. One month after moving to California I received word from Stanley's mother that his ship was sunk by a Nazi submarine. There were no survivors.

I felt awful about what happened between us. I know your heart belonged to someone else. So did mine. I could tell by how upset you were acting before we said goodbye. I don't know who the lucky girl is, but she is just that, a lucky girl.

My reason for writing this letter is to say thank you. Thank you for your kindness a year ago. Thank you for being the gentleman I'd always known you to be. I hope that wherever you are, you are safe and that you and that lucky girl will have a wonderful life together when this war is finally over. Oh, and Sal, please, don't worry about me and the baby. We are going to be just fine. I met a nice man, a very understanding man. He was 4-F. We intend to be married soon.

Take care,

Irene

Emily finished reading but didn't look up. Her brain was processing this new information. Hagen's heart galloped fast in his chest, and Emily's was neck-and-neck with his. Moments passed. It was quiet except for the train wheels clacking and their hearts thumping. She didn't look up at Hagen, not yet. She slowly re-folded the letter, slipped it back into its envelope and re-read the return address.

"Emily? Are you alright?" Hagen delicately asked her.

She slowly raised her head and looked him right in the eyes. "Sal… had a child." She said it without the intonation of a question.

"Yes, Sal had a child."

"Did he know about this child when he told you about his one night with Irene?"

Hagen shook his head. "No. This letter is the only correspondence Sal ever received from Irene and he was unaware of its existence until last December."

Emily frowned and cocked her head like a curious puppy.

"This letter arrived when Sal was a POW. It was placed in the bottom drawer of my father's desk along with the other letters Sal received. There were so many of them. Letters from his B-17 crew and their families. Letters from men he trained with and from men who had trained him. They were written at a time when Sal's condition and whereabouts were unknown. And they were written with the expectations that he would one day read them. They were prayers; hard copy, tangible, tactile prayers. He touched so many lives." Hagen paused. He was becoming emotional, and it was not about him at that moment. He dabbed a tissue at his eyes and continued. "Somehow this letter had fallen to the bottom, inside the desk. It was by pure accident that Dottie, Karl's wife, found it. She pulled the drawer out one day while looking for stamps to mail Christmas cards, and when she pushed the drawer back in, the envelope was poking out from underneath. Sal saw it for the first time when we went home for Christmas."

Emily sighed a big sigh. "So, again I ask, why should this matter to me?"

"Sal wanted to find out all he could about his child. Not for anything else but to just… know about him, or her. When we returned to New Mexico after Christmas, we hired a private investigator to find out whatever they could. While we were waiting to hear something from the investigator, Sal became ill. By the middle of January, we had received the information about Sal's child and a day later, the cancer diagnosis. Irene Wells married, like she said she was going to do. From what we gather and may assume, the man she married was understanding, just like Irene said. When he married her, he also adopted her child. Irene Wells and her son, Johnny, became Irene and Johnny… Connolly."

Emily's breath hitched, and she put a hand to her mouth.

"Emily, you see where this is going?"

She had felt it coming. Something had told her it was heading in this direction, but she kept putting a finger in a hole, plugging the leak, afraid to let it spill out into the open, but at the same time wanting to let it. She ran out of fingers and the dam broke open in her mind. The past three days whooshed in and swirled in a whirlpool as random flashes, snapshots of their time together, flicked on and off. She took a deep breath and let it out slowly, her hand still covering her mouth while the envelope jiggled in her other shaking hand. Shock made her speechless, then anger gave back her voice.

She dropped her hand from her mouth. "You KNEW… all… this… time?" Her voice wavered, revealing her pain. She felt betrayed.

Hagen wasn't prepared for this. He had played the scenarios in his mind, moving the chess pieces in different directions around the board. What he had done up until this moment was calculated and, in his opinion, the best way to have handled it. The next few minutes would be crucial to the direction of any continued relationship.

He remained calm. "Yes, Emily. I knew."

"Why didn't you tell me when we first met? Why did you wait until now?"

"I am sorry, Emily. We did not want it this way."

"We? *We*? Sal knew about me?"

"Yes. He knew, and he wanted so much to meet you. But his health declined very quickly, quicker than we had expected. This trip was intended to be about the three of us getting to know each other, from each other. He died before getting to meet you. He would have really liked you. And I believe you would have really liked him."

"Oh, GOD! You really know how to stick the guilt pins in the voodoo doll, don't you?!"

Hagen stopped, pursed his lips and bowed his head, his hands clasped under his chin.

"I'm sorry Hagen, that was mean. But, why wait until now to tell me? I would have been, I don't know, more emotionally invested in your family, *our* family, when you told me all about them. I didn't know jack about you or Sal until three days ago. And now, he's my *grandfather*? I—I don't know what to think. You lied to me."

"I withheld, Emily. At first, I thought I would tell you when we met, then get to know each other. Then, I thought, maybe you should hear the whole family story first; get to know Sal and me. I wanted you to like us as people before knowing us as family. Please forgive me, Emily. I never meant it to seem deceitful. And I believe you have been emotionally invested since I began to tell you everything."

He was correct. She had admitted earlier that she was emotionally invested. His being right again knocked down her defenses and lit another fire. "How much about me did you find out from your investigator? Did you already know everything about me and my mom and dad and make me tell you all of it anyway? Was that some kind of honesty test?"

"Emily, listen. I appreciate how you must feel. I have just thrown a very large boulder into your pond. Hear me out. Please?"

"OK." She wiped her tears away with the heels of her hands and folded her arms tightly across her chest. "Go ahead."

"I only asked the investigator for basic information. He found out names and dates; that's all. We didn't want to know any more than that. We wanted to get to know you, from *you*, not second-hand. This cross-country journey that we have been on was meant to be for the three of us to take together. Not just the two of us up here eating cold fried chicken while Sal lay downstairs cold in a box." He stopped. His frustrations were getting to him. He took a deep breath and continued. "Sal and I had already planned this birthday trip. His procedure may have given him the ability to be here, to meet you. We never made it that far. So, it's just me, and you. That is, if you still want that."

Inside, Emily knew that everything Hagen was saying was logical, that he was sincere, and grieving, and lonely; that he was dealing with two emotional fronts: the loss of Sal and the addition of Emily.

"Hagen, this is a lot to take in, on top of everything I have learned about you, and this wonderful man…"

She started to cry. Hagen tried to get up. She held up her hand to stop him. "I'll be fine, just give me a moment." She sniffled, blew her nose into a fresh tissue.

"…this absolutely wonderful man who has touched so many lives and now, through you, he is still touching people's hearts. I fell in love with your family over these last few days. I cannot undo that. Knowing that I am part of that family is a little… overwhelming… to say the least."

Hagen simply nodded as he listened.

"Does your whole family know?"

"Yes, they know. But only what I knew before meeting you. I haven't been secretly sending off late night communiqués detailing all of the information about you that I plied from you with beer and cabbage rolls, if that's what you are wondering."

She smiled. The storm was ebbing. "No, I just wanted to know who knew, what I was walking into."

"Family, Emily. Family. My family, Sal's family." He pointed a finger back and forth between them. "Our family. I have one more thing for you." He reached into his inside coat pocket and pulled out another envelope and handed it to her. On the outside, written by the shaky hand of an ill, elderly man was one word:

Emily

"Oh, God, is this from Sal?" She bit her lip to keep from crying.

"It is." He shrugged a little, pursed his lips. "It is his 'Plan B.'"

"Plan B?" Her lip biting was proving ineffective with Hagen sitting near her and on the verge of breaking down himself.

Hagen took a deep breath and let it out slowly. "I was instructed to give this to you when I felt the time was right. I didn't ask him what he wrote." He looked up to Heaven. "Huh, I can only imagine." Then back to Emily. "He found humor even in the shittiest—pardon my French—situations. When he was in the hospital in Kansas City, he joked that he was a better shot with a chair than the robber was with a gun."

They laughed through their tears.

Hagen composed himself and reached into his coat pocket again and handed her a letter opener. "Would you like me to leave you alone with the letter?"

"No," she took a deep breath. "I think I'd like you to be here." She slit open the envelope and pulled out the contents. An aroma wafted up to her face and she sniffed the paper.

"That's English Leather," said Hagen. "Sal is the only man I knew who scented his letters with cologne."

She put the letter on her lap and began to sob deeply into her hands.

Hagen put a hand on her shoulder. "Emily, what's wrong? What happened?"

It took a few moments for her to compose herself enough to speak. "When I came in earlier and woke you from your dream" —she picked up the letter and sniffed it— "I smelled this scent. He was there, in your room, and in your dream."

"Oh, my goodness. That doesn't surprise me. Sal was very persistent." He looked up again to Heaven then back down. "Emily, are you alright?"

"I'm OK, I'll be OK." She wiped more tears away with her hands and sniffed. "This is just... huh... so much to process." Another deep breath and she picked up the letter and began to read:

Dear Emily,

If you are reading this letter, then my wish did not come true. I hope you aren't reading it. I want so much to meet you. But, if you are, then fate played a better hand. I have no claim to be your grandfather other than in a biological sense. The paths life drags us down are impossible to predict. I have no idea why the Universe waited until now to bring us together with so little time left.

By now, you most likely have listened to Hagen talk about me. He's always been like a proud mother bragging about her son's accomplishments. Now it is my turn to brag about him.

If it were not for Hagen, you would not be here, because I would not have been me. He entered my life at its deepest and darkest time and turned my miserable existence into Heaven on Earth. Fifteen years later, he dragged me from death and brought me back to life. A friend of ours calls him her angel. She could not be more right. There is no other explanation for what he does. He just does it and people who have Hagen in their lives are better for it. I call it the Hagen Effect. If you decide to stay around for a while, you won't regret it. Hagen is the kindest, most generous person anyone has ever known. He will spoil you. Let him. He will go nuts without me around to spoil, so you'll actually be taking care of him more than he will be taking care of you.

Emily, there is another man you must get to know. Shilah Begaye. Yes, Hagen is my soulmate. But Shilah is my spirit brother. I cannot convey to you how much he means to me. He understands Spirit. He knows I will be traveling on to the next world. But he is human, and I know how much he will miss me in this world because I know how much I would miss him. Listen to him. Learn from him. He is wise. He is family.

I don't know what else there is to say. Hagen has given this letter to you because he knew it was right. He knows people, sometimes better than they know themselves.

I told him to give this letter to you ONLY if you captured his heart. I had a feeling that you would.

Take care of yourself and my Hagen,

P.S. Technically, I am your grandfather. Hagen and I discussed what his relation would be to you. He said Great Uncle. I said Grandmother. Thoughts?

Emily read the letter, and as she did, waves of emotions ebbed and flowed. She laughed so hard when she read Sal's *P.S.*

Hagen was watching the familiar scenery passing by outside while Emily read. As the train crossed the trestle over Rancocas Creek, he could see the bridge in the distance where Marta had passed away sixty-six years ago. *I love you, Mama. Take care of Sal.*

Emily's laughter caught him by surprise. She was looking at him. He rolled his eyes. "I told you he finds humor in everything."

"Yes, he sure does. Oh, Hagen. I wish I could have met him. I feel like I know him because of you. I wish I could have heard his voice and looked into those eyes you loved so much."

"I wish you could have, too. You may have seen a little of yourself. You remind me a lot of him. Your eyes, your facial expressions, your laughter. I don't think excessive ketchup usage is an inherited trait, but you share that quality with him as well. When I first saw you dragging your fried chicken through a Sal-sized lake of ketchup, there was no doubt in my mind you were a Cristoforo."

"Well, that's one mystery solved."

He looked out the window again. "We are getting close."

"Do you need to do anything?"

"I think I would like a drink."

Emily stood. "I'll go get some water."

"Not water. Help me up." He held out his hand. "I need something stronger. Follow me."

He led the way to the kitchen. "Have a seat. My turn to serve." From a cabinet, he retrieved two rocks glasses and a bottle of Jameson's Irish Whiskey and brought them to the table. "I take mine neat. How about you?"

560

"Same, thanks."

"I am impressed." He sat and poured two fingers into each glass. He held his glass up.

She touched hers to his and they held that pose.

"To Salvatore Cristoforo," said Emily.

"To my favorite Italian."

They sipped and put their glasses down. The warmth of the whiskey spread out from their cores. Hagen sighed as the soothing effect of the alcohol made its way to his head. "I needed that. I feel better already." The train slowed to a crawl. "We're home."

Emily stood and looked out the kitchen window. The farm came into view on the right side of the train. "Oh, my God. Hagen."

"What's wrong?"

"You have to see this."

He got up and stood next to her at the window. "Oh, Shilah."

The train made its slow turn onto the divergent track that led onto the farm. The track led right up to the house, separating the expansive front lawn from an enormous, empty corn field. What Emily had seen at the station in Lamy was nothing compared to what she and Hagen were witnessing now. On the lawn were hundreds of people. Entire families: the Beckenbauers and the Morawskis, the Ostermans' children and their families, surviving *Thor's Hammer* crewmen and their families, generations of neighbors and friends from the orphanage and their descendants—all had come to pay their respects. So many people whose lives were affected by one man were there to say goodbye. At the forefront of the expanse of people in winter coats braving that cold New Jersey day was Shilah Begaye. Shilah was wrapped in a long Navajo blanket. A feathered headband wrapped around his head and down his back. He sat high on a horse, holding the reins with one hand and a feather-adorned staff in the other. His face was stoic, never looking anywhere but in the direction of the peach orchard. A riderless horse stood next to his, with only a Navajo blanket over its back. Shilah's entire family, dressed in traditional Navajo clothing and wrapped in woven blankets, stood behind the horses in generational order from oldest to youngest. Backed up to the tracks, waiting to give Sal one last ride, was the old Sterling, with Karl at the wheel. Standing in the back of the truck were six strong Navajo men, in traditional warrior attire.

"Emily. It's time."

They walked to the elevator. They went inside and just before Hagen closed the door, she stopped him. "Wait. I'll be right back." She disappeared around the corner, down the hall to his bedroom. A few moments later she reappeared, carrying his overcoat and wearing Sal's bomber jacket.

Hagen's mouth opened. His eyes widened.

"Well? What do you think?" she asked.

"It's perfect. Absolutely perfect."

"Thanks. I feel much better now."

Hagen closed the door—Rosemary Clooney began to sing *I'll Be Seeing You*—and he hesitated for a moment before pressing the down lever. On the lower level, they exited the lift and stood at the exit door.

Emily turned to him. "Hagen?"

"Yes, Emily?"

"Thank you for letting me capture your heart."

"Thank *you,* my dear, for saving it."

He pressed the button and the door swung open. They walked down the steps arm in arm. Her new family gathered around her, welcoming her with open hearts and arms. Then Ryfka held Emily's face in both her hands and looked into her eyes. In her Polish-accented English, "Emily, you have Sal's light."

Emily hugged her tightly. "Thank you." Then she turned to Hagen. "Hagen?"

"Yes?"

"Would you tell Warren Ackerman I quit?"

Hagen smiled. "Of course I will."

"Thanks, Grandma."

He burst out laughing and looked up to Heaven. "God will get you for that, Sal."

...and so it begins...

Acknowledgements

Many people have cheered me on during the creation of this novel. They listened to my story, read some or all of it, gave advice, laughed with me at the happy times, and cried with me at the sad.

To Major General (Ret) Karen Ledoux: From the beginning you have been supportive of this endeavor. Your friendship, bendable ear, and advice on military protocol have proven invaluable. Thank you.

To Tonya Long: You did not know this, but a week into the writing of Ravelled, I almost gave up. You breathed life into my dying creative flame. Thank you.

To John Kube: Your enviable command of the English language, editing assistance, words of encouragement, and friendship—priceless. Thank you.

To Sara Lovitt and Julie Mooneyham: you are *my* Blue Angels. I can never thank you enough for coming to my rescue, but I will try anyway. Thank you, to the Nth degree.

To Chey Collar: Your helpful advice and knowledge about farms and dairy cows is so very much appreciated. Moo-Moo.

To Russell Stewart: You gave me a laptop that I so desperately needed and could not afford. Trying to write this novel on an eight-inch tablet would surely have driven my mind, eyes, and carpal ligaments bonkers. Thank you.

To Ken Houghton Rail Images: Thank you for the Choo-Choo image.

To Christie and Max Johns: I am one of those souls who believes that everything that will happen is a result of what occurred before. When John and I landed like refugees in Virginia, you opened your home to us until we found our footing. You were our safe haven physically but will always be our souls' safe harbor. We love you. I love you.

To Helen Jane Long: Your music—your luscious, sonic portraits—kept my soul alive and aloft and kept Emily, Hagen, and me company as we took the journey together across the country, and across a century. Thank you for sharing your amazing talent with the world. xx

To my husband, John (You get your own page for this.)

Thank you for all the late-night conversations that kept my heart beating.

Thank you for being by my side for the entire journey.

Ti amo, אני אוהב אותך, Ich liebe dich, Kocham cię,
愛しています，Ayóó'áníínísh'ní, Tá mé i ngrá leat—

I Love You

About the author

Seph Gannon is an American author born in Pennsylvania. At just three days old, he was adopted. Baby boy Gannon grew up in Southern New Jersey surrounded by cornfields, fruit orchards and pumpkin patches, at a time when life was less hectic; when you knew all your neighbours and they knew you.

He has since lived in New Mexico, St.Thomas and Florida. In his travels, Seph has worked in restaurants, been a Disney Puppeteer, and is now a licensed massage therapist. Among his passions, he lists photography, music, cooking, acting, and singing in the car.

His first novel Ravelled is inspired by his life experiences and compassion for all living things. This continues to be the inspirational backdrop to his writing.